Deadly Equations

Jeffrey Rosoff

This is a work of fiction. Similarities to real people, places, or events are entirely coincidental.

Deadly Equations

To my children, whom I love. Never forget.

In crisis, change finds its voice, for good…or bad.

Part 1: Butterfly Effect

Chapter 1: Luna

Monday, August 20

A single photon—the smallest unit of light—began its journey deep within the Sun's core. Born of nuclear fusion when the Earth was locked in ice, it carried the promise of warmth. For early humans battling the cold, its arrival would have been a gift from 93 million miles away.

But the voyage was slow. The photon ricocheted through dense plasma, its path broken by countless collisions, until at last it broke free—100,000 years later. From there, its final sprint across space lasted just eight minutes.

By the time the photon arrived, the world had changed. The Ice Age was gone, replaced by a planet reshaped by human hands. Civilization had advanced through the Agricultural, Industrial, Information, and finally, the Warming Age. The Earth needed no more heat. Yet this photon came with a gentler purpose.

It pierced the atmosphere, struck a gold band on the ring finger of a woman in a red dress, and reflected into the left green eye of a second woman. The second woman's name was Luna.

For the photon, its long journey ended in a fleeting moment of brilliance. For Luna, the journey mattered little. Yet it carried a hidden purpose, its glint drawing her gaze toward the woman in red. Its impact, yielding far less energy than a butterfly's wingbeat, was poised to alter Luna's trajectory—and, in doing so, humanity itself.

For a moment, Luna's world seemed to pause. She observed the woman on the bridge, poised yet unassuming, standing against the backdrop of a decaying city skyline. Sunlight leapt from her ring again, scattering more delicate sparks of light. Luna squinted. There was something about her—a familiarity cloaked in mystery, a magnetic pull that defied explanation. It felt as though the light delivered a message meant solely for her.

Wait—she's holding a baby.

Luna smiled warmly as her heart filled with joy. She had not seen a baby in months. It was such a treat. A rush of feelings pulsed within her—meaningful and undeniable.

Questions surged through Luna's mind. Who was this woman with the child? Why did she feel such an inexplicable connection? Perhaps an unseen force had aligned their paths, orchestrating a deliberate cosmic intersection. Luna, always the follower, passive and unassuming, followed once again.

Quietly, she moved toward the bridge, the woman, and the child.

The woman on the bridge stood with her back to Luna, her shoulders rising and falling in a steady rhythm.

How beautiful—she's laughing.

The way she cradled the baby in her arms radiated love— maternal and infinite. In a fractured world of restrictions and uncertainty, this simple moment felt rare, fragile. It captivated Luna, a fleeting glimpse into a bond she knew she would never experience.

Her own parents had been taken from her, lost in the Sacramento Valley fires. She had been only an infant and had no memory of them. Sometimes, she liked to imagine they had held her this way—secure in their arms, cherished.

An instinctual ache stirred in her chest, tempered by the sight before her. Luna knew she wasn't eligible to have children herself.

Genome testing had ruled it out—her markers, an unforgiving verdict etched into her DNA. Yet, instead of bitterness, she felt an odd kind of peace. Watching this woman cradle her baby was enough for the moment, like standing in the glow of a light she could never hold but could still feel.

The morning's quote echoed in her mind: "Sometimes a break from your routine is exactly what you need." It read like a set of instructions, prompting her to venture out for a rare early stroll—a deliberate break from her usual rhythm. To ignore it would feel rebellious; her pen had always sketched obediently within the lines.

Normally, she would be at home, curled on her grandmother's worn settee, sipping black tea and nibbling wheat toast, while the distant hum of the news played on her screen. Her routines were her sanctuary, a buffer against the chaos of the world. But today, the quote had pushed her, needling her with its quiet challenge to leave behind her cocoon of safety and predictability.

The quote, along with the glint that had initially captured her attention, had brought her here. And it seemed worthwhile.

Luna took a few cautious steps closer to the bridge, still within the seam of tall buildings, ever mindful of maintaining proper distance, and the specter of the next pandemic.

The woman in red wore a simple sundress, its sleeveless design fluttering slightly in the furnace-like heat of another hundred-degree morning. Her dark hair hung straight, obscuring her face and the baby. Something about her was striking—her figure slight but proper. She didn't look like a local, though Luna wasn't sure what "local" even meant anymore.

Luna caught her own reflection in a nearby window, glancing at herself the way she imagined others did. At five foot one, she didn't command much physical space, but her features often intrigued people. Her shoulder-length hair fell in soft, layered coils, framing her deep brown skin, which always seemed to carry a natural glow. But it was her green eyes that stopped strangers in their tracks.

People loved to tell her how "unique" she looked, how she was "a portrait of diversity," as if her mix of Black, Jewish–Eastern European, and Mexican heritage turned her into some kind of emblem. But she didn't see it that way. At twenty-six, her reflection wasn't remarkable; it was just hers.

Her attention snapped back to the woman when she noticed her shoulders still bobbing. The rhythm seemed unusual. Laughter didn't last this long. She continued forward, unknowingly stopping inside the government-mandated ten-foot distance rule.

The woman's head lifted slightly, giving Luna her first clear look at her face—Asian. Her almond-shaped eyes were swollen and red. Tears carved clean trails down her cheeks, cutting through the layer of sweat from the heat.

She wasn't laughing. She was crying.

The baby shifted in her arms as the woman whispered something that sounded like, "ching."

Luna tilted her head, confused. "I'm sorry, I don't understand."

The woman looked at her again, struggling to form words. "Please," she murmured, her voice thick with emotion and a heavy accent.

Luna's instincts as a speech pathologist awakened. The woman's accent and difficulty with the "L" sound were familiar. She moved closer, keeping her voice calm. "I didn't mean to intrude. Is there anything I can do to help?"

The woman's gaze dropped to the baby. "Pretty lady... hold baby?"

Luna hesitated. The offer was difficult to resist. The woman adjusted the blanket, revealing the baby's face—tiny, pink-cheeked, impossibly small.

"She's beautiful," Luna whispered. "How old is she?"

"One month old," the woman replied, her voice faltering. "Take?"

"I've never held a baby this young," Luna admitted, nerves buzzing with a mix of restraint and anticipation. "Are you sure?"

The woman edged closer, extending her arms. "Be gentle. Always."

Luna reached out carefully, noting that the word "always" didn't quite fit the sentence. She cradled the baby as if she were made of porcelain. The tiny weight in her arms felt unreal, and the baby let out a soft, contented grunt. Luna smiled, caught in the glow of this fragile life. "Her name?"

"Jade," the woman said softly.

"She's perfect," Luna whispered. Her thoughts shifted to the woman's tears. "Are you okay? Is Jade okay? Can I call someone for you?"

The woman's expression changed. Her eyes lingered on the baby before locking onto Luna's. "Inside stroller," she said faintly.

"I'm sorry?" Luna asked, confused.

The woman stepped back. Her movements were slow, deliberate. Her arms fell to her sides as she approached the edge of the bridge, her legs lifted high over the railing. Below, the river churned, jagged rocks breaking through the water's surface.

"No! That's unsafe. What are you doing?" Luna's voice cracked with panic.

The mother continued stepping back until her heels hovered dangerously over the water, like a gymnast poised at the start of a routine, with only the balls of her feet touching the bridge.

Luna pleaded, her voice trembling. "Please! Take Jade back! Your baby—please!"

The woman raised a finger to her lips, signaling silence. Her tear-streaked face was calm now, and she formed a heart with her hands, holding it briefly over her chest.

"Please... letter," she whispered softly.

Then, with one final step back, she fell.

Chapter 2: Simi

The unkempt, bearded man brushed red paint in flowing strokes with the same artful attention that a Japanese calligrapher might use. But his medium was not paint—it was blood. To him, the life-sustaining fluid had found another purpose, shimmering with a simple crimson message on a tan canvas. He stood inside his victim's tent, the inner surface providing a useful backdrop. The paint itself came from the sacrificial bodies at his feet—nothing wasted.

The early morning light seeped through the city haze, just bright enough for him to work without casting any noticeable shadows in the tent. It was too soon to unleash alarm; the job was not complete.

He stepped back, surveying his work. He had etched the numbers "14" and "88," deliberately mirroring the tattoos on his face. At first glance, they seemed unremarkable, but for those familiar with the code, they carried a menacing significance. The numbers also served a secondary purpose: when summed as individual digits, they totaled 21—inspiration for his call sign, Blackjack. Even better, his father's name, Jack, was embedded in it. Including him in an act he would have renounced felt fitting. He hated his father.

He considered the next steps. Blood alone would not provoke the reactions he craved. He patted his Italian stiletto knife—an almost affectionate gesture, like rewarding a loyal pet. The blade, slick with red, glistened even in the dim light. He almost wiped it on his tattered clothes to make himself appear even more menacing and unpredictable, but he reconsidered, wary of leaving a trail of evidence. Instead, he wiped the blade on one of the victims' shirts, the fabric soaking up the gore like a willing accomplice. Satisfied with the stiletto's performance, he tucked it into his pouch of tools and reached for the gut-hook skinning knife.

The next task required precision. After years of flaccid helplessness, of toiling in anonymity, he finally felt like he was doing something that mattered—something that would impress his boss and set things on the "right" course. His movements turned careful, almost reverent, each one a fragment of a private ritual he believed would lift him from faceless drudgery to a man of purpose. He would set the world straight—unlike his father, whose choices had dragged everyone backward.

The tent's air grew heavier with the metallic tang of blood mingling with the faint smell of mildew. Outside, the muffled sounds of the waking city began to penetrate the canvas walls. He felt insulated, as if this grisly chamber were a sanctum removed from the mundanity beyond. But Blackjack knew he couldn't stay much longer. The world outside would soon take notice, and when they did, they would see his message clearly—and fear it.

He paused, the gut-hook knife hovering over one of his victims. There was a moment of stillness and a brief hesitation. Then, imagining the approval of his distant master, he began again, carving his statement into flesh with meticulous care. The work was grotesque, but to him, it was righteous—a testament to his resolve.

He looked down at the dead couple. "This will change everything," he muttered, his voice low and gravelly, heavy with conviction. A grim smile crept onto his face. Soon, the rising political star Remi McCarthy would take the stage—delivering her speech before thousands. None would suspect his true identity: Simi Kremna—her trusted staffer.

Unlike her, he didn't need applause or recognition from the city he despised. It was enough to know he had turned this small corner into his own stage. A bloody performance, perfectly choreographed.

And when the curtain finally rose, they wouldn't just be afraid—they'd be terrified.

Chapter 3: Luna

Luna felt paralyzed, as if she were no longer the pilot of her own body. She couldn't bring herself to walk to the edge of the bridge and look down. The mother's fate was already sealed; there was no real need. The only sounds were the playful notes of song sparrows and the soothing rush of water through the rocks below—a stark contrast to the tragedy that had just unfolded.

Luna struggled to process the horror she had just witnessed. She felt her spirit lift from her body, suspended above, looking down at a distressed young woman holding a baby. Slowly, the surreal transformed into reality, and her predicament became crystal-clear. Overwhelmed, she became hysterical. Panicked, she cried out, "Help! Somebody, please help me!"

Still cradling the baby, she unintentionally startled the infant, who matched her cries with equal volume and intensity. Instinct took over—mother or not—and Luna turned her attention to the child with comforting, nurturing care. Tending to the baby felt as natural as breathing. Though she had no children of her own, her maternal instincts ran deep, embedded in her DNA.

After calming the baby, Luna tried to compose herself and resume the search for help.

Where is everyone?

The area was unusually deserted, ever since the homeless had been rounded up and redirected to the Washington Mall. She scanned her surroundings. In the distance, she spotted an older man approaching. Perhaps he could hear her, or maybe he was simply headed her way. For either reason, he would be there soon.

Thank God.

She needed help—and didn't trust herself to handle the situation alone.

While she waited, Luna recalled the woman's last words. She reached into the stroller and rummaged through diapers and formula until she found a red envelope. She broke the wax seal and pulled out a card decorated with magnolia flowers arranged in a heart shape, with a photo of Jade at the center. Inside were handwritten symbols aligned in columns.

Oh my God—I can't read this.

Luna assumed it was traditional Chinese.

She took a deep breath to steady herself, then clumsily retrieved her phone and loaded a translation app. Her nerves made it difficult to tap the commands accurately. Using the camera, she pointed the lens at the letter. An interpretation appeared almost immediately:

I'm sorry to make you take my responsibility. If I choose you, it means that I think you are kind and will take care of my children. A few months ago, my hometown Shanghai flood overly and I flee to your country. If I get caught, I will send back to China and place in jail. Jade's genome score is unknown and she conceived without proper approval. She will be executed if returned to country within. I have no money and my health is uncommon. Since I'm here illegally, I don't have health care. I am of no choice. Please take care of my child and love as you own her.

Although the translation was awkward, the message was clear—Luna could almost hear the mother's tears in the words.

Luna was torn, caught between two of her deepest beliefs. What began as distant admiration for motherhood had become a choice between a death sentence for the child and unlawful aiding and abetting. On one hand, kindness drove her, always willing to help others. On the other, she believed in following the rules.

Luna would determine the small child's fate. To save her, she would have to harbor an undocumented migrant. She had also witnessed a suicide, which by law had to be reported. Luna didn't see herself as courageous. In fact, she was often fearful—easily unsettled when her life lost its order and predictability. Spontaneity had never been in her nature. She lived her life terrified of repercussions and the unknown.

She remembered that help was coming and looked up. The older man was drawing closer, but his progress was agonizingly slow. Perhaps channeling her grandmother, Luna couldn't help but label his painful slowness a *schlep,* as Bubba would say. Luna nervously stroked one of her diamond earrings, an heirloom passed down from her Bubba. It was one of the few material possessions she truly cherished. But the jewelry offered no comfort or answers; her predicament was beyond any remedy. Not even a bowl of Jewish penicillin—chicken soup—could fix this.

With each step, the man's face shifted from blurry impressionism to sharp focus. He had gray hair neatly trimmed under a fedora, and deep wrinkles that seemed to mark a lifetime of accrued wisdom. His complexion was pale, leaving his bulbous red nose the only color in his worn face. Luna guessed he was in his early eighties. His furrowed brow made it clear he was concerned—and coming to help.

She had only seconds to make a life-altering decision.

Oh God, what am I going to do?

The man's voice reached her—distant, crackling, but audible. "Do you need help?"

Chapter 4: Remi

Senator Remi McCarthy stood just a foot behind the podium, poised beneath the grandeur of the Jefferson Memorial, its columns casting a stately frame around her silhouette. In her mid-forties, she radiated a sense of controlled confidence. Appearances mattered more than she liked to admit—especially when it came to her hair. Today, her stylist had worked wonders: a layered, mid-length cut with sun-kissed highlights that lent her an effortless edge. Her scarlet-red pumps clashed boldly against the measured tones of a tailored purple pinstripe suit—an intentional hint of rebellion beneath the sheen of professionalism.

She took a sip of water, cleared her throat, and adjusted the mic clipped to her lapel. In that brief pause, she felt powerful. Commanding. Ready.

Then she stepped forward. The crowd hushed, their breath held, waiting for her to speak.

"I'm Remi McCarthy, and I have a message for my Republican and Democratic opponents," she began, her voice cutting through the tension like a blade. "Find a mirror—and take a long, hard look. There, you'll see the reason. The reason for the disaster. The reason for our despair."

She paused, letting the silence settle, then swept her eyes across the massive crowd.

"But know this—every one of you here today stands to gain. Their infighting, their paralysis… it's brought something better to life. From their failure, a new force has risen—UnaTerra. A stronger party. A unified mission."

She brought her fist into her open palm, arms raised in a gesture of resolve. "This is our commitment. We call it the verdant salute.

The fist represents the earth—the covering hand, its protector. Together, they symbolize our shared duty to safeguard our future."

The crowd buzzed. A few fists mirrored her motion, testing how it felt.

She paused, smiling, before continuing. "Our vision is clear, simple, and bound to our name: UnaTerra. One land. Let me say it again—*one* land. It's all we have. Without protecting it, without safeguarding the very earth beneath our feet, we risk losing everything."

She let her words settle. The crowd murmured—she wanted them to feel the gravity of her warning.

"The other parties have bickered, pointed fingers, and failed to act, while our land—and the people on it—have borne the cost. Let me ask you—what did you think of their plan? How has their strategy reversed the erosion of our planet?"

She took in the crowd, letting her question hang in the air.

"You don't know what plan I'm talking about, do you?"

She allowed the silence to work for her—a moment of reflection.

Then she grimaced. "That's because there isn't one. They've done nothing. And the crisis grows worse by the day. Their weak policies have led to an out-of-control border, soaring energy consumption, reckless drilling, rampant crime, skyrocketing emissions, and—most disheartening of all—overpopulation. Aren't you tired of it?"

A voice shouted from the back, "Yeah!"

Remi smiled inwardly. She recognized the voice immediately—her star employee, hoodie pulled low as planned.

Thank you, Simi.

He was her most loyal staffer, always doing his part.

"Tired of the heat?" she called, her voice rising.

Another round of "Yeah!" echoed back—more voices this time.

"Tired of the floods and contaminated water?" The crowd roared, "Yeah!"

"How about the air pollution and wildfires?" The response was deafening.

The crowd was with her now—anger and frustration stoked with every word.

She paused, letting the energy build before cashing in on it. "But I'm not here to tear you down. No. I'm here to offer a way forward. You might ask—what way, Remi?" She almost never referred to herself in the third person, but this moment called for it. "My colleagues and I within UnaTerra have recognized the need for bold, decisive action. And we've dared to create a plan. A bold plan. One that links three key factors: carbon, productivity, and population. You know it as the Carbon Laws."

Her eyes flashed with conviction. "While other countries have resorted to cruelty, dictatorships, and violence in times of change and vulnerability, we've chosen a path of reason, balance, and justice. I've worked alongside brilliant geneticists, lawmakers, climatologists, environmental engineers, and economists to create a blueprint for the future. A future that feeds the hungry, preserves the Earth, and strengthens the greatest government ever devised—democracy."

She pumped her fist in the air to the chants, then lowered her arm. "Under the Carbon Laws, every productive American has a chance to lead a fulfilling life."

She leaned in, voice dropping to a near whisper. "But they must follow the law of the land—or rather, the land's law."

She straightened, her voice rising with a sense of finality. "The beauty of this plan is its simplicity. It rewards those who contribute—and isolates the freeloaders. Those who choose to live off the system will face consequences. But those who work— who contribute—will be rewarded with all of life's essentials. This is the essence of capitalism—of fairness, of evolution."

Her gaze swept the crowd, her next words edged with emotion. "Let me show you how UnaTerra's policies are already making a difference. Just this morning, we chartered buses to relieve the suffering on the D.C. Mall. Yes, folks, we've offered free transportation to my home state of Sustalia, where food, shelter, and meaningful jobs await. It's an opportunity for those displaced by chaos to trade labor for necessities—a fair, mutual exchange."

She paused, giving them time to absorb it.

"For those who take this offer, they'll find a new future in our modern town of Felicity. But those who choose to remain—who choose to leech off others—will continue to suffer. Even if they don't feel the pain, they represent a drain on society."

She let the silence stretch, a master at cadence. Then her voice softened, almost pleading.

"It's not too late. The buses are still running. All it takes is a signature. I personally invite anyone ready to change their life to join us. For them—and for *all* Americans—I ask you to follow UnaTerra. To live within the limits of our land. Only then can we revive the American dream. There is no other choice. UnaTerra is the only party with the answers. The Earth demands it."

The crowd erupted, applause roaring around her. Remi stood tall, eyes shining with resolve.

"Finally, I want to thank you for being part of this world tour," she continued, her voice rich with emotion. "Unlike others who

use the term, our world tour isn't about the distance we travel—
it's about protecting our home, our world. Please, join me in saving
this beautiful land. God bless you—and good Earth to you all!"

Her fist met her palm one last time in a farewell verdant salute.

The crowd jumped, arms thrusting, chanting her name: "Remi!
Remi! Remi!" The sound was deafening—and she reveled in it.

Remi waved, grabbed her notes, and stepped back, careful
never to turn her back on the audience. She removed her mic and
whispered with a small, satisfied smile, "Queen takes pawn."

Chapter 5: Zev

Zev watched the Senator on television from the empty lobby of a federal building near the IRS headquarters. He understood that the Earth needed TLC, but it was the Carbon Laws that had landed him in this mess. Senator McCarthy's face filled the screen, and Zev felt his pulse quicken. He wasn't a fan.

A feminine voice cut through the otherwise quiet room: "Number 16."

Zev looked for the woman making the announcement but saw only a diminutive, balding, and pasty male clerk in a light charcoal-colored smock. He stood in an open doorway connecting the lobby to the accounting offices. "16," the clerk repeated. His voice clearly didn't match his appearance.

Zev glanced at his smartphone; the electronic ticket read 91. There was virtually nobody else around, so he didn't understand why the wait was so long. He braced himself for what promised to be a frustrating ordeal.

The clerk repeated himself, eyeing Zev. "Number 16, please."

Zev jiggled his phone, activating the accelerometer; the ticket number flipped a full 180 degrees. Feeling like a complete fool, Zev muttered, "Yeah, here. Sorry."

"This way, Sir. Let's check you in."

Zev placed his thumb on an ultrasonic scanner, and his name appeared on the screen.

"Please review all the information before we proceed—height, weight, hair and eye color, birthdate, genome score."

Zev looked it over: 6 feet, 180 pounds, brown hair, left eye blue, right eye brown, 29 years old—today. His genome score appeared in blue, indicating he was in the top 1% of the population—an enviable value. Multiple boxes were checked, reflecting his race: Hispanic/Latino, American Indian, and Caucasian. Birth gender and identity were also displayed, listing him simply as male. "Looks right."

"Our carbon accounting specialist is ready—just down this hallway. She's waiting for you in office 29."

Zev noted, with a hint of irony, that the office number matched his age. Maybe a good omen.

He walked slowly, half-expecting this annual assessment to feel like a visit to a proctologist. Not that he'd ever been to one—his healthcare wouldn't have covered it anyway.

An overweight woman with a sourpuss expression sat behind her desk, focused on her computer. She barely acknowledged Zev. Without looking in his direction, she crudely extended her hand toward an empty, well-worn chair. A sign with an arrow pointed to the seat and read, "Old Sparky."

Zev imagined the countless tortured souls who'd sat there, facing their judgment.

Zev remained standing. The woman gave him a command as though he were a pet. "Sit!"

As she gestured toward "Sparky," she shifted slightly, sending a faint cabbage odor wafting his way. He tried to push aside his judgmental thoughts, but she rubbed him the wrong way.

With words polite but a tone disapproving, she kicked off the session. "Good Earth, Mr. Brighton. Thank you for keeping your appointment. My name is Ms. Pennington, and I'll be discussing your audit today. I have all your information up on my screen. Your carbon debits include gas, electricity, oil, flights taken, miles driven, etc. Of course, our ledgers reflect all of your credits— recycling efforts, labor contributions in offshore kelp offsets.

Even with these credits, your net carbon footprint isn't favorable. However, once you pay down your balance, we can restore your good standing."

She looked directly at Zev for the first time, her eyes scanning him like an X-ray. Her pug nose and round face reminded him of Miss Piggy from old reruns—but this woman, unlike the TV character, was mean-spirited and unlikable.

"Yes, I had a number of issues last year. My mother became ill and passed away. There were other setbacks as…"

Ms. Pennington interrupted, devoid of empathy. "Mr. Brighton, I can't be sidetracked with the details of your personal life. We're here to address your positive carbon balance. I am not a counselor or part of a support group. Now, as for your 4,463 pounds in excess, you need to zero the balance. What method will you use to pay this off today?"

Searching for words but finding none, Zev bowed his head, now the one avoiding eye contact. "I can't."

The auditor transitioned into full condescension. "When, then, Mr. Brighton? I'm sure you embody the character traits of a responsible citizen, and will do your fair part for our environment! When can you pay the amount owed?"

Old Sparky lived up to its name.

"If I could explain what happened… the funeral exp—"

Ms. Pennington's hand shot up, the traffic cop for unwanted words.

"I've made it clear this isn't a place for excuses. Answer the question, Mr. Brighton. When can you pay?"

Her tone made Zev simmer. He couldn't control most of the factors that caused his financial hardships, but this bureaucrat wasn't interested in helping.

"Mr. Brighton, are you listening to me?"

Zev fought to stay calm, but his mind drifted. He pictured a bear at a dinner table, fork and knife in its paw, the chubby woman tied up on a platter with an apple stuffed in her mouth. He nearly smiled.

"Back to Earth, Mr. Brighton. Hello!"

"I am unable to pay. What are my options?"

She shifted in her chair, then leaned back. "I see. Well, per state law, your medical care will be suspended until the balance is restored to a negative number. There will be other penalties listed in your summary report. Perhaps your choices to pay for your mother's medical care are the source of your predicament? Bad decisions lead to bad outcomes."

That did it.

"My mother isn't your concern!"

"I wasn't the one who brought her up. You did. There are consequences to our actions, no matter how well-intentioned they are."

Her smug expression was too much. Zev's restraint slipped, and he muttered, barely audibly, "You smell like cabbage."

"What?"

Recovering his common sense, Zev enunciated, loud and clear, "Savage. I said these rules are savage."

"I don't make them; I just enforce them, Mr. Brighton."

The sound of his own name now grated on him. She continued, "I've updated your records and sent you a copy of your statement. We have concluded our business. Good day, Mr. Brighton. Please see yourself out."

Zev finally lost it. "I understand that you have a job to do and that you're enforcing the rules. What I don't understand is why you choose to do it in such an unfeeling manner. You've assessed me—now allow me to return the favor. You're heartless. And... you smell!"

Not his best insult, but it flew out, raw and unfiltered.

"I suspect you're upset with yourself and taking it out on me. Please leave at once, Mr. Brighton... or shall I call security?"

Zev wanted to sweep his hands across her desk, sending her knick-knacks flying. Instead, he left—angry, but peacefully.

As he exited the building, his phone dinged. An email from the Office of Carbon Emissions Control. Ms. Pennington's parting gift.

Predictably, it confirmed that his medical coverage was terminated until the balance was paid.

But at the bottom, one more consequence was listed—one that stopped Zev in his tracks.

He stood on the sidewalk, staring at his phone, open-jawed.

Chapter 6: Luna

Luna didn't respond, so the old man asked again. "Miss, are you all right?"

Luna's tongue refused to cooperate, numb and stiff in her mouth. As a speech therapist, she knew exactly how to position it—press the midpoint against the roof of her mouth, tip pointing downward—but her body betrayed her. Her muscles were unresponsive. Paralyzed. Finally, forcing herself to speak, the words tumbled out—stuttered and broken. "Y-y-yes, I'm s-s-so sorry." She took a shaky breath, trying to steady herself. "My baby was choking but seems to be much better now. Thank you, though, for your kindness."

She silently willed him to leave. But he didn't.

"I'm a retired pediatrician," he continued, his voice warm. "Would you like me to take a look at your child?"

Luna's pulse quickened. She wanted to say no, to assert herself—but instead, she hesitated, her voice faltering. "It's not necessary. All is good now. But thanks—I really appreciate your offer."

"Well, I've come all this way," he insisted with a gentle smile. "Let me just have a quick look. I love seeing the bright young faces that will shape our future. I bet he has his mother's beautiful eyes."

Luna's stomach twisted, but she knew she had no choice. Resisting would only draw more attention. She forced herself to speak, steadying her voice with effort. "It's a she," she said, trying to sound calm. "Her name is... Karli." She stumbled over the name, scrambling for something—anything—but it was out before she could think. Lying was becoming easier, and that unsettled her. She peeled back the blanket just enough to show she was cooperating.

The baby's ivory skin and delicate Asian features were stark against the gray of the blanket—and against Luna herself. The doctor withdrew slightly, his smile faltering for a moment. He cleared his throat, then smiled again, softer this time. "Beautiful baby. I'll bet she makes her father proud."

The words hit her like a slap. He might as well have said she didn't look a thing like her mother, seeing through the deception. But the doctor's twinkling eyes revealed no malice. In fact, he reminded her of her late Zada—of better days, when things hadn't felt so... wrong. Still, she couldn't risk telling him the truth.

"I'm guessing she's about a month old? You and your husband's genome score must be the envy of many," he said, eyes alight with admiration.

Luna's mouth went dry as she spun another lie, hoping the web wouldn't trap her. "We both thank our parents for that."

"Well, she certainly looks healthy," the doctor said, his voice warm again. "A mother's love does wonders. Well, I'll be on my way now. I take a walk every morning to keep these old bones limber. Perhaps we'll meet again. Good day."

He tipped his hat with a polite gesture and left. His footsteps were slow, deliberate, as if he had nowhere else to be.

Luna watched him go, her heart pounding. Once he was far enough away, she let out a long breath she hadn't realized she'd been holding. Alone with the baby, the gravity of her situation hit all at once. She had made a decision—a deeply emotional one—and now she had to face the consequences. By not telling the doctor the truth, she had chosen a path of lawlessness, one that led her further from the life she had known.

Acid rose from her stomach, and she pressed a hand to her mouth to keep from retching. The simplicity of her studio apartment suddenly felt like a lost dream. No comfort of a cup of hot black tea, no quiet peace of normalcy. She had fallen victim to her own habits, chasing a random quote that had sent her out for a walk.

Her mind drifted back to high school—when her fear of public speaking first became evident. Despite her reluctance, she'd been pushed into the role of debate team captain. Nerves unraveled her composure. When it was her turn to speak, her voice trembled, barely rising above a whisper, and her words spilled out in a tangled mess. She'd felt unmoored, painfully out of place—no leader, just a girl caught in the spotlight with nowhere to hide. And now, that same raw exposure was creeping back in—stinging, unwelcome.

Luna needed a plan. She couldn't afford to waste time. She had to think. Moving away from the bridge, she pushed the stroller along and sank onto a nearby bench. Cradling the baby in her arms, she took in the delicate features, her mind churning for a solution. She cast out a mental line, hoping for a thought—any course of action that might tug and pull her from this mess. But instead of clarity, her thoughts tangled into a jumble of confusion and panic.

She had never done anything illegal before. She didn't know how to deceive, how to cover her tracks. She was in unfamiliar territory, with no experience to guide her.

Think, Luna. Think.

She found herself recalling the forensic cold-case shows she loved. But instead of offering a solution, they stained her thoughts with worry. She pictured a lab with blood-soaked swatches of cloth, eyedroppers, test tubes—threads of evidence everywhere.

Luna scanned the area. There were security cameras nearby. And an eyewitness. The child's DNA could be linked to the mother. She thought of the stroller, the blanket—all the tiny particles they held, each one a potential connection to the deceased mother.

She needed to get out of here. But her apartment? Out of the question. Too many eyes and ears. Nosy neighbors. If they sensed something was wrong, they might even call the authorities. She had to find somewhere safe—somewhere she could hide the baby and think.

But where?

Then, like a light flipping on, the answer came. "Of course," she whispered. A place where she could blend in—unseen, unnoticed. A place to hide in plain sight… even with the police around.

Lincoln Memorial sanctuary, the tent city.

Chapter 7: Kylo

Sergeant Kylo Cromley scraped the last stroke of his razor along his jaw and studied the mirror. The face staring back looked older than thirty-six—dark circles sagged beneath his eyes like permanent bruises. And no matter how close the shave, a stubborn shadow remained, giving his face a harsher, more intimidating edge.

But like a book in the wrong dust jacket, the outside didn't match the story inside. Beneath the imposing six-foot-five frame beat the heart of a man more teddy bear than tough guy—a teddy bear with lungs that had never pulled their full weight. Asthma had been his shadow since childhood, tightening his chest without warning. And this morning's humidity made each breath feel heavier, with the thought of another long shift outside not helping.

He reached for the inhaler, his thumb finding the familiar curve, and drew in the cool mist. Relief came in slow, measured rhythms. At least he still qualified for medical care. The genome test—the Carbon Law deciding who could have children—hadn't existed when his daughter was born. That door was locked now.

Thoughts drifted to Ingrid and Alma. Ingrid had been his anchor from the beginning, steadying him through every squall and giving him a child who became his compass. At home, there was always food on the table, nothing fancy, but she could turn simple staples into comfort. In a world that was fraying, their home still felt whole.

Before leaving, he made his rounds. A cop never knew if he'd make it back.

In Alma's room, her breathing was slow, hair fanned across the pillow. She looked older than the little girl who still lived in his mind. He kissed her forehead lightly. Back in the master bedroom, Ingrid stirred as his lips brushed hers.

"Don't forget it's Alma's birthday tomorrow," she murmured.

His eyes widened. "Tomorrow? I thought it was Saturday."

"That's her party, cloud hopper. The actual birthday's tomorrow."

He pointed to his head. "Too many dates rattlin' around up here."

"That's why you've got me—full-time corrections officer. But don't you ever forget our anniversary."

"I suppose that's tomorrow too?"

"Nope. Today."

His expression went blank.

She grinned. "Kidding. If it was, you'd be on the sofa."

"I'd say the garage."

Drawing him into a hug, she said, "Absentminded, but still a great dad… and a tolerable husband."

"High praise. And you—practically perfect in every way. My Mary Poppins."

"So true." Her smile eased, "Honey… she still wants a puppy—a terrier."

"You know we can't afford that."

"I think we could stretch the credits—gardening, composting…"

"We'll see." He said it, knowing full well he had no intention of adding a dog to the mix.

Shifting against the pillow, Ingrid said, "I had a dream last night. Will you promise me something?"

"Sure."

"Be careful today."

He bit back asking any questions. Her dreams too often ended badly.

"Ring promise." He laced his fingers through hers until their wedding bands touched, and she drew their joined hands to her chest. With her free hand, she gave his stomach a playful tap. "And skip that second helping of cake Saturday. We want you sticking around."

"To pay the bills," he said, grinning.

"True… and because I love you." He leaned in for a kiss—then pulled back, waving a hand. "Whoa! We could use you to take down the bad guys."

Her eyes narrowed, a smile tugging at her lips before she rolled away. "Ha! I can brush my teeth, but you can't fix being a cloud hopper. Can remember faces—uncannily—but never dates." Her words softened, blurring into something he couldn't catch, and sleep claimed her in seconds.

Kylo left her and headed to the kitchen. He poured himself coffee, swallowing too soon, and scalded his tongue. But the sting didn't stop him—he kept drinking in quick sips until the cup was empty. Coffee cost credits, and he wasn't about to waste it. It was still cheaper than the other boosts.

In the garage, he untethered his moped. At his size, the little machine looked like a joke, but with one family car eating most of their income, it was the only option. The short ride to the station barely registered—his body steered while his mind wandered to a cross-country trip with his parents, a lifetime ago.

By the time he parked, he was only slightly more awake. Another day of the unpredictable—what he loved most about the job. People were wild cards, especially in a collapsing world. Foot patrol kept him close to the city's pulse, though it also meant he couldn't avoid the ugly—homeless camps for the displaced, the raw edge of survival.

Through the PD doors, a voice boomed from behind.

"Yo, is that Bigfoot? Nuddah freakin' day."

Kylo didn't have to turn. "Hey, Trev."

Trevor's New York accent came through thick, with "freakin'" slipping into nearly every conversation. Kylo had noticed it years ago; now it was just part of the background hum. Trevor was built like a tank—broad, dense muscle stuffed into a frame with barely enough room for a neck. And he talked as if someone paid him by the word, a habit that had earned him the nickname Round Mound of Sound. Most people just called him Romoso.

"Wutcha beat t'day, bud?" Trevor asked.

"Mall." Short answers were survival.

"Aw, the tents again? Same here. Grab yaself some nose plugs, I'm tellin' ya. That smell—fuhgeddaboudit—it's like nobody's evah hearda soap. Disgustin'. An' Don's the worst, him an' all his freakin' johns. Ain't nearly enougha 'em, neither. Fecal matter everywhere. Gonna make me quit, I swear on my ma."

Kylo faced his locker, fastening his inner belt. Eye contact was a trap—one glance and Trevor would keep going.

Baton, pepper spray, taser, flashlight, spare batteries, gloves, pens, pencils, keys, multi-tool, Glock 17, two mags, two sets of cuffs, radio—the duty belt took its weight. His inhaler slid into its pouch. Fully loaded, it felt heavy enough to moor a boat.

Kevlar vest secured, he moved to roll call. Captain Iris Fonner stood at the front, posture straight but not stiff, a braid down her back. She scanned the roster, then the room.

"Quiet night," she said. "One BOLO—and I emphasize, Be On The Look Out. This one matters. Eyes to the screen."

A grainy photo appeared: long, frizzy brown hair, full beard, lazy left eye, and a "1488" tattoo on the temple.

"For those who don't know," Fonner said, "1488 combines two white supremacist codes: the '14 words' and '88' for 'Heil Hitler.' This man's been verbally threatening displaced residents near the Mall."

A slow weight settled on Kylo's chest. The camp had swelled after two Category 5 hurricanes—Tampa crushed first, then Miami drowned under a stalled storm. Puerto Rican families now filled many of the tents. They'd lost everything, and summer heat made the misery worse.

As she spoke, he noticed Fonner kept looking at him. "We don't know his name, but he's targeting non-whites. We need confirmation for a hate-crime charge. Take a handout. Stay safe. Dismissed."

As the room cleared, she called, "Sergeant Cromley, a word?"

"Yes, ma'am."

She waited until the door shut and they were alone. "You've got that face-memory talent. Do you know him?"

"No."

"Take a handout anyway. Show it around."

Curious, he asked, "Is there a reason you kept looking at me?"

Her frown deepened. "I didn't want to announce it, but... yes, there is."

She paused, as he spread his hands, palms up, a silent 'get on with it' in his eyes.

"That man was shouting your name. Repeatedly. He called you a racist."

Chapter 8: Zev

Morning always hit D.C. hard, a shadow of its former prestige. No politicians rushing past, no aides chasing them, no tourists clogging the sidewalks. Travel was for the rich; the carbon rules had killed it for everyone else.

Shops were boarded up, signs fading, awnings ripped and sagging. Over the years, Zev watched the city slowly hollow out—still crowded, but now desperate.

A siren wailed. A fight echoed two blocks away. Smoke and trash hung in the air. It was a city of duality. The 'haves' kept chaos at bay with guards and shuttles. The 'have-nots' scraped by in the gutters. Zev walked between them, catching perfume and piss in the same breath.

Even the wealthy were splintered. The ultra-rich hid in VR compounds. The rest—mostly government workers—risked the trek to their fortified offices where they shuffled papers on crime stats and immigration quotas, ignoring the world beyond the country's borders.

Like every morning, the crowd flowed like a river, and Zev was moving with it, up until his phone chimed. His eyes were locked on an email, stopping him mid-step, causing the people behind him to stumble into his back.

"Watch out, buddy."

He barely heard them. Instead, he was focused on a letter, every word feeling like a noose drawing in around his neck.

Mr. Brighton,

As a result of the audit conducted on August 20, your medical coverage has been terminated effective immediately. Additionally, due to your carbon balance shortfall, your reproductive rights have been suspended as well.

Both privileges may be reinstated upon payment of the balance due and successful reapplication for benefits. Thank you for your continued commitment to addressing the environmental challenges facing our nation—and the world.

Sincerely,

Ms. Florinda Pennington

Auditing Director, Office of Carbon Emissions Control

Zev staggered back as the email hit him with brutal force. Medical coverage—gone. That alone was devastating. But the suspension of his reproductive rights—the sheer absurdity of it— cut deeper. It wasn't even about wanting children. It was the principle. The idea that some invisible system could dictate something so personal.

His thoughts spun. He'd tangled with bureaucracy before— fought the slow, grinding machinery of red tape. He knew the game: endless forms, months of dead ends. A system built not to help, but to break you. The only time a human voice answered was when you owed money.

His legs weakened. How could he keep pushing when the system seemed hell-bent on crushing him? It wasn't just about survival now. It was about navigating a maze of control—a maze with no way out.

Zev felt closer than ever to joining the 'have-nots.' With his carbon audit going badly, he either had to pay the debt or risk joining the Mall's displaced, living in poverty and under curfews.

He looked around. A man shoved past, a cardboard sign hanging from his neck: FOOD OR WATER, PLEASE. Others begged for booze, meds, cash, even drugs. A barefoot boy slipped through the crowd, ribs showing, searching trash cans for anything of value. A woman cradled a baby on the curb, whispering unintelligibly. All around, the damage showed—swollen eyes, rashes on limbs, teeth blackened and broken. And that was only the surface. Zev couldn't imagine the damage he didn't see.

He felt hopeless.

Then, a torn poster caught his eye, crumpled in the gutter: NEED CREDITS? YE$$?

WORK, FOOD, CALL NOW.

He'd seen them before—vanishing as quickly as they appeared. But today, in his desperation, he felt a pull. Maybe, just maybe, this was a way out.

He picked it up. Underneath was something he hadn't seen in years—a penny, long out of circulation. This one was heads up.

A sign under a sign.

He dialed. A woman answered, monotone and impersonal. "Displacement Services."

"My name is Zev Brighton. I was inquiring about your ad. Do you still have job openings?" His voice sounded hoarse, not as friendly as he had hoped.

"I'm sorry," she said. "That was weeks ago. Those vacancies have been filled."

He pressed. "Is there anything else? I'll work long hours. I'm available now."

A long pause. The kind that made his heart pound faster.

"We have one commission-based opportunity," the woman said, her voice softer than before. "I was about to post it, but it's not the same job. You'd need to sign a waiver."

Zev straightened. "What's the position?"

"You'd be on a roundup team." Her voice faltered for a beat.

He'd heard rumors—but never met anyone who joined. "What does it involve?"

"Gathering the homeless. Getting them onto buses. Shipping them west to Felicity."

"Felicity?"

"Yes. They'll work in exchange for food, clothing, and shelter."

Zev's mind raced. "And the waiver?"

Her voice dropped lower. "The government's clearing the camps. They need to move people somewhere. This is about helping them… but it's not without danger. Not everyone goes quietly. Some fight."

He felt cold sweat bead at the back of his neck. The risks were real. But what else did he have left? The city—his future—it was all slipping away.

"What's the pay?" he asked.

"You get paid by the busload. It can add up—in carbon credits. But like I said… it's not without risk."

He felt a flutter in his belly. How much worse could it get? Maybe this was his one chance—to claw back some control.

He drew a breath. "How do I apply?"

"You'll need to meet Avi Sweller. We're temporarily stationed in the Archives building. He's out right now, but should be back soon."

Zev nodded instinctively, forgetting he wasn't visible. "I'll be there in half an hour."

"We'll see you soon," she replied before hanging up.

He slid the phone into his pocket. Ahead, the National Archives loomed, its granite columns guarding a country that no longer upheld the ideals it once stood for.

He made his way toward the entrance, where words were etched in stone—a harbinger of truth:

"What is past is prologue."

Chapter 9: Avi

Avi stepped into General Stuart's office. The General sat behind his mahogany desk, eyes locked on Avi. The pungent smell of wood polish mixed with the stale ghost of cigar smoke. Smoking was forbidden in the building, but no one dared remind the General of the regulations. His battle-worn scowl was fixed on Avi—today, the lines were deeper and darker than usual.

Before Avi could close the door, the General's voice ripped through the air like gunfire.

"What the fuck, Avi? You're like a nitwit fullback with too many concussions—charging the wrong way down the field!"

General Stuart had been a college football player, and his leadership style still lived in the locker room. There was no room for losing in his playbook.

Avi flinched, trying to absorb the assault, but the General's insult hit Avi's chest like a punch.

"Let me make this simple—DO... YOUR... FUCKING... JOB."

He stood, stabbing a finger at a photo on his desk.

"The aerial photos don't lie—this is expansion, not retraction. This isn't some damn charity game. You're not containing this thing—you're feeding it. We were supposed to be pulling the population back, yet it's up by ten percent. Ten. Percent. So tell me—what the hell do you think your job is? Because right now, I'm wondering if hiring your company was the worst damn call I've made this year."

Avi forced the words out.

"Sir, we misjudged the migration. Our calculations were based on the peak two weeks ago, but then the second hurricane—"

The General's fist slammed against the table. His nostrils flared, disgust flashing in his eyes.

"You assumed? What is this, Avi—some back-alley guessing game? You know the saying: when you assume, you make an 'ass' out of 'u' and 'me'." But here's the real problem: when more goes in than comes out, it gets bigger. Just like you, butterball. You're gorging on excuses instead of carving this problem down to size. Drop the fork, Avi, and fix it."

Avi knew he didn't fit the General's mold. At thirty-nine, he carried too much weight around the middle, stood five-eight in shoes with a lifting heel, and had a sweating problem that humiliated him daily.

"These are circumstances out of our control," he muttered, hating how small his voice sounded.

The General leaned forward, eyes locking on Avi with predatory focus.

"In football, we didn't get the luxury of excuses. Players went down—did that stop us from winning the championship? Hell no. We adapted. We found a way. You're not doing that. Fix it. This is your last warning. I don't give a damn how much your wife's daddy shields you. Now get those disgusting pit stains out of my office before I throw you out myself."

Avi left with his tail between his legs. He'd taken plenty of "Alpha Charlies" before—cheap shots—but this one had teeth. The insults were meant to wound, and they hit their mark. He was running out of ideas to salvage the mission.

He stumbled out of the Pentagon feeling eviscerated. The thought of losing everything—his career, his credibility—made him dizzy. He needed a plan, and fast.

His career was circling the drain.

On the Metro, the city felt like a pressure cooker, the Yellow Line groaning and shuddering beneath him. The lack of air conditioning made the sweat roll faster, sliding down his spine and pooling at his waistband.

He got off and began the short walk to the National Archives, rubbing his temples in a futile attempt to stop the headache forming in his skull. The humidity clung to him like a wet towel. He couldn't tell if the sweat was from the weather, the General, or the fear of the unpredictable homeless near his office—the dangers in his life were multiplying by the day.

Inside, he flashed his badge at security, trying to ignore the gnawing in his gut. Temporary headquarters once meant progress; now it felt like a trap with no exit.

His secretary sat outside his office. "Good morning, Mr. Sweller. A gentleman's waiting for you in the conference room. He's a referred applicant."

Avi nodded, taking the folder. "Send him in."

"Your wife is also on the line, waiting."

He rolled his eyes and sighed. "Okay. Just a minute."

In his office, he dropped the folder on his desk, his fingers trembling slightly as he wiped moisture from his brow. The General's words echoed: "DO YOUR FUCKING JOB." Filling the buses was critical. He wiped his face with a towel, trying to steady his heart rate before picking up the phone.

He sat down. "Hello, honey."

"Hi, love. How was your meeting with the General?"

"Good. Everything's fine."

"That's wonderful. I just found the perfect kitchen remodeler. He's a little more expensive, but worth it."

"What's it going to cost?"

"With your promotion, it'll be money well spent. You'll be eating like a king."

Avi's mind flashed to her father, who'd doubted him even on their wedding day.

"Okay, honey, listen, I need to go." He hung up, finances now added to his worries. The whole thing felt like a house of cards, one gust from collapse.

He studied the folder—references, résumé, clean record. Zev Brighton might be part of the solution.

Zev entered moments later.

"Hello, Mr. Sweller. I was told you might have a position available at the Lincoln Sanctuary?"

Avi nodded absently. "Mall IDP," he muttered.

Zev's eyes narrowed.

"Mall for Internally Displaced Personnel. The media calls it a sanctuary. We don't like the term."

"Got it."

Avi looked up. "You've worked as a kelp diver? I never got into scuba—couldn't get into the wetsuits. Why the change?"

"I'm in debt. My mother was ill. Bills piled up. I need my medical coverage back."

"Honesty… rare these days. Glad she's better."

"She passed away."

Avi studied his folder, not interested in the details. "Sorry to hear that."

After a beat, he leaned back in his chair.

"Here's the deal. My job is to relocate people—get them out of the Mall. Some of them are willing to go—jobs, shelter, food. Senator McCarthy's been running a program for that. But there's a stubborn group that remains. We don't want to resort to force, at least not yet. I need someone who can help move them voluntarily. Your job is to fill the buses. You won't be the driver, but we'll need you to ride along and see the job through to the end."

Zev didn't flinch. "Sounds good. I'll do it."

"There's a catch," Avi said, leaning forward. "It might get ugly. Down in the muck. These are desperate people."

"I need the money, sir. Whatever it takes."

Avi studied him in silence, not seeing any sign of hesitation, just what he needed.

"I doubt you'll thank me when it's over. Good luck, Zev."

As the applicant left, Avi leaned back in his chair, rubbing his chin. His plan was split in two, and Zev was only one half of it. The other branch—the darker, secret one—needed checking. It was time to see how far it had advanced.

Chapter 10: Luna

Luna made her way to the Lincoln Memorial sanctuary, pushing the stroller with Jade nestled inside. She knew she'd eventually have to abandon it—the wheels could be traced back to her—but for now, the carriage was essential for the long mile to the encampment. Soon, they would be just two more lost souls folded into the crowd, at least until she figured things out. She glanced at Jade, her heart racing at the memory of the mother's desperate final act.

My God, she didn't even tell me her name.

Luna gathered her strength and pressed on, stepping into the unknown.

The only thing Luna knew about the camp was from the news. She had never ventured beyond the safety of her walled-in life and didn't know what to expect. Thousands had found temporary refuge near the Reflecting Pool, and the government hadn't yet forced anyone to clear out. A longer-term solution was still supposedly in the works, but for now, the homeless were allowed to stay.

Luna was still struggling to adapt to this new reality, a headache brewing as her mind scrambled to form new pathways for the tasks ahead. Survival would demand careful planning. Fighting against her need for routine, she reflected on a quote by Alice Duer Miller, her favorite American poet and suffragist: *"The strongest will is the will that knows how to bend."*

But today, she preferred a humbler version, from Dolly Parton: *"We cannot direct the wind, but we can adjust the sails."* Now, those words felt urgent—a makeshift mantra, a reminder to keep moving forward, to expect the unexpected. She knew she had to summon an inner strength she'd never needed before.

As she walked, she began to consider how she might hand Jade—no, Karli—over to the police, recasting her as an American child. The name had to be changed, just in case. Identifying her as a Chinese citizen could mean deportation and, most likely, death. Luna could claim that both the child's papers and her parents had been lost in the storm surge down south, and that the infant was orphaned.

But how did I end up with Karli?

Nothing came to mind. *Maybe the walk will give me answers,* she thought, but the anxiety monster was already clawing at her again.

Luna felt like she was living two lives now. There was the studious, rule-following therapist—the friendly, law-abiding woman who had once been her. And then there was her desperate inner twin, a woman living in the shadows, her identity obscured and tested by overwhelming challenges. This shadow twin was no superhero—perhaps not even courageous. The only weapon she wielded was a willingness to shield the truth.

Call it what it is… lying.

She was determined not to cry, but the weight of it all fractured her resolve. She didn't like being secretive. She wondered if the mother's body had been discovered. If so, cameras might have caught her at the scene. Bile rose in her throat.

That stupid quote about breaking my routine got me into this mess!

Finally, it was time to abandon the stroller. Luna veered off the main path into a park where a rusted playground stood. Homeless men, women, and children were scattered about—sitting on benches, slumped beneath dead trees, sprawled across patches of brown weeds and grass. Many watched her, sensing she didn't belong. She approached the swings and stopped, quickly stuffing what she could into her pockets. Then she lifted Karli from the stroller, peeling away the blanket.

With Karli draped over her shoulder, she walked away, putting distance between herself and any trace of evidence. She paused and glanced back—at one of the last remaining ties between the child and her mother. A few displaced figures were already fighting over it, yanking the empty stroller like scavengers tearing at a carcass. She turned and kept walking. There was no getting it back now.

With Karli in her arms, she strode forward, urgency in every step, until the white marble columns of the Lincoln Memorial came into view, rekindling something that felt almost like resolve. Maybe she could draw strength from the president immortalized there—do what was right, even at the cost of her own needs. But then again, Lincoln's story hadn't ended well.

As she neared the Reflecting Pool, her stomach twisted.

There were too many people—far too many. Luna kept her head down, trying to move through the crowd without brushing against anyone, but it was impossible. Bodies pressed close, tents jammed into every available space. The air reeked—sweat, urine, feces, spoiled food, grass. It hit her all at once and didn't let up, thick and constant.

Most of the tents had laundry lines strung between them, sagging under stained shirts, threadbare towels, socks stiff with grime. The Reflecting Pool—if it could still be called that—was being used to wash clothes and dishes. Someone was rinsing their hair in it. The water was dark with algae, green swirls mixed with trash and filth. It looked more like sewage than anything safe.

Luna kept her eyes moving, scanning the mess of people and tents. This wasn't temporary. It wasn't being managed. People were surviving in filth, with nowhere to go.

This is no place for Karli.

Suddenly, Luna felt a touch on her shoulder.

She spun around, startled, and found herself face-to-face with a man wearing a calm expression. He stood out from the rest—well-dressed, striking, composed. His eyes held something unreadable—perhaps empathy, or something harder to place. He offered a soft smile.

"Hi. I'm Zev. I was wondering if you might be interested in hearing about an opportunity out West?"

Luna blinked, struggling to process his words as a wave of exhaustion hit her. *Out West? What kind of question is that?* She drew Karli in closer, eyes narrowing. Everyone had an angle.

Zev's voice remained gentle. "What's your name?"

Chapter 11: Kylo

A large crowd had gathered, forming a tight ring around a white sphere lying on the grass. It was no bigger than a ping-pong ball, with a ragged strip of pinkish tissue clinging to its side and a glossy, dark-brown disk staring out from the center. An elderly woman broke through the crowd and stepped toward it.

"No, Abuelita, no toques," the granddaughter warned, but the gray-haired woman refused to be told what she could or couldn't do. She bent down and scooped up the grisly fragment with one hand.

"Mija, es un ojo humano."

A voice from the crowd demanded, "Well? What the hell did she say?"

The granddaughter replied, her tone firm, "It's a human eye. Abuelita, put it down—es evidencia." She scanned the crowd. "Someone call the cops."

Kylo, on foot patrol nearby, was quickly ushered to the scene. Feeling like Moses parting a sea of bodies, he pushed through toward the object that had hypnotized the onlookers. He crouched for a closer look and confirmed what he'd been told. Without hesitation, he radioed for backup, then began scanning faces for anything—or anyone—out of place.

"Does anyone know what happened here?" he asked. The granddaughter translated into Spanish. Heads shook.

"Anyone see someone missing an eye? Or injured?" Another wave of silent headshakes.

"Did anyone hear a scream? See anything unusual?" Nothing.

Assessing that there was no immediate threat, Kylo knew he needed to establish a perimeter. That would be tricky—the tents were jammed so close that some might as well have been welded together, pitched exactly where he wanted to cordon off. Minutes later, Trevor arrived, moving with the urgency of a tank. After a quick exchange, he pulled out tape, ready to secure a fifteen-foot radius. They worked together, the result looking less like a circle and more like a lopsided octagon, its "spokes" stretching to tree branches, tent poles, and sticks jabbed into the dirt. More officers rolled in as they waited for the investigative team.

A young Hispanic teen reached over the tape and tugged on Kylo's sleeve. "Excuse me, officer… we found something you should see." His mother, standing just behind him, muttered, "Otro."

Kylo caught Trevor's eye and gave a quick nod. "Let's go. The others can hold this spot."

They ducked under the taut tape and followed the boy and his mother. Within seconds, they came upon a severed human finger lying on the ground. A smaller crowd hovered nearby, faces caught between fascination, disgust, and fear.

The victim appeared to be African-American.

Trevor shook his head. "Looks like our eyeball guy lost a few more parts, huh? Freakin' nightmare."

Kylo crouched for a closer look, keeping his voice low. "Clean cut. Whoever did this keeps their knives sharp. The killer—if this is a murder—knew exactly what they were doing."

From a short distance away, another voice shouted, "Officer! You'll wanna see this."

Trevor groaned. "Aw, c'mon, gimme a freakin' break. I told ya—I deadass hate this place."

Kylo shot him a look. "Stay here. Lock this down."

Walking toward the voice, Kylo found a severed ear.

Trevor whined from a few yards away, "I'm tellin' ya, our guy's tossin' body parts all over the effin' place."

Kylo shook his head. "I don't think so. These parts form a line. We're being led somewhere."

His instincts kept him walking, following the grisly breadcrumb trail. As the years passed, he had learned to listen to his gut—and he trusted it now. Soon, he spotted another finger—this time actually, a thumb, sliced clean away. A little further on, a fresh horror: a fleshy organ, hard to identify—maybe a kidney.

The trail ended at a tent. Something lay outside the entrance: human skin, spread flat like a rug, with the word "Welcome" written in red. The letters were neat enough to earn an English teacher's praise—if not for the horror they were created from.

Avoiding the display, Kylo pulled back the tent flap and peered inside.

"Bingo."

Chapter 12: Luna

Luna wasn't comfortable providing her own name for a variety of reasons—especially explaining the dire circumstances in which Zev had found her. Instead, she asked, "Are you with the Park Authority?" She had to get the child to safety—away from the chaos.

Before Zev could answer, the conversation was disrupted as they stood near the edge of the reflecting pool. A charity worker appeared, toting a wagon with a large container of water and a metal ladle. A crowd surged forward, cups thrust out like open hands, shoving for a better spot—like they were begging for porridge.

Luna instinctively tightened her grip on the child, pulling Karli closer against her chest. She recalled when water bottles were allowed—long gone now, since single-use plastics were banned.

Zev's voice cut through the noise. "I'm not with the police, miss. But maybe I can help." He sounded suspiciously eager. She wanted to brush him off, especially as his eyes flicked to the brochures in his hands. She saw the shift—this wasn't just about helping. He was pitching something.

Every part of her wanted to shut him down. This wasn't the time for offers or schemes. What she needed was to get the child to the authorities and return to her stable life. But walking away without a word felt impossible. She couldn't bring herself to be rude, even if he had an ulterior motive—whatever it was.

"Are you sheltered here?" Zev continued. "If so, I've got some information you might want. Plenty of rewarding jobs in the beautiful town of Felicity, Sustalia. We offer free transportation. It's a safe option for you and your child."

Luna felt her suspicions confirmed—he was clearly looking to cash in. But none of it mattered. Not the jobs or the town. Not the free transportation. Still, the word "safe" caught her interest. There was no safety here—not for her, and certainly not for Karli.

She glanced at him, trying to keep her face neutral. "No. And this isn't my child. Thank you, though." A plan—half-formed, but something—was taking shape. The words slipped out before she could stop them.

"I offered to watch the baby while her mother went to the bathroom. She never came back."

It was the only way forward—another lie. The words felt strange on her tongue, but they were believable.

No one needed to know the mother wasn't just lost—she was dead. World circumstances had claimed her, like so many others. But Luna didn't have to say that. She could hand the child over to the authorities, who'd assume the mother was American. Karli would be offered for adoption. It would be over. Luna could go on with her life. Her conscience could be clear.

"Have you seen the police?" she asked, forcing herself to focus.

Zev looked at her with concern. "Sounds like you've got a serious problem. What did the mother look like? Maybe we can find her together."

Luna wasn't interested in partnering up. He didn't seem like a threat—not exactly. But he was making this harder than it needed to be. She just needed to get away from him, find an officer, and then… it would be over.

"No," she said, harsher than she intended. She softened, "Thanks, but I'll look on my own. Shouldn't be hard."

"You sure?" Zev pressed. "What was she wearing?"

Damn it. How do I get out of this?

Luna forced a tight smile. "I'm good. Really."

Zev studied her for a moment, then leaned in slightly. "Mystery woman. Got it."

Irritated—and now letting it show—she started to snap back.

But Gandhi's words echoed in her mind: *"Speak only if it improves upon the silence."*

Luna drew a slow breath and turned to walk away.

"They'll want your name, you know," Zev called after her.

Luna's stomach twisted. She turned, keeping her face impassive. "What?"

"The police," Zev said slowly. "They'll need to know who you are—and what happened with the baby. I just figured... you seemed reluctant to give your info. Just trying to prepare you."

She'd been thinking ahead, plotting her way back to normal. But this—this she hadn't considered. Giving her identity to the police? That, she couldn't do. Her heart hammered as she bit the inside of her cheek, struggling to stay calm.

He stepped closer, voice soft. "Not to pry. I really do want to help you."

He seemed genuine—too genuine. And that's what bothered her. He could see the fear in her eyes. See the cracks. But what could she say? She didn't want his help. She didn't want anyone's help. She just wanted to disappear.

Before she could respond, a man burst from the crowd, slicing through with such force that Zev stumbled sideways. He was unkempt, his long, scraggly beard tangled and windblown. He didn't apologize—didn't even glance their way—as he shoved Zev aside, moving like someone who thought the entire grounds was his for the taking. Then he was gone, bulldozing through the horde, vanishing as abruptly as he'd appeared.

Luna didn't recognize him, but something about him set her on edge. His left eye looked wrong. And the numbers tattooed across his face... impossible to ignore.

"There are some scary folks around," Zev said, almost reading her mind. "It's just not safe here. Anyway, my offer stands." He handed her a brochure. "My number's on the back. Buses leave Constitution and 7th at 7 a.m.—first thing. If you change your mind..."

Luna took the brochure, seizing the chance to end the conversation. She nodded, fighting to steady her breath, to hold herself together. She needed to leave the Mall.

She opened her mouth to offer a final, firm thank you—and a blood-curdling scream tore through the air.

She froze. Every muscle locked.

The scream didn't stop. It echoed again—longer this time, louder, raw with terror.

Luna's eyes darted across the crowd, searching for the source. Nothing. Just a swell of chaos. But she knew the direction it had come from.

Zev scanned the area as well. "Wonder what that's about?" His tone dropped—soft, confused.

Luna swallowed hard.

Get away. Now.

Her feet finally moved—but curiosity snagged her, and instead of fleeing, she inched toward the scream.

Chapter 13: Zev

Zev watched the mystery woman head toward the commotion.

He let her go, seeing that she didn't want his help. "You've got your own problems," he mumbled to himself.

But the screaming didn't stop—harsh, raw, impossible to ignore.

Was this what Sweller meant? The risks… the violence?

He thought about the dangers of the tent city. Then his thoughts returned to the woman—and the baby. Their plight clung to him in a way he couldn't shake.

With some reluctance, he gave in and fell in behind her, weaving through the camp toward the uproar.

Within moments, they reached the heart of the chaos—an angry mob had gathered near a tent, yelling at the police.

A senior officer, his nametag reading "Kylo," stood at the center, trying to bring order. His voice rang out above the throng, steady but strained, as he motioned with both hands for calm.

"Please, everyone, give us some space. We need to secure the crime scene."

A harsh voice cut through the clamor: "Why the hell should we? You didn't protect us—just look at the bodies in that tent. What's left of them."

Zev watched Kylo pull out a small cylinder and lift it to his mouth, inhaling. His hand trembled slightly, but his voice held steady.

"I understand this is upsetting, but we need to preserve what happened here. The evidence we find might help us stop further violence. Please, everyone, back away a few steps."

Kylo's calm demeanor seemed to work. Slowly, people edged back from the tent.

Zev caught sight of a stooped woman nearby, her face etched with disbelief as she stared at the scene. He leaned in, his volume quiet so only she could hear.

"What happened here?"

Her lower lip quivered. When she spoke, her voice was barely a whisper.

"Two people… skinned… dissected… too horrible…"

The words broke off. She clutched the crucifix at her neck, her other hand rising in a slow, trembling sign of the cross. After a long, heavy moment, she bowed her head and seemed to fold inward. Zev stayed silent, watching her retreat.

Kylo finished roping off the area and stepped back, his eyes scanning the crowd. Zev looked at the scene—and froze.

A welcome mat lay outside the tent's entrance. The sight of it sent a chill through him, stirring up memories he'd buried—a Halloween long ago, shadows that still clung to him.

He shook his head hard, shoving the thought away before it could take hold.

He knew exactly what he was looking at: human remains.

His eyes snapped back to Kylo, then slid toward the mystery woman. How was she handling this? Would she still report the infant?

He was about to ask, when Kylo turned back to the crowd, raising his voice.

"Folks, can I have your attention?"

He waited for the murmurs to fade.

"My name is Officer Kylo Cromley. Thank you for your cooperation and for giving us some space. I know it's been difficult living here, but we want to make it as safe as possible. If you have information or witnessed anything suspicious, please don't leave the area."

He held up a photograph—a bearded man—and began walking in a slow circle, showing it to as many people as he could.

"Also, if you've seen this man, let us know immediately. One of his eyes drifts slightly—a key detail to help identify him. If you come in contact with him, don't engage. He's considered dangerous. If you have any information, Officer Trevor and I want to hear from you."

Zev squinted at the photo. An empty feeling formed a pit in his stomach. It was the same man who'd nearly bowled him over moments ago.

Goosebumps crawled along his neck and shoulders. He spun around, scanning the crowd for any signs of him.

Gone.

He turned to the mystery woman. "That's the guy that—"

But she was gone too.

He pushed through a few knots of people—nowhere. No sign of her.

She hadn't given her name. Hadn't spoken to the authorities. Hadn't said a word about the child.

She left—somewhere among the tents, with a baby—and a killer still on the loose.

Her story doesn't add up.

He decided to approach the officer.

Chapter 14: Avi

Avi sat at his desk, sweat darkening his shirt once more.

A soft knock, then the door cracked open.

His admin spoke softly, "It's the CEO on line one."

Avi had made it clear—never refer to him as "my father-in-law." Everything had to stay professional. No reminders he hadn't earned the job.

"Tell him I'm in a meeting."

"He said you'd say that. He's furious. Said he spoke to the General after you left."

Avi closed his eyes. "Fine. Put him through."

After a beat of silence, he lifted the receiver. "Yes?"

"Listen up, pantywaist," the voice hissed, low and cold. "I built this company from the ground up—before you were even a twinkle. And now you're about to burn it all down."

Avi swallowed hard. "I can deliver, sir."

"Don't 'Sir' me. You thought you'd coast to the top on my daughter's name. *My* name. Not anymore. Fail this one, and you're out. Got it? And Evelyn and Oscar will move back home."

"I have a plan."

"Well?"

"I—Sir, I have another call."

"Don't hang—"

Avi cut the line. The old man's temper was fierce, but Avi doubted he'd ever pull the trigger—not while Evelyn still believed in him. The old man's love for his daughter ran deeper than anything Avi could muster.

But right now, far worse problems loomed.

He had heard the news and initially felt angry—but now was mostly afraid. What began as a pleasant morning had twisted into a nightmare. It was bad enough the General and his father-in-law threatened his job—but far worse was the looming threat of his involvement in a murder. Prison was tough on the soft and plump, and he knew he wouldn't fare well with hardened inmates— especially if the specifics of his actions leaked out. The fact that the crime seemed racially motivated only made things worse.

He couldn't wait any longer. He exhaled and grabbed his burner phone, mind racing. As he started to dial, the outside line rang again—his admin's voice faint beyond the door.

He yelled out, "No more calls."

Then he punched in the number, praying this would be the last time.

An overly familiar male voice answered after one ring.

"Boss man!" Blackjack's cheery tone made Avi's stomach twist.

"What the hell did you do? I said scare them, not mur…" Avi bit off the word. Technology left trails. He couldn't risk it.

Blackjack sounded almost gleeful. "Oh, I'm sure they're scared, Boss man. Sure as the sun beats down and makes us sweat. You sweating?"

"Listen, Blackjack. I didn't ask for this. I'm out."

Blackjack laughed. "Oh, you're in it, Chief. Dead center. No undo button. After all, you hired me. We're linked. And lucky for me, I've got… let's call it an invoice. Just in case things go south."

A trail? How? He's bluffing. I've been careful.

"What invoice?" Avi's gut clenched.

"Let's just say I picked our first meeting spot for a reason."

The implication hit Avi like ice water. Cameras. Microphones. Evidence. His pulse hammered.

Goddamn it. How could I be this stupid?

"Okay, okay… Let's reset. Keep this friendly."

"I'm not the one upset, Chief. I'm your humble servant."

"Well… consider the job complete. I'll get you the final payment. Hopefully, the Mall rats decide to move on."

"Nope. They haven't fully heard the message yet."

"You've done enough. They're starting up again—on buses, headed west. Senator McCarthy in Sustalia actually wants them… God knows why."

Blackjack chuckled. "Don't think it'll be that easy, Boss. The disease is still spreading, creeping into the capital. Our message isn't loud enough. No… this is just the beginning. I've been brainstorming a few ideas, giving them more inspiration."

"What do you mean?"

"We could poison the water… or light fires around their camp at night. Maybe stir them up into a good ol' race war—ebony versus ivory. Oppressed versus authority. Catholics versus Muslims. Jews versus everybody. The possibilities are endless."

Avi fought to keep his voice steady. "No. We wait. See how the political winds blow first."

"No can do, Chief. Starting to think we're not even reading the same book. You're not going soft on me, are you? One of those Bible-thumping do-gooders?"

"I'm not a kill..." Avi stopped himself.

There was nothing but silence on the other end.

"Hello?"

"Tell you what. I'm going to pretend I didn't hear that. Take some time, reevaluate things. Don't call me—I'll call you. After all, we're partners now. Linked."

The line went dead.

Chapter 15: Simi

Simi hung up the phone with Avi. Now comfortably in his hotel room, he headed straight for the bathroom mirror. The reflection staring back at him was that of a man he barely recognized. Only one feature remained unchanged—the slight amblyopia in his left eye, drifting slightly inward.

He stripped off his clothing, hat, and wig. Then he removed his latex prosthetic nose, rubbing off the remaining glue on his skin. Next, he peeled off his false beard, feeling immediate relief from the tormenting itch that had plagued him since early morning.

He tossed each piece of his disguise into a bag and inspected the contents. Normally, he would burn it all, using an accelerant to torch the evidence. But this time, the plan was different, making his task much easier. He wouldn't have to worry about finding a remote location to burn it—and risk others smelling the distinctive stench of burnt hair. Still, he couldn't wait to get rid of the traces of the murders he had committed.

Stepping into the shower, he washed the darker foundation from his face. Occasionally, a splash of red swirled down the drain—a flash of Hitchcock crossing his mind. But he was no psycho. His actions had purpose. The blood was just a small memento from his nocturnal butchering.

The last steps took the longest. He scrubbed at the temporary henna tattoos—the numbers 14 and 88—knowing they could last for weeks if left untouched. Repeated strokes of soapy warm water, alternating with lemon juice, worked away the ink. He had to avoid creating a rash and stopped just short of rubbing the skin raw. Later, he would cover any stubborn remnants with foundation matched to his natural tone until the numeric hate speech faded.

Finally, he dyed his hair and eyebrows back to the blond color God—or his mother's genetics—had given him. Not his father's—the dark-haired sympathizer with blood on his hands. His mother's blood.

Shaking off the past, he reemerged as his true self and eyed his reflection for confirmation. "You handsome man." The murderer had vanished; the thirty-two-year-old blond had returned. Blackjack was gone.

It had been an exhausting day. He cracked open a celebratory beer, dropped onto the small couch, and reflected. He considered himself a mission-oriented man, not a cruel or sadistic one. War was war. Death, a byproduct. Sacrifices were sometimes necessary for the betterment of mankind. It was Darwinism—the strong defining the future genetic path.

For his part, he was proud he'd put his victims out of their misery quickly. They were dead while still standing, their bodies slapping the canvas floor like wet rags on a shower tile. He lived by the hunter's ethical code he'd been taught as a child in Wyoming: strive for a clean kill. He followed that rule whether in war or homicide. Although it mattered that his victims didn't suffer, it mattered more that their deaths had meaning. He ensured there was no waste. Killing for sport, while letting the meat spoil, was reprehensible. But hunting for sustenance—that was a justifiable need, a respectable code.

In the same way, the people he killed had died for a higher purpose. Their deaths weren't wasteful. They were, unknowingly, unsung heroes—unwilling martyrs.

Simi turned on the television and switched to the news. Predictably, the press was helping his cause. The banner headline read, "Murders on the Mall." Aerial footage of the Capitol's reflecting pool showed empty pockets in the massive crowds— crime scenes roped off in stark contrast to the masses.

An anchorwoman appeared onscreen. "Police are searching for the man pictured here. He's a person of interest and considered potentially dangerous. If you have any information on his identity, contact the authorities immediately."

The image showed a bearded man with long brown hair and a noticeably larger nose. Simi guessed the photo had been taken during his outburst—accusing Officer Kylo of racism. Planting that seed of discontent had been part of the plan, but he knew it would require careful tending to blossom into the chaos he envisioned.

Kylo was the perfect target. It was his beat. He was respected. To topple the system, you took out its strongest pillars. Kylo was ground zero. If all went well, he'd become the next sacrificial, unsung hero.

Meanwhile, weak, pathetic Avi would be devoured by the press—a savory scapegoat served up like mutton.

Glancing at the wall clock, Simi realized it was time to check in. He securely logged onto his government-issued laptop and accessed the encrypted messaging system for updates. Every move he made was reported to his boss.

He started running through possible disguises. Rabbi. Hispanic. Rich. Homeless. Aryan. His mind cycled through faces and accents.

But his attention snapped back to the news as they cut to another story gaining traction. A field reporter stood on location beside a detective, microphone in hand. The station's call letters loomed large on the screen.

"What can you tell us about the incident here?"

"Yes. At approximately eleven this morning, an unidentified female corpse was found floating beneath this bridge. She appears to be in her late twenties. Based on nearby security footage, she was accompanied by an infant—likely her child. We're concerned because this child was later seen in the arms of another woman. Foul play can't be ruled out—possibly homicide, kidnapping, or both."

The reporter retracted the microphone. "Thank you, Chief. Police have released two images in hopes of tracking down the suspicious woman."

The first picture appeared onscreen. "Here, you see the infant with the mother while the other woman watches—perhaps stalking from a distance." The image switched. "This second photo shows the suspect holding the baby and fleeing. The mother is nowhere to be seen. We'll bring you updates as they come in. Now, back to the studio."

Simi studied the suspect's face until the image disappeared.

The anchorwoman returned. "In more uplifting news, let's check in with our correspondent at the climate symposium…"

Simi muted the television, his mood darkening. This second story was a distraction from his mission—and he didn't like sharing the spotlight. The public's attention span was short. Now he'd have to escalate the situation on the Mall just to stay on top of the headlines.

Still, he couldn't help but wonder who this woman was, and why she had taken the baby.

Chapter 16: Luna

Luna fled the Lincoln Memorial sanctuary and walked the long distance to Dupont Circle. There weren't as many homeless people in the area, and she found a bench where she could steal a few moments to shake off the horrors of the Mall.

She turned her attention to Karli, longing for something positive to cling to—anything to give her hope. She couldn't resist the cute bundle she was holding, pressing Karli's tiny fingers against her lips and kissing her delicate pink cheeks. Luna spotted a small fleck of dirt on Karli's forehead and tried to scrape it off, only to realize it was a mole. She smiled and kissed it. Then she examined every tiny feature of the baby, from the soft fuzz atop her head to her wiggling toes. Everything seemed healthy—perfect.

But Luna's attention caused Karli to squirm, which escalated into a full-blown outburst. Luna's instincts kicked in as naturally as a laugh or a cry. She whispered, "You're hungry, aren't you, fuss-bucket? You're so cute. I'm going to keep you safe, I promise." She fed the child, calming her, and then changed her diaper. "There. You've transformed back into the angel you were—good as new."

Luna held Karli to her chest, gently patting her, waiting for a dainty, soft burp. Instead, the sound that erupted was more fitting for a grown man.

As Luna held the baby, her thoughts drifted to the flawed line from the mother's note: "Please take care of my child and love as you own her." It was clearly meant to read "love as your own"—but now, the idea of owning her felt strangely appropriate.

A surge of resolve filled Luna—a fierce determination to defend this precious miracle. With every glance at Karli, the bond between them deepened. Luna was no longer just an advocate; she had become Karli's protector—her guardian. Handing the child over would be emotionally impossible. But if Karli's life depended on it, Luna would do whatever it took.

Breaking her doting attention, Luna assessed her supplies. She needed more. Pulling out her phone, she used an app to locate the nearest market and quickly headed in that direction. Luckily, she still had her credit card, though she knew it was traceable.

Minutes later, she stood in front of a small shop and pushed the bell. With crime rates skyrocketing, she understood that businesses now required permission to enter—especially so close to the camp. The familiar buzz sounded, the latch clicked, and she pushed the door open. The bell chimed as she stepped inside, the door locking shut behind her.

A tattooed, scruffy clerk glanced up from his phone as Luna entered, eyeing her from behind the counter. When she grabbed a basket, he dropped his gaze, mouth slightly open, absorbed again in whatever mindless game had him hooked.

She turned down the infant aisle—an unfamiliar landscape. Premixed formula, diapers, wipes, bottles, nipples, blankets, toys. She hesitated, then began filling the basket with items she could only guess she needed, including a soft blanket she spotted near the endcap—and a tote to carry it all.

She moved quickly, grabbing what she could, each item another pull on her already fragile carbon limit.

Karli began to cry again. Luna froze, bracing for a reaction from the clerk—but he didn't even flinch. She reached for a shelf and placed a fuzzy stuffed animal in Karli's hands, her touch soft and steady. The crying eased.

By the time she reached the checkout, she knew she'd blown past her monthly limit. But she kept going.

Satisfied she had everything, she walked up to the cashier. A television mounted high on the wall behind him blared the news, though he seemed to tune it out.

"Ts'all?" His mumble was neither disrespectful nor engaging.

"That's it." Luna fished her card out of her pocket, bouncing Karli as she handed it over.

Her eyes drifted toward the television screen. A woman's picture flashed, a banner beneath it: PERSON OF INTEREST.

Life froze—no sound, no movement, not even her own breath.

Her heart hammered against her ribs.

It was her.

Chapter 17: Zev

Zev, still working roundup, felt a sudden pang of guilt. The murders—horrific as they were—had boosted his business, promising him a small windfall. Profiting from the fear and desperation of others wasn't how he'd chosen to make his living.

He found himself questioning whether he was exploiting the homeless, profiting off them like some modern-day carpetbagger. In the end, he decided his ethics were intact. After all, the homeless weren't paying him—he was simply administering government assistance. At least he could take comfort in knowing he was helping displaced people, moving them away from degrading conditions. He'd even given his eyewitness account of the man authorities were hunting to Officer Cromley, doing what he could for those who chose to stay. He opted not to mention the lady with the baby, thinking the police had their hands full.

He thought about the scene of horror he'd witnessed. Since childhood, Zev had been squeamish. It was that nightmarish Halloween when his life was turned upside down—the one that also fell on a Friday the 13th.

His older brother, just two years ahead of him, led him outside to the family shed. Although it was after nightfall, Zev was blindfolded—kept from even catching a glimpse of the city lights. He tried to resist but was overpowered. Then his brother and friends forced him to touch things—gooey, foul-smelling things placed in bowls.

He couldn't decide what was worse: the slimy, cold body parts or the warm ones. He'd had to touch eyeballs, intestines, skin, human bones, and brains—which, in reality, were nothing more than peeled grapes, cooked and cooled spaghetti, flour tortilla pieces slathered in oil, chicken bones, and a warm, slightly mushy head of cauliflower. To his young mind, someone had just died and been dismembered—exactly like what he'd recently seen on the Mall. And the killer? Most likely waiting under his bed later that night, ready to claim his next victim.

They also made him break a tiny mirror, laughing that he'd be cursed with seven years of bad luck—the exact number of years he'd been alive. He fought back tears, not wanting to give them the satisfaction, but they came anyway. Then they forced him through an obstacle course, where he had to open an umbrella indoors and walk under a ladder—continuing their hazing, an endless punishment for no better reason than being the youngest.

In the end, everything might have been fine—if not for what happened later that night. The curse found its mark, and it wasn't Zev. But Zev witnessed karma strike. At first, he laughed, oblivious. In fact, had he acted right away, he might have saved his brother. But he didn't. That hesitation became a death sentence. That was the last day his brother drew breath. The family, already hollowed by their father's loss in a car accident years prior, was now reduced to just Zev and his mother—her favorite child gone. Even after twenty-two years, the memory burned as fiercely as the day it happened.

It was then that superstition became his unwelcome wingman—an association forged by the tragic death of his sibling and the series of bad omens that had led to it.

He shook off the details, as he'd done countless times before, and reviewed his list. There were enough commitments now to fill nearly five busloads—people willing to relocate to Sustalia. The limit was eight buses total, mainly due to the capacity of the train during the longest leg of the journey.

He didn't know much about the country's fifty-second state, other than that it had been carved out of the Oklahoma Panhandle. Word had spread quickly, and the new state had drawn national attention, triggering a gold rush of homeless people seeking a fresh start. It was like Steinbeck's *Grapes of Wrath* in reverse—desperate people heading into the Dust Bowl instead of fleeing it. Recent elections had brought UnaTerra, a new political party, to power, securing key positions like governor, senator, and House representatives.

Zev knew even less about Felicity—the utopian town within Sustalia. He would find out soon enough; he'd have to deliver the recruits himself. The town was shrouded in secrecy, with politicians claiming that if its exact location were known, it would be overrun by people desperate to improve their lives. True to its political message, UnaTerra enforced rigid border control.

Zev was tired, but he pushed on. The more signatures he gathered, the more carbon credits he earned toward restoring his healthcare benefits.

Earlier, he had referred to the documentation he'd been given to answer questions. Now, he could field inquiries without looking. He walked to a visible spot on the Mall, beneath the shade of one of the few remaining trees, and held up a sign that read, "Sustalia: Work, Shelter, Food. Questions Answered Here." A group gathered. Zev waited until the crowd was large enough. Finally, he spoke.

"Hello, folks. On behalf of the senator from Sustalia, I'm here to present an opportunity out West. She's offering free transportation to her state in exchange for your labor. I trust you've looked over the brochure I've been circulating. It explains the opportunity—and the provisions in the contract each of you will need to sign. I'm here to answer any questions."

The first question came quickly: "Why do we have to hand over our IDs, like passports?"

Zev anticipated this one. "The buses will take you to the train station, where you'll be processed. The fastest way is to collect your IDs so we can move large groups through security efficiently."

Another question rang out: "Why can't we keep our phones?"

Zev nodded. "As the contract states, you're giving up communication to protect the site's location. We can't risk it being compromised. Once you arrive, you'll be given more details."

A third question: "Will you still take us if we don't sign?"

Zev's response was firm. "No."

A man, looking militant, raised his hand. "Why can't we at least carry a knife to protect ourselves?"

Zev met his eyes. "Everyone's safety is our top priority. Weapons could be a danger to you and to others."

A small, elderly woman called out, "What time do you leave tomorrow?"

Zev answered with a smile. "7 a.m., on the dot, ma'am."

More questions followed, one after another.

"Will there be room on the bus?"

Zev glanced at his clipboard, scanning the signatures. "There's still space, but the buses are filling up fast. I suggest getting on the list soon—first come, first served."

A mother asked, "Are there bathroom stops?"

Zev replied, "The train station and the train itself have restrooms. The buses do not."

"When do we get to Sustalia?"

Zev relayed what he'd been told. "It'll take two days to reach the destination."

"One more question," Zev added, "then I've got to move on."

The final question came: "When's the first meal?"

Zev hadn't gotten a clear answer for this recurring question. "I'm not sure. I recommend bringing a small amount of food and drink for the trip."

It was late, and Zev had had enough. "Folks, you'll need to make your decision. I can't make it for you. I'll be near the buses on Constitution Avenue tomorrow morning. Like I said—we leave promptly at 7 a.m."

Chapter 18: Luna

Luna exited the store with her purchases, relieved the clerk hadn't noticed the television behind him—her face broadcast in full view. If he'd seen her picture, she wouldn't just be on the run—she'd have to literally run.

Although she felt alone and vulnerable, an inner strength was taking root. Luna was adapting, adjusting her sails not only to capture the shifting winds but to find pride in her moral compass. Her Paps would be proud. He'd been the one who got her interested in inspirational quotes. She thought of one he often used—a favorite from Martin Luther King Jr.: *"The time is always right to do what is right."*

It felt surreal. She was trying to do the right thing... only complicated by the police.

She figured there was only a narrow window of time for her next move. A plan began to form. Knowing her credit and debit cards could be traced, she quickly found an ATM and withdrew her limit from each. She rolled the bills with blue and red rubber bands, placing the wad of cash in her pocket. Then, one by one, she destroyed her cards, bending them until the microchips were useless. Next came her phone—she pulled the battery and SIM, then smashed it against the pavement. These remnants of her old life went straight into a trash bin.

Her outfit also had to go. Spotting a clothing store, she peered inside, relieved no news was flashing on the screens. She rang the bell and felt the subtle vibration of the lock disengaging beneath her fingertips. With the child in hand, she entered to the calming sound of a classic, a Rachmaninoff concerto she recognized—a refuge from the chaos outside.

She moved quickly down an aisle, grabbing a few items, when a voice startled her, "May I help you, darlin'?"

A middle-aged, motherly clerk seemed genuinely eager to assist.

"I'd like to try these on. Do you have a dressing room?"

"Certainly, hon. It's in the back. Please follow me. What a beautiful child. What's his name?"

Luna realized that when she grabbed the stuffed animal, the toy had blue ears. Blurring the baby's gender might slow down anyone searching for her.

"Zev," she answered. She was shocked at what came from her mouth, but it was the first name that popped into her head.

The clerk smiled at the baby. "Hi, Zev. Such an adorable little peanut."

Luna was relieved the woman didn't comment on the child's dissimilarity.

In the dressing room, she changed into jeans, a T-shirt, and a sweater, then approached the register in her new outfit.

"I'd like to purchase these. I spilled something on my other clothes, and I'd prefer to wear these out."

The clerk smiled warmly. "I hadn't noticed, but no problem at all, dear. I'll get you a bag for your old clothes."

"I'd also like to pay with cash."

The clerk paused. "Well, that might be a problem. I can't make change since we don't carry cash in the store."

"It's okay. You can keep the balance."

The clerk hesitated. "I'll also have to charge you extra, you know, since it won't register against your carbon balance."

"That's fine. Just ring me up."

"Of course." But the clerk's expression betrayed her suspicion, her eyes narrowing. She finished the transaction, and Luna left the store. Her old clothes went straight into a nearby garbage bin.

It was at that moment Luna realized her shadow had surfaced—steering the course ahead. The risk-averse, rule-bound speech pathologist was now just a passenger in this new reality.

Shadow-Luna pulled out the brochure Zev had given her. It read: *"Relocation Services, sponsored by UnaTerra,"* with Zev's name scrawled underneath. The back listed the bus departure time. She wasn't that desperate. There had to be other options. Instead, she'd use the cash to catch a different bus to Texas, where her Abuelita lived. But she still needed a place for the night—the Union Station schedule only showed an afternoon departure. Reluctantly, she headed back to the sanctuary, hoping someone might offer shelter. Clutching the cash, she figured someone would.

Once again, the smell of the camp reached her before actually seeing the grounds. The closer she got, the heavier the air—a mix of sewage and dinner.

Sewage had the upper hand.

Her mind drifted to the cozy apartment she'd left behind—soft blanket, mint tea. For a moment, she wondered if she'd made a mistake. But then she looked at Karli… and knew she hadn't. The child gave her a higher purpose.

The sun had fully set, and the darkness transformed the area. Using the lit Washington Monument as her beacon, she approached the camp, weaving between tents—a patchwork of color and decay. There were makeshift shelters of every kind: dilapidated, patched, new; green, blue, stout, wide; canvas, polyester—a hodgepodge that would've horrified any homeowner's association.

She ducked under laundry lines, skirted portable stoves, and was careful to respect the claimed spaces. She was searching… though for what, she wasn't sure.

Eyes followed her every move. With her stylish clothes, freshly washed hair, and makeup, she didn't blend in. She felt exposed. Luna wished she'd chosen something less noticeable—especially the tight jeans that drew attention to her figure.

She heard a rattling sniff from below. "Purdy smellin'. Git me some of dat."

A toothless man reached for her. Luna didn't know if he wanted money or worse—but she didn't stick around to find out. She moved on, scanning for someone kind, someone safe.

A teen caught her eye. When he looked up, she held his gaze. He seemed wasted—too far gone.

He mumbled, "Rock, Smack, Weed?"

Luna forced herself to keep walking, though part of her longed to help.

Faintly, she heard him mutter after her, "Cunt."

For the first time in her life, she wanted to turn back and kick the little punk in the teeth. Where that feeling came from, she had no idea.

A catcall from ahead. "Hey, sweet dumpling. How 'bout some jelly fillin'?" A man jerked his pelvis at her.

Her nerve was unraveling fast. The place had been unsettling by day—at night, it was terrifying.

Then—without warning—a hand groped her from behind.

She spun, ready to strike—only to watch another man punch the offender in the mouth.

Her would-be savior looked to be in his forties; the attacker, younger, now crumpled on the ground.

"Sorry, miss, but I gotta say—it's not safe for you here. Dressed like that, you stand out. Some guys can't handle themselves."

Luna pleaded, "Can you help me? I have nowhere to go."

"What are you doing here?"

She couldn't answer—just stared.

The man's stance softened. "Secretive type, huh? Well… at least tell me how long you're staying?"

"Just until morning."

"Ah, so you're catching one of those UnaTerra buses."

Luna let him believe it.

"No matter," he said. "I can get you to a safer spot. First things first—this section's for loners and drug dealers. Family section's over by the Capitol. Believe it or not, there's a code of conduct. Looks rough, but most follow the rules—at least there."

She couldn't hide her fear.

"Don't worry. You'll be safe with us. Come on, I'll introduce you to my wife and son. We're from Tampa—trying to figure things out after Hurricane Alois wiped us out."

Luna held up the wad of bills. "I can pay you for your trouble."

The man immediately covered her hand and pushed it down. "Miss, please don't flash that around."

He glanced around before letting out a slow breath. "You're gonna get us both mugged. Stealing'll get you banished—but for that kind of cash? Someone might risk it."

He started walking away, then turned back. "Well? You coming?"

Chapter 19: Simi

It was late, and Simi was exhausted. Clutching his second Red Bull, he sat alone on the bed, hoping it would push him through the night ahead. The instructions were clear, so he headed to his closet to review his options. When he opened the French doors, he peered inside and smiled.

His preparations had been meticulous. The perfect blue shirt and pants stood out as the obvious choice. Everything he needed was in his hotel room—no more last-minute supply runs. With shoes that would add a few inches to his height and a bit of brown hair dye, he was good to go.

Simi thought about Senator Remi McCarthy. Earlier that day, when he saw her, it was from a distance—she'd electrified the crowd with her inspiring speech. He watched her ascend the steps of the Jefferson Memorial, radiating confidence. She was wearing those blazing red pumps—her favorite—and his, too. The crowd erupted as she spoke, but it was the look in her eyes before she even opened her mouth that Simi couldn't forget. She was a force. On cue, as they'd rehearsed, he yelled to get the crowd involved and energized. He had to be careful, though; he was still in costume, so he kept his "14" and "88" covered.

The speech itself was a success, and he knew she was pleased with her performance. Life was good when she was happy—and even better when she glowed.

Simi served on her staff, advancing her cause. Deep down, he believed she would lead the masses back to their former greatness. She was a visionary, a gifted orator—especially when championing her proven reconstruction plan. And he was part of it all. Remi often said that people like him—operatives working behind the scenes—were indispensable.

In time, she would become a historical figure, compared to Thomas Jefferson, the author of the Declaration of Independence. Her doctrine would be the Carbon Laws. But unlike Jefferson, she had no ambition to become president. Her drive was purely for the good of the cause. To Simi, her reluctance to seek the presidency was a flaw.

But she had many strengths. She wasn't just a great collaborator in pushing this reform. Perhaps even more impressive was that Senator McCarthy was a master at reading people. She was like a human X-ray, scanning others to their core. She gathered information, then leveraged it to bend them to her will—whether through mutual goals or political blackmail.

It didn't take long for Simi to recognize that Remi had discovered his vulnerability. Simi was drawn to her, aware of every movement, every word she spoke. Though it wasn't obvious, he could feel a subtle shift in his pulse—a quiet attraction he couldn't quite ignore. But Simi had no interest in being just another piece on someone else's chessboard. Somewhere in Felicity, he was sure, lay the real answer.

Snapping back, he knew he needed to focus on his instructions. He picked up his phone but delayed dialing. He needed to reboot, reorient—to embody his character. He mouthed a line of simplified, prolonged speech: "Well hey there, Mr. Boss Man!" Satisfied, he dialed the number. A man answered, his voice hesitant.

"Blackjack? I'm glad you called. I—"

Simi cut him off. "Boss Man, I've been thinkin'. I decided to grant your wish—to sever our ties."

He heard a long exhale. Messing with Avi was always fun. Predictably, Avi said, "Thank you. That would be great. I can pay—"

Simi interrupted again. "Hold up. It comes with a condition."

"A… condition?"

Simi laid it out. "Simple task." He knew it wasn't simple. "I need some items from an officer named Kylo Cromley. He works the Mall."

"Who?"

"Write this down. Kylo, C-R-O-M-L-E-Y. I need something with his DNA—blood's best. I also need something he owns— maybe his mace, cuffs, comb, pen… anything he uses on patrol. You're the contractor in charge of the Mall's drawdown. You have access to him, so I need these items tonight. Deliver, and we're done. We can part ways."

Avi hesitated. "Tonight? Come on, Blackjack. Be reasonable. Give me a few days—"

Simi's voice hardened. "Tonight."

"What if I can't get them tonight?"

"Well, then you'd be unfinished business. And we both know how that goes."

Avi's voice wavered. "If I do this, how do I know you'll hold up your end?"

"You have my scout's word." The words came out too quickly, stirring up memories he hadn't meant to summon. Simi's mind flashed to his father—not present the day he earned his Eagle Scout badge at just thirteen, a record pace. His dad had been too busy, "saving lives" at the hospital. Blah, blah. Still, Simi had embodied the oath: duty to my country. He was, if nothing else, a patriot. It was just which country that was in question. The oath itself, of course—like all important things in life—had to be prioritized. Just like his father had prioritized the Brunner Syndrome over him. Over his mother.

He forced himself back—discipline over self-pity. "But really, Boss Man, what choice do you have? You've seen what I'm capable of. Besides, you wouldn't want to disappoint your family, would you?" He knew how to expose raw, paternal issues. "Prove everything your father-in-law said about you is true?"

"What? How do you know about that?"

"I know plenty. But surely you'd agree—things would smooth out if he were gone, wouldn't they? Maybe an accident... a slip from his penthouse balcony. Or perhaps your wife passes first—that would make the inheritance far messier, wouldn't it?"

There was a long silence.

Bullseye.

"Okay, Blackjack. I'll do whatever you need. Just... don't involve them."

"Excellent. Then we have an accord. Leave the items at the drop-off site by midnight."

Simi hung up, chuckling. He stood and changed into his blue attire, preparing for the next phase.

Chapter 20: Avi

Avi sat at his desk staring at his phone, willing it to light up—this time with a message that would undo everything. "Never mind," he imagined Blackjack's voice saying, words that would somehow release him from the impossible task he'd just been given. But no such message came.

Instead, his wife, Evelyn, came up behind him and interrupted his thoughts.

"That was a late call. So rude. I hope it didn't wake Oscar. Who was it, darling?"

Avi bristled at the sound of her voice, but he was practiced at not showing it. "Just a coworker. No worries."

She swiveled his chair to face her, holding up two small marble blocks, one in each hand. "Which one do you like better?"

"What?"

"For the kitchen, silly—this one's Calacatta Borghini. Gray veining with hints of gold."

"And the other?"

She lifted the second. "Thassos. Also white, but ultra-pure. Almost no veining."

He forced himself to sound interested. "I like the first one. Wait… which costs more?"

"The Calacatta. And I agree—it's better quality. I love the way the gold shimmers. Thanks, sweetie."

His stomach clenched, but this wasn't a fight worth having. Not now. "Fine."

"I'm going up to brush my teeth. You coming to bed, honey?"

He fought the urge to look at her. He didn't want the reminder of her father in her face. Some features had become hard to look at.

He turned back to his screen, eyes bloodshot, fighting to focus. "Got some late-night work. I'll be up in a bit."

He braced for her complaint.

"That's ridiculous. You've been at it since early this morning. They don't deserve you."

The sting in her words landed, but he didn't let it show. He muttered, eyes on his research. "Just a bit longer. Things'll ease up once the Mall population thins out."

She rested a hand on his shoulder—a connection he wanted no part of. "Avi... everything okay? You seem... distracted."

"It's all good. Please... go to bed. Don't wait up." He offered no kiss, only his back.

She withdrew her hand, a question etched beneath her words. "Okay. Good night, then."

He didn't respond. She disappeared upstairs, leaving him with the cold glare of his computer.

Avi exhaled slowly, pulse pounding, nerves on edge. His gaze drifted to the photo on the monitor—Kylo Cromley. Broad, muscular, intimidating. Avi's stomach clenched. *This guy?* The cop looked like he could crush him with his pinky. If this got physical, Avi wouldn't stand a chance. He'd have to outthink him—collect DNA without raising a flag.

He wanted out, but had no choice. Blackjack cared only for results. If Avi didn't deliver... God knows. For months, he'd shielded Evelyn and Oscar from the truth, letting them see only the façade. Now the truth was closing in, ready to expose him.

Her father already suspected—quick to figure things out. Blackjack had been dead right about the old bastard. The crusty old man showed his contempt loud and in public, even from the start, during that humiliating wedding toast. No subtlety. No grace. Just a warning in plain sight. The man had seen through Avi the moment they met.

Sometimes Avi wished he'd just die—with Blackjack's offer tempting. But he didn't need Blackjack's help. At least in theory. But the kidney failure was just taking its sweet time. Then again, maybe slow agony was exactly what he deserved.

His gaze dropped to a photo on his desk—Evelyn. Not radiant. Not the woman of his dreams. But rich. She had no idea what kind of man her husband was—or worse, what he'd become. To her, he was the driven contractor they toasted when he landed the Mall relocation project. Never mind that Daddy had set it up. She never knew about the backroom arguments, the midnight threats, the reckless promises.

The irony burned. He'd done it all for the lifestyle she grew up with—to prove her father wrong. And yet, deep down, he was sure she'd have lived in a tent if it meant being together.

He glanced at the clock. It was time. Avi gathered a small bag and scissors, then popped a stick of gum in his mouth. He listened for sounds upstairs.

Nothing. Good.

He slipped out of the condo, careful not to make a sound. The door creaked faintly, but not enough to wake anyone.

He felt like a kid sneaking out past curfew. This wasn't meant to be violent—just unpleasant. He had plenty of flaws, but cruelty wasn't one of them—at least not yet.

The night air hung heavy as he walked toward the Mall. The displacement camp stretched before him, an alien world after dark. The air reeked of things he couldn't name. Every step felt wrong. Worse—it felt like his fault.

Kylo Cromley.

The name alone sent a jolt of anxiety. The cop's presence could shrink any man. Avi prayed he'd be on patrol at one of the crime scenes tonight. It was his only shot.

He moved between various roped-off areas until finally he spotted him—big, imposing, impossible to miss. Avi swallowed hard and approached him.

"Officer Cromley?"

Kylo turned to him, squinting. "Yes?"

"My name's Avi Sweller. I'm overseeing relocation." He extended a hand, noticing the tremor in his fingers.

Kylo's wary look softened. "Heard of you. Pleasure, Sir."

Avi smiled, though his mind raced. "I was hoping to borrow a minute. My superiors want a report on today's events. Just a few questions."

Kylo rubbed his eyes. "Been on duty fourteen hours. Go easy on me."

Avi caught the fatigue in his voice. "Rough day?"

"One of the worst. On my feet since morning."

"Understood." Avi pulled out a notebook, jotting. "About the two victims..."

Kylo interrupted. "Can't release names yet—active case. I can share that we've got some witness statements."

Avi nodded, scribbling. Then—the window opened. "Mind if I borrow your flashlight? Hard to see out here."

Kylo handed it over without hesitation. "Sure."

Avi tucked it under his arm, carefully, and kept writing. Then glanced up, feigning surprise.

"Officer, I don't mean to embarrass you, but... I noticed something."

Kylo frowned. "What's that?"

Avi pointed. "Looks like you've got something in your hair."

Kylo started to reach for it.

Avi stopped him. "I wouldn't touch it. Let me take care of it for you."

Kylo nodded, and bent slightly. "Go ahead."

"It's gum. Don't move. I've got scissors—I can get it out. No trouble."

Kylo gave a tired laugh. "Figures. Story of my day."

"It's not a problem," Avi said, his voice warm. "Lower."

Kylo leaned down further.

Avi slipped the flashlight into his back pocket and palmed the gum he'd been chewing while Kylo bent down, unaware. He pressed it into the officer's hair, working it in as if he'd found it there. One quick snip, and the gum was mostly gone—leaving only a small chunk behind. He held up the piece he cut. "There's still a bit left. I'll have to pull."

"Go for it."

Avi tugged hard enough to yank a few follicles.

"Ouch!"

"Sorry," Avi said softly. "All done. Though... you've got a slight notch now. It'll grow out soon enough."

Kylo felt the spot and gave a low chuckle. "Figures. Gum's not even legal on the Mall—and I've been wearing it like a hat."

Avi offered a faint smile, hiding the surge of relief. "I'll tell you what, I'll leave you be and check in tomorrow. Hope you get some rest. The brass can wait."

Kylo nodded. "Thanks, Mr. Sweller. Take care."

Avi walked away, heart hammering—not from fear, but excitement.

Cakewalk.

He had the hair. And the flashlight. He'd deliver his package and be done with Blackjack once and for all.

He walked with his chest lifted. He felt proud of himself.

His father-in-law never saw the good—the cleverness it took to game the system. But tonight, Avi had saved his family's reputation, maybe even their lives. Most of all, he had secured his inheritance.

Chapter 21: Simi

Simi watched Avi and Officer Kylo from a distance, eyes narrowing as he tracked their exchange. The body language suggested an ordinary, uneventful conversation, but Simi knew better. The officer—unaware of the play being made on him—tilted his head slightly, allowing Avi to approach, even to touch his hair—an oddly intimate gesture of trust. Simi couldn't fathom how Avi had convinced the cop to voluntarily offer a hair sample, but whatever it was, it worked. Fear was a motivator, capable of producing creative solutions.

"You've got some spunk after all, Chief," Simi muttered softly to himself, a habit he'd honed during long, solitary stakeouts.

Simi noticed the officer's flashlight, now tucked into Avi's rear pocket. "That'll work, my man. You probably think you're out of the woods now, don't you?" His voice dropped, almost conspiratorial. "But you're not. Never will be. I can't leave loose ends. Still, sleep well tonight, Boss. You've earned it."

Soon after, Simi held a small lunch bag—the proof of a job well done, hidden in a planned location by Avi. Simi melted into the night, his mind already churning with the next move.

The Jefferson Memorial steps were quiet when he arrived, but his thoughts were insistent, consumed by the image of Remi. He pictured both of them standing there—her commanding a crowd, him shadowing behind her. The thought anchored him, holding him steady. Patience, he reminded himself, was paramount. The timing of his next move had to be flawless, to keep his dream intact.

He closed his eyes and rocked slowly, letting his body settle into the rhythm of meditation as the minutes slipped away, then hours, advancing unnoticed.

At 3 a.m., he rose, ready. His mind was clear; every detail of the plan rehearsed into memory. He'd already scouted the perfect location. He knew where the cameras would be—and where they wouldn't. The tragedy had to happen in the family section. The media would feast on it. Anywhere else would barely make a ripple. This wasn't just a crime. It was a narrative.

The camp's silence felt thick, almost suffocating. He slipped rubber gloves over his hands with practiced ease, his movements calm, deliberate. His eyes swept the grounds until they landed on a large green canvas tent—its fabric newer than most, sturdy.

Perfect.

With a practiced hand, he peeled back the entrance flaps, careful not to make a sound. Inside, the scene was still, almost serene. Four sleeping bodies lay undisturbed, their shallow breaths the only sign of life. The soft sound of snoring was comforting— a green light to proceed without fear of being caught in the act.

Simi slipped inside, moving with quiet grace. His eyes fell on the first sleeping bag. The man inside had positioned himself near the entrance—the protector, the shield. But protection meant nothing here. The man, fit and strong, didn't stir as Simi knelt down. Simi drew his knife with practiced precision, and in one smooth motion, ended the man's life from ear to ear. A rag over his mouth stifled any sound as life drained from him. No cry for help.

Next lay the woman. Simi worked quickly, the knife a blur. Her death came as quietly as the first.

The third was a boy—no older than fifteen. An easy target. His slumber was deeper than the others. Another swift motion, and it was over.

One left.

A young woman—Black, mixed, maybe in her twenties.

But then—he saw it.

A child, cradled against her chest. He hadn't noticed the child before. Both slept peacefully, the child nestled close.

Simi froze, his knife hovering. Her beauty struck him—a calm expression that made him wonder, for the briefest moment, if he would regret this later.

But no. He pushed the thought away. There were higher principles at play. Her death—and the child's—were necessary.

Still... something caught his eye.

A wad of cash, rolled neatly in the woman's hand. Unexpected.

In a split-second decision, he changed course. The woman, he realized, would serve a better purpose alive. She had money. She would tell the authorities it was stolen. The fear of robbery—combined with murder—would ripple through the camp. That would be priceless. The homeless had their own code. Theft wasn't tolerated. The chaos this would spark couldn't be overstated.

His hands worked quickly. He slipped the money from her grasp and tucked it into his pocket. He glanced again—diamond earrings. Too chancy. Better to leave them rather than risk waking her. But the cash—he would take that.

He stepped back, surveying his work. Normally, he would have carved a scene—something grotesque, an artistic flourish of death. But tonight, he needed only one thing. A scalp.

With swift efficiency, he sliced it off—the long hair of the woman beside the protector. He would plant it outside the tent come morning. In daylight, it couldn't be ignored.

Next, he retrieved the lunch bag Avi had provided. He scattered its contents throughout the tent, touching each victim with traces of Kylo's DNA. The flashlight he dropped beside the teen's body—a perfect touch.

A rush of satisfaction swept over him, almost too sweet to believe. This was going to be glorious. The headlines screamed in his mind—a cop implicated in a massacre. The homeless would turn on him—and on each other. The chaos would be absolute.

Before slipping away, he made a mental note. One last disguise—a tunic and jet-black hair should do it. And one final detail: planting the stolen money on Kylo. A little extra effort. A stop at the officer's home. A small price for a perfect story.

Part 2: Blood Diamond

Chapter 22: Luna

Tuesday, August 21

Deep beneath the crust of Earth's lone supercontinent—Rodinia—a deposit of carbon lay entombed, sealed a hundred miles below the surface. Subjected to unrelenting pressure and heat, it underwent a transformation only time could orchestrate. Over a billion years, the carbon hardened, molecule by molecule, into its most coveted state: a flawless diamond—radiant, enduring, and seemingly eternal.

Curiously, though carbon would later dominate political discourse, the Carbon Laws made no mention of this glittering manifestation of their focus.

Yet the diamond's value was not discovered from transformation alone. A chain of improbable geological events followed. Tectonic plates shifted with slow determination, stirring the Earth's mantle and propelling the gem's host rock—kimberlite—upward. For millions of years, it traveled in darkness, sealed in igneous stone, until a volcanic surge finally carried it near the surface.

It remained untouched for epochs, as if waiting for humanity to arrive.

Eventually, in what is now modern-day South Africa, the diamond was unearthed—raw, unassuming, and buried in soil that had lain undisturbed. Extracted from the ground, it passed through the hands of the De Beers Mining Company, one of the few entities with the appetite and reach to control such a prize. Shipped without incident in the late 1800s, the stone made its way to Europe, where it was cut, polished, and placed beneath the sterile glow of a glass display case.

There, under cold light, it caught the eye of a young Orthodox Jewish man searching for a ring worthy of his beloved. He bought the stone, mounted it with care, and offered it in a quiet proposal. The conversation ended with a single word: "Da." Their shared joy was sealed as he slid the ring onto the fourth finger of her left hand.

The diamond remained with her through the decades—through the births of twelve children, the laughter of sixty grandchildren, and the long, peaceful twilight of a life fully lived. After her passing, the ring was passed down, generation by generation. At one point, it was carefully split in two and recut, transformed into matching earrings.

Now, those earrings rested gently against Luna's ears as she slept, soundly and unaware of their origin. To her, they were simply a cherished gift from her Bubba—a beautiful heirloom, a resilient symbol of love. She had no inkling of the stones' ancient journey, nor of the quiet power they held.

Unseen, unmarked, and unimaginably old, the diamonds were poised to become more than decoration. They would be a catalyst—a pivotal domino not only in Luna's story but in the fate of the Carbon Laws themselves.

Chapter 23: Luna

Despite the hard, uneven tent floor, Luna's exhaustion overtook her discomfort, though her rest came in shallow, broken stretches. Karli had fussed several times during the night, and each time, it had been a struggle to lull her back to sleep.

Now, she stirred again—this time roused by a murmur outside the tent.

It took a moment to clear the fog of sleep and register the sound. Voices—low at first—rose in volume, more frantic. Some even sounded angry. Luna's first instinct was to check on Karli, but the soft, steady rhythm of the baby's breath against her chest reassured her: warm, damp, alive. Karli was fine.

Strangely, the host family hadn't woken. They must've been used to this kind of noise.

The voices swelled in volume, but Luna pushed them aside, focusing instead on Karli's needs. She patted the infant's belly.

"Good morning, beautiful. Sweet little Karli. Are you hungry?"

She reached for the bag with baby supplies. Moving quietly, she changed Karli's diaper, prepared a bottle, and fed her—pressing soft kisses to her cheeks, forehead, and tiny fingers. Every small ritual centered Luna, even as her world unraveled.

After feeding, she lifted Karli onto her shoulder to burp her. As she bounced her gently, Luna's mind wandered back to the night before. Something felt off—an unease she hadn't noticed until now, a wrongness she couldn't shake.

She realized that when she woke, her hands were empty. Panic overtook her.

She reached into her pocket—empty, too.

The cash was gone.

A chill ran through her—immediate, yanking away the fog of sleep. Her worst fear, realized. She felt duped. Naïve. Her new reality crashed down around her: penniless. Hunted by the authorities. Homeless. And still the sole guardian of a helpless child. Worse, Karli wasn't even a citizen—an illegal alien, a term once outdated, now revived in a world that no longer tolerated the tired, the poor, the huddled masses.

Fear turned to anger. She was working up the courage to wake the family, to confront them, when—

The voices outside cut through the air—now shouting with an edge of chaos. Yet the host family remained still. Too still.

A man's voice rose above the noise. "Coming in!"

The tent flaps flew open. A white man with salt-and-pepper hair appeared, his expression hard. A second man stood behind him.

He scanned the tent. "There's dead bodies here," he barked over his shoulder toward the tent opening. "Including the owner of that scalp. Someone, get the cops."

Then his eyes landed on Luna. He yelled again.

"There's a survivor—a young woman, with a baby."

He stepped forward, over the dead man, gaze fixed on her. His voice had a hint of suspicion.

"What happened here?"

Luna tried to process what she'd just heard. Her voice barely held steady. "I'm not sure."

He narrowed his eyes. "Not sure? How's that possible? Did you hurt these people?"

"No, sir. They let me stay the night. I just woke up. I didn't hear anything. I didn't know they were… dead until you came in. It's… horrible."

His frown deepened.

"Hold on. You're telling me that just now—sitting there—you didn't know you were in a tent with dead people?"

"Yes—I mean, no. It's the truth."

"How could you not know? They're inches from you."

"I just woke up—and realized my money's been stolen."

"Money?"

Luna struggled to remember. "Yes, it's gone. It was in a roll, in blue and red rubber bands."

"Why stay in a place like this if you had cash? And why would a murderer leave you alive but kill the rest? Makes no sense!"

Luna stood with the baby in her arms, legs trembling. That was when she finally saw it—the blood, dried and dark, only inches away. Her eyes locked on the woman's bare, exposed skull, the scalp torn off in a brutal, jagged wound.

"I don't know. But I can't stay in here."

As she moved toward the exit, he stepped in her path.

"You're not going anywhere, little miss. Not until the cops arrive."

"Please… let me out. The blood—I can't breathe in here."

The other man put a hand on the first's shoulder, speaking low. "Let her out."

The first man studied her face, searching for something—guilt, maybe. But his eyes softened, doubt eased, if only slightly. With a grunt, he stepped aside.

"Don't go far."

Luna slipped outside among the onlookers, careful not to step on a scalp laid out like a rug. The crowd, now shouting, surged forward for a glimpse inside the tent. She backed away—slipping outward, one step, then another.

She had no idea what time it was—her phone was long gone—but instinct pulled her toward the buses. Maybe Zev would remember her. Maybe he'd still be willing to help.

Right now, the buses were the only shot she had.

Maybe, just maybe, she could get off somewhere along the route and make her way to Texas. Her Abuelita would take her in. Although her grandmother never had a formal education, she was a survivor, with wisdom that could humble any Ivy League degree.

Luna distanced herself from Independence Avenue, angling toward Constitution. As she drew closer, a line of purple buses came into view—each bearing an oversized image of Senator Remi McCarthy cradling a basketball-sized Earth.

Even longer than the line of buses was the queue of people waiting to board. At the very front, Zev stood with a clipboard, processing each person one by one—collecting papers, taking signatures.

Luna didn't hesitate. She bypassed the line and walked straight to him.

"Hi, Zev. Do you remember me?"

A voice behind her snapped,

"There's a line, lady. Get the fuck back."

She ignored it.

Zev looked up, squinting.

"Don't worry, folks," he called out. "I'm going in order."

He then spoke to her:

"The mystery woman. Yeah, I remember you. I'm kinda swamped here. Can it wait?"

"How do I get on? I'd like to go. I've changed my mind."

He shook his head.

"Sorry. You're too late. We're maxed out. Eight buses. All full."

Her legs suddenly felt weak, and she feared she would collapse. "Please. I have to go. For my baby."

Zev hesitated. "I thought that wasn't your kid? Look, I'm really sorry. We're chock-full. I wish I could help."

Luna nodded, accepting defeat and her dire circumstances. With a resigned breath, she turned away.

But something shifted inside her. Before she took a step, she reached up to feel her diamond earrings, grateful they were still there.

Forgive me, Bubba.

Chapter 24: Remi

Remi McCarthy was back on familiar soil, her itinerary packed so tight she could almost hear the clock ticking behind her. Today's battlefield was a glossy morning talk show set—bright lights, biting questions. The producers had promised a "lively discussion," their polite code for an ambush.

In the Mix at Six came right after the five o'clock Channel 6 news, when early risers and political diehards were sipping from their mugs and hanging on every word.

Remi took the center seat, framed by two hosts. To viewers, the blue-haired progressive occupied the left, bracelets chiming with each flick of her hands. On the right sat the redheaded conservative, with dangling earrings catching a glint with each head turn. Behind their jewelry, Remi knew they both concealed a cutting edge.

Remi smoothed the leg of her deep-purple jumpsuit, feeling the silk stretch beneath her palm. Purple—neither the left's banner nor the right's—was her quiet declaration. A blend, not a side. A color meant to show them that compromise was not weakness, but unity was strength.

What the show couldn't seem to escape—its Achilles' heel—was its reliance on scripted arguments, each side clinging stubbornly to its corner and dragging the nation nowhere. Remi thought in solutions, even when confined to soundbites. She wasn't swayed by ratings or ad revenue—the real engines behind the program. She had come for something better.

The show's producer counted down aloud: "Five, four, three…" Then he held up two fingers, followed by one, and finally a fist, signaling the start of the broadcast. The red camera light glowed to life.

The redheaded hostess spoke first. "Welcome to *In the Mix at Six*. We're excited to have our next guest in the studio. She's making waves across the country."

The blue-haired co-anchor picked up seamlessly. "You know her as the author of the Carbon Laws—please welcome Senator Remi McCarthy." The live audience erupted in applause. "Good morning, Senator, and thank you for joining us so early."

Remi smiled warmly. "It's a pleasure. Good Earth to you both."

The camera swung right as the redhead began the questioning. "Senator, before we jump into the fray, could you explain the Carbon Laws? Many are still confused about how they work."

Remi's eyes gleamed as she launched into her well-rehearsed response. "Thank you for giving me that opportunity. I appreciate that your show is fact-based. By asking that question, you demonstrate a real commitment to getting the facts out."

She paused, meeting the hosts' eyes—a subtle appeal for leniency when the tougher questions came. Both women smiled.

"The Carbon Laws consist of three main articles; all aimed at preserving humanity's healthy relationship with the Earth. The first addresses our largest issue—overpopulation. We've devised a formula to reduce our numbers to sustainable levels, using measures like immigration control and procreation rights."

The blue-haired host cut in. "Many in the community criticize this tough stance on immigration, especially considering most of us are not native to this land. They find it cruel and hypocritical."

"We're focused on preserving life for Americans—regardless of ancestry. The past cannot be changed, and national lines have been drawn. This land can sustain only so many. God gave us the ability to reason, and we must use it for our survival. Caring for our own isn't cruelty—it's the most compassionate path forward."

The blue-haired woman looked ready to object, but Remi pressed on. "If I may, let me explain the second article, which—in concert with population reduction—focuses on protecting the human genome. With medical advancements, we've become overly reliant on surgery and pharmaceuticals. We must reverse the dilution of our DNA."

The redhead interjected. "That feels morally wrong."

"Yet, it's the most humane thing we can do for future generations—to preserve the species. And I remain open to a better way."

Both hosts fell silent.

"Finally, the third article outlines incentives designed to reduce our carbon footprint. You may know the Keeling Curve, which tracks atmospheric CO_2 levels—a major driver of global warming. To help reverse this trend, carbon emissions are now measured per capita, with each person responsible for generating enough offsets to reach a net-zero—or even negative—carbon balance."

The blue-haired co-anchor quickly interjected: "Thank you for summarizing the laws. But many believe your approach is harsh— even unconstitutional. How do you respond?"

Remi kept her expression neutral, careful not to betray what she felt. "It's important to remind your audience that without these laws, our planet will become uninhabitable. The signs are everywhere—floods, contaminated drinking water, toxic air. Statistically, we've seen increases in almost every category of natural disaster: hurricanes, wildfires, and more.

As for the Constitution, including the Bill of Rights, my party upholds the principles that matter for all Americans. The difference now is that with every right comes responsibility. If you don't protect our precious resources, you'll be considered an adversary to national interests. But for those who put the Earth first—they will have our protection."

The redhead jumped in. "It seems incredibly un-American to tell a woman—or a couple—they can't have children. How do you justify that?"

Remi leaned forward slightly, her tone steady. "Two factors determine eligibility to procreate. First, financial means—measured through your carbon balance. It's unjust for a child to be born into poverty. Second, if your genome score is low, you risk introducing weakened genetic material into the population.

We considered gene-editing tools like CRISPR but found them unethical and unreliable. Instead, we focus on strengthening the most resilient members of our species. We must put our best foot forward."

The redhead continued, "Your platform is gaining every day in popularity. What about you personally? With all the excitement you've brought to politics—do you have your sights on the presidency?"

"None at all. My focus is getting this country back on track—breaking free from the political deadlock we've created."

The blue-haired co-anchor shifted the focus. "Senator, we understand you offered to relocate the homeless living in 'Lincoln's Sanctuary' in D.C. State. But there's secrecy around where you're sending them—the ranch in Sustalia. Can you clarify?"

"Thank you for asking," Remi replied smoothly. "We don't believe in Sanctuaries. We call it the Mall for Internally Displaced People—Mall IDP. As for where we send them, it's a small city named Felicity. 'Feli' means luck; combined with 'city,' it stands for happiness. We felt it was the right name for a safe haven for refugees willing to help the environment."

"But why the secrecy?"

"A fair question. I've traveled all 52 states and seen immense suffering. In Felicity, we're thriving—no hunger, no flooding, no polluted air or water, no wildfires. Our policies work. They've become the envy of the world. But like with border control, we have to avoid becoming victims of our own success.

We know we can't handle an uncontrolled influx. Our hope is to replicate these methods nationwide. Once that happens, and people have other options, perhaps we'll ease security."

The redhead cut in, urgency in her voice. "I'm sorry, Senator, but we've just been informed of a triple homicide on the Mall. I know you visited recently. Any comments or insights on what's happening near the capital?"

Remi's eyes dropped to the floor, offering the perfect visual of compassion. She answered, "I'm saddened by any senseless murder. When I visited, I saw desperation—which leads to desperate acts. I don't expect the violence to end soon. I urge my colleagues to take a hands-on approach to the environment. Maybe then we can prevent these crimes before they spiral out of control."

The blue-haired co-anchor caught the producer's signal to wrap up. "Senator, thank you for your time."

"Certainly. It was an absolute pleasure," Remi replied, offering a confident smile.

"Thank you for tuning in. We wish you a Six-cessful day."

Remi stood to unclip her mic, satisfied with the interview. She'd only had to lie once.

Chapter 25: Kylo

Kylo grabbed the assailant's wrist, locked in a desperate struggle for the skinning knife—the same weapon that had carved the Mall IDP victims. The bearded man's blade hovered inches above his wife Ingrid's throat. Kylo's hand trembled while he fought to hold the knife back. Sweat beaded on the man's 1488 tattoo, dripping onto Ingrid's cheek. In the corner, Alma shivered, knowing she would be next. Then—a tap on his shoulder.

His eyes snapped open. He jerked, seizing a limb.

A voice broke through the confusion, firm and steady.

"Ouch—you're hurting my arm. Kylo, you're having a nightmare. Wake up."

Kylo blinked hard, groggy but keyed up. Ingrid sat over him, her wrist clutched in his hand. He let go. "Oh no… sorry, honey."

"I hope that doesn't bruise," Ingrid said, rubbing herself. "Trevor's here. Says he needs to talk to you."

Still shaken from the dream, he felt a flush of embarrassment and frustration. He had always treated her gently.

"Trev? About what?"

"Wouldn't say."

"Gimme a sec." He pulled on a shirt and pants, brushed his teeth quickly, and stepped out of the bedroom.

Trevor was waiting on the couch, ramrod straight, hands clamped in his lap. The usual wisecracks were gone. His eyes kept darting toward the door.

When Kylo entered, Trevor stood. "Mornin', Kylo."

Kylo tried to lighten the mood. "No Bigfoot greeting today, Romoso?"

Trevor didn't smile. "They want ya down at the station for some questionin'. I told 'em I'd bring ya myself—beat 'em to showin' up here."

Kylo scratched his unkempt hair. "Not even a knock-and-talk?"

"Nah. They want ya in person—face ta face."

"What's this about?"

Trevor hesitated, voice low. "Kylo… it's bad. Real bad. Had more trouble down at the Mall last night. Three dead. They think you might know somethin' 'bout it."

Kylo's felt a pit in his stomach. Violence wasn't new to him—but this felt different.

"Alright. Just… give me a minute." He grabbed his wallet, keys, and jacket. Before heading out, he gave Ingrid a quick kiss, catching the deep creases between her eyebrows—lines he'd only seen on the darkest days.

"It'll be okay."

She hugged him tightly, longer than usual. He let her hold on as long as she needed.

The drive to the precinct was silent. Neither of them spoke—until halfway there, when the gut punch hit.

"Dammit."

Trevor glanced over, nodding. "Yeah, I know… it's freakin' ridiculous."

"It's not that. It's Alma's birthday… I didn't give her the gift. Still in my pocket. Didn't even tell Ingrid. A surprise."

Trevor gave a quiet grunt. "Hey, you'll give it to her when ya get home."

When they arrived, Trevor led Kylo through familiar halls to the interrogation room—cold, gray, sterile. The place where people unraveled.

Kylo looked around and gave a weak chuckle.

"The Box, huh? Didn't think I'd end up on this side of the glass."

Trevor didn't return the smile. "Go ahead, grab a seat. The agents'll be heah any minute." He stepped out, closing the door behind him.

Alone, Kylo fidgeted. He checked his watch, then rubbed his palms on his jeans. The air felt more humid with every passing minute. He knew the game—make you wait, make you squirm. Give silence time to curdle into doubt. He felt like a field goal kicker, the opposing team icing him with a timeout.

Then the door opened.

A plainclothes investigator stepped in. "Good morning, Kylo."

Kylo gave a half-hearted shrug. "Not sure it is, but thanks."

"Do you know why you're here?"

"I heard about the triple. Figured you'd want to know if I saw anything suspicious."

The man sat down. "What time did you leave the Mall last night?"

"Late. Around one."

"Anyone see you leave? Anyone verify when you got home?"

Kylo frowned. "No. My wife and kid were asleep. Why?"

"Did you enter any tents after midnight?"

"No. I just monitored the murder scene."

"The first scene? The Black couple?"

"Yeah."

The investigator nodded slowly, then reached into a plastic container.

"Can you explain this?" He held up a flashlight—Kylo's name etched into the side.

Kylo stared. "What the hell? That's mine. I keep it clipped to my belt."

The investigator's gaze didn't budge.

"Do you keep a large amount of cash on you?"

Kylo narrowed his eyes. "What? No. Why?"

"I'm going to need to pat you down. Just protocol. No weapons, I assume?"

Kylo stood slowly. "No weapons. Go ahead."

A second officer entered. As hands methodically searched him, Kylo felt the eyes behind the one-way mirror.

"Would you consent to a search of your home and vehicle?" the investigator asked. Polite tone. Razor-sharp eyes.

"We can get a warrant if needed."

Kylo didn't hesitate. "Sure. But can I call my wife? Let her know you're coming?"

"We'll inform her," the investigator said, his tone shifting ever so slightly. "I'm sure this is all a coincidence, but we have to be thorough. In the meantime, you'll need to stay put."

Kylo's stomach knotted. "Wait. What coincidence? Am I under arrest?"

The man leaned in, calm but firm. "You're not. But if you're innocent, you'll want to stay ahead of this—voluntarily. Can we get you anything? Coffee? Sandwich?"

Kylo shook his head. "No, thanks." His thoughts spun. Nothing made sense.

The investigator turned to leave.

"Wait," Kylo blurted, standing abruptly.

The man paused, glancing back. "Yes?"

Kylo's pulse hammered. "I remember something. About the flashlight…"

Chapter 26: Luna

Luna approached Zev for the second time, her nerves fraying thin at the edges. She was afraid of annoying him with her constant interruptions, but desperation left her no choice.

"I'm sorry, Zev. I should've introduced myself earlier. I'm Luna, and this is Karli. I'm sorry if I was being rude."

He offered a faint smile, lacking the warmth he'd shown when she first approached him. "So, part of the mystery unfolds."

She felt embarrassed and wanted to leave—but forced herself to stay. She needed help, even if she couldn't bring herself to say it.

"Quick question—can I board if I convince someone to give up their place?"

"Sure, but good luck with that," Zev replied, his fatigue softening his voice. "There're a lot of people here who want the same thing."

Luna hesitated, scanning the throngs of weary faces. She turned, then stopped, a question pulling her.

"Would I need two spots, or just one?"

"Sorry?"

"The baby. Does she need her own seat?"

"Oh, I see. No, she'll be fine on your lap."

Luna nodded, but a knot tightened in her chest.

Sorry, Bubba. I'm sure you'd understand.

Her fingers trembling, Luna pulled out one of her diamond earrings. She glanced at the glimmering stone, knowing what it meant—she'd be left with only the matching gem, her last possession of value.

A glint of movement in a bus window caught her eye. She barely recognized the reflection. A woman she would've pitied stared back—a homeless woman, wearing her face.

Bracing herself, she walked the line, arm extended. The faces around her were empty, unreadable. Now, she was one of them— the displaced, the desperate.

"Would anyone be willing to trade seats for a diamond earring? Half a carat?" Luna called, her voice trembling despite her efforts to steady it.

Most didn't even glance her way. Hollow eyes stared forward— exhausted or indifferent. Her stomach twisted. For a moment, it felt like begging.

But she kept going, repeating the offer. Her voice grew stronger—firmer, more urgent.

A shrill voice cut the air.

"How do we know that's not just glass? We're not jewelers."

"You have my word," Luna said, forcing calm into her tone.

"Empty promise," the man snapped. "Worth zero carbon credits. No thanks. Probably just costume junk anyway."

The words stung, but she didn't stop. She couldn't. She walked on, scanning the crowd, hoping—just hoping—someone would see either the value or the desperation.

Behind her, a softer voice murmured, "Gems won't feed us, miss. Not anymore."

Then another—snide, mocking.

"Yeah, why don't you shove your diamonds up your designer-jeaned ass and get lost."

Laughter followed—brittle, cruel. It sliced through her— deliberate, meant to wound.

She kept moving until a large man stepped from the line, blocking her path. She tried to go around him, but he shifted, forcing her to meet his eyes.

"We're hungry," he said, voice like gravel. "Our days of galas and fancy dinners are long gone. We've been standing in this heat for hours. No one's trading their place for sparkle. Bribes don't work. Spare yourself the shame—and catch a later bus."

Each word landed like a blow. Luna said nothing. When he stepped aside, she walked on, legs like lead, pulse hammering.

By the time she reached the end of the line, no one had taken her offer.

She wanted to collapse. To vanish into the heat and dust. But there was nowhere else to go.

She just needed one person.

Just one.

Luna turned back toward Zev, desperate—but composed.

He was speaking with a man in his forties—his nose hairs catching the sunlight in a way she couldn't unsee. She caught the tail end of their exchange, her heart sinking.

"...broken hip. He fell last night—the old poop tripped over his own boots outside the tent. I heard the crack." The man pointed toward a bench. "That's him."

Zev's voice was kind but firm. "I'm sorry, he can't go. Even if we had someone to help him, it would be too painful. We'll need to free that seat for someone else. You should stay and find help for him."

The man's tone turned bitter. "First off, his ticket's mine to give, not yours. And I've got my seat," he snapped. "My responsibility for him ended when my wife died in the storm.

That's her uncle, not mine. I owe him nothing. He never liked me anyway. He can rot in Hell for all I care."

Zev didn't flinch. "Fine. The seat's yours to give away. What's your name?"

"Clive. Why? I've done nothing wrong."

Zev turned to Luna, their eyes meeting for a brief second. "This young lady wants on the bus."

Clive looked her over, bottom to top, a greedy glint in his eyes. "Highest bidder gets it."

Luna stepped forward, swallowing her disgust. "I'll trade you this diamond earring for the seat."

He rubbed his chin, weighing the offer. "I suppose I could sell it. Throw in that blanket?"

Luna stared. "This is for the baby."

"Fine, whatever. Yeah, alright, it's a deal."

She hesitated, glancing toward the man on the bench, his body stiff with pain. "Should I leave it with your uncle?"

Clive chuckled darkly. "Weren't you listening? He's not my uncle anymore. I'm the one who made the arrangements. I'll take the earring."

Luna's breath caught. "But... what about him?"

Clive's face hardened. "Miss, he was dead the moment he tripped. His own doing."

The words were uncaring and disrespectful. But she nodded, swallowing a desire to lash out. "Fine. It's a deal."

She dangled the earring. Clive snatched it, his grin spreading as he examined it under the sun.

Luna turned to Zev, keeping her voice steady. "Thank you. What do I do now?"

Zev gave a genuine smile. "My pleasure, Luna. You'll need to fill out some forms. I'll get you an electronic pad."

Luna raised a finger. "Great. Just give me a second."

She walked over to the bench where the old man lay, his breathing shallow, pain evident in every breath. Gently, she placed her hand on his arm.

"Sir, I'm so sorry about your injury. Give me your hand."

She pulled out her second earring, placed it in his palm, and curled his fingers around it, clasping her hands over his.

"I hope this helps. My prayers are with you."

A tear traced down his cheek. His voice came soft, thick with gratitude. "God bless you."

Luna turned away, her heart heavy—but also oddly light.

Clive caught sight of her and sneered, holding the diamond up to the light. "What was that all about?"

She didn't even glance at him as she reached for the electronic pad.

"I just wanted to wish your uncle good luck." She let the word "uncle" hang in the air, knowing it would chafe.

She scanned the consent forms—dense with legal jargon designed to protect Sustalia from lawsuits.

Halfway down, a clause jumped out at her—and she finally understood why so many had been reluctant to board.

Chapter 27: Avi

Avi had slipped into bed just after 2 a.m., careful not to wake his wife. Though physically exhausted, his nerves refused to settle. Sleep never came. When her alarm finally rang, he was still lying there, eyes open in the dark, feigning a stir as she rose.

Despite the sleepless night, he felt oddly invigorated—almost euphoric. Instead of slipping out the door like he usually did, he made his way to the kitchen. To everyone's surprise, he didn't just pass through; he pulled up a chair and sat down for breakfast.

It wasn't a planned choice—just a sudden urge to celebrate. To be free from critics, and most importantly, from the threats. Last night, he had silenced them all. His home remained his quiet refuge. That was enough.

"I think I'll have three eggs this morning," he said, with a rare smile.

His wife, Evelyn, raised a brow and grinned. "Well, someone's in a good mood. I love having you here, but… weren't you trying to cut back?"

"Sometimes you gotta stop and smell the roses, my dear."

For the first time in weeks, he looked at his son—really looked—without flinching from shame. Of course, what he saw offered nothing inspiring. Oscar, unaware of his father's stare or turmoil, sat contentedly at the table, focused on his cereal. He pressed each puff beneath the milk, watching with fascination as they bobbed back to the surface, one by one. At eight years old, it struck Avi as a bit simple.

The boy has her genes.

Evelyn plated the food, and Avi didn't hesitate—slathering butter on his toast, inhaling the eggs like a starving man. Her hand settled on his shoulder, kneading gently in slow circles.

"At last," she said softly, "my cheerful husband is back. We've missed you."

As she walked away, he slapped her rear.

"Not in front of our son." But a faint smile gave her away.

Oscar looked up, mouth open, curious what he'd missed—then resumed drowning the next puff with his spoon.

She nodded toward the TV. "You must've seen the news."

Avi blinked. He hadn't. He'd been thinking of Blackjack. But curiosity tugged him toward the screen.

Footage showed buses filling up on the Mall—overflowing. The reporter said the homeless population was finally thinning out. Progress, they called it.

Strange how fast things change.

Avi thought of the General—could almost picture the crusty old man smiling. The thought alone was so absurd it bordered on surreal. Smiling? The General? Might as well imagine unicorns prancing up marshmallow mountains.

No—more likely he'd settled into Defcon 4. Back to a baseline grump instead of full-blown outrage.

Avi's thoughts drifted over the past two days. Hurting people gave him no satisfaction, and after what he'd done that morning, he felt far from heroic. Yet one truth remained: his actions had given him a lifeline. All he could do now was hope the DNA sample provided enough of a distraction—and that Kylo, whoever he truly was, had an alibi that would hold.

He was still lost in thought when a knock snapped him back.

His wife turned. "Sweetie? Are you expecting someone?"

Panic surged.

Blackjack?

He bolted toward the bedroom, yanked open the drawer, grabbed his Glock. Hands shaking, he checked the magazine, shoved it into his pajama pocket, and hurried toward the door.

Too late. She'd already opened it.

"Good morning, ma'am. I'm Officer Iris Fonner. I'm looking for Avi Sweller. Is he here?"

Avi stepped from the hallway, forcing composure. "I'm… him. I'm Avi."

The officer's face stayed neutral, her voice firm. "Sir, we'd like you to come down to the station. Just a few questions."

Avi's stomach twisted. "Questions about what?"

"It's in connection with the triple homicide at the Mall. We believe you may have information."

"Triple homicide?"

His heart slammed. He hadn't heard a word about a murder.

His wife's voice snapped, "He was here all night. I don't see how he could help you."

"We understand, ma'am," Fonner replied calmly. "But this isn't a conversation to be held in a doorway. Mr. Sweller, you're not under arrest—you're free to change, and we'll take you in when you're ready."

"Right… yeah," Avi muttered. He retreated to the bedroom and locked the door behind him.

He unloaded the Glock and shoved it back into the drawer, then yanked a hoodie over his head. "That piss-hole lunatic Blackjack," he hissed. "He's behind this. Did he kill Kylo too?"

But then a thought struck—sharp, cold.

The flashlight… Fuck. It's even worse—Kylo's still alive.

Chapter 28: Luna

Luna sat near the center of the packed, idling bus, suffocating in the noxious brew of diesel fumes, body odor, and stale breath. The windows were fogged with condensation, and the air inside clung to her skin like damp cloth.

A greenhouse on wheels—minus the green.

Directly in front of her, the nephew, Clive—loud and bitter—voiced his grievance to anyone willing to listen.

"If I'd known we had to give up valuables, I would've traded this seat for food. Don't let that pretty face fool you. She's a conniving thief."

It was clear that Luna was seated behind him. That was the point.

She said nothing, though the accusation throbbed in her ears. She had been just as shocked when she'd read the fine print in the relocation agreement. The mandatory forfeiture of personal items hadn't mattered much—she had little left worth keeping. But other clauses in the contract had unsettled her more deeply. Still, like everyone else, she had signed. She had no real choice.

But the man wasn't ready to move on. His resentment boiled.

He suddenly twisted around, jabbing his finger inches from her face. "You knew, didn't you?"

"Not when we made the deal."

His finger pushed closer. "You cheated me!"

Luna snapped.

She grabbed his finger and bent it backward with enough force to cause his shoulders to lower in pain. She held him in submission for a beat to make her point.

She finally let go, startled by her own reaction—but she didn't back down.

"Don't ever point at me like that again," she said, her voice clipped and fierce. "As for our transaction—the one where you traded your uncle's life for jewelry—I hadn't read the onboarding details at the time. You had. You signed hours before I did. So next time, read before you deal." She realized, with a surge of surprise, that this was the first time she'd ever gone on the offensive with a stranger.

A few people clapped quietly. The man turned and shrank in his seat, saying nothing more. Whatever dominance he'd tried to exert had completely dissolved.

The tension broke when Zev entered through the bus door.

"Ladies and gentlemen," he called out, his voice clear and practiced, "we'll be departing for Union Station in just a few minutes. From there, armed escorts will guide us to the train. I'll be stationed outside the first car to check you off the list. Please board quickly—there's no assigned seating, and some of you may not be able to sit with your companions. I apologize for that."

He paused, his tone softening. "I know this journey is difficult, but I'm asking for your cooperation along the way. I've been authorized to remove anyone who becomes disruptive. Please remember—this opportunity exists because of Senator Remi McCarthy. It's a second chance, a gift. If you look out your window, you'll see people who would do anything to be in your place."

A woman from the back raised her hand. "Will there be meals? My daughter hasn't eaten since yesterday."

"I'm sorry, I don't know. Communication has been limited," Zev admitted. "We'll find out soon. I'll be with you for the next two days, until we arrive in Felicity. I'm riding on bus 55, right in front of you. There are over eight buses. Once at the station, we'll transfer to the passenger train."

He scanned the faces around him, waiting. There were no more questions. He nodded his thanks and gave a look to the driver, who opened the doors so Zev could exit.

Luna turned to the window.

Outside stood the ones who hadn't made the list.

She studied their faces—raw emotion barely masked: desperation, disbelief, and fear. Some paced, others sobbed, and many simply stared as if willing the buses to open their doors for more. Their hopelessness mirrored her own from moments ago. She'd nearly been one of them.

Then came the pounding.

Angry people surged forward, slamming fists against the side of the bus. Shouting. Demanding. Others nearby caught the mood and joined in. What started as frustration was rapidly becoming a mob.

The peaceful ones were shoved aside. Chaos rippled outward. Luna watched bodies stumble, some trampled beneath the swarm. The bus rocked violently. Passengers gripped the backs of seats to stay upright. Heads bobbed in unison as the vehicle tilted under the pressure.

"Driver!" Luna shouted. "You have to leave. People are going to get hurt!"

"I haven't been authorized to move."

"Forget authorization—look! They're trying to flip the damn bus!"

Her voice cracked with command. The driver hesitated, then threw the bus into gear, easing it forward, steadily gaining speed, giving time for people to move so he didn't crush anyone.

The other buses followed, wheels groaning as they pulled away. Through the rear window, Luna watched the riot ignite—people swarming the vacant space like a storm. Then, almost as if summoned, reservists swept in to regain control. But before they fully secured the crowd, another bus lurched forward, less careful. She caught a glimpse—just long enough to register a man's legs buckling, his body vanishing under the wheels—before she wrenched her gaze away.

A man three rows back stood, his teenage daughter clutched to his side. "Ma'am," he said, looking at Luna, his voice thick with emotion, "I don't know who you are, but thank you. We wouldn't have gotten out if you hadn't stepped up."

Others nodded in silent agreement.

Luna felt something inside her change—a quiet but certain shift in confidence. A threshold had been crossed. She'd trusted her instincts, and they hadn't failed her.

She turned and kissed Karli gently on the forehead.

For the first time in a long while, she felt something close to hope.

The road ahead wasn't just survival anymore. It was a beginning.

And this time, she was ready.

Chapter 29: Avi

Officer Iris Fonner led Avi into the humid interrogation room and left without a word. The door clicked shut behind her, leaving him alone with his thoughts.

Avi scanned the room. He wasn't a detective, but even he could tell the purpose of the large pane of glass on the wall. A two-way mirror—others watching him as he watched his own reflection. Every shift in his seat broke the silence, the chair's creak a grating rasp, ruffling him like fingernails on a chalkboard. The room seemed designed to keep him on edge.

Overhead, fluorescent lights buzzed faintly—sterile, harsh, surgical. There was no comfort in them, only exposure. The manufactured daylight stripped him bare, as if to spotlight every misstep. They were going to dissect him, piece by piece.

He steadied himself, forcing his features into neutrality. No cracks. No panic. But his palms were clammy. The sweat had returned—a familiar curse he couldn't shake.

The minutes dragged—thirty, maybe, he didn't know. Even the faintest sounds—the hum of electricity, the distant clatter of footsteps—were sharpened by the stillness. Finally, the door opened.

A man entered, dressed in business casual, holding two cups of coffee. "Good morning, Avi. I appreciate you coming in. Sorry about the wait—I had a stack of paperwork to get through." He set one of the cups in front of Avi. "There's cream and sugar if you want it."

Avi didn't touch the coffee. The gesture felt off—too familiar for the circumstances. "Am I being held?"

"No. This is voluntary," the agent said smoothly. "We're assuming you had no involvement in what happened, but we figured you'd want to help clear things up."

He paused, eyes locked on Avi's, voice calm but focused. "Before we go further, I'm going to read you your Miranda rights. Not because you're under arrest, but because it protects the integrity of the case."

Avi frowned. "I don't get it, but okay."

The agent's tone turned flat, rushed, almost robotic. "You have the right to remain silent. Anything you say can and will be used against you…"

Each phrase fell like a stone in Avi's gut. The room seemed to shrink, more like a prison with every word.

"…If you cannot afford an attorney, one will be provided…"

The word "afford" got him thinking about his finances.

The agent finished and leaned back in his chair. "You understand what I just read?"

"Of course."

"Good, with that out of the way, I'd like to ask you a few questions."

Avi nodded again, trying to appear nonchalant. "Go ahead."

"What's your role concerning the Mall?"

"I'm a senior contractor brought in by General Stuart to oversee the drawdown of the displaced population. I've been coordinating with UnaTerra and working out of a temporary office in the Archive Building—it's close to the encampments."

The agent raised his eyebrows slightly. "How's that effort going?"

"The relocation? Poorly—until recently. But I heard people started leaving after the latest incident."

"So, you know about the triple homicide last night? A husband and wife, and their teenage son?"

Avi's stomach turned. "I heard about it this morning. Didn't realize it was a family." He tried to show an expression of concern by thinking of his own wife and son. It wasn't working.

The agent leaned forward. "It seems the murders are accomplishing what your operation struggled to do—moving people off the Mall."

"That's not how I would've chosen to make progress," Avi replied, jaw tight. "But yes, the incident has accelerated things."

"Do you have any idea who might be behind the killings?"

"No, sir." The lie felt believable.

"When was the last time you were physically in the tent city?"

Avi hesitated. His mind scrambled to align his answers with his wife's memory of the night. "A couple of weeks ago. I've mostly been in my office. Haven't been out on the actual grounds lately."

The agent nodded, reached into his coat, and pulled out a few photographs. He slid the first one across the table.

"You recognize this man?"

A bearded Caucasian with a lazy eye stared up from the photo. Avi's pulse stuttered. Blackjack. He kept his voice flat. "No, sir. Doesn't look familiar."

Another photo.

"And this one?"

Kylo.

Avi's gut clenched. A bead of sweat traced down his back. If Kylo was still alive—and talking—Avi's lie would collapse. He'd never wished death on anyone but his father-in-law. Now there was another.

He kept his expression neutral. "Nope. Never seen him."

The agent didn't react. Instead, he slipped on a glove and reached into a black bin, pulling out a flashlight between his thumb and index finger.

"Does this look familiar?"

Avi's throat closed. He swallowed hard. "I've seen many flashlights in my life."

"We found this one near the crime scene. We ran prints on it—just waiting for the results. You wouldn't expect to see yours on it, would you?"

"No, sir." His mind raced. Did he wipe it down? He couldn't remember.

"Would you be willing to take a polygraph?"

Avi hesitated. "I don't think that's a good idea. I don't handle pressure well. Medical issues—I can't even exercise."

The agent lifted an eyebrow, clearly unimpressed. But he didn't press.

"Last thing, then you can go. I'd like you to meet someone—one of the officers on the case. Just in case we need to follow up."

Avi nodded, too relieved by the word "go" to argue. He needed to regroup.

The door opened.

Kylo stepped inside.

The trap had been sprung.

Avi avoided eye contact with the big man. "I'd like to leave now."

Chapter 30: Luna

Luna was among the first to reach security at the train station. The screening process was relentless—metal wands, latex gloves, hands probing where no one should ever touch. She endured it for the sake of safety. Then came a sudden tug.

A guard had his hands on Karli.

Luna's grip tightened instantly, yanking the child back, both alarmed and defiant. "What do you think you're doing?"

"Hand over the child." The man wore camo, but it was the patch that caught her eye—a deep purple emblem stitched onto his shoulder: a palm encircling a clenched fist, with the word "UnaTerra" curved beneath it. It felt more like conquest than protection.

"I'll do no such thing."

The guard lowered one hand to his belt, eyes locked on hers. "You'll do as you're told."

Luna bent protectively over Karli, unwilling to let him lay a finger on her again. The guard reacted instantly—one hand now on his taser, the other clamping onto her arm, firm and unyielding.

Then Zev appeared.

"I'm in charge of these passengers. What's going on here?" His voice was confident and edged with authority.

"Then you'd better get them in line. We're required to search every passenger," the guard replied, eyes still fixed on Luna as if she were at risk of escaping. "That includes the child."

Zev glanced between them. "You'll give the baby right back, yes?"

"If nothing's suspicious," the guard said. "Protocol applies to everyone—even this entitled princess."

Zev extended his arms toward Luna. "Let me hold the baby. Just for a moment—it'll be okay."

Luna hesitated. She didn't know why, but something about him felt trustworthy. Slowly, she passed Karli over.

The search was brief—clinical, impersonal. Karli whimpered once, then fell silent. A moment later, she was back in Luna's arms. Zev immediately moved on, heading toward a louder dispute further down the line.

Luna drew a slow, deliberate breath, trying to shake the confrontation from her shoulders. Once cleared, she boarded the train and found a seat near the front of the lead passenger car, holding Karli close. Her jaw ached; she hadn't realized she'd been clenching it.

Was something truly wrong with this place, or was fear conjuring shadows where none existed? She couldn't tell. Still shaken, she felt grateful that Zev had appeared when he did.

Across the aisle, a handwritten "saved" sign caught her eye. Beneath it sat a backpack she recognized instantly—Zev's. There were no official seat assignments, but she guessed he'd claimed the spot to be visible and accessible to travelers.

Her focus returned to Karli, who had started fussing again. Luna fed her quietly, trying to soothe her. The crying eased to whimpers, then faded into long, sleepy blinks.

But Luna still felt tense. She retrieved her tote and inventoried the supplies security allowed her to keep: enough formula, enough diapers for a few days. That was something, at least. But there was no food, no water for herself. She'd have to manage. Like the woman who had asked earlier, Luna couldn't help but wonder when—or if—food would be served. Breakfast had already passed.

More passengers trickled in, and Luna was surprised by how many the train could hold. Once every seat was filled, the stragglers were ushered into another car. The process was slow and discouraging. After the cabin was packed, the train remained motionless, its doors still open.

Out the window, she spotted Zev on the platform, locked in a heated exchange with a man she didn't recognize. He wore a jacket nearly identical to Zev's, with "RELOCATION TEAM" stamped across the back in bold purple letters.

Even from a distance, she could sense the tension. Zev's arms were crossed as he stood firm. The dispute escalated until an armed guard intervened, clearly admonishing Zev. Zev was visibly frustrated, shaking his head slowly before climbing aboard.

He addressed the car almost immediately.

"Folks, I'm really sorry," he began, voice tight with tension. "We have to take on additional people. Another group will be boarding shortly, and as you can see, we're out of seats. I'm asking anyone who can—especially those without small children or elderly companions—to give up their spot. I tried, but I couldn't prevent this."

The car grew even more crowded as more passengers squeezed in, forced to stand in the narrow aisles. No one offered their seat—except Zev himself. Luna's stomach twisted at the thought of reaching the bathroom, especially with Karli. This violated every reasonable safety regulation—but no one spoke up.

Once the final passengers crammed in, the doors sealed shut. A jolt ran through the car as the train lurched into motion. Zev, having given up his seat to an elderly woman, found a small space near Luna to stand.

She offered a faint smile. "We can take turns, if you'd like."

"Thanks, but you've got your hands full with the baby. I'm good," he replied, warm but resolute.

"I doubt you'll want to stand for two straight days."

His voice was low and tired. "Okay, Luna. Let's see how it goes. Thanks."

Something about the way he said her name made her smile—unforced, genuine.

"No, I should thank you."

"For what? Getting you into this cattle pen on rails?"

"For helping me with Karli, and getting us on the bus. I know it hasn't been easy."

Zev exhaled, part weariness, part apology. "It was my pleasure. Though honestly, I'm not sure what I've gotten you into. Hopefully, in two days, we'll all be a little more comfortable." He scanned the train. "This is far too packed. And there are some… unusual characters." He nodded in a certain direction.

Luna stood, pretending to adjust her pants and gather herself. She scanned the cabin, trying to locate who Zev was referring to.

Through a break in the crowd, her gaze snagged on a man seated a few rows back, not far from Clive, the nephew. He stood out for some reason—his plain cotton tunic noticeable even in the dim light—and something about him held her fast.

His jet-black hair seemed at odds with his pale skin. When their eyes met—lingering just a breath too long—a chill ran down her spine. One eye locked onto her, steady and unnerving. The other drifted, slightly misaligned, as though keeping watch on someone else.

That single, unblinking eye seemed to be taking her apart piece by piece, quietly cataloging her.

She broke the stare first, the act feeling like a concession. There was something about him she almost recognized—a darkness she couldn't name, just out of reach.

Chapter 31: Aldric

The air in Felicity buzzed with anticipation, felt by everyone—from top officials to the humblest workers.

"Sir, Senator Remi McCarthy is moments away. The caravan's approaching."

Even Aldric Heister, CEO of Felicity and the embodiment of its rigid order, couldn't hide the tension in his stance. He had prepared for this day with the focus of a man who knew exactly what was at risk. The city's future—and his own—rested on Remi's approval. In truth, he secretly resented his dependence on her, but if all went according to plan, that would change.

"You've doubled the armed sentinels, including those in the towers?"

He could see the reinforcements from his vantage point, but he needed to hear it confirmed.

"Yes, sir."

"And Town Hall? Every detail?"

"Clean. Staff reminded about posture and conduct, as you directed."

It was still not enough. It never was. He feared something intangible had slipped past him. This wasn't just a visit—it was a reckoning, a stage where the carbon-free vision would either triumph or fracture.

He straightened, shoulder still sore from yesterday's workout, and let his hand rest on his firm abdomen. At six feet tall, with a Nordic frame and every blond hair in place, Aldric imposed the same discipline on his body that he demanded of his city.

At just thirty-two, he was young to be leading one of the most ambitious urban projects on the planet. His success never relied on charm or rhetoric—only on results. No excuses. No delays.

His relationship with Senator McCarthy was carefully structured and symbiotic. She needed Felicity to prove UnaTerra's model could scale. He needed her political capital to expand its reach. Together, they made the perfect front.

But behind the alliance lay a quiet truth: they did not share the same approach. Only one was willing to make the necessary sacrifices.

As the crowd grew restless, a sleek black electric-powered limousine glided through the compound gates, flanked by dark Suburbans. The entourage came to a stop just outside Town Hall. Even Aldric's heart rate quickened, but his expression remained impassive, a mask of professionalism.

The limousine door opened with ceremonial precision. A young aide stepped out briskly, opened the rear door, and Senator Remi McCarthy emerged—tall, poised, unmistakably in control. She adjusted her jacket with practiced grace, then stepped toward Aldric, her purple heels clicking against the asphalt as she took in her surroundings.

The long ride from the television studio had done nothing to dim her focus. Her attention was locked on the CEO standing before her.

Aldric stepped forward, offering the verdant salute with a slight bow, then extending his hand for a firm handshake. "Good Earth, ma'am. It's an honor to welcome you back. Your presence means everything today."

Senator McCarthy returned the salute with smooth authority. Her staff followed suit. Then she took his hand, her smile warm but calculated.

"Green fields, Mr. Heister. Last time I visited, it was all projections and sketches. I've heard your progress has been… formidable. I look forward to seeing it for myself."

Aldric kept his voice steady, but he was uneasy. Had he overlooked something in the preparations?

"I hope everything meets your expectations."

Remi's smile widened. "You've created life from dust—I'm sure it will."

Aldric began walking, motioning for his guest to follow. "We'll start the tour here. You just passed through our primary checkpoint—security's been significantly upgraded since your last visit."

"I noticed."

He nodded. "The perimeter wall is a necessity. It keeps the city secure and shuts out those who don't belong here."

"Remind me—how large is Felicity now? And have you reached your development limit?"

Aldric shielded his eyes from the sun, scanning the skyline.

"About 160 square miles. Los Angeles is nearly 470, but unlike L.A., we hold to a strict density—four residents per acre. That's the ratio we must maintain to stay carbon neutral."

He slipped in a pointed comment. "I still act as mayor in all but title. Of course, to change that would require political support." He watched her closely, hoping the message would register. But Remi remained staring at the landscape, absorbing the city with clinical fascination.

To regain her attention, he pivoted to rhetoric she could use as a sound bite.

"This city proves that UnaTerra's ideals are achievable. No hunger. No idle hands. Every citizen a contributor."

That caught her. Their eyes locked. "Impressive."

Satisfied, he gestured outward. "Beyond the pasture there, you'll see the turbines. They're dual-purpose—powering our facilities and maintaining water flow for the aquaponics system. We're even exceeding our carbon benchmarks and selling surplus credits."

Remi glanced at her staff with pride. "See? Proof of concept."

Aldric pressed on. "Also, you're technically standing on the roof of a high-rise structure. What looks like our entrance road is actually an engineered roof deck—multi-functional and heavily reinforced."

Instinctively, everyone glanced downward, seeing only asphalt.

"Below us lies a subterranean network, modeled loosely on Disney's utilidors. But unlike Disney World—crippled during Hurricane Stella—our infrastructure is built to withstand future climate catastrophes."

Senator McCarthy's eyes snapped back up. "I'm eager to see the interior."

"That's Town Hall ahead—very functional. It's vast, yet modestly decorated in a minimalist style."

Remi raised an eyebrow. "No windows?"

"Exactly," Aldric replied. "We conserve energy wherever possible. The design philosophy here is utilitarian—every structure, every surface has purpose. We've eradicated distractions. Nothing is ornamental, and waste is anathema."

He had looked up the word *anathema*, hoping it would land. Politicians loved their words—windsocks of action—and she was no exception.

They entered the building together. Inside, they bypassed biometric turnstiles flanked by armed guards. The space opened into a towering, dove-white lobby.

Aldric turned, letting the height of the room emphasize his next point.

"Our color palette reinforces a culture of cleanliness. White surfaces reveal the slightest contamination instantly. We've gone 255 days without a single case of flu—and not a single positive test for any known pandemic variant."

He continued walking, shoes echoing across the tiled floor.

"This lobby accommodates up to a thousand. You'll notice the benches and tables are unupholstered—functional, not comfortable. That's intentional. We encourage efficient communication and purposeful celebration. No idling."

He paused, letting that sink in.

"Mall IDP passengers enter here after processing and sanitation. They arrive via the lowest level, where they're tested, cleansed, and issued standardized garments. Personal belongings are disposed of responsibly—buried, never burned."

One of Remi's aides furrowed her brow. "Sanitized?"

"Absolutely. Full-body decontamination, followed by vaccination. Then, aptitude and genome assessments. This ensures optimal role assignment. Every individual contributes." Aldric purposely left some of the steps out.

He continued down the corridor, gesturing toward a glass atrium up ahead.

"This," he said, pausing, "is one of our proudest features."

Through the glass shimmered a lush atrium, sunlight cascading through overhead panels. A small bird darted between the branches.

Remi's eyes lit up. "Is that a woodpecker?"

"Yes. Red-bellied."

"Its head is red, not its belly."

"You'll have to take that up with the taxonomist who named it, not me," Aldric said, allowing a rare smile. "Our ecologists maintain every element of the habitat. The goal is harmony. Controlled biodiversity. Not just a symbol—an operational ecosystem."

He led the group a few steps farther. "And now, the cafeteria."

They entered a spacious dining hall with modular seating and a clean, industrial aesthetic.

"This is where our citizens eat. Two meals per day—breakfast and dinner. Calorically optimized. Efficient."

He gestured, and a man in green approached, his tall white chef's hat blending in with the surroundings.

"It's my honor," the chef said, "to prepare meals that nourish minds and bodies. But first, please try one of our creations."

He offered a tray of appetizers. "Goat cheese and pecan-stuffed mushrooms."

Remi picked one up and popped it in her mouth. "Exquisite."

The chef beamed. "Everything you taste is grown or raised here. Zero imports. High yield, no waste."

Still chewing, Remi asked, "What's for dinner tonight?"

"Hungarian mushroom soup—a warm savory dish. Then, baked sweet potato with Northern Pike in lemon butter. Garnished with burdock and dandelion."

Remi smiled, looking at her staff. "Yum."

He continued, "For dessert, we're serving 'death by chocolate'—moist layers of chocolate cake, frosted with dark chocolate buttercream, and coated in mini chocolate chips. Did I mention the cake's main ingredient is chocolate?"

Laughter rippled through the group.

"As filling as that sounds," the chef added, "breakfast is actually our heaviest meal. We front-load calories for the workday."

Remi nodded appreciatively. "Very smart. But how do you produce so much, given the harsh environment?"

Aldric stepped in, confident. "Our biosphere engineers designed vertical grow systems and greenhouses. Nothing here relies on unpredictable conditions. Everything is controlled. Calculated."

He gently touched the Senator's elbow and smiled. "We're just getting started. The power plant, the farm, the labs, the fishery— they're waiting. This is only the beginning."

As they moved on, Remi leaned closer, her voice lower, more personal.

"Later, I want the full tour. Just you and me."

Aldric met her gaze, pulse steady.

"Of course, ma'am."

Chapter 32: Avi

Avi sat rigid in his chair, heart hammering as Kylo loomed inches away, voice booming with barely contained rage: "Tell them we talked last night. Tell them you were there, used my flashlight."

Avi met his glare, masking the terror running through his body, and replied evenly, his voice forced calm: "No clue what you're talking about. You've mistaken me for someone else."

Kylo's eyes pinched into slits, fury radiating throughout him. Kylo lunged, but a stocky officer barreled in, yanking him back, arms locking around his shoulders, muscles straining. Had he not had protection, Avi knew he wouldn't have a chance.

The outburst created the opening Avi needed. He seized it like a lifeline. "You said I wasn't being held here. I'd like to go home." More questions came, but he repeated his words like a mantra. He was finally released, with a warning not to leave town.

Avi stepped out into freedom, senses on edge, shaken by the confrontation at the station. The man he had helped frame— Kylo—had stood inches from him, ready to strike, and Avi had lied to his face. In that moment, a decision was cemented in his mind: he would no longer cooperate with the authorities.

It came down to his word against Kylo's, and the investigator didn't have enough hard evidence to prove either side. He walked free—but Avi knew the fingerprints on the flashlight could still betray him. He had only a day or two before his lies unraveled completely.

Behind the wheel, he cycled through worst-case scenarios: what might unfold in the next few hours, days, weeks—even years. In every imagined future, he saw himself drowning in humiliation, facing a lifetime in prison—or worse, execution. The longer he drove, the more obvious it became: there was no escape. If he went home, he'd eventually have to explain everything to his wife. She would likely leave him, taking their son, and their money, to her father's care.

Fine. Good riddance to her—and her whole shitty family.

As for going into the office, that seemed pointless too. His career was doomed.

His thoughts spiraled into the bleak reality of his impending arrest—not just humiliating but physically terrifying. He imagined being twisted into a submission hold, his body contorted, his dignity shredded, even if he didn't resist. He could almost feel the law's grip closing in on him, arms forced behind his back.

And with these thoughts came a plan. He would need to hide—preferably in plain sight—but first, he had to relieve himself of the emotional weight crushing him.

First stop: the pharmacy, then a bar, then a letter to write, and finally a place he hadn't set foot in for years.

He made his way to the drugstore, still neatly dressed enough to be let in. That would change soon. He bought a few items with his credit card, no longer caring about money. Then, glancing at his phone for directions, he headed to the next stop.

Soon, he spotted the Black Cat Pub. He parked right in front, disregarding the fire hydrant, and shuffled to the entrance. Head down, thoughts heavy, his defeated posture made his misery obvious to anyone watching.

Inside, the dim light and stale air suited his needs. The place was dingy, worn—a perfect match for his state of mind. The only thing he regretted was being sober—but that wouldn't last long.

He slid onto the least worn pleather stool and scanned the room. A few lost souls sat scattered around him, each absorbed in their own thoughts. The décor was cheap and mismatched, utterly uninspiring. Above the liquor shelf hung a crooked print of Van Gogh's Night Café. Avi recognized it instantly—he'd admired the original during a visit to Yale. The painting, with its figures, struck a chord. One man in particular: slouched over a drink, alone, consumed by despair. The figure's face was hidden, but his posture said it all.

Avi stared. He saw himself in that isolated man—surrounded by people, yet completely alone. It was as if Van Gogh had reached across time to capture Avi in that lonely moment. And just like that, he knew he'd found the perfect place to disappear.

The bartender gave him a quick once-over. "What'll it be?"

"Double Scotch. Straight up," Avi replied flatly.

"Got it." The bartender nodded toward the front window. "That's gonna be a problem for you."

"What?"

"They'll tow your car if you leave it there."

Avi didn't care. "Yep," he muttered, pulling a bottle of pills from his pocket. He popped a couple into his mouth and began spreading out stationery on the counter. His mind raced. The letter had to be written quickly—before the drugs dulled his focus.

Time blurred. The drink vanished, and Avi flagged the bartender for another. Then another. The plan in his mind was now complete. But he needed liquid courage to carry it through. Courage had never come naturally. He had to manufacture it.

Ironically, the final step wasn't about bravery at all—it was about avoidance. As always, he was running from confrontation. Deep down, he knew the truth: he'd always been a coward.

He caught his reflection in a mirror: ugly, pitiful. His fears, his regrets, his refusal to face consequences—they had defined him.

He had lied, cheated, and looked the other way—anything to avoid life's challenges. Today was no exception. The truth was too big to face.

"Another," he called, hand raised.

The bartender narrowed his eyes. "Looks like you've had a rough one. Why not go home, sleep it off? Maybe things'll look better in the morning."

Avi waved him off. "Another, I said."

"Okay, fine," the bartender sighed. "But this'll be the last one. And you'll need to settle up before I pour it."

"I'm good for it."

"Square up now or that glass won't see another drop."

Avi's head swam. He mumbled, "What, you think I can't be trusted?" A bitter laugh slipped out. "Join the fucking crowd." He pulled out some bills and tossed them across the counter. "Take it and stick it wherever you want."

The bartender shook his head. "I'll let that slide—this once. Finish your drink. After that, you're done here." He took the cash and pushed back the extra.

Avi threw back the fourth drink in one motion, rose unsteadily, and staggered toward the exit. "Who needs this shithole anyway?"

"OUT!" the bartender barked, stepping from behind the bar.

Avi hurried outside, not wanting to risk a physical confrontation. Letting his rage dissipate, he returned to the mental checklist. One more task down. Only one remained—he wondered if it would hurt.

Chapter 33: Kylo

Kylo sat alone in the locker room, his eyes locked on the duty belt hanging in his open cubby. He wasn't really seeing it. His thoughts still circled the wreckage of his conversation with Avi.

Kylo had believed he was immune to that kind of rage—always in control. But today, he'd found the line and crossed it, and he did it in front of his colleagues.

The door creaked open. Trevor entered, his usual energy gone. "Cap'n Fah-nuh wants to see ya," he said flatly.

Kylo gave a slow nod, keeping his inner thoughts to himself. "Figured. Thanks for stopping me, Trev."

Trevor shrugged with a nod. "Fuhgeddaboudit."

Kylo stood, grabbed a few things from the locker, and headed toward Fonner's office. He didn't need to guess what this was about.

Inside, Fonner was hunched over, flipping through a stack of files. She glanced up—barely reaching his chest—then returned to her paperwork without making eye contact.

"Kylo," she said, "I need your badge and weapon."

Already holding them, he set them gently on her desk. "I figured," he replied, calm but with an edge.

"You're on administrative leave until further notice." Fonner's voice was steady, almost clinical. She snapped a folder shut and leaned back, finally meeting his eyes.

"Are you lying to me, Kylo?"

"Don't tell me you believe that coward."

She looked away. "No."

"Then why ask?"

"There's been a new development—we found money at your home. The same money reported stolen during the triple, bundled with blue and red rubber bands." Her tone remained neutral. "I can't overlook that."

"That doesn't make sense. Where exactly?"

"In your car."

"I don't even drive that car. That's my wife's. He's framing me."

"Avi?" Fonner exhaled through her nose. "Honestly, I believe you. There's something sneaky about him... more to uncover. There's even motive. But there's just one problem—he's not the profile for this type of crime. The suspect we're after is physically imposing. Avi doesn't fit that mold, does he?"

Kylo felt the sting of the implication. "But I do," he muttered.

Fonner's voice softened. "Your outburst didn't help. I've never seen that side of you. It complicates things." She turned her eyes back to the desk, squaring the folders into a neat stack. "Let's see what we can recover from your flashlight. If we're lucky, maybe there's something usable."

Kylo hesitated, then spoke. "There's something I haven't told you. It's been eating at me."

She stopped moving, eyes lifting, listening carefully. "Go ahead."

"Last night on the Mall—when I saw Avi—he offered to pull gum out of my hair. I now think it was a setup. I think he was trying to get my DNA."

Her expression shifted slightly.

"You think he planted your hair at the scene?"

Kylo nodded, frustration simmering beneath his calm. "That's exactly what I think. He knew what he was doing—follicle and all." He bent down. "The notch is still there."

Fonner stood, looked at it, then turned her back to him and walked to a small fishbowl on a filing cabinet. She scattered a pinch of food into the water, causing small ripples. "If that's true, you've got a tougher road ahead than I thought. I'm sorry."

Kylo watched the fish dart near the surface. "I feel like that fish. A glass house, everything on display."

"It's a Siamese Betta. Male. That bowl isn't just his home—it's his territory. Put another in there, and he'll fight to the death."

He raised a brow. "Is there a message you're trying to send?"

She didn't answer that. "You're a good man, with a wonderful family. Let's hope your instincts are wrong."

"Or that Avi didn't wipe down that flashlight."

"Kylo, one more thing. Like Avi, I'd be remiss if I didn't ask you to stay in town."

Kylo shook his head. "Right."

He left the office with a staid demeanor. But once the door clicked shut, anger surged again.

"That gutless liar," he muttered under his breath. "Looked me dead in the eye—as if daring me to hit him… Fuck Trevor for stopping me."

He caught himself and quieted. The station walls had ears. The last thing he needed now was to come off as vengeful. His family was on the line.

He pulled out his inhaler and took a quick spray. Relief hit instantly, like a smoker's first drag. His lungs came alive.

One thing was certain—he hadn't killed anyone on the Mall. He hadn't gone near that tent. The truth was still on his side.

But truth didn't matter if no one believed him.

Now he had to prove it—and prove Avi was the one framing him.

Kylo sped home on his moped, the small bike feeling all wrong. He should have been tearing down the street on a Harley, loud and angry.

When he arrived, the house was empty—his wife at work, his daughter at school. At least he had space to think.

In his office, he opened his laptop and typed: "Avi Sweller." The screen filled with articles—Avi's role in the Mall's relocation efforts, interviews, political backing, his father-in-law's company.

Kylo leaned back, eyes narrowing. It all fit. Violence on the Mall helped Avi. It cleared the camps, pushed people out. But murder? That didn't track. Avi lacked the nerve. Something else—someone else—had to be behind this.

He shifted his search. Where were the displaced being sent? Why was UnaTerra, with its hardline stance on population control, backing the effort? Didn't they enforce strict border policies? Now their public messaging seemed to turn humanitarian, but the undercurrent felt strategic.

Kylo frowned. None of it added up. This wasn't just about Avi. There was a bigger machine at work. Bigger players. Bigger stakes.

And he was running out of time.

Watching from the sidelines wasn't an option. Like the Betta, he would fight—for his family, and for his territory.

Chapter 34: Aldric

Two hours had passed, and the tour was nearing its conclusion. Senator Remi McCarthy was invited to make an announcement over the PA system from the control room on the second level. Aldric watched her with a mix of admiration and contempt. She never tired of promoting the Carbon Laws, delivering the same rhetoric as if reciting gospel—blind to the sacrifice required to realize the very goals she so fervently championed.

Shallow, he thought. *Idealism in words, not action.*

Her speech was well-rehearsed—Aldric had heard every line before. When she finished, the control room clapped in polite applause. Everyone, that is, except him, tucked away in a shadowed corner. Politicians could try to confine him with their view of his potential, but he saw them for what they were: weathervanes, turning with each shift of the political wind.

"Human melatonin," he muttered. Reassuring. Empty. Yawn.

Still, there was something about Remi. Her endurance was rare among politicians. She repeated the same lines, the same messages, over and over—as if they still held meaning. Aldric found that both irritating and admirable. She didn't just go through the motions like the others—she believed them.

After the speech, they were led back to the entrance lobby where the tour had begun.

Aldric had tuned out, but mention of his name pulled him from his thoughts. He heard Senator McCarthy's graceful tone.

"Mr. Heister, I want to express my appreciation for your outstanding overview of this impressive operation. I love that you're based here in the heart of Sustalia. Your team has created a successful trailblazer for us all to admire. I truly believe the work you've demonstrated will pave the way for others to follow and replicate across the country."

His lips barely moved in acknowledgment as applause rippled around them. He had no interest in being part of the performance. Still, as much as he wanted to dismiss her, he couldn't ignore her influence on others—it was the very force that had propelled her upward, the discriminator that elevated her above the rest.

The Senator glanced at Aldric, then turned to her entourage.

"I'm sure many of you are exhausted," she said with a knowing smile. "It's been a long day. I've arranged a private meeting with Mr. Heister. While we talk, he's suggested you join the residents for dinner to recharge. I should be done within the hour, and then we'll return to headquarters."

She's got stamina, too.

Aldric extended his arm, guiding Remi away from the group. While the others headed toward the dining hall, the two of them slipped away for the private portion of the tour.

He led her to an elevator, and they descended into the utilidor system. Aldric could tell Remi was still processing the scale, structure, and control of the operation—her mind alert, despite the day's demands. He wanted to move quickly—highlight the basics, avoid difficult questions, and send her on her way. She had her sound bites.

"We'll transfer briefly to Basement Level 1," he said. "But our real destination is B2."

Once on B1, they navigated a maze of hallways. Aldric observed Remi as he spoke—wondering what she'd seize on. She listened the way few people did—fully engaged, as if every word mattered. That could be dangerous. Or useful. He wasn't sure which. But for now, he was grateful she hadn't yet posed the questions he didn't want to answer.

They stopped at a set of secured double doors. Aldric entered a code, then pressed his thumb to the sensor pad, waiting for the green light to flash. A metallic click echoed down the corridor, followed by a buzz.

"Dual security protocols," he said. "Two layers to gain entry." They stepped into the elevator. The doors shut, and they descended one more level.

Once on B2, he said, "It would be a bit of a walk from here, so I've secured an electric cart just ahead."

They boarded the cart, and Aldric took the wheel. He accelerated smoothly, his voice steady as he began his narration.

"The system runs east to west. We'll start at the far end—Station One. These narrow tunnels alongside us? That's the intake route for newly arriving immig—"

He stopped short.

"Go on," she said, arching a brow. "You were about to say 'immigrants.'"

"Sorry. Mall IDP. Both processes use the same protocol," he said, correcting his language. He couldn't afford more mistakes.

"They arrive outside under heavy guard and descend two flights of stairs. Anyone unable—aside from infants—is turned away at ground level. The rest are funneled through those tunnels. We monitor their progress through the viewing windows." He gestured toward the glass. "It's straightforward."

Remi interrupted, "Each train carries 3,000 passengers. The city's not that large. How do you accommodate that many people? With your density caps to stay carbon neutral, it's never added up for me."

Bingo. She's sharper than most.

He picked up the pace.

"I'll explain that shortly," he deflected with math. "We process one person every fifteen seconds. With the 3,000 arrivals, that's roughly twelve and a half hours of uninterrupted throughput."

Remi frowned, deep in thought.

"Ah, here we are." He nodded toward the next station. "One by one, they enter that chamber."

As the cart slowed, Remi leaned forward, eyes narrowing at the room beyond a pane of glass.

"Is this one-way glass?"

"Yes. Keeps them from feeling exposed—especially at this stage."

She gave him a look, but said nothing.

"Here, each new arrival removes their clothing and drops all belongings into the disposal chute. The room holds thirty at once. After undressing, they step into automated showers with biodegradable disinfectant. That's Stage One. Then they move through forced-air dryers. Stage Two. Think car wash."

Remi smiled. "Well, that brings back some old memories!"

Aldric didn't return the smile. He accelerated again.

"After drying, they undergo health evaluation—Stage Three. If they pass, they're routed to inoculation, Stage Four."

They entered another corridor. Aldric's thoughts began to outpace the cart. "This area is for vocational and psychological assessments. Once we assess their potential contribution to Felicity's needs, everyone gets compound-issued clothing. Skilled workers wear blue smocks. Unskilled—orange. That all happens in Stage Five."

"What kind of experience qualifies someone as 'skilled'?"

"Energy systems—solar, wind. Medicine. Agricultural engineering. The list goes on."

Remi's brows drew together.

"You might want to hold your questions until after the next stop; we have a lot to see," he said quickly. When they reached the lab, his tone shifted. "This is my favorite step in the process." That was a lie—it was his second favorite.

"Why?"

"For viable candidates—young, healthy—we collect blood samples and analyze DNA here in the Genome Lab. It's all automated—seconds for results. It determines who's eligible for procreation. Cutting-edge. Efficient."

Remi peered through the glass at green-smocked technicians.

"Looks like a cross between a data center and a medical lab. What are those machines?"

"Chemistry and hematology analyzers, CRISPR stations, and much more, integrated into one system. It's all backed by a full complement of IT support—servers, racks, routers. You see now, they're prepping for the next Mall IDP intake."

Her lips parted, but he kept going, keeping a fast pace.

"Here, we generate each candidate's genome score. Those who qualify—age 32 and under—are documented for birthing rights. About 1.5% make the cut. That's roughly 45 out of every 3,000. It aligns with your Carbon Laws—better genes, stronger future. Qualified candidates are housed in upgraded quarters near Town Hall."

Remi took it all in, then summarized.

"Greens can procreate, blues are skilled labor, orange means unskilled."

Aldric nodded once.

"Exactly. Final scores are based on genome, age, health, cognitive ability, psychological profile, and carbon footprint. Greens get the most freedoms, healthcare, and reproductive rights. Blues get modest medical support and decent housing. Oranges live on B1 and work factory shifts."

She fell silent. Aldric drove on toward the next stop.

Finally, she spoke.

"Earlier, I asked about capacity. You dodged it. You also said those who can't manage stairs are turned away. What happens to them—or the ones who fail the screenings? The numbers don't make sense."

She hadn't forgotten.

Aldric's voice cooled.

"Illness is expensive. So is sustaining an unproductive population. It's not unlike denying visas to those with medical burdens—except we implement it at the city level. To comply with your Carbon Laws, we make hard decisions. Those who don't qualify are isolated. We pursue repatriation strategies. Many simply have no role here. States that reject your vision inherit the consequences of their leniency."

"Repatriation?"

His second slip.

"Sorry. 'Relocation' is the better term."

Chapter 35: Avi

Avi stumbled out of the bar, his steps unsteady, the pavement tipping and swaying like a ship in rough waters. He blinked hard, trying to bring the street into focus, and scanned for his car. Relief hit him when he spotted it—or maybe them.

His vision warped. Two cars—identical, side by side—shifted in and out, blurry and overlapping like a faulty hologram. He squinted, struggling to steady his eyes, until the double image snapped back into one.

He made his way over, trusting his phone to unlock the door. It did. He opened it and collapsed into the driver's seat, the worn leather exhaling a death rattle beneath his considerable weight.

He shoved aside whatever caution remained and pressed the ignition button. The engine roared—too loud, splitting through his skull like a drill. It felt like both cars had come alive at once, the noise pounding inside his head. The first hints of a hangover were already throbbing at the edges of his brain.

He slapped the steering wheel. "I'm not fit to stand, and yet you let me start the car," he muttered. "Smart tech on, judgment off. For shame." He laughed out loud, with no one to hear.

He shifted into drive, bracing for the final steps of his plan. The car lurched, then stopped with an abrupt clunk of metal. Avi pressed harder on the accelerator, another jolt—a mechanical standoff. The car seemed caught between his command and its refusal to obey. On his third try, a loud thud shook the frame, vibrating through his spine.

Drunk but determined, Avi dragged himself out of the car and found the source of the noise. "Fucking cops booted me," he muttered, scanning the area as if it might offer a loophole. He looked up at the sky, a hollow laugh escaping his throat. "Nope. You won't stop me. You'll have to do better than that."

His pockets offered some comfort. He dry-swallowed another handful of pills from the small bottle. As he placed the container back, his fingers brushed against the folded letter—his revenge—and it gave him a sliver of solace. But he needed more. More numbness. Less thought. His eyes swept the street, catching the neon glow of a nearby liquor store.

Minutes later, he was inside, rummaging through the shelves in search of relief. The store was empty, and the shelves were nearly the same—bare. In the background, he heard the clerk double-lock the door. Panic shot through his chest at first, but the clerk explained.

"You're our last customer, sir. You'll need to make your selection so I can close up," the man said.

Avi's tension loosened. He grabbed a pint of scotch and paid without meeting the clerk's eyes. Once outside, the door clicked shut behind him, and Avi staggered toward a corner, managing to wave down a cab. The yellow car pulled up, and he slurred, "Iwooo Jeeema." Speech was getting harder. The driver wrinkled his nose but said nothing, waiting for the door to close before pulling into the night.

In the backseat, Avi poured whiskey down his throat, spilling some on his lap. He didn't care about the mess. Anything to drown out the voices. The bottle drained quickly, and he let it fall to the floor, nearly empty. But then he noticed there might be one last sip left and retrieved it.

The driver glanced at him through the rearview mirror. "Easy, buddy. You're going to regret this tomorrow."

With a thick slur, Avi shot back, "I c'n guarantee ya I'm not."

The cab dropped him off at the memorial statue, silhouetted against the warm night. It loomed over the Capitol grounds—a place once proud, now littered with tents, laundry lines, and trash. Avi stumbled across the area, looking for a quiet spot. He leaned back, eyes fixed on the WWII memorial, the words "Operation Detachment" echoing in his mind—eerily fitting for what he was about to do.

He pulled the letter from his jacket—a confession, of sorts, but full of lies. An explanation for why he had to walk away from Evelyn and their son. It all traced back to a murder-for-hire scheme—commissioned, ironically, by her own father to save his company. Revenge had never really been Avi's style, but hatred? That ran deep. And when it came to his father-in-law, the temptation was impossible to resist.

Blackjack left no trace, so there was no sense in naming him. A cleaner scapegoat was Sergeant Kylo Cromley of the Park Authority—a cop he would describe as dirty. The evidence was already in place. He was the logical fall guy, with the physical stature to get the job done. According to the letter, Kylo handled the job—the killing.

Avi didn't feel much guilt. He hadn't chosen the man. Blackjack had.

As for the old bastard? He was the real subject of his wrath. He brought it on himself. Cancer or not, Avi would hit him where it hurt the most.

Legacy: shattered.

And Evelyn? Well, she'd be fine. She'd survive like the rest of her hoity-toity family—but without marble countertops and voice-activated appliances. Let her see how the real world lived, the one he came from. She needed that lesson.

Far from her state-of-the-art kitchen.

His fingers trembled as he unscrewed the cap on the bottle of pills, letting most of the capsules spill into his mouth. He tried to swallow, but some got stuck in his throat. He grabbed the bottle of scotch, knocking back the last sip, coughing as the alcohol burned its way down. His vision blurred, and a numb heaviness settled over him. He'd made his choice. He would pass the blame—and become the victim.

The line between bravery and cowardice twisted in his mind, but the truth became clear: he'd spent his life avoiding pain, avoiding confrontation. And so, he would end it the same way. He downed the few remaining pills, then chased them with air from the empty whiskey bottle. Crashing onto the grass nearby, he lay back, staring at the stars, and waited for his final escape.

Part 3: Bad Seed

Chapter 36: Avi

Wednesday, August 22

A solitary samara—more commonly known as a twirly or helicopter seed—hung limp and forgotten from the branch of a dying maple. It might have gone unnoticed, just another quiet surrender in the vast theater of dying trees. Yet even in its final, futile act, it obeyed the rhythm etched into its bloodline.

For 60,000 years, maples had endured cold epochs and fleeting thaws. Born in an age when mammoths still roamed beneath unbroken skies, their lineage adjusted to a world that changed at a glacial pace. But now, the old rhythms had been broken—no longer shaped by season or sun, but overwritten by a single, accelerating force: humankind.

Human hands had brought a new kind of crisis. Not one of ice or fire, but of combustion and consumption—a crisis without precedent, fueled not by tectonics or orbit, but by extraction and excess.

For most of Earth's history, its climate had followed a pattern—warmings and coolings stretched across epochs like breathing. These shifts shaped life, yes, but they never unraveled it. Not like this. In the last 150 years, the change had become severe, jarring, and unmistakably artificial. It began as a whisper—barely measurable, but it accelerated with a ravenous industrial appetite.

The factories. The coal. The forests stripped to stumps. Humanity's ambition, once hailed as progress, had tipped the scales. The Earth, once able to absorb its own fluctuations, now reeled from a force it hadn't evolved to withstand. The damage gathered momentum—quietly at first, then all at once.

A fire here. A flood there. Initially, it was easy to dismiss them as anomalies. But the pattern grew too frequent to ignore. Wildfires became seasonless and ravenous, devouring landscapes in days. Hurricanes gathered strength over warmer oceans and returned again and again like relentless, bloodied fists. Droughts stretched on. Ecosystems buckled. The balance was no longer delicate—it was irreparably broken.

By the middle of the twenty-first century, the signs were everywhere. Ice caps were breaking apart, their edges collapsing into the sea. Coral reefs were bleaching, their colors fading to bone. Forests that once stretched uninterrupted for hundreds of miles now stood as scattered islands—remnants in a world no longer their own. Entire species vanished before they could even be named. The Earth groaned, strained, and warned of worse to come.

The maple tree, once a symbol of steady endurance across North America, began to fade too. It needed cool nights, slow springs, and consistent rainfall—routines that no longer existed. Droughts lengthened. Temperatures climbed. The seasons turned erratic. Even the samaras, once elegant travelers on the wind, now dropped into desolation. They spun toward soil that no longer offered nourishment.

This one had clung longer than most, as if reluctant to surrender to the parched ground that had betrayed its kin. When it finally let go, it spiraled half-heartedly, tugged by a limp breeze, drifting left, then right—its motion more hesitation than flight. It was too late in the season. Too dry. Too warm. It carried no promise now—only a silent collapse.

But its fall marked more than the end of a seed. It was a quiet crossing—where the decline of one species brushed against the fragility of another.

Where one bad seed met another.

The samara twirled through the thinning air and came to rest on the open eye of a man lying motionless on the grass.

At first, a couple strolling by barely noticed. The man seemed peaceful, perhaps asleep beneath the early morning sky. The park was silent, the hour barely brushing 4 a.m., the air still holding the cool hush before sunrise.

But as they neared, a wrongness settled over the scene like mist. His eye was open, with the seed resting on it.

His skin, pale in the half-light, looked drained of warmth. His chest did not rise. His mouth hung slightly open, but no breath passed through. His eyes were wide, fixed, unblinking—unseeing, detached from the world around him.

The woman's voice barely found breath. "Is he...?"

The man with her pulled her back. "Leave him," he said quickly, his voice catching. "We need to call 911."

He stepped away, fumbling with his phone, fingers trembling as he dialed. The sound of the wind returned, soft and indifferent.

When the paramedics arrived, they checked for signs of life. There were none.

In the man's hand, they found a letter, folded with deliberate care, as if meant to be discovered. It was addressed to the park police.

The author, they would later confirm, was Avi Sweller.

Chapter 37: Kylo

Kylo woke to the sound of a ringing phone and reacted immediately, careful not to disturb his wife. It was Trevor, the Round Mound of Sound.

"Yo, sorry to wake ya, buddy, but somethin's come up I think you gotta hear, real quick."

Kylo sat up against the headboard, rubbing his eyes, keeping his voice low. "I'm listening."

"They found Avi Sweller's body down in Rosslyn. Even if his prints're on that flashlight, it don't mean nothin' now—mook offed himself."

"Damn," Kylo muttered, a little too loud. His wife stirred and turned on her side, her back to him.

"Kylo, I'm callin' ya this early for a reason, a'ight? An' 'cause I'm your bro. Off the record—you're in their crosshairs now. They got more dirt linkin' ya to that triple. DNA from your hair, right there on the kid. Just like you said, that rat Sweller had to plant it. Between that an' the cash, I'm tellin' ya—it ain't gonna be long before they're bangin' on your door."

"Thanks, Trev. You've had my six since day one."

"One more thing—Sweller left a letter, clenched tight in his stiff hand. Wrote it to be found. Straight-up dropped your name. Called ya the killer. Said ya were hired."

"By who."

"Now that's the real kicker—his father-in-law."

"Thanks, Romoso."

Kylo hung up and slipped out of bed without further disturbing his wife. She slept soundly, unaware of the deep trouble he was facing. He didn't wake her or Alma, choosing instead to let them enjoy what could be their final hours of peace. To Ingrid, he was just a bystander in the investigation—a witness, not a suspect. Kylo wasn't a liar, but he let her believe what she wanted. Lying by omission, perhaps. Better that than watching fear consume her.

It was 6 a.m. when Kylo sat alone at the kitchen table, robe draped around him, staring blankly at a box of corn flakes. His thoughts drifted to prison food—gray trays, soggy bread, bitter coffee—and the cardboard taste he figured would define his future.

Needing comfort, he stood and opened the fridge. A carton of eggs caught his eye, and he decided to make one of his signature omelets. A little ritual from better days. A thought nagged at him: could this be his last breakfast as a free man?

He wished his family were awake, sharing the morning. Ingrid pulling him in, with a sleepy kiss—bad breath, messy hair, all of it. Alma bragging about her soccer goal.

Focusing on the omelet helped calm him. In the past, he'd dice celery, mushrooms, Vidalia onions, and orange bell peppers, stir them gently in butter, then add chopped ham for depth. He missed pork—especially bacon, smoky and indulgent. But these days, he stuck to basics due to cost: yellow onions and standard peppers. He gave them a quick stir, then poured in three vigorously beaten eggs. Timing was everything.

When the eggs hit the sweet spot, he flipped the omelet into the air and caught it smoothly in the pan. One clean motion, just like always. He plated it, sprinkled shredded cheddar and fresh basil in the center, and folded it into a perfect half-circle. Steam curled up into the kitchen air. He poured himself black coffee, hot and bold.

It was all gone in much shorter time than it took to make. Despite the meal, he felt far from satisfied.

"This can't be happening," he muttered. He drifted quietly down the hallway, pausing outside Alma's room. His daughter lay peacefully asleep. He'd planned to wait for her party and surprise her with a gift. A gift that would surprise even Ingrid. Now, he wasn't sure he'd be around.

A lump formed in his throat. She didn't know. And he didn't know how to protect her from what was coming.

Anger surged. "Coward. Sets me up and then checks out. I hope he's rotting in Hell." Again, he'd spoken too loudly. He paused, listening. Stillness. He grabbed his inhaler and drew a steadying breath.

His mind spun, looping in on itself. He thought of a version of himself that existed just days ago—the man who trusted too easily.

Why'd you let him touch your hair? Idiot! Water under the bridge.

He thought of the news, and the woman who jumped.

Then Avi stormed back in his thoughts.

I oughta jump too—track the coward down in Hell and finish the job.

He wanted a front-row seat to see Avi burn—and cursed Romoso for stopping him from punching Avi in the mouth.

He recognized the pattern. The five stages. Denial was gone. Anger was here. What came next?

Not bargaining. No. Retaliation. He wasn't a victim. Not yet. There was still fire in him.

Thinking of Ingrid pulled him back. He had to fight. For her, and Alma. That meant figuring out who benefited from the Mall killings.

Sure, fear served Avi's cause—but UnaTerra had plenty of reason to want the tent city gone. They'd offered free relocation to Sustalia. Pushed hard. Too hard.

Kylo sat at his computer and pulled up the UnaTerra website. He clicked through event photos, most featuring their golden politician—Senator Remi McCarthy. The face of the Carbon Laws. Charismatic. Clever. Dangerous.

One image stopped him cold. A posed shot of McCarthy and her staff. Kylo leaned in, studying a blond man standing beside her—impeccably dressed. Something familiar, slightly off.

The eye. Amblyopia.

His pulse spiked. He raced to the laundry room, dug through a basket of dirty clothes, and yanked out his work pants. He fumbled through the pockets. First, he found Alma's gift. Relief washed through him. At least he hadn't ruined it. Then his fingers found the paper.

He pulled out the crumpled handout—the bearded man from the Mall. Same face. Same lazy eye. No question.

Kylo's breath caught. Adrenaline surged. This was it.

He grabbed his phone and dialed.

Trevor picked up. "Y'ello?"

"I need a favor. Two photos. Can you run them through facial recognition within the hour?"

"Facial recognish'n?" Trevor snorted. "Listen, Kylo, I ain't no tech guy, but I know a dude who's a whiz with software. Gimme an hour—less if he ain't still eatin' his mornin' burrito."

Kylo hung up and stared at the kitchen, remembering the breakfast he'd made. A fragile routine of normal life.

"To make an omelet," he said aloud, "you've gotta crack a few eggs."

Chapter 38: Luna

Twenty-eight hours into the train ride, the air had grown thick and suffocating. Passengers had learned to share seats in shifts, but the reek of sweat clung to every surface, and the car felt stifling. Reaching the bathroom had become an ordeal—every step meant navigating a maze of tangled limbs to reach the lone, filthy stall. With no attendant in sight, it had descended into squalor in mere hours. In a grim twist, the lack of food and water almost seemed merciful.

Luna stood beside Zev, having just given her seat to a man fighting his own fatigue.

"You've been on your feet this entire trip."

He frowned. "I got everyone into this mess—it's the least I can do. These conditions are brutal."

Luna rocked Karli gently. "It's not fair they put you in this position—doubling up, no support. None of this is on you. I would've thought there'd be at least a conductor," she said, keeping the exhaustion out of her voice, not wanting to add to his burden.

"There's a lot more wrong here than just the lack of a conductor," Zev muttered, rubbing his eyes. "If I'd known what this would be like, I never would've taken the job. I'll be having words with the guy who hired me—Sweller. But more importantly—how are you two holding up?"

Luna reached for the formula bottle and placed it in Karli's mouth.

"I'm okay. Just hoping we reach the final stop before I run out."

From a few rows back, a voice cut through the clatter of wheels passing over rail joints.

"Incredible. You've got something to drink, and I'm about to die of thirst. You still owe me!"

It was Clive again, clawing for a fight.

Zev turned toward him.

"She's not giving you anything, so settle down. And I don't think you've stood once this whole trip. Maybe let someone else have a rest."

The man sneered. "You're the one who lured us here. Greedy opportunist. I saved that baby's life—the least she can do is give me a drink. I haven't had anything in over a day."

Luna interjected, her voice calm and measured.

"Nor have most people. Including me."

The man narrowed his eyes.

"If you think I'm just going to sit here while you feed that baby, I can produce a fist that says otherwise."

Zev, now fully turned to face him, his voice loud enough to carry, said, "You just threaten her?"

Clive stared at him, wide-eyed and motionless.

Zev prepared for confrontation, shoulders back, ready. "What the hell is wrong with you?"

Clive slumped into his seat.

Luna tugged at Zev's shirt. "Don't waste energy on him."

Zev paused, letting the tension bleed out of his frame, then asked, "Tell me something—what's really going on?"

Luna hesitated. "What do you mean?"

"I see you. I see the baby. It doesn't add up."

She shifted. "I appreciate your concern—and your help—but I'd rather keep things private."

Zev raised his hands. "Sorry. I overstepped. I'll keep to myself."

She exhaled. "I didn't mean to sound cold. It's just been... a lot."

He gave a small nod, voice gentle.

"Fair enough. But I think you're running."

Her heart stilled. She said nothing.

"From someone—or something. To protect that child. I don't need the details. Just—if you need help, I can be here for you."

She looked at him then. Really looked. For the first time, she noticed his mismatched eyes—one brown, one blue. Kindness lingered there, dulled by fatigue but unwavering. How little she actually knew about him struck her. Why was he working this job? Who was he when he wasn't dog-tired, standing watch over strangers? Was someone waiting for him back home, wondering if he was safe?

She opened her mouth, then closed it again. She had no right to ask—not when she kept herself so guarded.

The train rocked beneath them, the trip long and merciless. Luna felt the weight of her secret sink deeper into her bones. It wasn't her nature to be deceitful—especially not toward someone who hadn't earned her suspicion. She looked at him again—broad shoulders, quiet steadiness. Her walls weakened, and emotions long kept in check began to stir.

She leaned in slightly, voice barely above a whisper.

"You're right," she said quietly.

Zev looked at her. "About what?"

She glanced down at the sleeping baby in her arms.

"This isn't my baby."

Just then, they heard the sound of broken glass.

Chapter 39: Kylo

As promised, Trevor called Kylo just shy of an hour after their last conversation. When Kylo answered, the familiar energy in Trevor's voice was a welcome sound.

"Good news, Bigfoot!"

Kylo's lips stretched into a smile for the first time in a couple of days. He hadn't realized how much he'd liked hearing that nickname—it pulled him back before everything began to unravel.

"What's that, Romoso?"

"That facial recognish'n program says there's, like, a 99 percent chance dat botha those photos're the same guy."

"Thanks, buddy," he replied, the words coming easily, like slipping into the more familiar rhythm.

Trevor kept going, his excitement evident.

"This could be somethin' big. We got ourselves a solid lead now. If we can link dis bearded guy ta McCarthy's crew, it might jus' be the break we been lookin' for."

Kylo let the words sink in. It was undeniably good news, yet the implications began to spiral through his mind.

"Yeah, definitely," he muttered, "but it's not as simple as just a match."

Trevor paused. "I hear a bit o' hesitation there. What's botherin' ya, bro?"

Kylo leaned back in his chair, steepling his fingers as he weighed the stakes.

"If McCarthy's team is involved, I can't just hand this over to the cops without thinking it through. The fallout would be massive. McCarthy has connections, and she won't make this easy on us."

There was a moment of silence. Then Trevor's voice returned, softer now, more cautious.

"You ain't thinkin' 'bout takin' this on by yourself, are ya? That'd be freakin' suicide."

Kylo hesitated, rubbing his forehead. The decision grew heavier with every second.

"Yeah, I am," he said after a moment, his voice barely audible. "I'm not sure I have another choice. The cops would be bogged down with red tape, and who knows how long it'd take to get real answers—if we ever do."

Trevor's tone softened.

"I don't wanna know. Jes' take care, a'ight? Don't do nothin' you'll regret come sundown."

Kylo exhaled slowly, leaning forward.

"I'm just trying to stay one step ahead." He paused. "Thanks for the help. I'll be in touch."

The line went silent, and Kylo sat for a moment, staring at his phone. It was easy to tune Trevor out sometimes—his words spilling in his edgy dialect. But beneath the chatter was something deeper: a fierce pride, forged through generations of firefighters and through tragedies like 9/11. Kylo realized he had misjudged the man, letting volume and speech cloud his perception of the loyalty and courage that ran through him. Sacrifice—for family, for community.

Then, without wavering, the decision was made. He could no longer afford to wait on anyone else. This was his mess to clean up—and he would do it alone.

He grabbed a backpack and loaded it with essentials: a change of clothes, toiletries, and cash from a tin they never touched, saved for a vacation dream. He packed no liquids or weapons. Then, he scribbled a quick note to his wife, cryptic on purpose. The less she knew, the less police would learn.

Love, I need to take care of something. I'll be back, but it might take time. Please don't worry. I'm sorry. I love you.

He moved through the house quietly, every motion deliberate. Once outside, he was relieved to find no uniforms lingering. He started his moped and let his thoughts narrow. No room for doubt now—the journey had already begun. He'd need to catch a plane.

The ride went quickly, his mind racing through all the possibilities of how this could end. At the airport, the foggy morning seemed to work in his favor; security moved with mechanical routine. He made his way to the ticket counter, where a young woman greeted him with a smile.

"Hello, Sir. How can I help you today?"

"I need a ticket for the 8:30 a.m. flight to Albuquerque," Kylo said, keeping his tone even.

She nodded, typing into her system. "Yes, we've got availability. Might I suggest a bulkhead seat for more legroom?"

Kylo was used to people noticing his height without saying it outright.

"That sounds great," he said, handing over his credit card and ID.

She processed the transaction with what felt like an excessive number of keystrokes, finally sliding his boarding pass across the counter.

"You can proceed to Gate D20."

"Thanks," Kylo said, tucking the ticket into his pocket.

He passed through security without incident, raising no red flags. Beyond the checkpoint, he noticed a flight to Denver departing earlier. He took a seat in the lounge and began scanning the nearby passengers.

His search landed on a young man sitting alone, scrolling his phone. Kylo approached with slow, purposeful steps.

"Excuse me," he said, his voice smooth but direct. "Can I ask for your help with something?"

The young man looked up, brow furrowed. "Huh?"

"I was supposed to fly to Albuquerque, but my father's become seriously ill in Denver. I need to change my plans. I'll give you $3,000 if you swap tickets with me. The bus from Albuquerque to Denver takes about six and a half hours, or you could grab a short flight. Not a bad way to make some fast cash."

The teen hesitated, eyeing the roll of bills in Kylo's hand.

"$3,000?"

Kylo nodded, extending his hand closer. "Easy money."

The young man looked torn, glancing toward the boarding area. "But we're at the gate. Not sure they'll let us swap."

"They won't check IDs again. You take my seat—I'll take yours. Simple as that," Kylo said, his voice low and reassuring.

After a moment, the teen sighed and nodded. "Okay. Sure."

Kylo handed him the money, and they traded tickets. As the kid walked off, Kylo felt a pang of guilt. He hoped the teenager wouldn't face any consequences. There was no turning back now.

With the new boarding pass in hand, Kylo felt a fresh surge of resolve.

Next stop: McCarthy's office.

Time to finish this.

Chapter 40: Luna

Neither Luna nor Zev could locate the source of the shattered glass that had echoed through the car moments before. They stood side by side in the vehicle—less a train than a cramped metal coffin—shuddering along the tracks beneath them. The compartment was packed beyond reason, like overstuffed cans of sardines, carrying a pungent stench of rot. With each sudden lurch, the train jolted unpredictably, at times, forcing them together in an unintended intimacy.

Luna was shocked at her own confession. The words had burst free, releasing what she had buried for far too long. She could still feel the warmth of Zev's gaze on her, though she hadn't looked up. His voice came softly, close to her ear, stirring something deep inside.

"I kinda figured it wasn't your child," he whispered, his tone careful, measured.

Relief swept through her, carrying with it an unexpected sense of comfort and safety. Admitting it aloud had loosened a tension she still struggled to control. The tears broke free without warning.

"It's been terrible," she said, her voice cracking.

She felt his hand on her shoulder—steady, grounding.

"It'll be okay. We'll get there, and everything will fall into place. Can I ask… whose baby is this?"

Luna tried to collect herself, but it was harder than expected. She wiped her eyes and shook her head.

"I'm not sure you'll believe me."

He waited, his hand still resting lightly on her shoulder.

"You can trust me."

For the first time since the suicide, Luna let her guard fall completely. The sensation was strange—equal parts liberation and dread. She didn't hold back.

"I don't actually know. I was out walking in the morning and saw a woman with this baby. I held the child for a moment... and then the mother jumped off a bridge. There was a note in the stroller. She said she was undocumented, in poor health, terrified of deportation. If caught, both she and her baby would be sent back—and she said they wouldn't survive. It was heartbreaking... They found her body in the Potomac later that day."

Luna glanced at Zev, bracing for alarm or judgment. Instead, she saw only empathy.

"I heard the story on the radio. You really are the mystery woman."

She nodded and went on.

"The next morning, I was identified as a suspect. Security footage showed me as the last person with her. I've been running ever since. It's been horrible. Please believe me—I just want to protect the baby. I'm afraid of what might happen to Karli if she's sent back."

"What country was she from?" Zev asked, voice low and serious.

"China. I think she was a refugee—a victim of the Shanghai typhoons."

"Yeah... that tracks." He pressed his lips together, thoughtful.

For a second, Luna sensed she'd touched something deeper— a ripple beneath his calm.

"China's population policies are brutal now. Makes the old one-child rule look merciful."

He looked at her, his expression softening.

"I gotta say—you're tougher than you look. I believe you. And I admire what you're doing." He hesitated, then added, "How about…"

Luna, worn out from the confession, looked down. She didn't want him to see the desperation behind her eyes. But Zev didn't let her hide.

He gently lifted her chin, coaxing her to meet his eyes. A tear slid down her cheek.

"When we get to the final destination," he said quietly, "we won't say a word of this to anyone. It's behind you now."

His manner was disarming.

"You've been so kind to me. Thank you," she whispered, voice thick with emotion.

"Tell you what," Zev said, "why don't you let me hold Karli for a while? You look like you could use a break."

Luna's arms ached from hours of holding the baby. After a moment of hesitation, she passed Karli to Zev. He cradled her easily, his arms steady and sure. Luna noticed how natural he looked with the child. An unanticipated thought surfaced—he'd make a loving father.

It struck her then: without realizing it, she had been evaluating him—some quiet calculus unfolding in the back of her mind. What startled her most was the subtle pull she felt toward him. She wanted to know more.

"How did you end up in this mess?" she asked, the question slipping out before she could stop it.

She panicked, then relaxed. Now that she'd told her story, maybe it was okay to ask his.

Zev didn't flinch. His voice stayed even.

"My mother got sick. Bitter as she was, she fought. I did everything I could for her. But the cancer didn't care. It took her—leaving me in debt, and carbon auditors knocking at my door."

He gave a humorless laugh. "This job was supposed to clear my account and restore my healthcare."

Luna was silent for a moment. His story, though brief, revealed a theme—compassion. The bitterness went unexplained, and she didn't press; she hadn't earned that question.

"That's… important. Prioritizing family. Helping her through her final moments. Admirable," she said softly, almost too soft.

Zev nodded, grateful.

"I wasn't her favorite—my brother was. She blamed me, I think. That always stung. But I loved her nonetheless."

"I'm sure she didn't have a favorite." Again, Luna steered clear of probing deeper, letting him decide what to share.

He opened his mouth to say more—but was cut off by a commotion a few rows behind them.

Luna flinched as she turned.

Clive was pushing his way forward again.

"Move. I'm going to the front," he barked.

An elderly woman—hair white as paper—collapsed when he shoved past. She cried out in pain as he stepped carelessly on her ankle. Her husband, equally frail, tried to help, shooting the man a glare full of fury.

"Whatcha gonna do, old man? Throw your dentures at me?" Clive sneered.

Luna winced as the woman wailed, "My leg!"

She couldn't stand. People nearby muttered in disbelief, but everything fell still when someone called out from the back, "Give 'em space. He's got a weapon!"

Luna's heart slammed against her ribs. She looked up just as the man reached her, towering over her, eyes wild.

"I told you I was thirsty," he growled. "Now give me something to drink—or you get hurt."

Her eyes dropped to the makeshift weapon in his hand—a shard of broken glass taped to a pen. He reached for the bag of baby supplies, but she yanked it back. The blade hovered inches from her stomach, his breath sour.

But Luna didn't flinch.

She stared him down, her voice cold, unshaken.

"How much intestinal fortitude do you have?"

The man blinked. "What?"

She clarified.

"Guts. Do you have the guts to kill me? Because that's what you'll have to do to get this baby's formula."

The words came without filter, courage surging through her like adrenaline. A tremor of fear followed close behind. Her meek, cautious instincts surfaced briefly: Who are you? You never talk like this. This shadow version of you is going to get us killed.

From the corner of her eye, she saw Zev trying to hand Karli off—getting ready to intervene.

But before he could act, an arm reached in behind Clive, snatching the weapon.

In one brutal motion, the stranger wrenched the man's head back—and sliced the jagged glass across his neck.

The only sound that followed was the wet gurgling of blood bubbling in his throat.

The assailant looked at Luna, with jet-black hair flowing over his eyes like a veil. He held up the bloody glass, pointing it at her. "The bridge murderer, the kidnapper."

Luna was petrified and couldn't move or speak.

"You'll bring problems."

Zev suddenly reappeared, fist raised. The black-haired man hesitated, then headed for the rear of the train, away from the chaos.

She looked down.

Clive had fallen to his knees, clutching his throat, blood streaming between his fingers. He gagged, coughing violently, choking on his own blood. The surrounding passengers froze, horrified, unsure whether to step forward or flee.

"Hold on, Clive. Just hold on," she urged, her voice cracking. He convulsed, gasping, struggling for air.

He slumped further into a curled fetal position, blood pooling beneath him, his head resting against Luna's shoes, sweat mixing with the crimson streaking his face.

Luna grabbed a cloth from someone nearby and pressed it to the wound, heart hammering. Blood soaked through almost instantly.

When she looked up, scanning the car, the killer was gone— lost in the sea of passengers.

He knows.

Chapter 41: Aldric

Aldric Heister sat in silence behind the controls of his electric cart, stationed deep in B1—a sector deliberately left off the Senator's polished itinerary. The industrial bay loomed around him, its cavernous ceiling soaring high above staging zones lined with heavy-duty production equipment. The sheer scale rekindled memories: the Lockheed Martin Air Force Plant in Fort Worth, Texas—though this place lay buried underground.

His military service had shaped him, teaching him both what to emulate and what to avoid. Back then, his tours had taken him overseas, responding to catastrophic weather events—a futile endeavor. The difference now: he wouldn't tolerate wasteful humanitarian efforts. But he did govern his city with the same disciplined rigor.

Still fuming over the time lost to the Senator's distracting visit—albeit politically unavoidable—the CEO was determined to inspect every inch of the plant before the incoming passengers arrived the next day. He'd begun his walk-through at the far western end of B1, the midpoint of a food assembly line that started on the level below, B2.

For logistical efficiency, the preparation occurred directly beneath the main building, allowing the product to be transported seamlessly up one level to the cafeteria.

Aldric watched yellow powder churn inside a row of mixers, each nearly the size of his cart. The machines moved steadily as he calculated the nutritional output required for the impending influx. He always found their motion carried an odd calm, almost hypnotic in their rhythmic whir. But today, something was off. He focused on one machine—it was making an unusual noise.

Nearby, a supervisor in blue was directing his orange-smocked subordinates. Upon spotting Aldric, the foreman straightened and approached with a trace of unease.

"Sir, good Earth," he said, offering the verdant salute.

Aldric returned it with crisp precision. "Blue skies, Foreman. Did you get the corn and cereal quantities you were expecting?"

"Plenty of corn, Sir. A little short on barley and wheat, but we'll adjust the ratios. No worries."

Aldric gave a curt nod. "What about labor?"

"We're good, Sir. There'll be more staff in the morning."

Aldric held his gaze. "We'll need to ramp up production. The group from D.C. is arriving early. They won't have eaten in days. A lot of mouths to feed."

The foreman didn't flinch. "We'll be ready."

Aldric acknowledged with a short dip of the chin, then motioned toward the loud mixer. "That one is hissing."

"Yeah, mixer three started making that noise this morning. Probably the bearings—maybe just lubrication. It's scheduled. But there's a bigger issue with one of the extruders downstream."

"I'll head there now. Brace for long hours."

The worker dipped his head. "Calm seas, Sir."

Aldric depressed the accelerator, steering his cart toward the next station further down the production line. He pulled up beside a technician in an orange smock seated at one of the super extruders. The man was covered in oil and food residue, a wrench in hand. Spotting Aldric, he stiffened and quickly stood, offering the verdant salute—but avoided eye contact.

Aldric didn't return it. "Where's your boss?"

The man remained upright, but uncomfortable. "Good Earth, Sir. He's in logistics, tracking down a part."

"What part?"

"The die-cast plate cracked. The foreman's bringing a replacement."

"What's your target?" He knew the answer, but was testing him.

"Stamp-sized pellets, four cups per person. That's fifty cubic feet in twenty-four hours—figuring fifteen hundred. Three shifts will cover the incoming passengers, of course distributing to the blue and orange smocks first. Reserves will buffer any shortfall."

Aldric tilted his head slightly. "Can the coating stations keep pace?"

"Yes, Sir. It's the rendering and grinding stages that slow us down. Those are always the bottleneck. They're unmanned right now."

Aldric knew the production process better than anyone. "We'll staff the abattoir first thing tomorrow, when we're at full tilt."

He turned to leave, then saw the man starting to sit back down. The casual motion struck him as insolent.

"Why are you idle?"

"The machinery is broken, Sir."

"Did you make sure no metal shavings contaminated the mix?"

The man's voice began to quiver. "I didn't think of that, Sir."

"Clearly not—nor did your foreman. Come here."

The man froze.

"Here, I said."

He approached hesitantly, still avoiding Aldric's gaze.

The CEO demanded, "Let's see your arm."

The man in orange extended his arm, as Aldric jotted down his identifier. Then, he pulled out a permanent marker and scrawled a bold "R" on the technician's forehead.

He left without another word, the man's quiet sobs fading into the distance.

Aldric felt exalted—certain he'd just eliminated inefficiencies.

He mumbled, "Two birds, one stone." Cliché, perhaps—but as clichés went, it fit.

He decided to bypass the packaging station—the only area that never gave him trouble. Tonight's inspections were complete. The real work would begin tomorrow with the train's arrival.

His plan was already set: he'd start the day on B2, the far western perimeter. First stop: the underground disposal area that stretched beyond Town Hall grounds. Technically classified as a landfill, most just called it "No-Man's Land." The name wasn't just a nod to history—it captured its desolation perfectly. Entry required top-tier security clearance.

From there, he'd move east, ending in the entrance tunnels just in time for onboarding—where the true assembly line began. There, he'd oversee processing and ensure that Felicity's protocols were followed to the letter. Every measure would be enforced. Every inefficiency stamped out.

As his final act of the day, he dialed the site manager.

He didn't offer a salutation, just an order. "I want two deliveries to Stage Nine. You'll find both working the mixers, a Blue and an Orange."

Aldric ended the call, satisfied. Tomorrow, nothing—and no one—would slow the line.

Chapter 42: Simi

Simi decided it was best to retreat into another passenger car, still gripping the dead man's weapon as he slipped away—he knew he'd need it again soon. He pushed through the crowded aisles, shouldering past passengers and forcing his way through multiple sliding doors, until he finally reached the last coach on the train.

Once there, he removed the black-haired toupee and stuffed it into a bag. He wanted to hurl it from the train—anything to sever ties with the identity it embodied. But the windows were sealed. Instead, he tucked the bag under his tunic, tight against his belt. There'd be opportunities to toss it later—once he reached a place where help could be found.

Killing the defiant man had sent an unmistakable message: compliance was the only path to survival. It would establish order for what lay ahead. Stalin, Mao, even Hitler—they hadn't hesitated to use fear like a scalpel, whether to motivate or pacify. Dictatorships and fascism were their machinery of control. Under a democracy, fear was a more elusive tool. Simi would need to work harder.

Some of Simi's colleagues—the idealists—didn't understand the utility of emotional manipulation or how it could be weaponized to produce results. But Simi understood. After all, he'd filled the very train he was riding by stoking terror, capitalizing on the panic triggered by the homicides he'd committed on the Mall. Weaklings like Avi, left to their own devices, would never have finished the job.

Though his actions were ruthless, they always adhered to one of Simi's core objectives: plausible deniability. He never shared his methods with the Senator, keeping her insulated from any legal or political fallout. Her vision—and her career—were paramount. But not for her sake—not for Senator Remi McCarthy, but for his true boss. Aldric was the true visionary, the one who had pulled Simi from darkness and given him purpose. With Aldric's help, he quietly secured a position on Remi's staff—she never suspected he was a mole.

From there, Simi would feed her policy, shape her talking points, craft her beliefs—so she could do what she did best: communicate a vision. Remi was merely the face. A pretty one at that. She had no idea that much of her platform originated from Aldric, though she had been led to believe it was hers. That illusion was essential—and Simi made sure it endured.

Tucked into a corner at the rear of the train, Simi began to visualize the next phase of his plan. He needed to eliminate any resistance—if not literally, then psychologically—leaving the rest rudderless and compliant. He scanned the car, evaluating the passenger dynamics, watching for natural influencers.

Two men near the middle of the coach caught his attention. Both were angry. The first, in his early forties, was broader than the other, with bulging muscles stretching his tight green shirt. Simi listened carefully as the man spoke.

"When we get to the last stop, we need to stick together. We won't let them treat us like cattle anymore. Actually, cattle get treated better! They at least get water and food. UnaTerra's going to be in for a shock when we arrive."

The man he was speaking to looked to be in his mid-thirties, leaner but still built, his camouflage shirt hinting at military roots. His body language was assertive, his posture aggressive, feeding off the larger man's outrage.

"I'm with you, brother. I'm pretty pissed right now—wish I'd brought my iron. That's my wife over there, hunched over in the seat. She needs water—she's sick from dehydration."

Simi took it all in, locking every detail into memory. These two were more than loudmouths—they were catalysts. One speech. One thrown bottle. That's all it took. Then fists would fly, guards would panic, and the whole train would dissolve into chaos. Not a protest. A contagion.

He'd handled threats before—quickly, quietly. The shard of glass in his sleeve hadn't dulled. It would be used again.

And this wasn't the only pocket of defiance. In the first car, he'd already marked Zev—the rounder man, arguing loudly about the overcrowding, looked to by others for guidance. Then there was the woman from the news—with the baby, and her secret. She was a wild card, dangerous for reasons the others weren't. He decided she would need to be disposed of; she could draw attention at the worst possible moment. He had missed his first opportunity; he wouldn't miss his second.

As for the coach he was in now, he'd added two more to the list. They'd be dealt with once the train arrived—ideally during the chaos of onboarding, when noise and confusion would drown the screams.

He felt lucky. Words were meaningless. Action was everything—and he had the will to act. He thought of his father, and the only gift he'd ever given him: the experience of breaking through hesitation—the moment he killed him. Justified. Without guilt.

Chapter 43: Kylo

Sleep-deprived and worn thin, Kylo arrived in Denver with bloodshot eyes and heavy lids. The two-hour time difference from the East Coast had only extended an already punishing day. As he deplaned, a brief wave of relief washed over him—no sign of law enforcement. Not that he'd expected a welcoming committee.

His thoughts turned to the poor kid using his ticket. After a thorough interrogation, the FBI would surely uncover the swap. They'd trace his trail to Denver soon enough. He had bought himself time—but those grains of sand were already slipping through the hourglass.

One of the few remaining rental car counters still operated inside the terminal, tucked next to a row of vacant booths once claimed by now-defunct competitors. Kylo handed over his credit card and rented a compact EV. It was traceable. This would be its final use.

It would take three hours to reach Kansas—not the shortest route, but the fastest exit from Colorado. Once across the state line, tracking him would become harder.

Before getting into his assigned car, Kylo slipped his phone into the trunk of a nearby vehicle. A decoy; he hoped it would mislead authorities if they tried to trace the signal. Back in his rental, he settled in for the long drive. Six hours to Guymon, Sustalia. He knew border security there would be tight—tighter than U.S. immigration had ever been.

What he'd do once he reached UnaTerra's headquarters remained uncertain. For now, he had time—and the quiet sprawl of the plains ahead.

The terrain was as flat as the omelet he'd eaten for breakfast. With no mountains to blunt the horizon, he was grateful the sun was setting in the west, its glare behind him rather than in his face.

As he drove, Kylo reflected on the devastation wrought by climate change. Different regions faced different catastrophes. California burned: wildfires, drought, ash-choked skies. Each fall, the Gulf states and East Coast braced for hurricanes, brutal storm surges swallowing towns whole. D.C. and surrounding states buckled under the weight of climate refugees, people fleeing uninhabitable homes for safer ground.

West of the Mississippi, fresh water had become a luxury. With limited water, agriculture—which normally consumed 80% of the resource—now made farming untenable across vast stretches of land.

He couldn't help but think of the irony: a planet covered in water—even rising—yet less than one percent of it was drinkable.

Driving through the Great Plains, the drought's toll was impossible to miss. As a child, he remembered lush fields of corn, wheat, hay, sunflowers, and sugar beets. Cattle grazed beneath shady trees, indifferent to the passing traffic. Now, the trees were gone. So were the cattle.

All that remained were dry riverbeds, parched earth, and abandoned machinery—hulking, rusting relics of a bygone era. Tractors sat motionless, idle for years. Like the Tin Man, they waited for the miracle of an oil can that would never come.

The ground had cracked and splintered, deep fissures carving jagged scars into the soil. It looked as if the land itself were reaching upward—desperate curls forming shallow bowls, pleading for rain.

Where a vibrant farming community once thrived, only dust remained. Without water, nothing survived.

Then came the hum. At first, he thought it was a flaw in the rental's electric motor, but it grew louder—higher-pitched, mechanical. He glanced up through the front windshield and saw its source: a black drone buzzed overhead, shadowing him like a vulture. Military? Police? Whoever it was, it was unmarked.

He tapped the brakes. The drone slowed too.

He veered onto a frontage road and accelerated. The drone followed for another half mile before suddenly ascending—straight into the sky—then vanishing behind a bank of dry clouds.

Someone knew he was coming.

The sun dipped lower, the sky taking on a dusty orange hue. In the rearview mirror, a glint caught his eye. Headlights. Far behind, but closing fast.

He sat up straighter. The road had been empty for hours. Now someone barreled toward him, the engine growling like a predator—emerging from the shadows of the setting sun. He gripped the wheel tighter. An unmarked car. The Kansas border was just minutes away, but he wouldn't make it.

They've got me. This rental stands no chance against it.

The vehicle closed the distance quickly—an old, gas-guzzling muscle car, patched with matte black paint. It swerved as it approached, then honked twice, the sound ear-splitting and mocking. When it passed, he caught a glimpse of two kids—maybe late teens—one howling with laughter, the other flipping him off as they roared by.

The car fishtailed once, corrected, then disappeared over the rise ahead, kicking up a long plume of dust behind them.

Kylo let out a breath he hadn't realized he was holding. Not law enforcement. Just joyriders—probably bored out of their minds, burning gas without a thought for Carbon Laws.

But the near miss left him on edge. Someone was going to find him eventually. Someone who wouldn't be laughing.

When he crossed into Kansas, the border guards had pulled over the speeders, paying little attention to him. The drone, which he'd feared was tracking him, was now resting on a small platform nearby. The teens would soon learn of the impact on their health care.

After some distance into Kansas, he spotted a broken-down car on the roadside. He pulled in behind it, fished a coin from his pocket—his makeshift screwdriver—and replaced his license plates.

Now his rental wore Kansas tags. A small change, but maybe just enough to buy him time. With more miles crossed, he turned south toward Sustalia. The tightly controlled checkpoint loomed ahead. He needed a plan.

Kylo had spent years suppressing emotions—a lesson drilled into him as a cop to minimize mistakes. But now, as he approached, he welcomed the fury heating his blood. Anger had never come naturally. But here, now—it felt… good.

He veered off-road, cutting through an open field—not even a dirt trail in sight. He entered Sustalia through a narrow, unmonitored stretch near the border. A risk—but one he had calculated carefully.

He drove until a light hiss broke the silence. Two tires gave way, defeated by the brutal terrain. Guymon—and the UnaTerra headquarters—lay twenty miles to the south. He would go the rest on foot. The vehicle had served its purpose.

With nothing but a backpack, Kylo stepped out without a backward glance.

The barren land stretched endlessly, but nothing would stop him now. He had come too far. He would reach the compound. Soon, he would stand face-to-face with either Simi Kremna—or the Senator herself, Remi McCarthy.

Only then would he learn who they truly were—and their involvement in the Mall murders.

Chapter 44: Luna

Blood streaked the floor beneath Clive's body, snaking in jagged lines across the aisle. No one moved. No one spoke. The passengers remained frozen, staring, each too shocked to react.

A voice shook as it spoke: "Is… is he dead?"

The question came from the white-haired woman still crumpled on the floor; her ankle bent at a wrong angle.

Luna was crouched next to him. Her fingers found his wrist, but she already knew.

"I think so," she said softly.

From the rear, someone muttered, "A slow death. Had it coming."

Luna's chest sank. She hadn't killed him, yet somehow it still felt like her fault.

"We can't just leave him here," she said.

Another voice cut in, louder—almost feral. "Toss him out the window. Make more room."

Murmurs rippled through the cabin. A girl sobbed, a man cursed.

Zev's voice rose above the chaos, trying to restore calm.

"Okay—okay. Let's be civil. The man just died. We're not throwing anyone out the window; they don't open anyway."

She nodded. "We need to move him. Not leave him here."

Her thoughts spun, but instinct took over.

"Someone strong—maybe two volunteers. Wrap him in spare clothes to contain the blood. Then lift him into one of the overhead racks. Above my seat is fine." She hesitated. "We'll need to know who is willing to sit below as well."

No one answered right away. Only the soft rattle of metal on the rails filled the cabin.

Zev's eyes darted around the cabin, distracted, but he said, "I'll sit underneath as well." He hesitated, then continued, "Luna, I need to go after the guy who did this. He was a jerk, sure, but this isn't right. We can't just let a killer walk free. I think I saw him— black hair, tunic." He started to move.

She reached for his wrist, stopping him.

"Please don't. He's dangerous. We're close to arriving. Let the authorities handle it."

Zev shook his head, his lips pressed thin.

"What if he hurts someone else before then?"

She leaned closer, in a whisper. "Zev… he recognized me. From the TV. He knows who I am. I don't feel safe."

Zev stilled. His expression hardened.

"Okay. I'm not leaving your side. But we should block the back compartment. In case he doubles back."

The elderly husband had been silently clutching his cane. At last, he spoke—his voice thin but urgent.

"Can someone help my wife?"

Luna turned, seeing her in pain.

"Oh my gosh, of course. We need to get her into a chair."

A kind father with a young daughter stepped forward to help, as did Zev. The cabin was overcrowded, with two bodies stretched across the floor—one alive, one dead. The move wasn't easy.

The woman's cries sliced through the car as they carefully lifted her. Luna's gaze landed on her husband, still gripping his cane with trembling hands.

His lower lip quivered. Tears welled in his eyes and slid down the deep lines etched into his weathered face.

"Please… be easy with her."

He was distraught and confused—helpless.

To Luna, it was painfully clear: this man's whole world was in that woman's existence. Their bond—timeless love—meant everything. And now, in the moment she needed him most, he could do nothing.

Luna felt something catch in her chest. Not only sorrow. Not just pity. But envy.

She admired that kind of love—the kind that endured decades of hardship, that survived storm after storm, and still held fast in quiet tenderness.

She longed for it.

Maybe someday, she'd find someone like that. Someone whose empathy didn't fracture when things fell apart.

Hardship revealed character.

She'd seen it in the man now lying dead—his brutal end an exclamation mark on the life he'd led. Brash. Greedy. Leaving his uncle stranded. Selfish to the last breath.

Her thoughts drifted—to Zev.

She remembered what he'd said about his mother. The way he'd reacted when things spiraled. That overriding instinct to protect.

In another life, maybe they'd have been more than two people caught in a storm.

Luna's eyes swept the cabin again. It landed on the father of the young girl—still helping lift the elderly woman, but always glancing toward his daughter.

There was tenderness in that, too. A love that didn't concern itself with his own worries, only hers.

Parental love. Quiet. Constant. Infinite.

The world was unraveling in fragments around her. Blood on the floor. Fear in every corner. But love still survived—fragile, yes, but intact.

She saw it in herself too—the same devotion. Unspoken and all-consuming.

Her eyes shifted to Karli.

Part 4: Rain Check

Chapter 45: Kylo

Thursday, August 23

A tiny droplet of water traveled with a tight-knit group, drifting like a lone minnow in a school, weaving and darting with its companions through invisible currents. It bent and swirled, a quiet participant in a silent pilgrimage, guided by unseen forces. But this was no ocean; the currents it followed were made of air, not water. High above the earth, the droplet was caught in a relentless wind tunnel. The jet stream gripped it firmly, pushing it eastward, defying gravity's pull. For many miles, it hung suspended—a delicate act of defiance against the world below.

Once, these droplets had risen from the vast Pacific with regularity, but now the journey was far more perilous. Many of its companions had already succumbed to the inevitable—lost to gravity's tug, pulled together by condensation into larger, heavier masses. Some tried to climb the jagged peaks of the Sierras, but the air was thin and dry, and even those who persisted couldn't hold their shape against the cold, unyielding peaks of the Rockies. The mountains had become merciless gatekeepers, their summits shredding through the clouds, leaving only the most elusive, the most determined, to continue the long trek toward the Great Plains.

A subtle shift in the air marked a truth no one could ignore: the seasons were changing. Winters were shrinking, their cold breaths shorter, less forceful. Snowfall grew less frequent, and what had once been a steady rhythm of nature now seemed erratic and uncertain. But even though droughts had taken root where green life once flourished, this droplet pressed on, clinging to a migration encoded in memory, a path etched long before it had ever traveled. Then it reached the cold front. The wind shifted. The temperature dropped. The droplet, like so many before it, joined a larger companion—a single tear from the sky. It was as if the heavens wept for what the earth had become.

Combined with others, it became too heavy to remain suspended. Gravity won, and with it, the droplet's fate was sealed. It fell, a single raindrop among a few others, and as it descended, it carried the weight of all that had come before.

It landed softly, almost imperceptibly, on the left elbow of Kylo Cromley. The brief contact with his skin—cool, unexpected—was enough to break the quiet stillness of his slumber. His body stirred, a soft breath escaping as his eyelids fluttered open. In that moment, the droplet had done its job, rousing him just in time.

Had he remained asleep, the Senator would have come and gone, unnoticed. The raindrop, an unlikely herald of change, had completed its journey—and its purpose.

Chapter 46: Kylo

Kylo jerked upright as a second cold drop of rain slid down the back of his neck, finding its mark through a ragged tear in the roof of a battered 2030 Chevy Camaro, an obsolete combustion relic. He hadn't chosen the car—it had chosen him. Abandoned and half-swallowed by weeds in a junkyard a few blocks from UnaTerra Headquarters, it was the only shelter he'd found after a long night of wandering.

For a man of his size, the contoured seats were a cruel joke. His back throbbed from the awkward angle he'd curled into. Still, it beat sleeping in the open.

Had he been in a bed, he could've easily slept another couple of hours. But today's mission left no room for luxury. He forced himself upright, grimacing at stiff joints, then shoved open the car door.

Despite the few drops, the surroundings were still bone dry. His boots crunched against the gravel as he stepped out onto the ground. The sky was dull and leaden; he glanced around, relieved to see no one nearby.

It was 7 a.m.—or so the old clock tower on the corner claimed. His mouth felt like sandpaper. He rifled through his backpack, hoping for a thermos, but came up with a toothbrush instead. It would have to do. He gave his teeth a quick scrub, barely able to spit, doing his best to freshen up. A stretch followed, though it did little to loosen the knot in his spine.

After slapping dust from his clothes and smoothing out the worst of the wrinkles, he gave himself a quick once-over in the side mirror. Not great—but not suspicious either. He nodded at the reflection, then set off at a steady pace toward UnaTerra Headquarters, careful not to kick up dust as he crossed the lot.

The red-brick structure loomed ahead—an imposing monolith that dominated the skyline. Once the Texas Courthouse, its top floor had housed a jail. Now, it housed Remi McCarthy's office. A symbol, Kylo thought, of how UnaTerra had risen—transforming old power into something sleeker, more attractive. As the fastest-growing political party in the country, their influence spread like wildfire, and this building stood as both throne and fortress.

He reached the front doors and pulled one open, stepping inside. Immediately, his eyes landed on the security guard seated behind a long black desk. Above the guard's head hung two portraits: a modest photo of the President, and a larger, more commanding image of Senator Remi McCarthy.

Kylo approached, an uneasy mix of confidence and nerves. He knew the drill.

"Good Earth, Sir," the guard greeted politely.

Kylo gave the proper response: "Fertile lands. I'm looking for Simi Kremna—he's on Senator McCarthy's staff. We were supposed to meet in Washington during the rally, but wires got crossed. I was told he has an office here."

The guard's fingers danced lightly on the touchscreen embedded in his desk. "Certainly, Sir. I'll call upstairs. May I ask who's requesting the visit?"

Kylo recited a name from the UnaTerra website. "Tom Meyers, Boise City UnaTerra election support staff."

"Ah, near Felicity. I've heard it's quite the underground wonderland. Never been authorized to visit myself." He tapped a few more keys, then lifted the receiver. The one-sided exchange was brief, and his face turned into a frown.

"Sorry, Sir. Looks like he's out. Won't be back for a couple of days. Would you like to leave a message?"

Kylo hesitated, then asked, "Any chance of seeing Senator McCarthy?"

The guard chuckled. "She's in, sure—but getting a meeting? That's a bureaucratic Everest. I've been here four years and only see her when she walks to her Cadillac for airport runs. And wouldn't you know it—she's headed to a rally in Dallas this morning. Busy lady."

"I understand," Kylo replied, his optimism thinning.

He stepped back outside and circled toward the rear lot. There, parked in a clearly designated VIP space, was her unmistakable Cadillac limo, sleek and spotless, its glossy black surface catching what little light the gray sky allowed. The chauffeur sat inside, head bent, eyes locked on his phone.

Kylo assessed the scene, then turned and scanned the adjacent lot. A glint in the gravel caught his eye—a rusted nail.

Perfect.

He palmed the nail and crept low toward the limo, careful to stay in the chauffeur's blind spot. With steady hands, he wedged the nail between the rear tire's tread and the ground, setting the trap.

Once done, and after a short puff from his inhaler, he approached the driver's side window and tapped lightly.

"Excuse me?" Kylo said, calm but urgent.

No response. The chauffeur remained absorbed in his phone. Kylo rapped again, louder. "You've got a flat. Just thought you should know."

Finally looking up, the driver cracked the window just an inch, and mumbled, "What?"

"You've got a flat. Nail in the tire."

The man glanced down at his dash. "Pressure looks fine."

Kylo stepped back, gesturing toward the rear tire. "I'm just telling you—check for yourself."

The chauffeur hesitated, then opened the door. His hand instinctively brushed against the weapon at his belt as he stepped out. Kylo didn't flinch. He kept his movements easy, leading the man toward the back of the limo.

"There. See it?"

The chauffeur crouched and peered at the tire. "Doesn't look flat to me. Nail might not've pierced."

"I hear a hiss," Kylo insisted, voice steady. "Get closer. Listen."

As the chauffeur leaned in, Kylo struck—a single, brutal punch to the base of the man's skull. The chauffeur collapsed instantly.

Kylo dropped to a knee, his fingers pressing against the man's neck.

Pulse—steady. Good.

He dragged the unconscious driver toward the trunk, grunting at the weight. The man was big. Both a blessing and a complication. He'd wake up hours later, bound and gagged, stripped to his underwear—but alive.

Kylo changed quickly, slipping into the chauffeur's crisp uniform. He adjusted the collar, tucked the weapon under his belt, and slid behind the wheel of the limo.

Soon, the Senator would arrive—and he'd get the truth out of her. Not with charm. Not with patience. But with something he'd never used as a tool before—anger.

Chapter 47: Aldric

Aldric Heister awoke and, for once, skipped his morning workout—too much demanded his attention. The break irritated him, though. Even as a boy in his family's sprawling estate, he had rarely neglected his body. He'd learned early that money could bend most people, but some yielded only to strength. He wanted both, and that ambition set him apart from weaker classmates. Being called a bully was simply confirmation of their inadequacy—and his superiority.

But money and strength weren't the only tools of influence. As a tween, he saw his housekeeper steal his mother's gold bracelet. Instead of reporting her, he covered for her, biding his time. Then, when the moment was right, he coerced her into doing his bidding. She became an unwilling accomplice in a series of attacks against his enemies—those who refused to comply with his demands. The chef, in particular, needed to go. After all, there was no reason for Brussels sprouts to be served on a plate. So why not sabotage a few meals? It was oddly satisfying watching his family retch night after night, until he was let go.

Over the years, he refined his habits that cemented his dominance. It was the little things, the details. This day was no different. He picked up where he'd left off the night before.

His first stop was B2. From there, he climbed into the utility cart through the tunnel system, tires crunching over clods of dirt scattered across the floor as he headed west toward the landfill. The low hum of the super augers grew steadily louder—deep, mechanical pulses marking the relentless excavation two levels below.

At the site, he pulled his collar over his mouth, though it did little against the choking dust. It hung in the air despite the ventilation, clinging to every surface in a fine film that slipped past even the best filters.

He paused in the cart, watching the augers at work. Towering machines bored through soil with brutal rhythm, drills rising and plunging with tireless precision. The zone was all motion—noise, grit, and a vibration he could feel in his legs.

His mind wandered to the land's grim legacy. The Oklahoma Panhandle, once the Dust Bowl's ground zero, had been carved from Texas under the Missouri Compromise—excluded so the land below could join the Union as a slave state. But the Panhandle lay north of the 36th parallel, where slavery was banned. Misfit land. Orphaned. Officially "No Man's Land." Unclaimed. Unwanted.

Later, the territory became part of Oklahoma. After the 1929 market crash, waves of migrants fled west to escape dust and drought, chasing salvation in the Salinas Valley. Now, ironically, people were returning—trying to plant roots in a soil where real roots had once failed.

Aldric's gaze settled on three red-coated figures seated on the ground, shackled together. Their exhaustion was unmistakable. Cogs in the machine. They watched the augers with vacant eyes, disconnected from the moment, as distant as the buried histories beneath them. Few locals even knew this drilling existed. Those who learned of it never resurfaced.

"Good Earth! What's the drill bit size?" Aldric called, his voice crisp and authoritative.

A nearby worker in a green coat snapped to attention, offering the verdant salute. "Harvests plenty. Three-foot diameter, Sir," he said, flat but respectful.

"Number of holes?"

"Five done of fifteen—each above the water table. That should cover the abattoir waste."

"Trucks?"

"Three. One for runs from Stage Nine, two to haul soil."

Aldric gave a short nod. He already knew each hole's depth— a hundred feet down. The cycle never stopped. The land absorbed it all, and the excess dirt was simply hauled out to the parched land.

He turned toward the abattoir and rendering stations, the final legs of his inspection. Soon, the train would arrive. A few more hours to ensure the assembly line ran without flaw.

He loved the efficiency of it all, thinking of how meticulously he had carved his place in the world. He thought of a pivotal moment when he changed his name—from Thomas to Aldric Heister—adopting the initials of the man he most admired. The name was a ritual of allegiance, a reminder that perfection, order, and ruthlessness were virtues to cultivate. He would improve on this visionary. Correct his missteps.

Aldric looked again at the red-coated workers. "Need more?"

"Sir?"

"Turnips."

"Oh, the Morlocks. No, sir, we're good. They'll work the dirt, then be processed as backlog."

As he walked away, the image of the shackled workers—seated on the very soil that would soon consume them—remained etched in his mind.

Nothing wasted. Compost.

Chapter 48: Luna

The train jerked to a halt, its pneumatic brakes hissing as everyone bobbed forward in unison. The last stretch had been bumpy, and the stop delivered one last jolt. Cheers and applause erupted. Luna woke with a start, pulled from a light sleep. She'd managed to wedge Karli between her leg and the armrest so the baby wouldn't fall. It had been a rare few hours of peace—precious and quiet—without fussing.

The crowd's excitement felt distant, a blur of noise and motion against her bone-deep exhaustion.

At the front of the car, the door slid open with a mechanical whine. A guard in camouflage stepped in, blocking the exit, his M16 held tight across his chest. His voice rang out, loud and commanding.

"Stay where you are. You'll be escorted to our facility shortly. Before we proceed—is Zev Brighton on board?"

Luna heard a cough, then saw Zev awkwardly clear his throat. His lips moved, but no sound came. He tried again.

"That's me," he rasped, his voice hoarse and unsteady. He rubbed his throat, his tone ragged and worn down.

"Do you have the paperwork?" the guard asked.

Zev lifted a clipboard. "Holding it."

"Good. Exit and follow the other guard to the front office."

As Zev moved down the aisle, Luna caught him looking at her.

"You alright?" he asked.

"I'll be fine. Thank you for everything. You've been very kind."

He gave her a tired smile. "Good luck to you and Karli. I wish you both—"

Before he could finish, the guard grabbed his arm.

"Keep moving." The guard turned to the rest of the passengers. "Single file to the Felicity entrance. It's a half-mile walk. Once there, you'll descend two flights to be processed inside Town Hall. Keep pace. The faster you move, the faster this ends."

The line began to form outside the car. From near the back, an elderly man's voice called out in distress.

"Sir, my wife—she's hurt. She can't walk. Can we wait for a lift?"

"Leave her," the guard snapped. "We'll send someone after everyone is off the train."

A lump formed in Luna's throat. She saw the woman—white-haired, frail—clutching her husband's hand.

"Don't go," she whispered. "I'm scared."

He squeezed her hand, lips trembling. "I'll meet you inside. Be strong. We've survived worse. We'll get through this." He kissed her forehead, then turned and walked away—head bowed, shoulders heavy.

Luna, now carrying Karli against her chest, was pushed forward with the crowd. The elderly woman's face—pale, devastated—stayed fixed in her mind as they were herded into line. Guards flanked them every thirty feet—a show of order, or perhaps control.

"Move it."

There was no choice. She started walking.

The path was dusty and dry. Luna kept her eyes forward, locked on the horizon. The land stretched on—no trees, no shade, no signs of life. Just cracked earth and gusts of wind that threw dust into their eyes and mouths.

Her mind drifted. She'd never been west of the Mississippi. There was nothing here, except the distant walled city, its outline shimmering in the heat.

Someone behind her muttered, "Feels like Mars."

It made her remember the reports—droughts, once-fertile valleys now dust. Bakersfield, in the west, had already collapsed. On the coast, desalination plants were being built, but it was too little, too late—musicians still playing as the Titanic sank.

And yet… she kept walking, still hopeful.

A guard's shout cut through her thoughts.

"Get up!"

A man's voice, weak, barely audible: "I can't… I can't walk anymore."

"You need to stand."

A young woman cried out, voice shaking. "He hasn't had water in two days! He's eighty-five! What's wrong with you?"

Luna attempted to see what was happening, but an arm in a camouflage sleeve pushed her forward.

A voice behind her continued.

"Leave him. Keep the line moving."

"I'm his granddaughter! I'm not abandoning him!"

"Move, I said."

Luna couldn't see what happened next, but she heard it—the sudden crack of a slap.

A beat passed, then a pained scream.

"Don't you dare touch me!"

"Raise your hand again, and you'll lose it. Understood?" The guard's voice hardened, ice-cold this time.

Silence followed.

The line continued moving, but faster now, fear saturating the air.

They reached the city's outer perimeter, thirsty and worn. Felicity loomed behind a thick wall. Concrete and steel surrounded it like a fortress, with a large multi-story building in its center. Guard towers rose even higher, rifles tracking the train passengers.

Once through the outer gates, they approached two massive doors—metal and flush with the ground. This was not the front entrance of the building, but more like a bomb shelter entrance. Each door swung open. The large building loomed ahead, still distant.

"Left or right," a guard barked. "Pick a side and move. Don't stop."

Luna chose right, Karli pressed close to her chest. The stairs were steep and dim—no handrails—so she focused on each step, careful not to slip. She descended into the earth.

At the bottom, a tunnel stretched ahead. No visible end—just a pale passage and harsh fluorescent lights. Around her, people groaned. The march wasn't over.

They were guided forward until finally they could see the tunnel's end. A sterile room waited—lined with showerheads. On one wall, a one-way mirror watched like an eye. Luna shivered.

A guard stood at the entrance, clipboard in hand. "Thirty per unit," he said, counting bodies.

Near the back, a teen girl held her father's hand.

"We're together," the man said.

"She'll be in the next group," the guard replied without looking up. "Thirty only. Move."

The door shut with a hiss, separating them. Inside, the guard tapped a wooden baton on a steel bin.

"Remove all clothing. Put everything in here. You'll get a standard smock after disinfecting."

Luna froze.

A woman near her whispered, stunned as well: "You want us to strip? In front of everyone?"

"That's right," the guard said flatly. "You have fifteen seconds before the water turns on."

Another voice protested, shaking. "There are men and women here. That's not appropriate."

The guard didn't blink. "Refuse, and you'll be escorted out. Your choice."

Nobody moved. Then—slowly at first, then in a rush—people began to comply, zippers sliding, buttons coming undone.

Luna kept her head low. Just like everyone else, she began to disrobe.

She had no choice.

No one did.

Chapter 49: Aldric

Aldric remained stationed at his post in the observation deck, hands resting loosely behind his back, the very image of composure. Below, the first group of passengers began their slow, deliberate march toward the wash stations. Through the one-way glass, he watched and listened—orderlies giving crisp instructions, footsteps shuffling forward, murmurs rising and fading as heads turned to catch directions.

Stage One. The point where hope still clung, where no one yet understood they were stepping into a human assembly line designed to sort the useful from the expendable. They assumed the rough treatment was temporary—merely the price of entry into something better.

Aldric's mind drifted back to military service, where efficiency had been his blueprint and order an unwavering principle. At the time, he had seen himself aligned with most—working toward the goal of benefiting mankind. He had volunteered in humanitarian efforts, convinced he was making a real difference.

Thinking of those efforts now, his eyes swept methodically across the crowd—faces, movements, interactions—each detail carefully cataloged. A girl and her father had been separated. A woman carried a baby—he noted the risk that one might progress farther than the other through the stages. But it was the man with the cane who held Aldric's closest attention. His voice rose in a plea, a display of helplessness. One spark like that could ignite empathy—and empathy could breed something far more dangerous: teamwork.

Aldric slipped back into his memories. Years in the field had taught him harsh lessons. Tuvalu, in particular—a flooded island where his unit had tried to ease suffering, only to see their efforts fail. The Earth exacted its toll regardless of human intervention, claiming countless lives. To Aldric, it was an epiphany: it wasn't destruction, but rebirth—a cleansing.

He pressed the button on his belt. "What's going on with the old man in batch Q?"

A crackled voice replied, "He's upset about his wife. She was left behind—with a broken ankle."

Aldric felt a surge of excitement. "Good. Reunite them—mark him as Red."

Seconds later, the voice returned. "What about the woman with the baby?"

He hesitated, then said, "Let them through. We'll see how they test in genome—if they make it that far."

He was the architect of the real Carbon Laws—the harshest accountability ever imposed on humanity. Born of his conviction that only ruthless control could halt the planet's decline, those laws demanded sacrifices most could never stomach. Over time, Aldric had not only accepted the cost—he relished it, even prolonged it despite Simi's discomfort with anything but a swift kill. He kept that joy buried; Simi remained useful. For now. Aldric had invested heavily in that loyalty, another form extending his own influence.

Aldric thought back to the time he had saved Simi, assembling a defense team so skilled that the younger man would never see jail time for killing his father. Beyond his hunting code, Simi was a blank slate Aldric could shape to his designs.

His gaze returned to the glass as the first group edged forward, step by measured step, deeper into the system. He'd missed the chance to identify the Red Coats with Simi's help—but there would be other opportunities.

Chapter 50: Zev

Zev was escorted alongside the exterior wall of the massive Town Hall until he reached its center—the front entrance. A guard guided him through the front doors, where a round, hairless man with brambly, untamed eyebrows greeted him.

"Good Earth, Mr. Brighton. I'm Varek—city treasurer and your host today. On behalf of the Felicity Chief, we thank you for your service to our community and to Earth itself. Welcome."

"Didn't feel very welcoming for the passengers on that train," Zev replied.

Varek's smile held firm. "Ah. We see it differently. We've rescued them from poverty. A few hours of discomfort seems a small price, wouldn't you say?"

Zev frowned. "No. And it was days, not hours. Completely unnecessary. No food, no water."

Still smiling, Varek waved the comment away. "Let's not bicker, Mr. Brighton. Before we proceed, I trust you have no phone or communication device?"

"Confiscated before boarding your splendid train," Zev said dryly.

"Of course. Weapons?"

"Really? Also not allowed. So, no."

Unbothered, Varek continued, "No offense intended—protocol demands these questions. Now, follow me. You'll have access to showers. Afterward, a clean smock—purple, in accordance with our policy. We maintain strict uniform regulations within the city walls."

"Purple? I've seen people in blue. You're wearing green."

"Colors denote role. You're a visitor—purple marks you accordingly." He shifted the conversation. "Once you've changed, you may dine in the cafeteria while we reconcile the headcount and calculate your payment. We should be done in a few hours—just in time to catch the eastbound train home."

Zev took in the surroundings as they moved through the expansive lobby. He stopped before a breathtaking multi-story atrium.

Varek paused with him. "This glass enclosure is a replica of nature's splendor. Dozens of tree varieties thrive here."

"I haven't seen an atrium in years," Zev murmured.

"Yes, and you'll find some rare species—red and sugar maples, white and pink dogwoods, even a black willow. That waterfall is fed by a stream from the second story, emptying into a koi pond and generating the fine mist you see before you. Alluring, isn't it?"

Zev heard a high-pitched, toy-like squeak and spotted a tropical bird. "Is that a toucan?"

"Indeed. Not quite the call one expects—closer to a puppy's yip," Varek said. "We also keep familiar creatures. Squirrels, for instance. Remarkably clever little rascals."

Zev watched a monarch butterfly, resting on a rock, pump blood into its wings. Others glided in lazy zigzags toward flowers. Inefficient, erratic—yet somehow precise in landing.

Varek noticed. "They're spared the rigors of migration here. It helps preserve their beauty."

To Zev, the atrium was a bittersweet jewel—a curated miracle. Millennia of evolution, reduced to décor.

His awe soured. "It's tragic. Earth can no longer sustain the very life it once bore."

"And that," Varek said solemnly, "is why Felicity—and UnaTerra—exist. Samples from precious ecosystems like the Amazon now only live here. A museum of what once flourished freely."

Zev thought of the species slipping away. Extinction had become mundane. He had to admire UnaTerra's intent.

"Sir," Varek said gently, "we must continue."

They passed through the atrium into the men's wash area. Varek handed him a bag.

"Place your belongings inside. It's biodegradable. Your clean garments will be waiting after your shower."

"You laundering what I have on?"

"No, sir. They'll be disposed of. New clothing will be yours to keep."

Varek lingered as Zev undressed, making him uneasy. Zev disrobed quickly and handed over the sack, relieved when Varek finally left. Alone for the first time in days, Zev stepped into a vast, tiled chamber, large enough for fifty. Only one of the many showerheads along the three walls poured—he headed for it. The water was lukewarm, underwhelming, but still a relief. He scrubbed away dirt, grime, and who knew what. He let it pour into his mouth but didn't swallow—not sure if it was safe.

No towel awaited him. Instead, Varek returned and pressed a button. Air jets blasted from the floor and ceiling, reaching every crevice. Zev wasn't sure if it was disturbing or pleasant—or both.

Thirty seconds later, he was dry. Garments, including a purple smock, sat on a nearby bench, along with slip-on shoes.

He paused. Varek was still there.

"You mind?"

"Mind what, sir?"

"Watching me dress. It's invasive."

"In Felicity, we practice full transparency. Nothing to hide."

Zev let it go. At least the shoes fit perfectly.

"This way, sir," Varek said. "To the restaurant."

He actually craved a bed, but none was offered.

They passed by the women's quarters. Zev wrinkled his forehead.

"So men and women are separated?"

"Yes, unless you wear green. A passing genome score allows cohabitation."

"I see you passed."

No reply. Zev pressed for a better understanding.

"I get that the Carbon Laws limit procreation. But people can't even sleep beside each other?"

"Correct. No temptation, no expectation. Our focus is communal."

"Sounds like a blast."

"Many still face hunger, Mr. Brighton. They would welcome such a life."

Zev grunted.

Varek gestured ahead. "Since the atrium intrigued you, perhaps you'll appreciate our fishery."

Zev's eyes widened. It resembled a public aquarium—immense and multistoried. A school of fish, shimmering in their metallic scales, moved in perfect unison, while other species scoured the bottom alone, drifting like dreams.

"What are you breeding?"

Varek beamed. "All freshwater: salmon, trout, tilapia, catfish, bass, pike. Some are separated to avoid predation."

Zev admired the tank's design and the careful engineering.

He glimpsed outside. "That lake—is it connected?"

Varek nodded. "Our largest man-made reservoir. The wind turbine on the hill powers the system, pumping water to simulate current. Fish can travel between the tank and lake via transparent pipes. A peaceful life—right up until harvest."

Zev tracked a trout gliding toward the tank's bottom, drawn to a chunk of meat dangling from a hook. Suspended by a thin rope, it swayed in the filtered current. The chunk's size made Zev wonder if it came from their livestock. Around it, fish darted and snapped, each trying for a bite.

"This way," Varek said.

Finally, they arrived at the cafeteria.

"Here you can enjoy replenishing nutrients for your safe return."

Zev muttered, "Sounds yummy. Don't oversell it."

"Pardon?"

"Never mind."

"I can't respond if you mumble, sir." Varek seemed irritated for the first time.

"You'll be seated shortly. It's required that you remain here. If you leave the restaurant, an escort is required."

A young woman in blue approached. "Just yourself, sir?"

"Yep."

"Follow me to your stall."

Zev laughed. She gave him a puzzled look. He explained, "You said stall."

"Yes. Isolated stalls reduce airborne illness."

"Right," Zev muttered. His thoughts turned to Luna. This was her future.

"Can I ask something?"

"Of course."

"What do you do for fun? Movies? Bowling? Dates?"

Her demeanor remained flat. "As a Blue, I'm not permitted to date. But I live in a shelter, safe from the weather. I'm never hungry or afraid. My work benefits the community. We consider ourselves fortunate."

Her answer was polished—too polished.

"Rehearsed that?" Zev muttered.

She turned toward him, frowning.

"Sorry. I didn't mean to offend."

She said nothing more, stopping at a small table built flush against the wall, flanked on both sides by partitions. A narrow slot was embedded in the wall at table height.

Zev sat. No menu appeared; she simply turned and walked away.

Above the slot hung a sign: "Efficiency in all we do," beneath which sat a framed portrait labeled Aldric Heister, CEO. Blond, fit, and stiff.

Zev studied the man's face.

Arrogant.

He wasn't opposed to judging a book by its cover. He was usually right.

Moments later, a tray slid through the slot—holding nothing but a bowl of brown pellets and a glass of water.

It looked like kibble.

He stooped down, trying to peer through the slot, wondering if he could catch the person serving it. It slid shut quickly.

This wasn't living.

At that moment, he made a decision.

I can't leave Luna here.

Chapter 51: Simi

The doors to the last passenger car remained shut, and the stillness inside grated on Simi's nerves. He stood at the rear, his gaze darting between the nervous crowd and the guards unloading their human cargo from the forward cars. The first two cars had already emptied, their passengers sent off to meet their fate—the selection. They were probably already scrubbed clean in the showers—or, if they were fortunate, undergoing genetic testing. He'd missed the chance to share his findings, and with each added second, more people were being processed without him.

He needed to move—he was missing out. An immediate solution sparked in his mind. He couldn't execute it literally, but Aldric's metaphor still applied. Tightening his grip on the cold weapon he still carried—the glass now dark with dried blood—he scanned the room. His eyes locked on a target.

The car was packed, everyone desperate to get off, eyes pinned to the doors. Simi didn't hesitate. He moved, a shadow among shadows, until he stood behind one of the troublemakers he'd been watching earlier—the angry man in green, too eager to command. His posture radiated quiet dominance—the kind that needed to be cut down. In one smooth motion, reaching low and angling across a passenger between them, Simi drove the jagged glass deep into his side. The shard pierced clean through, punching into the kidney. The man recoiled—instinct taking over—struggling to make sense of the sudden pain.

Simi left the glass lodged in flesh, watching as alarm spread in a chain reaction of gasps and screams. He didn't pause. He kept moving through the shifting crowd, unnoticed amid the confusion, the writhing man behind him now a useful distraction.

As others, slow to understand, surged to assist the wounded man, Simi reached the front of the car. The guards, seeing the chaos, opened the door—just enough. A narrow gap allowed for a quick exchange. He pointed to the injury, then identified himself quietly.

They let him through. No one else.

He stepped off the train into daylight.

The job was done. Efficient. Clean. He allowed himself a silent moment of satisfaction. "Two birds, one stone," he muttered. The phrase wasn't perfect, but close enough. One eliminated threat. One timely exit from this metal box on wheels. The move itself was definitely something his boss would approve of—might even enjoy.

Outside, the air was oppressive and dry, but at least he was free from the train. Simi spotted his ride—a lone guard stationed in an electric vehicle. Without a word, he climbed in, and they sped off, heading west toward Felicity. Dust curled behind them, mixing with the haze of passengers still marching toward the eastern gates, their feet kicking up a steady cloud.

They bypassed most of the crowd, the vehicle veering smoothly toward the expansive walled city. As they approached the sentries, Simi studied the alert figures. Rifles were raised, and the air seemed to tighten with every passing second—until the driver flashed a badge. The rifles dropped, and the gates swung open, granting them entry through the perimeter.

The vehicle veered right to avoid the main entrance of the Town Hall, cutting instead toward a rarely used side access near the eastern side of the building. Simi's mind was already racing ahead. His only hope was to observe as many batches as he could, before they disappeared into the system.

He jumped out, every movement purposeful, and headed for a ciphered doorway. He pressed a few swift keystrokes until he heard the satisfying click of the release. He signaled the driver to leave him, then stepped inside.

Two flights of stairs descended before him, each step drawing him closer to where he needed to be.

At level B2, he paused at another door—this one requiring biometric clearance. He pressed his thumb to the pad and waited.

The door slid open.

Inside, Aldric stood at an observation window, watching the flow of train passengers.

Aldric's face twisted as he took in Simi's appearance. "You look horrible—and you're late," he said firmly, though a smirk tugged at one corner of his mouth. "You also smell like Stage Nine." He handed him a bottle of water, which Simi drained in seconds.

Simi grimaced. "That train's a disaster. Needs a cleanup crew before it rolls again."

Aldric's attention was elsewhere. "You missed the first batch, and I suggest you miss the second."

"What?"

"Go shower. Maybe you can make it back for the last loads. We'll catch up on the other immigrants later. Hurry."

Simi nodded. "It'll be quicker if I use your cart."

Aldric waved him off. "Fine. But wipe the seat down after. I don't want that smell soaking in."

Simi was already moving, intent on reaching the showers fast, his mind pivoting toward what came next. He hated when the selection ran without him.

Chapter 52: Kylo

Kylo didn't know how long the Senator would keep him waiting, but he decided to make use of the time by checking the limo's supplies. A small refrigerator drew his eye—what he found inside felt almost illicit. Luxuries he hadn't tasted in years, things far beyond his means now.

So much for the Senator's carbon neutrality.

He mumbled out loud, "Do as I say, not as I do."

His eyes locked onto a carton of ripe, red strawberries. His mouth watered. Pavlov would've been proud. He glanced outside to make sure the moment was his.

All clear.

He closed his eyes and placed a berry on his tongue, letting it rest there. For once, he didn't rush. He pressed it gently against the roof of his mouth, savoring the burst of sweet-tart juice as it spread across his palate. The sensation stirred something faint and distant—a childhood long gone.

Next, he found a wedge of Manchego cheese. He broke off a piece and placed it in his mouth, chewing with deliberate care. The briny, nutty flavor filled his mouth, and he let it saturate his senses. If heaven had a flavor, it might be this.

Imported from Spain. Shame on you, Senator.

Another glance around. Still alone. His eyes landed on dark chocolate bark with almonds. From Belgium. He snapped off a piece and let it melt slowly on his tongue, the cacao's richness clinging stubbornly before giving way to the soft crunch of almonds. Pleasure exploded into something almost painful—the kind of indulgence that tasted better for feeling forbidden.

When the chocolate was gone, he looked up again. The minibar called. After a quick scan of the shelves—everything in its place— he muttered to himself, "Now that's what I'm talking about."

He spotted a cocktail shaker. Ice. Olive juice. Gin. Vermouth. He'd have loved it, and even knew the right proportions. He glanced at UnaTerra headquarters through the window. No signs of movement.

Then reason set in.

Too messy. Too easy to lose control.

He pulled himself away from temptation and tidied the area, careful to erase any sign of his private feast. Then he returned to the driver's seat, a bottle of water in hand. A simple plastic container, familiar in a way that felt almost strange—he hadn't held one in years. The seat clicked as he adjusted it, and he flicked on the radio.

Vivaldi's *The Four Seasons* filled the cabin. The music wrapped around him, refined—a strange contrast to his reality. He loved the classics. Fitting, really. Vivaldi, born in Venice, a city that had warned of rising seas centuries ago—its warnings ignored.

The music swelled. Kylo found himself moving subtly with the rhythm, the silent conductor of his own private orchestra, letting the symphony drown out the memory of what—and who—he'd left in the trunk.

He took a gulp of water, set the bottle in a cup holder, and closed his eyes, imagining a better life with his family. But the fleeting peace couldn't last. He thought of his daughter, his wife.

A morning kiss from Ingrid. Candles on a cake, blown out by Alma—her gift still in his pocket.

All of it more precious than anything the Senator's world could offer.

He wondered if he'd ever see them again.

Then came the guilt—piercing and sudden—as he pictured the police tearing through his apartment, searching for clues. For him.

The door opened, interrupting his thoughts, and Senator Remi McCarthy stepped inside. He was grateful her eyes didn't meet his.

"To the Guymon Palace Hotel, please," she said, settling into the back seat.

Kylo gripped the steering wheel harder than necessary, his fingers taut with tension. As he pulled away, he wasn't sure which way to turn. He had a fifty-fifty chance. He turned left.

"What the hell are you thinking?"

He panicked—then realized she was barking at someone on her phone.

"If I go into Congress with that speech, I'll incite a war on the Capitol grounds! We're trying to appeal to both parties, not unite them against us. Highlighting sterility as part of the Carbon Laws is idiotic. Honestly, I'm starting to wonder if you're the right person to be my speechwriter." She paused. "Hold on."

Kylo caught a quick glance in the rearview mirror. She was looking out her window, frustration etched on her face.

"I said the Palace Hotel. Where the hell are you going?" she demanded. She returned to her phone, her tone no less irritated.

"And why am I stuck next to that decrepit old fool from Wisconsin? He's out. I need someone with a backbone, not dead weight. Think, people!"

Kylo made a U-turn and headed northwest on Highway 412. He kept his movements fluid, trying to buy time as the Senator vented. His hand rested on the chauffeur's gun at his waist, the discomfort from it a stark reminder of the task ahead. He needed to make his next move carefully.

Kylo continued along Highway 412 as it curved from a northbound stretch into a westward route. Boise City lay about 45 minutes ahead, and he drove steadily, waiting in silence for the Senator to finish her call. When she finally hung up, he spotted a secluded stretch of road, veered onto a dirt turnoff, and cut the engine.

From the back seat, an annoyed voice snapped,

"What the fuck is this? I'm on a schedule! If you had to piss, you should've planned better!"

Kylo slid open the partition between the front and back, turning in his seat as he leveled a gun toward her.

"I'll need your phone."

The Senator stiffened, startled—but quickly tried to mask it.

"You're not my chauffeur. Who are you?"

"You'll find out soon enough. For now, don't test me."

She held his gaze, then slowly handed over her phone, posture tight with defiance.

"You realize my team will raise the alarm the moment I go silent. This won't end well for you. Let me contact them. Whatever this is about, I'll listen. I can make sure you're treated fairly."

Kylo's eyes narrowed.

"Fair treatment? Like the kind you offered the people in D.C.?"

Her composure slipped, her voice rising.

"I gave those people a lifeline. The National Mall is a death trap—disease, gangs, starvation. Felicity is a chance. A real one. Not perfect, but better than what they had."

Kylo didn't respond right away. He studied her, weighing her words.

"You made your political move. But no one wanted your 'golden ticket'—not until the murders started. You know exactly what I mean."

She scoffed.

"If you're accusing me of orchestrating that violence, then you're not just wrong—you're delusional. Is this some half-baked conspiracy theory?"

"It's not a theory." His tone was cold, flat. "One of your people slipped up: Simi Kremna. He was directly involved."

That name made her laugh outright.

"Simi? Please. He's harmless. A puppy. His job is to rally warm bodies and smile for cameras."

"Or pack them into buses." Kylo's voice hardened. "After the murders, people couldn't leave fast enough. Simi knew exactly what fear would do. You knew. And you exploited it."

"You're out of your mind," she snapped, but her confidence wavered for the first time. She drew a breath, trying to steady herself.

"What do you want from me? This is insane."

"Your cooperation," Kylo said simply. "We're going to Felicity. I think Simi's already there."

A beat of silence. Then her voice dropped, quieter but still laced with disdain.

"You really think you'll get in? Felicity has walls, checkpoints, eyes everywhere. It's a fortress."

"That's where you come in." His tone turned colder still. "You're the chink in their armor."

Chapter 53: Luna

After the showers, Luna's group—left bare and exposed—moved to the next phase. She gripped Karli tightly as they stood over a grate where jets of air blasted upward, accelerating the drying process. Luna kept her head low, deliberately avoiding eye contact, hoping the others would do the same. The guards stood in silent observation, waiting out the cycle.

When the drying stopped, they were ushered into a new room.

A sign above the entrance read: Stage Three – Health Assessments.

Along the walls, pairs of workers in orange smocks stood at stations. Luna, still holding Karli, was the only one allowed to pair with another—an apparent exception. A no-nonsense woman in her forties grabbed Luna's left forearm and scrawled "Q0024" with a permanent marker. She did the same for Karli: "Q0025."

She barked, "Q24, on the plate. I'll take the child."

Luna hesitated. "My name is Luna," she said softly.

The woman glared. "See this button?" She pointed to a device on her belt. "One click and you're gone. Got it? Down here, you're Q24. Now shut up and step up."

Luna, not fully understanding, swallowed hard. "Understood."

The woman grunted and turned to her coworker. "One-oh-five pounds. A pipsqueak," she muttered, typing it in. "Now height."

Luna stood stiffly against the wall, still without a stitch of clothing, trying not to show how exposed she felt.

"Five-one," the worker called out.

The checks continued—blood pressure, heart rate, temperature—each step carried out with clinical indifference. The process was modified for Karli and completed quickly.

Handing the baby back, the woman snapped, "Move along." As they shuffled away, Luna overheard her say, "They both pass."

As the group advanced, Luna noticed some people being led through a door on the side. She caught a glimpse of them being handed red coats. The elderly man who had left his wife behind, several other older folks, and someone with an arm in a sling were among them. She wished she had been given clothing like theirs, too. The group of thirty had become twenty.

The next space was smaller. The sign above read: Stage Four – Inoculation.

Workers stood by platforms arranged with medical supplies.

"Over here. Shots for you and the child," one of them said.

Luna hesitated. "For what?"

The woman furrowed her brow. "Do as you're told." She nudged Luna onto the platform. A needle went in without warning. Karli cried out as she was injected next.

Before Luna could react, they were pushed forward once more.

The next door was marked: Stage Five – Psychological and Aptitude Screening.

Here, Luna was guided to a station where the workers wore blue smocks. Still naked, she stood shielding herself—with Karli—as best she could.

A man looked her over, his eyes lingering a moment too long before speaking. "Age. Don't lie."

"Twenty-six," Luna replied, trying to keep her voice steady.

"Any history of mental illness? Or drugs you might take?"

"No."

"Education?"

"Speech pathologist. JMU, Virginia."

"Speech? Not useful."

"I shifted to acute care in a hospital—with patients who'd suffered strokes, head injuries, or MS …"

The man in blue shook his head. "Still not useful."

A chill slid down her spine, and her instincts cried out an alarm. Her shadow twin came to life.

"After the Carbon Laws, they trained me for our genetics lab."

"Doing what?"

"Testing and interpreting DNA results for markers."

He scribbled something on his clipboard and glanced at Karli. "Who's the kid?"

Luna was ready for that one. "Karli. My brother's daughter. He and his wife died in an accident. I was left to care for her."

"She doesn't look like you."

"My brother was adopted."

"Why are you here?"

She took a breath and continued to weave her lies. "My apartment complex burned down. Housing's been scarce in D.C."

The man paused, then nodded. "Lucky for you. We can use your genetic background. Move along." He gestured to the next station. "We'll assign you a color after genome."

"What?"

"Just move."

Luna obeyed with a mix of confusion and unease. She still didn't know what this was building toward.

At the next checkpoint, she noticed more people being pulled aside. Some were handed orange coats and guided out a south exit. Others, fewer, received the red. Only a small group—including Luna and Karli—were waved forward.

She tried to make sense of the pattern, but no one explained anything. She was afraid to ask.

Another room followed—colder, more clinical. The sign read: Stage Six – Genome and Lab Work.

Blood was drawn from both of them, their vials labeled Q24 and Q25. The samples were placed into machines. Luna wasn't told what they were searching for.

Afterward, she was handed a blue smock, which she put on. Karli, now fidgeting from the cold, remained naked.

"Take the child to immigration," a worker said. "Then you can return for final instructions."

Luna's confusion deepened, but she followed the directions.

The new room looked like an office cubicle, with chairs in front of desks. The sign said: Stage Seven – Identity and Citizenship Processing. Workers here wore green. A young Asian man invited her to sit, nodding politely, noting their numbers. He typed at his terminal. After a few moments, he slid a form across the desk.

"Sign this. It's a request to instate the child as a Sustalia citizen."

Luna blinked. "Sustalia? That's a state—you mean U.S. We're already citizens, so it's reinstate."

He looked up. "You signed away your rights."

Her stomach turned. "What? I had no idea."

"Yet, you signed."

"What are you saying? I'm not a U.S. citizen anymore?"

"Correct."

"Then we need to be reinstated."

"Ma'am, you're not listening. First of all, there's no 'we.' This paperwork is for the child only. As for citizenship, this is for Sustalia, not the United States. You are here as an illegal alien."

"Illegal? You brought me here."

"Please sign, ma'am. For the child's sake."

Chapter 54: Zev

Zev couldn't stomach the bland, synthetic meal in front of him. The fish in the aquarium were clearly better nourished than the purple-clad human guests. Instead of eating, his thoughts drifted to the people he'd convinced to relocate here. His worst fear was that he'd led them into a tedious, hollow existence they might come to regret. That guilt pressed on him, especially where Luna and the baby were concerned.

Assuming the treasurer would take a while to calculate his earnings, Zev ignored the man's request to stay put. Finding Luna mattered more than following rules. He owed her that much.

He flagged down the hostess. "Where are the bathrooms?"

"You'll need to head back to the men's quarters, outside the restaurant. But…"

"Thanks. This might take a while."

The hostess scowled slightly. "TMI," she muttered, as she walked away.

Zev cringed inwardly at his own implication, but he needed to manage her expectations of time.

He rose with the faint sense of being watched but brushed it aside. His first task was to find where the passengers were being processed. Perhaps some had already cleared. If luck favored him, Luna and the baby would be among them. In this sterile world of rules and lifeless faces, she would be a welcome sight.

As he left the cafeteria, he noticed heads turning—and then understood why. It wasn't just his mind exaggerating. The neon-purple smock he wore screamed "outsider" amid the muted blues, greens, and the guards' camouflage. It practically glowed, as if powered by its own battery pack, pulsing a single word into the room: WARNING.

People stared openly. Some halted mid-step as he passed, gawking as if he were a three-headed lizard. He didn't meet their eyes, didn't flinch—just kept moving toward a supply room he'd noticed earlier. But before he reached it, something else caught his attention.

A two-story expanse opened up ahead. From his vantage point, it resembled another atrium, but the interior was pure function over form. A greenhouse. Zev recognized it immediately— practical, efficient, built for crop production.

Stretching up to the second level, pallets of dirt rotated on a vertical conveyor system like a slow, soil-filled Ferris wheel, giving each plant its share of sunlight. Below, blue-coated workers moved methodically through rows of corn, broccoli, carrots, and kale. Some plants he didn't recognize. Zev's eyes caught on the fruit trees—branches heavy with apples, apricots, and figs.

His stomach growled. "None of that ended up on my plate," he muttered. "Though they can keep the kale."

A young female guard approached, slicing through the moment. "Sir, what are you doing?"

"I was looking for the bathroom. Found this greenhouse instead—looks like a Garden of Eden in there."

The guard wasn't amused. "It's a biome. Didn't your host explain that you need an escort?"

"To use the bathroom? I think I can manage, thanks."

The guard's expression hardened. "Where were you quarantined?"

"Quarantined?" Zev lifted an eyebrow, playing dumb. "I was shown to a table in the dining hall, then needed to see a man about a horse, if you catch my drift."

He leaned into being crude, hoping to shake the guard off with sheer obnoxiousness.

It worked. The guard just shook her head. "Use the facility and return to your assigned post."

Zev moved on. It was safer than the chaos he'd left behind in D.C., sure—but it lacked the one thing he craved: freedom. The walls weren't just sterile—they felt like they were closing in, a prison in disguise.

As he walked down the antiseptic corridors, the absence of warmth made him feel even more uncomfortable. No murals, no color, nothing human—just framed photos of the same man, rigid and unsmiling, with slogans beneath each: "One realm, one leader." "Work yields food." Every image listed the name, Aldric Heister—CEO. It was as if the entire place revolved around him.

Narcissist, too.

Zev passed a door labeled "Laundry." Just beyond it: the men's bathroom. After a quick restroom break, he backtracked to the laundry door and tested the handle.

It was unlocked.

He slipped inside, flicked on the light, and found what looked like a clothing store. Stacks of blue smocks lined the shelves, sorted by gender and size. Uniformity by design. It seemed no one here had more than one acceptable option. He could guess why there were no camouflage uniforms—for security reasons—but the absence of green attire puzzled him.

Zev picked one that fit, traded his neon smock for the safer blue, and folded the purple into his pocket. He felt an instant change. The blue made him invisible.

He moved like a chameleon now—unremarkable, untracked. But his goal hadn't changed: find Luna.

The maze of cold, featureless corridors was easy to get lost in— but he was watching, learning. He passed what looked like a medical wing—an annoying reminder that he no longer had health coverage, a fact he pushed aside before anxiety could settle in.

Then he saw her.

The young girl from the train. She was walking with a small group—all women, all in blue—no father in sight. They had just emerged from a door in the southwest corner, escorted by a green-smocked worker and a guard in camo at the rear.

Zev didn't dare approach—too many eyes. Instead, he followed at a distance, his instincts guiding him. His pulse picked up, each step pulling him closer to the possibility of finding Luna. If the girl from their coach had made it through, Luna couldn't be far behind.

He circled back to the southwest corner and found the door they'd come from. It was locked.

Everything about the place warned him not to push further. The lines of authority were invisible but unmistakable. Crossing them could have consequences. Still, his resolve didn't budge.

With a new plan forming, Zev turned toward the supply room. He wasn't going to stop—not until he found her.

Chapter 55: Luna

Luna couldn't believe the words she'd just heard. She insisted, "I was born in the U.S.—I am a citizen."

The agent in the green smock didn't flinch. "No longer."

"So that's it? Poof? Citizenship revoked?" The words slipped out loudly, before she could stop them. Luna's mind spun, struggling to absorb the weight of the statement.

The agent looked around, then said, "Please lower your voice."

She drew a breath, trying to stay calm. Better to understand the system—and bend it to her advantage. Being a citizen somewhere was better than nowhere. She could fight for the U.S. later. She narrowed her eyes. "You've got forms for the baby. I want mine. What's the process?"

The agent's tone remained unchanged. "There is no process."

"You're telling me I have no country?"

"Correct. You are stateless."

Something inside her shifted. Her pulse quickened, muscles tense as fury erupted. "Wow. Fascist, yet polite. I want to speak to someone above your pay grade. Someone who isn't a glorified mannequin." The boldness in her own voice surprised her.

"I'm your assigned agent," he said flatly, his eye twitching slightly now. "And I should warn you—we don't tolerate outbursts from immigrants. Lower your voice and watch your words. Consider this your first warning."

Luna's thoughts whirled, every question branching into more, none with answers. "What happens now? Where will we go?"

The agent's response was again robotic. "You'll be housed on Level G, since you're assigned Blue. Consider yourself fortunate. Most arrivals are classified Orange and sent to Level B1, or worse.

Level G offers amenities: a restaurant, an atrium, a biome, a fishery, medical access, and limited internet viewing."

Luna barely heard him. One fear swallowed all the others. "What about Karli?"

His voice shifted—smoother, almost celebratory. "She passed the Genome test. That qualifies her for full citizenship. She'll be free to live within city boundaries—inside the outer walls. She'll receive a full education through the doctorate level, access to premium recreation, and high-quality meals. Steak. Lamb. Fresh fish from our tanks. She'll thrive here."

The words cut like glass. "You're separating us?"

His face remained unreadable. "Yes. She'll be adopted following a brief trial period."

Luna's arms locked tighter around Karli. "Not if I can help it."

He leaned back in his chair, sweeping aside the paperwork in front of him. "These forms are a courtesy; we don't need your consent." He motioned to a nearby guard in camouflage. The guard stepped forward, face set, eyes cold.

"Escort the child to Green processing. Deliver her to the nursery."

Luna's heart pounded. The guard reached out, but she gripped Karli tightly. The baby stayed curled in her arms, sleeping through the very moment that could fracture both their lives.

The agent's voice sliced through the air. "Don't make a scene. That would be... unfortunate. This is your second warning. The next one has consequences."

Luna's teeth clenched, her body rigid. "You're not taking her," she said, her voice taut but resolute. "We stay together."

The agent exhaled, cold and dismissive. "There is no 'we.' And that's your third warning. That's a violation."

He began typing briskly at his console. The guard didn't move. "What are you doing?"

"I'm revoking your Blue status. You're Orange now."

Luna's stomach lurched. She didn't know exactly what Orange meant, but the chill in his voice made it clear—it was worse.

He glanced up, voice low and deliberate. "Trust me—you don't want to go Red."

Luna's mind raced. Red. It sounded final.

But how could she let go of Karli? She couldn't. Her thoughts scrambled, hunting for any path forward—a way to survive and reclaim her… daughter.

She looked down at the girl—not her child by blood, but something far deeper than before—and spoke the words she'd never dared to say aloud until this moment.

"I love you," she whispered. "Do you hear me? We're together—forever."

Then, slowly, she handed Karli to the guard. Though her arms emptied, her heart didn't. Even as pain carved its way through her chest, her mind stayed grounded, calculating.

Cry. Give in. Play the game. Let them think they've won.

The agent gave a curt nod as Karli was carried away. Then he gestured to the guard, pointing at Luna. "She's a Morlock now."

Luna flinched—another word that sounded like a slur, an unknown label. But that wouldn't stop her. Not ever.

She straightened her spine as the guard approached, unblinking. The fear didn't vanish—it calcified. She was led back to where she had come.

You think this is over? You have no idea who you just made your enemy. Time to adjust the sails.

Chapter 56: Simi

A fully showered Simi stood beside Aldric, his damp blond hair slicked neatly back, the faint scent of soap still clinging to his skin. Together, they faced a small pane—a window built into the chamber wall. Through the glass, people stirred inside. Simi's eyes moved over the crowd, searching for anyone he recognized.

Every person—whether terrified, grieving, or angry—had one thing in common: they all wore the same red smock.

After a long pause, Aldric broke the silence.

"You're looking through four layers of transparent aluminum composite glass, over an inch thick. The same material used on the International Space Station."

Simi glanced at the glass, then through it again. He wasn't in the mood for a science lesson. Still, he feigned interest.

"Why go to the trouble?"

"It's a thermal vacuum chamber," Aldric said, his voice tipped with pride. "Less messy. No gas, no contamination."

Simi gave a slow nod, his expression blank, though his jaw flexed. He made sure Aldric didn't catch his discomfort.

"How many in this first run?"

"We can cram fifty in. Checking your list?"

Simi squinted. "Most of the leaders from the last three cars are in there. But I don't see any from the first two. Should've skipped the shower. We need to find them."

"Trust me, the shower was necessary," Aldric replied, a wry edge in his tone. "One task at a time. Let's handle this group first. The rest will turn up."

Simi was struggling to pay attention. "Did you say turnip?"

Aldric frowned. "'Turn up.' But speaking of turnips, you'll see—we do get blood from them."

Simi didn't blink. "Blood I can handle."

Aldric shook his head. "I meant metaphorically, blood from a turnip. No actual blood. But water boils when there's no air pressure."

Simi frowned, again with the science. "What?"

"The human body is about sixty percent water," Aldric said, clinical as ever. "Tongue included. It boils when the pressure drops. Not instantly—slower than you'd think. A few minutes sometimes, while the turbines finish depressurizing. Don't worry, nobody explodes. Movies get that part wrong. We've even had cockroaches survive. Repressurize in time, and they crawl away."

Simi stared into the chamber—a cold, metallic enclosure. Some people inside were elderly, others teens or younger. A frail, white-haired woman clung to her husband, the two embracing tightly, both quietly sobbing. Nearby, the angry man—who must've survived the stabbing—slammed his fists against the glass, rage carved into every line of his face. He raised his middle finger toward the observers above. Off to the side, a young girl stood silently, clutching a worn doll to her chest.

Simi fought his discomfort. They were scraps—but cruelty was needless.

"This isn't one-way glass?" he asked.

"Nope," Aldric said. "They can see us. Tinted glass reduces visibility. Doesn't matter. They won't be around long enough to pick us out of a lineup."

"When does it start?"

"They're just waiting for my signal. Figured I'd explain first. Some people find the technology… interesting."

He pressed a button at his belt. His voice came low and smooth into the headset.

"Activate Stage Eight."

The chamber rumbled to life. A low hiss gave way to a rhythmic pumping, mechanical and deep. Like a train engine drawing breath. Simi shifted his weight, his pulse quickening with the sound. Pressure dropped. Panic bloomed behind the glass. People gasped.

He made himself watch.

It wouldn't be quick.

Out of the corner of his eye, he saw the faint smile stretch across Aldric's face.

Simi had heard the explanation before. It was evolution. No different than a lion pulling down the weakest wildebeest. Pain wasn't always brief. The prey sometimes died slowly. At least, that's what he kept telling himself.

But that smile had never made sense.

Not until now.

Aldric liked this. The helplessness. The drawn-out terror. He liked watching it stretch. He savored the elimination of... waste.

Aldric's phone buzzed. He glanced at the screen, then answered with a curt, "Yeah." A pause, then he hung up.

He tapped his headset again. "Shut it down. Hold them here."

Simi turned to face him. "What's going on?"

Aldric's jaw tightened. Irritation laced his voice.

"Looks like we've got company."

Simi's interest piqued. "What kind of company?"

Aldric didn't answer right away. His scowl deepened.

"Your other boss," he said finally. "The Senator. She just pulled up to the gates."

He spat the next words. "Wants to chat."

Chapter 57: Zev

After seeing where the new arrivals had entered the ground floor, Zev slipped into a supply room and was quietly relieved to find it unlocked. He grabbed a pair of rubber gloves, a mop, and a wheeled bucket. Returning to the door where the train's passengers had just entered, he tested the handle again—still locked. He stood motionless for a moment, careful not to draw attention, his eyes scanning the corridor.

A sudden realization hit him: the bucket was empty. If a guard happened to walk by, it would be painfully clear he wasn't doing anything useful. He relaxed his grip on the mop, uncertain of what to do next.

Then luck intervened. The door swung open again, and more passengers in blue smocks were ushered out. About ten emerged, their escort this time bringing up the rear—a makeshift caboose in the single-file procession. The escort let the door swing shut on its own, then hurried ahead to lead them with new instructions.

Zev saw his chance. Without hesitation, he thrust the mop head into the narrowing gap between the door and the frame, jamming it just before it latched. He adjusted his gloves and assumed the posture of a man ready to scrub floors—head bowed, eyes fixed downward, every inch the dutiful worker. The escort's attention remained fixed on the arrivals. Not a single glance drifted in his direction. He held the position, feigning focus, until the group disappeared.

Once the group had cleared the area, Zev cracked the door open just wide enough to slip through, pulling the equipment behind him. He fully understood the deliberate risk he'd taken—a gamble not easily explained if caught—but it felt justified, especially for Luna and the child.

Inside, he found himself in a large, barren room—completely alone. The most remarkable thing about the room was how utterly unremarkable it was. No windows, no furniture, no decorations—not even wall outlets. Just a light switch, another door, and an entryway to a stairwell. The door bore a ciphered label: "L2." It was locked.

He turned toward the stairwell that led down. Zev took the stairs, carrying the mop and bucket, each step echoing in the stillness. The air grew cooler as he descended, the damp concrete scent closing in around him. If anyone found him here, there would be nowhere to hide.

The staircase descended far deeper than Zev had expected, suggesting the basement extended into a chamber with an unusually high ceiling. At last, the stairs ended at a landing with two doors: one secured with a keypad labeled "B2," the other unlocked but marked with a sign—"B1."

With no other option, he pulled open the "B1" door and slipped inside. On the other side, a corridor ran beside another supply room before opening into a vast factory. The factory's immensity caught him off guard. Its purpose was yet to be determined.

Lost in wonder, he froze at the unwelcome click of the door closing behind him. He spun back and twisted the knob. It wouldn't budge. Too late—he had locked himself out. No escape. His pulse hammered in his temples.

Pushing aside the panic, he was relieved to find the supply room empty. It was an ideal location to stash his cleaning gear. He rolled his mop and bucket inside. Now unencumbered, he began to explore.

The factory's corridor led into a massive area alive with industrial clamor. The metallic noise grew steadily louder—grinding, chopping, whirring, clanking. Zev watched in awe as machinery worked in relentless rhythm.

Scanning the factory's layout, he realized it was divided into numbered functional stations. He found himself at the edge of Stage Eleven, dominated by large, rotating mixing bowls.

Hiding behind a forklift, Zev studied the workers. Something new caught his eye: they weren't in the usual blue or green smocks. For the first time, he noticed orange. As each mixing bowl churned, an orange-clad worker stepped in to scrape the inner walls with a paddle, then moved to the next. In fact, most of the physical laborers wore this new color.

Zev worried he might stand out but relaxed when he spotted a man in blue—like himself—barking instructions and taking notes on a clipboard.

Zev moved east toward Stage Twelve, where hulking metal machines revealed themselves as commercial extruders. The factory appeared arranged in a long, linear sequence, each stage flowing into the next like links in a mechanical chain. Numbered signs were posted above steel support beams, guiding the eye along the length of the corridor—Eleven, Twelve, Thirteen.

He recognized the extruders from childhood—his grandmother had used a much smaller version to make pasta: penne, spaghetti, farfalle, fusilli, and his favorite—linguine. His thoughts drifted to her Italian linguine with clam sauce. The faint aroma of garlic seemed to float in his memory. He missed his

Nonna—unlike his mother, she never blamed him for what happened.

A loud mechanical snap yanked him back to the present. A truck dumped its contents into a hopper, feeding a conveyor belt lined with small pellets—similar to what had been served at lunch. Zev realized he was inside a food production facility, likely the engine that kept Felicity nourished. While much of the world starved, this city had found its solution—however bland it tasted.

He followed the conveyor east to the next station. Ahead, the corridor narrowed slightly, then widened again into the next staging area. Thirteen—his least favorite number—whether justified or not. Sprayers coated the pellets before they reached the final stage: packaging and distribution, Stage Fourteen. There, the pellets dropped into a large bin manned by orange-clad workers on either side.

The workers shoveled the product into a chute in the wall. The sight reminded Zev of old black-and-white footage of railway workers hammering the same spike in rhythm, alternating in perfect choreography, never striking each other's mallets.

Once they'd filled the chute, the orange workers pulled a rope while a blue supervisor observed. The mechanism worked like a manual dumbwaiter, carrying food up the wall, presumably to the kitchen above—a low-tech, energy-efficient solution scaled to meet the city's demands.

Zev turned his attention back to the people—specifically, to finding Luna. He needed to understand what the smock colors meant. He already knew green denoted those allowed to procreate, blue meant those who couldn't, and purple was for visitors. Now he saw blue smocks giving instructions to orange ones.

A caste system.

He had noticed no orange workers on the ground floor.

Steeling himself, Zev headed north, now assuming confident strides to embrace his role, shoulders squared and chin raised. Passing an orange worker, the man lowered his gaze—a silent gesture of submission. Zev adopted the air of his newfound status and embraced it. He knew it was wrong, but it oddly felt good.

He found the men's quarters—bunk beds stacked three high, cramped compared to the glimpse he had caught upstairs at the more spacious living accommodations.

Nearby, a laundry room held only orange clothing. No blue, green, or purple.

He moved on to the women's quarters, equally tight.

Then he spotted a familiar face from the train. He stepped forward but froze as a group of orange newcomers entered, escorted by a blue supervisor barking orders.

"You'll each be assigned a bunk and a single dresser. No personal items allowed."

Zev's heart sank at the harsh tone, but then his eyes caught a flash of the curled, beautiful hair he recognized. His emotions surprised him—an unexpected warmth blossomed deep inside, beyond anything words could describe.

He'd found Luna.

Chapter 58: Kylo

Kylo climbed over the front seat into the back of the limo with the Senator, the vehicle now idling just inside Felicity's perimeter walls. They'd been waved through the city gates and escorted to a side lot, where they were swiftly surrounded by armed guards in urban camouflage.

With Kylo's gun trained on her, Remi spoke calmly into a phone. She was connected to a liaison regarding the locked, bulletproof vehicle.

"He wants to see Simi. Send him." She hung up, then turned to Kylo. "You've taken this too far. You realize you're not walking away from this, right?"

Kylo didn't flinch. "Then neither are you, ma'am."

Remi, coolly recalibrating, asked, "What's your name? You could at least give me that."

He saw no harm in answering. "Kylo."

"Why the theatrics, Kylo? What's really going on? Did you know the people at the mall?"

He gave her just enough to keep her talking. "No. You tried to frame me. Now my family's hanging by a thread."

"Why would we frame you?"

"Maybe to protect your golden boy, Simi."

She leaned in, eyes narrowing. "You mentioned your family. Why are they at risk?"

Kylo wanted nothing more than to bash her teeth in, but he held back. Let her have her little performance—for now.

"Two reasons. First: I live in the real world. I need a job, and I've got a kid to raise. Even if I'm cleared, no one will hire me— or my wife—because the suspicion will stick. We'll be ruined."

Remi's posture stayed composed, even with a loaded weapon inches from her skull.

"And the second?"

Kylo's voice turned to steel. "Even if I'm found innocent, someone out there won't believe it. Vigilantism's growing. You didn't just wreck my life—you've painted a target on my family."

Remi's expression softened—just briefly. "I assure you, I had nothing to do with this."

A knock sounded on the window. Simi stood outside, arms folded.

Kylo locked onto Remi. "Here's what happens now. I keep this gun aimed at the back of your head. It's loaded. The safety is off."

He paused, letting his words settle in. "You move, I shoot. You blink wrong, I shoot. Cooperate, and maybe this ends like a fairy tale."

She nodded, tension tightening her jaw.

Kylo pressed the muzzle against her. "Tell Simi to call you."

Remi shook her head. "He doesn't have a phone. They're banned on the compound."

"Security does. We'll wait."

She gestured to Simi through the window, forming a phone with her thumb and pinky. He walked off, speaking with the guards.

Minutes later, Simi returned, dialing on a cell phone.

Remi began to lift her phone, but Kylo held her wrist down. "Speakerphone."

Remi complied. "Simi."

"Good Earth, ma'am."

"Calm seas. Listen carefully." Her voice stayed composed. "I need you to enter the vehicle—unarmed. Tell the guards: no weapons, no tear gas. Use my door and lock it behind you. I'm under gunpoint. If you don't follow that exactly, I die."

"Understood, ma'am. Give me a moment."

She added, suddenly, "Wait—call Aldric. Have him direct the guards. They'll need to hear it from him."

"Will do, ma'am."

While they waited, Kylo couldn't resist a jab. "Carbon Laws don't count for much in here, huh?"

Remi glanced over. "What are you talking about?"

Kylo nodded toward the mini-fridge. "The imports. The excess. Doesn't exactly scream sacrifice—for all that poetic garbage you preach. Word salad, really."

Remi said nothing.

Outside the limo, Simi made a call that dragged on longer than expected. At last, he gave a thumbs-up.

Remi turned. "Well?"

Kylo nodded. "Scoot to me. Give him space."

The Senator unlocked the door, then edged over until their hips touched.

Simi climbed in, seating himself with Remi now between both men. He shut the door behind him.

"Lock it," Kylo ordered.

Simi obeyed.

Kylo's tone cut through the air. "Why did you kill the people at the mall?"

Simi didn't blink. "I don't know what you're talking about."

Kylo leaned forward, studying him. "We've got a photo. Ninety-nine percent match. Puts you at the scene."

Simi scoffed. "Ninety-nine percent? That leaves one in a hundred. Twenty thousand people there—do the math. That's two hundred suspects. Stellar detective work."

"The guy in the photo has a lazy eye. Just like you."

Simi barely cared. "So? You've probably got some grainy image of someone nearby. Not exactly a smoking gun. Lazy is right— lazy detective work. Disappointing, for a veteran cop."

Kylo froze. Something clicked. "Funny. I never told you I was a cop."

Remi turned, her full attention snapping to Simi.

Simi's confidence wavered. "You're well known around there."

"Yeah, but you're not from there. You're from here—Sustalia. You'd have to research our precinct, our operations. Why?"

Simi scowled. "You're trying to rattle me. Won't work."

"Already has. You're flustered. Even your boss can see it."

Remi, who had been watching like a tennis match, was now locked on Simi. "How *do* you know who he is? I only asked you to stir the crowd."

Simi hesitated. "Like I said, ma'am—we needed to understand the setting to guide the evacuation."

Her voice grew harsh. "I never ordered an evacuation. People were meant to board the buses—voluntarily. Look at me. Are you involved in the murders?"

Simi's tone turned measured, careful. "Ma'am, our only mission has been to support your platform and enforce the Carbon Laws."

Remi turned to Kylo, her face drawn and pale, dread blooming beneath her practiced calm. "You're in charge. I'd like to make a call."

Chapter 59: Luna

After being ushered up a single flight of stairs to B1, Luna stepped into a bleak, sterile room lined with wooden bunk beds and dented lockers. Faded orange tags hung from each frame. The air carried a faint stench of bleach and oil.

She stood still among the others, all of them dressed in matching orange smocks, blinking beneath the harsh, unrelenting hum of fluorescent lights.

A mutter came from somewhere beside her.

"Chahmin' place, huh?"

Luna turned slightly.

The speaker was a middle-aged woman—mid-fifties, perhaps—with narrow, watchful eyes, sharper and more alert than the others. Her voice carried an accent Luna rarely heard: thick, clipped, and dry, neither warm nor unkind.

She slid open the drawer beneath the bunk labeled Q0021 and made a face.

"Good news," she said. "Four Q-tips and a smear of Vaseline. Friggin' real generous."

Luna gave a brief nod. "Doesn't matter. I don't plan on staying long."

That earned the faintest, almost reluctant smile.

"What's the rush? You got a date or somethin'?" the woman asked, the Boston accent now unmistakable.

A face rose in Luna's mind—Karli.

"Just someone I miss," she said softly. Then, to pivot, "You pick up the order here?"

"Yeah. Greens're top tier—like we're s'posed ta worship 'em or be wicked scared. Blues do the supervisin'. We're orange—

bottom rung. Workahs, I guess. Actually… maybe we're second to last. The reds? They're beneath us."

Luna nodded once. "I saw them pulled during sorting. Sent back, I suppose."

"Yeah," the woman said. "Or dumped somewhere else."

"Where else would they go?"

Before she could answer, the scrape of wood against concrete ripped through the air. A Blue Coat stepped onto a crate at the front of the room—posture stiff, voice harsh.

The middle-aged woman leaned in.

"Here it comes. Our big welcome speech."

The Blue barked, "You have fifteen minutes to prepare for the evening meal. All assignments begin tomorrow morning. Noncompliance can result in expulsion. And trust me, you don't want that."

The middle-aged woman muttered under her breath,

"I dunno, expulsion don't sound so bad."

The Blue Coat heard.

"Q21, is it?"

"What of it?"

"I can show you if you want. Right now. Got it?"

A pause. Then the woman bit her lip.

"Yah. Got it."

"One more disruption, and you're gone. You too, Q24."

Her voice lifted, addressing the room.

"You will all learn to listen. There are designated times for talking. This isn't one of them. Now, get familiar with your provisions. Be ready in fifteen."

Luna crouched beside her drawer—Q0024—and slid it open. Everything Q21 had listed was there. But there were other things she hadn't mentioned: a toothbrush, sanitary pads, socks, a folded shirt, pants, and underwear. All neatly arranged.

At least they're clean.

She was about to shut the drawer when something caught her eye—her label, Q0024, was peeling at the corner. She pinched the edge and peeled it back, revealing an older identifier underneath: P0015.

A beat passed. Then she pressed the label back down.

The next few minutes passed in a blur. Then came the march to the cafeteria—down gray corridors, past bolted doors and silent surveillance cameras.

Inside, they sat on backless benches alongside other orange-clad women Luna didn't recognize. These ones looked like longer-term residents. Their heads hung low. Gaunt faces. Pale skin. On some were small circular black welts—some with one, others with two.

The walls were bare cement, a space that offered no warmth. For everyone present, the room sank into complete silence.

A tray landed in front of her: a bowl of dry pellets and a cup of cloudy water. Her stomach clenched despite the food's lack of smell. She hadn't eaten in days.

Two seats away, a young woman raised her hand timidly.

"Excuse me," she said, voice trembling. "Can I please have more water? We haven't—"

A crack of a baton against the metal table stopped everything cold.

"Q43 just made a request," the Blue called out, stepping over to her. She reached into her pocket and pulled out a metal device, then pressed it against Q43's temple. A spark cracked, and the Orange cried out in pain. As the device withdrew, a single small black dot was branded on her temple, the skin raised like a spider bite.

The Blue then stood on a bench. Her voice sliced the air like a blade.

"I'll answer loudly so everyone understands. You all get three demerits, then you're gone. You've just witnessed one. In Felicity, consumption isn't a right. It's earned. If you don't work, you don't eat. You don't drink. That's our law. No questioning our rules."

A pause, deliberate.

"But today, you're fortunate. Our green leader has granted a gift: one extra glass of water. Everyone except Q43 will receive a refill. Tonight only. Then—lights out."

No one moved.

"You now have ten minutes to eat, drink, and return to your bunks. Any delay results in a demerit."

The shuffle of silverware and scraping of trays began all at once. The pellets were tasteless, but Luna forced them down. When her water was refilled, she drank every drop, careful not to reveal how badly she needed it.

Then came the scramble.

Chairs screeched. Trays clattered. Movement surged through the room. The veterans bussed their plates with practiced efficiency. The rest tripped over each other trying to catch up.

Luna hesitated—just half a second too long.

A Blue Coat stepped in front of her, baton raised, the tip placed beneath her chin.

"You're slow, Q24," the woman said flatly. "I'll be watching you."

Luna held her gaze for a moment, fury rising. But she said nothing, just dropped her eyes.

The baton pulled back.

She rose, bussed her tray, and followed the crowd back to the sleeping quarters. Watching the others, she disrobed down to her underwear, hung her smock on a hook, and climbed into bed.

The lights cut out almost immediately.

Darkness settled. Whimpering and shallow breathing filled the room. Luna lay still, battling her own thoughts.

Ten minutes passed.

Sleep should have come easily. Exhaustion usually made it inevitable. But someone nearby snored—loud, wet, unrelenting— and it kept dragging her back from the edge of rest.

Then a hand touched her shoulder.

Panic surged—but a whisper followed.

"It's me."

She couldn't see, but she knew the voice.

"Zev?" Her hand moved toward him.

"Get your smock on. We don't have much time."

She didn't hesitate.

Quietly pulling back the sheet, she put on her smock and followed him out of the dark, heart hammering. She didn't know what came next—only grateful she wouldn't face it alone.

Chapter 60: Kylo

Kylo sat in the back of the limo, the air conditioner keeping him cool. Everything smelled new and fresh—the leather, the fruit—a stark contrast to the chaos of D.C., with its stifling heat and cloying human odors. Yet, like the Mall, tension lingered here too, dense and suffocating.

Remi sat beside him, shoulder to shoulder, with Simi on her other side. She dialed a number, speaking with quiet precision—each word composed. Kylo felt torn: he admired her steadiness under pressure, yet despised her, still holding her responsible for his situation.

She was too calm. Either she knew something he didn't, or she was better at bluffing than he could ever be.

"Aldric. Remi here. You're on speaker. I've got Simi with me—and another man. He's armed. We need to speak in person. I'm asking you to let all three of us in, unharmed, so we can all talk face-to-face."

They heard an exhale. "Senator, you know we can't have weapons in the Town Hall, with the exception of our own security forces," Aldric's voice was clipped, professional.

Remi didn't flinch, continuing without hesitation. "I'm asking that you, as the CEO, temporarily waive that rule. Are you not the one in charge of the city? I don't believe the man with the gun will harm anyone. I'll take full responsibility."

Kylo remained silent, tension coiling along his spine as Aldric's pause stretched longer than it should have. If this fell apart, he had nothing left but desperate options.

His grip tightened on the gun. One wrong word, and this would turn into blood—his own included.

Then, finally, the sound of resignation:

"Okay. Give me a minute to prepare my team. You'll all be guided in."

"Perfect. We'll also need some zip ties."

"Why?"

Kylo interjected, "For my safety."

Remi hung up and turned to Kylo. "Satisfied?"

Kylo shifted, not entirely comfortable with the agreement, even though he'd been the one to define the terms. "It'll do."

But his gut said otherwise. Too clean.

A guard knocked on the limo door a moment later, handing Remi the zip ties. She was about to pass them to Kylo when he pressed the muzzle against her side. He spoke in a voice low and controlled.

"Bind your boy's wrists behind his back. Tight."

Remi moved swiftly. Simi, seated beside her, didn't resist. He just stared ahead, unreadable. When she was done, Kylo grabbed the ties. "Your turn. Hands behind your back."

She complied without a word as he looped the zip tie around her wrists and cinched it tight. His voice was flat.

"Let's go."

Simi moved first, scooting awkwardly with his hands bound. Kylo watched, impatience rising. The man was slow—too slow. Deliberate, maybe. A signal? Or just trying to get in Kylo's head.

Kylo reached over Remi and yanked Simi's arms upward in warning.

When Simi finally stepped out, he started forward—but Kylo hauled him back, hand hooked through his arms, voice firm.

"Keep it tight, Speedy."

Without another word, he slid out with Remi, keeping her close. Once clear, Kylo turned to a guard, positioning himself so Remi and Simi flanked him—acting as a buffer against any threat.

"Left a present in the trunk. It's hot—don't wait too long."

Remi turned her head, eyes locking on his, realization dawning. "My driver?"

Kylo nodded. "He'll have a headache, but he'll live."

They were led through the lobby, bypassing the usual security checkpoints. Kylo stayed watchful, eyes sweeping each corner, still surrounded by Remi and Simi. The elevator ride was brief and silent. When the doors opened, they faced a long, quiet hallway. They moved quickly, ushered into a large, enclosed room.

The door clicked shut behind them, and Kylo's eyes snapped to the man at the head of the table—a muscular blond man, confident, in command. Aldric. The CEO's seat was larger than the rest—clearly a statement. He didn't rise. He didn't offer pleasantries. His gaze swept over them, cold and calculating, measuring every detail.

The room reflected his control: clean, clinical, and organized. Whiteboards lined the walls, filled with neat columns and scrawled sections labeled "Observations," "Root Cause Analysis," "Options," "Timeline," and "Actions." The only decorative touch was the dark oak table at the center, like a pillar anchoring the room.

Aldric finally spoke, voice smooth and measured. "We run a complicated, interconnected city—power, water, sewage, food production, living environments, livestock, and more. You might have noticed the boards. This is where we troubleshoot. Any serious issue ends up here. With that said, I've just suspended operations and waived a major security policy for that gun you're holding. I believe I'm owed an explanation."

Kylo didn't answer right away. His eyes stayed locked on Aldric. Remi looked to him—no words, just a quiet prompt. He gave her a small nod.

"Go."

Remi turned to Aldric, her voice firm. "I believe Simi joined my staff at your recommendation."

Aldric's eyes flicked to Simi. "True."

Remi continued. "This other man is Kylo…" She motioned to him.

Kylo spoke up. "Cromley. Kylo Cromley."

Remi's voice held steady. "He's a park authority officer in D.C. As you may know, there was a double homicide near the Lincoln Memorial. Soon after, a family of three was murdered. Kylo believes Simi is connected to both."

Aldric looked at Simi, then to Kylo, his eyes sharp and piercing. "And what makes you think that?"

Kylo's tone didn't waver. "He matches a photo of the suspect."

Aldric leaned forward slightly. "Not standard to resort to kidnapping to solve a crime, is it?"

Kylo's jaw stiffened, but his reply was calm. "He tried to frame me. I believe he was hired by Avi Sweller—the man assigned to draw down the Mall's climate migrants. Avi, through Simi, planted my prints and DNA at the crime scene." Kylo pulled out the photo.

Remi's voice cut in, sharp. "You didn't say you had a photo."

Kylo shrugged. "Not much time for a full conversation in the limo. But if you look closely, it's Simi." He handed it to the senator, who studied it, then passed it to Aldric.

Aldric examined the image, his expression shifting almost imperceptibly.

Simi's face flushed, irritation rising. "What do you have—a crappy photo of some random guy? His nose is completely different."

Kylo's reply was cold. "Putty. Any costume shop has it. We ran it through facial recognition, which uses other landmarks—distance between eyes, contour of the lips—not so easily fooled. In fact," he added, "look at him under this light. You can still see faint numbers on his skin. Fourteen and eighty-eight."

Remi leaned in, narrowing her eyes, then turned toward Simi. "He's right. I see it. Simi, is this you?"

Simi scoffed. "I'm not the one with the gun. He's the threat."

Kylo added, "I'm sure if we collect a sample, we'll also find his DNA at each scene."

Remi turned to Aldric. Her voice was calm. "I believe the cop."

Aldric gave no outward reaction. Then: "Actually, so do I. Simi, I'll need to detain you. You'll get your chance to explain." He turned to Kylo. "Mr. Cromley, I understand your actions."

Kylo felt vindicated, relieved. "Thank you."

Aldric tapped his belt communicator. "Send three security guards at once."

Moments later, the door opened. Three guards stepped in. Aldric pointed to Simi.

"Arrest him. Take him to B2 staging. Replace the plastic cuffs with metal ones."

The guards hesitated, brows raised.

Aldric said sternly, "I'm not used to repeating myself, gentlemen."

The guards snapped into action, cuffing and leading Simi away.

"Hold on." Aldric turned to Kylo. "May I ask for your weapon, now that he's been secured?"

Kylo glanced at Remi. Her support steadied him. He handed over the Glock without a word. Two of the guards left with Simi. The door shut behind them.

Aldric's tone shifted. "I appreciate your cooperation. That'll make this much easier."

Remi straightened—Kylo could see she was thinking ahead. "Well, hopefully we just ferreted out a problem. I need to return to my office."

Aldric studied her, holding out a hand to signal her to stop. Then, with a darker edge: "Ma'am, do you know what this room is?" He stood for the first time.

Remi's voice was steady. "As you said—where you solve problems."

Aldric looked between them. "It's called the War Room. It's where we handle our biggest, most dangerous problems."

"I understand."

Aldric's eyes lingered on Kylo, then settled on Remi. "I don't think you do, Senator. You see, you and your new friend just became mine."

Kylo felt the air shift, colder now. This wasn't over. This was just the beginning.

Chapter 61: Luna

Luna and Zev left her sleeping quarters. Almost immediately, Zev, still clad in his blue smock, jerked her forward as if she were nothing more than a subordinate. A wave of nausea swept over her. Had she misjudged him? Was he just another cog in this merciless machine? Was his compassion all a ruse?

Zev gave nothing away. His voice snapped out at her, hard and mechanical above the factory noise. "Pick up that screw." Then, "Food pellet." He spoke as if she were nothing—just debris. The harshness in his tone felt practiced, almost second nature.

She scanned the floor and caught sight of another blue-uniformed worker nearby. After a beat, it clicked. This was a performance. She lowered her eyes and folded herself into the role of a compliant Orange.

Zev directed her with rigid authority, guiding her through a labyrinth of towering machinery and the relentless clang of metal on metal. The air was thick with the industrial bite of oil. He led her back to the supply room. Once the door closed behind them, Zev's shoulders sagged. The bark vanished from his voice, replaced by quiet concern.

"Are you okay?"

Luna threw her arms around him, her body trembling. The hug lingered, equal parts relief and fear. For an instant, he felt like home.

"Thank you for coming for me," she said, her voice low. "There's something terribly wrong here. The passengers—everyone—we've been stripped of our names. Reduced to numbers. We're treated like we're in prison. Worse." Her voice faltered. "I was told I'm not even a US citizen anymore. They threatened us. Said if we disobey, we'll get a red coat. What does that even mean?"

Zev's face darkened.

"Not a citizen? That's bullshit. But I agree—this place is rotten. We need to get out. Tell the FBI. Anyone." He dragged a hand through his hair. "God, I feel sick. I got you and everyone else into this."

Luna met his eyes, tears welling, her voice barely holding together.

"Zev… They took Karli."

His brows pulled tight.

"What the hell for?"

The pain hit her like a blow to the ribs. She opened her mouth, but no sound came. Zev gently placed his hand over hers.

"Don't worry. We'll find her."

Luna swallowed, steadying herself.

"She passed the genome test. I didn't."

Zev's expression snapped from confusion to fury.

"Fucking Carbon Laws—sorry. Where'd you last see her?"

"There's a level below us. B2, I think. That's where they process arrivals. It's brutal—communal showers, assessments, then immigration. But only for those who pass the genome test. That's where they separated us."

"Then that's where we start."

"There's an elevator near these mixers," Luna added.

Zev nodded, motioning for her to take the lead. As they crossed the main floor, he slipped back into the role of hard-nosed supervisor, his act now carrying a sharper edge.

Halfway across the floor, a blue-smocked worker stepped into their path, eyes narrowing at Luna.

"Where are you taking her?"

Zev didn't blink.

"This Orange left something near the mixers." He shoved Luna forward with enough force to make her stumble. The gesture was convincing. Ugly, but convincing. Luna bit down hard on her lip, jaw tight with rage.

The worker grabbed Luna's arm, scanning the numbers inked on her skin.

"Fine, but make it fast. She's a Q. Past curfew."

"I will."

"And knock that spirit out of her. I can see it in her eyes."

They moved on. When they were clear, Luna turned to face him.

"I appreciate the rescue and the improv, but the domination act? It needs to stop. You're a little too good at it."

Zev pressed a finger to his lips.

"I have to sell it. If they catch on, it's over."

Luna exhaled, some of her tension easing.

"I know you're trying. Just… not like that."

They continued in awkward silence until they reached the freight elevator. Zev glanced at it, visibly relieved.

"No cipher needed. Thank God. Let's move."

They stepped inside—walls of brushed steel, a faint chemical tang in the air. The hum of hidden motors rose as the elevator descended. Luna leaned against the cold railing, her mind racing: Karli's little face. The absurd green smock.

The elevator shuddered as they reached B2.

The doors slid open and Luna stepped out first, followed by Zev. They heard the doors close behind them.

Zev turned and muttered, "Damn, I did it again."

"What?"

"You can go down no problem. But getting back up? You need a cipher." He pointed at the keypad—a code was required to ascend.

They stepped into what looked like another open factory. But the air was different—more humid, tinged with something foul and sweet. She couldn't place it.

Then she studied it more closely—and froze. A conveyor belt, moving sluggishly, carried heavy, glistening chunks of red meat.

Zev scanned the machinery.

"This is a rendering plant," he muttered, eyes narrowing. "Those are grinders—" he nodded toward the machines, his voice dropping—"they chew up most everything. Meat, bones, organs. Very little is wasted."

He swallowed hard, his face drawn tight with disgust. "Makes me sick just thinking about it."

Luna's stomach lurched. The floor was slick beneath her shoes, red lights blinking in slow rhythm, accompanied by the relentless crunch of bone.

"This is awful."

Zev frowned.

"Close. Technically, it's called offal. O.F.F.A.L. Internal organs and entrails from slaughtered animals. It's efficient—less killing, more recycling. Usually it goes into pet food, but—" He scratched the back of his neck. "Pretty sure that's what they served me upstairs. Tasteless as hell."

"I had some too." Luna's voice was hollow, far away.

Zev shifted uneasily. "I don't want to stay here. Besides, we need to find the genome lab."

Luna added, "If we spot someone in green, we might be able to trace where they're being taken."

Zev nodded. "Good thinking."

They moved past the grinders toward the eastern end of the building. A concrete stretch led them deeper, heavy machinery pounding and gnashing around them. Luna quickened her pace. "Finally, I recognize this hallway. There—on the left. That's the genome lab."

She pointed. A few passengers were filing out, all wearing green smocks.

"They're still processing arrivals. We need to follow them."

Zev hesitated, scanning the area.

"No, Luna. We'll stand out. We're not in green. If they spot us, we're done. Let's look further down. Maybe we can find a laundry closet with smocks."

They continued, the roar of machinery fading as the corridors narrowed.

Then a voice barked from behind.

"Where's your number, Blue?"

Zev turned too fast—his reaction edged with alarm. A guard stood ten feet away, rifle slung across his chest, eyes flat and unreadable. A shadow of guilt crossed Zev's face, but his voice stayed firm.

"They didn't give me one."

The guard didn't move.

"We'll tag you later. Proceed to the next station."

"For what?"

The guard bared his teeth. "Sterilization."

Chapter 62: Kylo

Kylo and Remi stood stiffly as the guard tossed red coats into their arms. His voice was clipped, emotionless.

"Put these on."

Remi's lips pressed thin. She glanced down at the coat, then around the unfamiliar corridor. It was colder here. Darker. "Where are we? I was given a full tour of your facility—including B2. This wasn't part of it."

The guard flared his nostrils. "I'll ask once more. Put on the smocks. I won't ask again."

Kylo stepped forward before thinking better of it. His voice was calm, deliberate. "You do realize she's the Senator of Sustalia."

The response was instant. A rifle butt cracked against his chin, snapping his head back. Pain detonated through his skull. His tongue was caught between his teeth, and blood spilled into his mouth—warm and metallic.

He tested his jaw. Not broken. But every movement sparked fresh pain.

The guard reeled back, ready for another blow if needed. "Shut up and follow instructions."

Kylo swallowed the blood and his anger. Remi, stunned silent, slipped into the red coat. Kylo followed.

The guard gestured forward. "Walk. Straight down. Don't stop."

They moved through a corridor, each step echoing off the concrete and sterile walls. No signs. No sound but their footfalls. A hallway engineered to dehumanize.

Then, almost conversationally, the guard muttered, "Yeah."

Kylo turned toward him—reluctant to ask, yet wary of another blow if he ignored an order.

"Are you…"

But the guard wasn't looking at him; his hand was pressed to his ear. "We're on no-man's path now. Approaching Stage Eight."

A pause.

"Correct. They're in red."

Another pause. This time, a slight crease formed in the guard's brow—not irritation. Something closer to unease.

"The chamber's still in use. If you want these two alone, I'll need to clear the others back to staging."

A brief silence. Then a sigh.

"Copy."

He turned to them. "Keep moving."

Kylo locked eyes with Remi and noticed the shallowness of her breath. She hadn't spoken since the guard struck him. But he saw something he hadn't until now—fear.

They passed through a wide doorway into a bare room. Two signs hung on opposite walls:

"No talking."

The second sign read more like cruelty than instruction:

"Remain standing." There were no chairs.

The guard stopped beside them. His expression had turned grim. "We wait here."

Moments later, the door in front of them creaked open. A group shuffled in—maybe thirty of them. Each clad in red, each bearing the same sunken expression. Hollow faces. Mechanical movements. Their steps carried no will of their own.

Kylo watched them pass, unease mounting. Who were they? Survivors? Detainees? Test subjects?

The group disappeared back the way Kylo and Remi had come. Silence returned.

The guard motioned them forward into a vestibule. One wall was featureless; the other housed a single circular hatch—like a ship's porthole crossed with a vault door.

Kylo frowned. "What is this?"

The rifle butt smashed into his kidney. White-hot pain shot through his side. He staggered, gasping for the air that was punched from his lungs.

The guard pointed to the chamber.

"Get inside."

Remi went first, wordless. Kylo followed, one hand pressed to his ribs. As soon as he stepped through, the opening was sealed with a thud.

Inside, the air was stale, heavy. The chamber was smaller than it looked—metallic, barrel-shaped, cold as a tomb.

Remi broke the silence, her voice softer than before. "I'm sorry I didn't believe you sooner. I overlooked the signs with Simi—he was one of my most productive employees. And Aldric... I should have paid closer attention."

Kylo rubbed his side. "You've managed to surround yourself with sociopaths."

Her lips trembled. The veneer was cracking.

"Why put us in here? And those people we passed... who were they?"

"No idea." Kylo's voice was rough. "But I'd guess they came at your invitation. From the train. The mall in D.C. They looked like they've been through hell."

Remi scanned the chamber, jaw tight. There were no cameras. No vents. No clock. Just the echo of their own words.

Then a voice rang from a speaker mounted above, rich with static and smugness.

"Greetings once again, Senator."

Remi went still.

Kylo turned toward a small window in the steel wall. His stomach sank.

On the other side of the glass, two men stood side by side.

One of them was Aldric. That, Kylo expected.

The other—

Simi.

Unrestrained. Steely-eyed.

Watching them.

Chapter 63: Luna

The man in camouflage pressed the muzzle of his rifle into Zev's shoulder, shoving him forward into a stark, windowless room. Fluorescent lights buzzed overhead. A green-uniformed attendant looked up as the guard barked, "These two failed genome. Fix them."

Zev stiffened. "We don't need fixing. We're fine."

The guard's eyes narrowed. "Then it's extradition."

Zev scoffed. "Perfect. Get me the hell out of here."

The guard grinned, his lips peeling back in a way that made Luna's stomach flip. "No problem." He turned his head and called out, "Get me a red coat."

Before she could second-guess herself, Luna stepped forward, clasping Zev's arm, her fingers digging in—not in anger, but in warning. Her voice came out controlled. "He doesn't know the system yet. Downgrade him to orange. That'll make your point."

The guard looked her over, then glanced at Zev.

"Well, hotshot?" the guard said, his voice like gravel. "You listening to the smart lady, or am I putting you in red?"

Zev hesitated, then muttered, "...Fine."

Luna didn't expect the word to sting—she had urged him to agree. She'd made peace with not having children years ago, yet beside him now, that concession now felt heavier.

The guard seized Zev's arm and yanked him forward, then looked at the attendant. "Skipped numbering in batch processing somehow." He pulled a pen from his belt, then—pressing harder than necessary—marked Zev's forehead.

Zev flinched. "What the hell are you doing?"

Suddenly, an alarm blared. A voice crackled over the PA:

"Attention all Felicity residents. Guards, report to your stations. All others remain in assigned areas. Security is seeking a Caucasian male, six feet in height, with brown hair, late twenties, wearing purple. Name: Zev Brighton. Considered unpredictable and potentially dangerous. Last seen on the ground level. All color classes are eligible for reporting. Rewards apply. This is not a drill."

The message began to repeat.

The guard's expression shifted from smug to alert. Without a word, he bolted toward the elevators.

Zev stood frozen. "That's me they're looking for."

Luna looked around the room, then a thought struck.

"We need to keep moving. There aren't many greens down here. Karli's almost certainly in the city, outside Town Hall." She glanced towards the path they'd come from, tracing it with quiet calculation. "Those hoppers—we saw them carry animal by-products. Trucks must load them somewhere. A dock. That's our way out."

Zev blinked. "You're right. That's damn good reasoning."

Luna caught herself grinning, proud of herself. They retraced their steps, moving with caution. Then she smiled for a different reason.

Zev gave her a sideways look. "What could possibly be funny?"

Her grin widened. She pointed at his forehead. "The guard didn't number you. He marked you with a question mark."

Zev's eyebrows arched. "Seriously?"

"It makes you look a bit… simple."

He wiped at the mark. "Glad someone's kept their sense of humor."

"Still there," Luna said, shaking her head. "Just leave it. But don't ask me any questions."

"Haha."

They moved across the operations floor, ducking behind equipment, shadows stretching long under the industrial lights. Finally, they reached the rendering area.

Zev pointed. "There. Two massive hoppers. See the double doors behind them? That's where the haul is coming from."

They crept forward, stopping behind a low partition.

Without warning, the double doors burst open as a front loader trundled in, beeping harshly. It dumped its cargo into one of the hoppers—a slurry of bone, tissue, and gore—then wheeled around and drove back through the opening.

As the doors started to close, Zev lunged forward, wedging his foot between them just in time. Metal pressed against his shoe. When the loader disappeared, they slipped in.

Ahead was a second set of double doors. These were unlocked. They passed through.

What lay beyond froze them both in place.

The air was dense with bleach and blood—the iron tang so thick it burned. Luna gagged, swallowing down the bile rising in her throat.

They were inside the slaughterhouse.

Carcasses in various states of disassembly hung from hooks or sprawled across steel tables. Torsos were methodically segmented. Intestines slithered into labeled bins. Severed heads sat askew, their blank eyes open.

Zev stared, mouth open.

"They don't need a loading dock," he said quietly. "The meat just walks in on its own."

He swallowed hard.

"And it's not cattle."

Chapter 64: Aldric

Aldric had just received the alert about the missing visitor moments before it blared over the PA system. His reaction was instant—rage surged as he punched in his treasurer's number.

"What the hell, Varek? How'd you manage to lose him?"

The treasurer's voice crackled with nervous static. "I left him in the restaurant with instructions to stay put."

Aldric gave him no slack. "You know the rules. Visitors require an escort at all times. Which part of that don't you understand?"

Varek stammered. "I didn't want to raise suspicion. Hovering around him might've sparked rumors—rumors he'd take back to D.C. I was trying to protect our reputation."

Aldric's voice hardened to steel. "You know, a treasurer is merely an accountant—a word rooted in a larger principle: 'accountability.'"

He hung up without another word and called security. "Status on the missing guest?"

The reply was tight, strained. "No sign yet, sir."

Aldric scowled. "What's his name again? Sev?"

"Zev. Zev Brighton."

"Right," Aldric muttered. "Where's the Senator's driver?"

"Recovering in the lobby. He was locked in the trunk for quite a while—suffering from heat exhaustion."

"With an escort?"

"Yes, sir."

Aldric's tone eased slightly. "Good. Apprehend both Varek and the chauffeur. Assign red coats to each. Take them straight to the chamber. No detours. And keep me informed about our missing guest."

"The treasurer, sir?"

"You heard me."

"Copy that."

Aldric turned to Simi, standing by his side.

"Find this Zev Brighton. The situation is unraveling. I want him in the chamber too. I'll deal with the Senator. Move."

Simi dipped his head in a quick motion. "On it."

Aldric gave a curt nod back, and Simi vanished down the corridor.

Alone now, Aldric stepped toward the glass observation window and peered in at his two prisoners. He activated the intercom, his voice devoid of warmth.

"We've hit a slight delay, my uninvited guests. While we wait, allow me to explain your surroundings."

The Senator scoffed. "Now you explain, Aldric? I guess the private tour skipped a few details."

Aldric's lips curled into a humorless smile. "You've never understood what it actually takes to meet your lofty carbon goals. You talk a big game, but you've never had the will to act. I'm the one who made your vision real. Not a single thank-you."

Still defiant, Remi jabbed, "What do you want, Aldric—a medal?"

His voice dropped to a cold simmer. "Mayor would've sufficed. The system needs someone who gets things done—not more empty suits. If you'd created a post and backed my campaign, this operation could've scaled years ago. We'd be global by now."

He paused.

"But you were only ever focused on your own ambitions."

Remi's voice was steady. "I care about the planet, Aldric. But I care about humanity too. You've stripped that side out entirely."

"Tough times, tough decisions," Aldric replied. "You think you wrote the Carbon Laws? We spoon-fed them to you."

"So, what—Simi was your mole?" Remi said, eyes narrowing.

Aldric's tone turned smug. "Not just a mole. Simi is my COO. Embedding him on your staff was strategic. He kept you in line. His loyalty was never yours."

Remi's jaw clenched. "My real mistake wasn't failing to promote you—it was trusting you at all."

Aldric stepped closer to the glass. "You never saw the details. That's always been your blind spot. Even this chamber was chosen for a reason."

"What do you mean?"

"You're in a thermal vacuum chamber. Soon, the oxygen will drop. Suffocation. No mess."

Kylo, silent until now, spoke. "If you wanted us dead, you could've shot us. Why all the theatrics?"

Aldric's voice took on a clinical edge. "Because waste is inefficient. Bullets leave shrapnel. Poisons contaminate tissue. We don't waste—ever. We're carbon-negative. More efficient than anything you've dared to imagine." His eyes bore into Remi. "We gave you a platform, and you used it to step on us."

The Senator frowned. "How does killing me help your future?"

Aldric's expression didn't change. "You preach about overpopulation, remember? Each person adds roughly four tons of carbon emissions per year. But you're worse than most. All those motorcades, flights, secret indulgences—your exotic food stash. You've been a useful face, but now you're a liability. And liabilities get eliminated."

"You're evil."

"I'm efficient. Felicity is a prototype we'll replicate nationwide. We cull the weak. We reward strength."

Kylo sneered. "So you're a modern-day Hitler."

Aldric's face softened. "Hitler targeted race and religion. I don't care about either. My focus is genetic degradation. We've enabled the weak to thrive—defects spreading unchecked through the population. Tay-Sachs, sickle cell, Huntington's, Down's, cystic fibrosis... If your DNA shows signs of any of it, you're out."

Kylo's fists clenched. "You're playing God."

"Not God. Just honest." Aldric's voice stayed eerily calm. "The Earth can't support uncontrolled growth. My plan actually results in fewer deaths. It eliminates the problem before our resources are drained. As for your demise, you will continue to serve. A negative becomes a positive."

Remi hesitated. "How so?"

Aldric's tone dropped to something even colder than before. "Your body becomes food. Rendered into protein meal. No bullets. No toxins. Just... utility. Recycled."

Kylo muttered, horrified, "So we're long pigs now."

Aldric didn't recognize the reference and didn't care to ask. He glanced at his phone. "Ah. You're about to have company."

The vault door hissed as it unsealed. Two more figures were shoved inside—one clearly the chauffeur, the other unfamiliar. The Senator's face crumpled as she placed a hand on the chauffeur's shoulder.

"I'm so sorry."

The chauffeur shot Kylo a glare. "No thanks to him. Sucker-punched me. Still got a bump the size of a peach."

Aldric watched from behind the glass, expression unreadable—a man observing theater, not a crime. "If only I had popcorn," he murmured.

The Senator shook her head, disgusted. "You're enjoying this."

"Thankless work. One of the few perks."

Kylo turned to the newcomer. "Who are you?"

The man's voice was heavy. "Varek. Treasurer of Felicity."

Aldric's stare fixed on him like a vise.

"Accountability, Varek. Accountability."

Chapter 65: Simi

Simi began his hunt for Zev, the missing visitor's face still vivid in his memory from the train. He had watched the roundup worker from a distance, noting his conversation with the wanted woman featured in the news. There was a subtle pull between them. To Simi, she had earned a red coat—not only because she was a person of interest, but because she had stood her ground under pressure. Delayed on the train, he had missed her during selection. Had she been there, he would have sent her straight to the no man's land corridor.

Simi suspected that Zev had formed an attachment to the woman and was now searching for her. Instinct told him that wherever she was, Zev wouldn't be far. Her name escaped him for a moment, then resurfaced—Luna. To reach her, Zev would need to descend into the basement levels and bypass a couple of security checkpoints. But Simi knew that getting down was always easier than going up, especially with security focused on keeping the Morlocks buried below. No one marked red or orange was ever meant to reach the surface.

As he formulated a plan, Simi quickly realized he couldn't do it alone. He approached one of the men in camouflage.

"I want all production equipment shut down."

The man nodded. Simi studied the guard's gear before adding, "Give me your utility belt."

Now armed, Simi began a methodical sweep. He would clear each floor, starting with B2, and work his way upward. He followed the path of the train passengers, retracing each processing stage. Zev—and Luna—were now priority targets. As

Felicity's COO, Simi prided himself on knowing every corner of Town Hall and the grisly machinery that churned beneath it.

He passed through the observation deck and entered the first shower enclosure. Thirty naked bodies huddled on the cold tile floor, shivering. None fit the profile. He moved on to Stage Two—the blowers—then Stage Three: health assessment. Stage Four was inoculation. In each room, he barked at the guards, "Nobody leaves or enters unless I say so."

"Yes, sir. Good Earth, sir," they replied, mechanical and obedient. The assembly line had ground to a halt.

Simi moved west along the chain—Stage Five: aptitude and psychological screening, then the genome lab at Stage Six, until he reached immigration at Stage Seven. He knew those labeled red would be routed next to Stage Eight—the chamber—under Aldric's supervision. He skipped it. Instead, he advanced to rendering—Stage Ten—then circled back to the abattoir: Stage Nine.

Rendering was quiet. But just outside the abattoir, he spotted a group of orange-clad workers lined up under the watchful eye of a man in a blue smock. Simi's gaze swept the line, intense and fast, then landed on the supervisor.

"Anything unusual here?"

"Good Earth, sir. Nothing out of the ordinary."

Simi's good eye fixed on a set of double doors.

"Why is that door open?"

The man glanced at it. "I hadn't noticed, sir."

"That's Stage Nine. You were told to keep it sealed at all times."

The man's shoulders drooped. "I'm sorry, sir."

Simi knew the man had no idea what went on in there. He likely believed it was an animal slaughterhouse.

"Take me in."

The man hesitated. "Sir, I don't have the clearance."

Simi's voice turned to ice. "What did I say?"

The man flinched, body stiff with fear, and shuffled toward the doors. He stopped, a silent plea written across his face—hoping, praying, that he might not have to go through. Simi's shove sent him stumbling forward.

"Move."

He obeyed, each step heavy, as Simi followed close behind into the abattoir.

"Next doors."

The man opened them—and froze. His face drained of color, lips trembling. He sobbed quietly.

Simi's voice was flat, devoid of pity. "Remove your smock."

His hands shook violently as he obeyed, setting the clothes on a nearby table.

"Kneel."

He understood without question. Falling to his knees, he whispered a prayer, words choked with terror. Simi raised the cleaver and brought it down. Warm blood splattered across his shoes, dripping onto the smock laid aside. The man crumpled, lifeless. Without a word, Simi collected his clothes, unfeeling.

Returning to the orange-clad workers, he addressed them.

"This is your station. Know everything that happens here."

He tossed the blood-streaked smock at a random woman, fixing her with a menacing look.

"It's yours now. Mind it well."

He turned to leave, but a faint, almost imperceptible sound cut through the silence.

Simi froze—listening for any clue to locate its source.

Chapter 66: Luna

Both Luna and Zev had just returned from the abattoir, the reek of blood still seared into their sinuses.

Luna looked at Zev. "It all makes sense."

"What?"

"Batch. Their terminology. What they called us. And I ate some." She swallowed hard, forcing down the acid rising in her throat.

Zev looked down. "Oh God. Me too. We didn't know."

They both heard something in the distance and fell silent. A blond-haired man was confronting a blue-clad supervisor. Without a word, they dropped behind one of the hoppers, crouching low to watch. The man's words were harsh, cutting through the quiet as he marched toward the slaughterhouse with the supervisor in tow. Moments later, the blond emerged alone, a blue smock clutched in one bloodied fist. He returned to the group, berating the orange-suited workers with cold authority. It struck Luna at once—their leader was gone.

Zev watched the man with a strange intensity, eyes narrowed like he was trying to summon a memory. When he finally spoke, his voice barely carried, so Luna had to lean close.

"That's him. The one who killed Clive on the train. I'm sure of it. He's blond now, but that drifting eye…" His voice trailed off. "What do you think?"

Luna didn't answer immediately. Her stomach twisted, the coppery stench of the abattoir still hanging in the air like a curse. She'd worked in a hospital—but this was not triage or trauma. This was horror.

She tried to steady her breath. She swallowed hard. But the image of the kibble returned. The scent from the hopper surged again—and this time, it hit with force. Human remains. Not theory. Not metaphor. Real.

Her body revolted. A harsh retch tore from her throat before she could stop it.

The blond-haired man froze mid-gesture. His palm shot up— a clear command: silence. Even the machines, already powered down, seemed to obey. The entire factory was still. Luna did the same, praying her body wouldn't betray her again.

Zev moved at once, silent as a shadow. He reached into the hopper, pulled out something slick with red, and crept behind a loader truck. He hurled it far—away from them, away from the group.

On impact, the blond man turned toward the sound. Then he began moving in that direction, his steps slow, deliberate, predatory.

Luna clenched her jaw, willing herself to stay still. But the air— thick, foul, death-soaked—wrapped around her like a shroud. Her stomach heaved again.

From a distance, Zev held up a single finger to his lips. A silent plea: Don't.

Luna nodded, trembling, but another gag escaped. This time, louder.

The blond man stopped cold, head snapping toward the noise, his face taut.

Luna shrank back, then froze.

A gunshot rang out.

The bullet struck the hopper with a metallic clank. Luna flinched, the vibration rippling through her bones. Worse—a startled yelp broke from her lips.

Suddenly, he was there—looming above her, gun drawn, eyes wild. The Glock gleamed under the industrial lights, sleek and merciless.

"Gotcha. Where's your pal?" he growled.

Luna raised her arms slowly. She tried to steady her voice.

"Who? I just work here. Not sure who you mean."

"Don't insult me, Luna. You just got off the train. No one's assigned you anything yet." He pressed the barrel to her forehead. "Where is he?"

Luna was petrified, but tried to buy time. "Who are you?"

"Simi. The last person you'll ever see if you don't tell me right now." His voice was monotone, but sharp as glass. "Tick-tock."

Then she saw it—a shadow moving behind her assailant. She locked eyes with Simi.

"Okay," she said. "You're right. I know where he is."

Simi pressed the muzzle harder. "Well?"

Zev struck.

He crashed down on Simi's arm with all his strength. The gun flew from Simi's hand, spinning into the hopper. The two men collided—a savage blur of fists and fury. Strength met rage.

They toppled to the ground, panting, bloodied, neither willing to give an inch.

Simi spat onto the floor, never taking his eyes off Zev. "You fight well. But you're no hunter."

Zev called out. "We're not done."

"No," Simi said, rising slowly. "But you are. Unlike you, I know what it takes to survive. Only the fittest."

Simi staggered toward the hopper and hauled himself into the vat of human remains, plunging his hands into the grisly mass. It didn't take long before his fingers closed around cold steel.

"I'll make it quick." He aimed the gun at Zev, finger curling on the trigger.

Then the machinery roared to life.

Luna stood by the control panel, eyes locked on the dial. She had activated the corkscrew conveyor beneath Simi's feet. The machine obeyed.

The teeth churned into motion, locking onto Simi.

He screamed as the mechanism caught his boot, twisting flesh and bone. He tried to pull free—but it was too late. The conveyor dragged him inch by inch into its gnashing maw.

In desperation, he fired.

The bullet hit Zev in the thigh.

Simi howled. "Turn it off! Or I'll shoot again, in the heart."

Zev crawled beneath the truck, out of view. Luna didn't move.

"You can join the others," she said coldly, "in the dining hall. In a bowl."

She turned a dial.

The machine screamed, dragging Simi deeper into the gore. He thrashed and shrieked as metal chewed through flesh. His legs vanished. Then his hips. His screams dissolved into wet gurgles.

And then—silence.

Eventually, only scraps remained.

Zev pulled himself out from under the truck, blood soaking his pant leg, his face resolute.

"A slow, agonizing death. Serves him right."

She stood upright, fierce. "Serve, yes, as a meal. Bon appétit."

Zev looked at her with a mix of awe and concern.

Chapter 67: Luna

Luna stared at Zev, adrenaline cutting through her fatigue. She gripped his arm, steadying him onto the truck's side step. Then the truth hit—final, irrevocable. She met his eyes, lips parting, but no words followed.

He studied her face. "Are you okay?"

Her voice was quiet, hoarse. "I just killed someone."

Zev lifted her chin with a forefinger. "It was self-defense."

"But…"

"But what? You had to."

"There was a part of me that felt… satisfied." Her eyes dropped, the confession heavier than the act itself. "I didn't know I was capable of that. And the things I said… they were mean."

"You're finding a strength we'll both need if we're going to survive this. Don't doubt yourself now."

Her eyes dropped to his leg, shifting focus to anything else. "We need to take care of that wound. Let's get your pants off."

He arched a brow, lips forming a half-grimace. "No dinner first?"

She gave him a dry look, though a hint of warmth softened it. "I know what you're doing."

With grunts and winces, she helped him ease out of the pants. Once he was settled, Zev managed a faint smile.

"Can't say I didn't picture this… just under better circumstances."

Luna rolled her eyes, but a small smile escaped her. "Using humor to pull me out of this abyss. And yes—it's working."

She crouched to examine his leg, then nodded.

"The bullet went straight through—a clean exit. You're lucky. Another inch and it might've hit your femoral artery. Or worse."

She left him sitting and walked toward the group of orange-clad workers. "We need help. Something to clean his wound."

The Orange holding the blue smock spoke. "We have bleach."

"That'll work."

She hurried off and returned with a gallon jug. "We use it to clean up after an operation."

"Thanks." Luna walked back to Zev. "This is going to hurt."

She poured a few drops of bleach, using its cap, into the wound. Zev groaned, his face contorting in pain.

Luna removed her orange belt and wrapped it tight over the wound and around his thigh, now serving as a bandage.

"There. That'll slow the bleeding and keep dirt out."

She turned back to the workers and approached them. "Are you happy here?"

The response was instant—and unanimous: no.

An emaciated woman, late twenties, stepped forward. "We're prisoners. But we're afraid to fight back. Those who do disappear."

Luna studied her—the hollow cheeks, the faint quaver in her voice, the trembling hands barely able to stay still.

"When's the last time you ate?"

"We get two rations a day, but it's not enough. I've been here the longest, batch 'A', and you can see what happens over time." Two small black welts marred her temple.

"What about going outside?"

The woman broke down, her face crumpling, a sob catching in her throat. "None of us have seen the sun. Or the moon. Or smelled fresh air since we got here."

The room fell silent—thick, suffocating.

Luna hesitated. She didn't feel like a leader—just a mother searching for a child in a place that had forgotten mercy. Her voice wasn't practiced. Her hands still shook. But if she didn't speak, no one would. She stepped forward, drawing in a breath that steadied her shoulders and straightened her spine.

"They're starving you. Isolating you. Even high-security prisoners get time outside. You have a choice: fight for your freedom… or wither away down here. I'm not going to be part of it. I'm fighting. Who will join me?"

There was a long pause.

Then Zev, still seated a few yards away, spoke, his voice distant but resolved. "Count me in."

A tall, broad-shouldered woman shook her head. "I've seen people try. They were handed red coats and escorted out. We never saw them again. I'm out."

The silence returned—uneasy now—but then cracked.

The gaunt woman stepped forward again, voice trembling but steady.

"We'll die anyway. Look at me—I'm halfway there already. Let them give me another demerit. Death is better than this. They're starving us while we help them hurt others. I'm done being scared. I'm in. Even if I can't help much."

Luna's smile was small but sure. "You just helped more than you know."

Others volunteered, one by one, until only the tall woman remained.

She pressed her lips tight, then sighed. "Damn it."

She raised her hand. "I'm in too," she said, lifting her chin. "What, you think I'm gonna be left with all your work assignments? I'm way too lazy for that."

Strained laughter rippled through the group. Hands clapped her back. They gathered in a ragged hug, bound not by physical strength, but by shared suffering.

Then they turned to Luna.

She took a breath. "We outnumber the guards. They're posted near the exits on this floor. Before we move, we need numbers. First target is B2. Then we push upward, one level at a time. Eventually we deal with the perimeter wall."

She scanned the room. "Who here has military experience?"

A young, gangly man stepped forward. "Good Earth, ma'am. Four years in the army."

Luna's expression darkened. "First off—don't ever say 'Good Earth' again."

He nodded quickly. "Right. Sorry. Yes. I can help."

Luna studied him. "What does your training suggest?"

"If it's numbers you want, we need structure. Squads of six. Each with a leader and a chain of command. We move in waves. Overwhelm them before they can respond."

Luna nodded. "Good. Focus on recruiting. Anyone who's willing—red, orange, blue. Even green, if they'll stand with us. Smock color means nothing now."

"Understood. I'll build a platoon."

She looked at the group. "In the meantime, I'm going to find another way out. I'll be back."

She returned to Zev. "Ready?"

He'd managed to pull his pants back up over the bandage. He gave a half-salute. "Yes, General."

She grinned. "Believe me, I'm surprising myself."

They retraced their steps toward the slaughterhouse. The air grew thick again—the scent of bleach mingling with the metallic stink of blood.

Zev leaned into her, arm wrapped over her shoulders for support. Inside, they moved carefully—eyes alert, nauseated at the gore still smeared across the floor.

Zev paused near the place where the blue leader had fallen, bracing himself against the wall.

"Luna. You need to see this."

She moved to his side. "A door?"

"No—a window. And it's not good."

Through the glass was a small chamber. Inside, four people struggled for air, hands pressed over their ears.

Luna's voice dropped. "That's the state Senator. They're suffocating."

Zev scanned the area, spotting a forklift.

"I can break it by ramming the glass, but it'll be dangerous."

Luna's eyes narrowed. "Why?"

"It's like a plane, but in reverse—the pressure is lower inside. Hit it hard enough, the glass blows inward, shards everywhere."

She nodded, jaw set. "If we don't do this, they're dead anyway."

Zev climbed onto the forklift. The machine buzzed to life. He rolled forward, fork raised to glass height. The first hit cracked it.

Inside, one man threw himself over the Senator, shielding her.

Zev reversed, then slammed forward again. The second hit—harder—and the pane gave way with a deafening crash.

The glass exploded inward, shards spraying the chamber like tiny knives. Blood spattered the walls. The man shielding the

Senator took the brunt—badly hit. Another was cut deep at the neck.

Then Luna saw it—through a second window on the far side, outside the chamber.

The man from the posters.

Aldric.

His voice spilled from a nearby speaker—unguarded, unfiltered.

"Simi. Simi, report. Simi, come in."

Then realization struck: Aldric's tone hardened, panic shifting into anger.

"Security. Station Nine, now. I've located our visitor. He's not alone. The fugitive has help. Approach with caution."

He drew his weapon and vanished from view.

Chapter 68: Luna

Aldric had disappeared, so Luna raced to the portal. She spun the wheel hard until the lock gave way with a metallic clunk. The heavy door creaked open, revealing the trapped survivors inside.

Luna entered the chamber and dropped to her knees beside the Senator as Zev rolled a man off her, leaving him on his back. He was injured but conscious.

"Are you all right?" Luna asked, scanning Remi's face.

"I'm fine," Remi replied breathlessly, then nodded toward the bleeding man beside them. "Thanks to my chauffeur. I owe him everything."

Luna leaned in. "Ma'am, I'm Luna. We're fighting for our freedom. Judging by your red coat, you're with us?"

Remi's eyes were heavy with fatigue, but a spark of resolve lingered. "I don't condone any of this. Tell me how I can help."

"Who are the others?"

Remi rested her hand on another man's shoulder. "This is Kylo Cromley. Park Police officer from D.C. Framed for the Mall murders."

Luna scanned him—nonfatal wounds, glass in his arms. Then her eyes landed on another.

"And him?"

"Varek," Remi said quietly. "City treasurer. Crossed Aldric."

A deep shard was embedded in his neck. Luna checked for a pulse… there was none.

A mechanical whir buzzed across the room. The opposite portal wheel began to turn.

Luna sprang up. "We need to move." Pointing at Varek, she added, "Leave him—he's gone."

They all exited, supporting the chauffeur's arms over Kylo and Remi's shoulders. Once out, Luna spun the wheel and sealed the chamber behind them.

Moments later, Aldric entered the very chamber they had just left—only to face a locked door. The broken window was far too small for him to climb through.

Luna let out a breath. "There's no release from inside. We just bought some time."

She turned to Kylo, looking up at his height. "Which Mall murder was the senator referring to?"

"A couple and their son," he said.

Her stomach dropped. "I was there. Slept in their tent. It was…" She blinked hard. The scalp outside still haunted her.

Kylo gritted his teeth, pulling glass from his arm. "I know who did it. Works for Aldric. Name's Simi Kremna."

Zev's face twisted in recognition. "Lazy eye?"

Kylo nodded.

"Well, he's burger meat now. Got caught in the cutter."

Kylo's lips thinned. "Then that's one less monster. Just wish I'd seen it."

Remi turned to Luna. "The Carbon Laws were supposed to advance us forward. But—" Her voice cracked. "This is evil. Aldric's twisted everything."

Luna remained focused. "Kylo—you're a policeman. We need someone to secure this floor. Can you help? Lead even?"

He hesitated, hands shaking slightly. Then he straightened. "I've seen some horrific things. But never like this. I'm in."

Luna glanced upward, mind racing. "There's an Army guy in orange. Young, military. He's recruiting others. Find him, build a force so we can take B2."

She turned to Remi. "Senator, you and your driver should go with Kylo." She pointed. "Through those doors—it leads to the rendering station."

Remi looked Luna up and down, then glanced at Zev. "I like her fire."

They helped the chauffeur to his feet and disappeared down the hall, leaving the bloodstained abattoir behind.

Luna turned to Zev. "We need to find a way out of the Town Hall."

Zev scanned the room. His eyes fell on a door. "There."

She approached and rattled the handle. "Locked."

Zev climbed into the forklift, waved her to move, and rammed it. After a few more strikes, the door cracked, splintered, and collapsed.

Luna walked through the wreckage into a tunnel—broad enough for two trucks. It curved west, vanishing into black.

Zev wedged the forklift in the hole, leaving himself enough room to slide out the front. "That'll slow them down." He pocketed the key.

Luna's gaze was fixed ahead. "Can you walk?"

"I'll need a shoulder."

He draped an arm around her. Together, they stepped into the dark. Footsteps echoed in the hollow tunnel.

Zev smirked. "Arm in arm. Just like I pictured it."

Luna rolled her eyes, but a smile crept in. "Keep moving, Romeo."

"Headstrong. Like the senator said."

His weight pressed into her, heavy but familiar. She didn't mind. His humor kept the horror at bay. She needed it.

The tunnel opened into a vast underground field.

Zev glanced around. "Like Luray Caverns, just without the charm."

Ahead, a worker in green operated a giant auger. He hadn't noticed them. They ducked behind an idle front loader.

Nearby, a backhoe dumped soil into a truck. Two mounds flanked a pit—one brown, one stark white.

"What is this?" Luna whispered.

Zev's face darkened. "I'm guessing it's a mass grave. Waste from the plant—clothes, hair, bones. Dumped, packed, buried."

"The white pile?"

"Probably lime. For decomposition."

A beam of light pierced the tunnel behind them.

Luna tensed. "Aldric. He's coming."

Zev scanned the open space. "There's no cover—just holes."

Luna whispered, "Still got that purple smock?"

"Yeah. Why?"

Her eyes lit with a plan. "We're going to pull the rug out from under him."

Chapter 69: Aldric

Aldric ran down the tunnel, flashlight in hand, lungs burning in the dusty air. Behind him, in the chamber, lay the treasurer's corpse—an end that disappointed. The man was meant to choke... slowly. Instead, he bled out on the floor, throat torn open by broken glass. Sloppy. Wasteful. Much too fast.

Even more upsetting, it wasn't his kill.

And worst of all—he had seen them. His fugitives. Slipping out of the abattoir. Escaping. In his own facility. Within a system he had designed. A design that now betrayed him. That stung.

They would pay.

He kept running, steady and intent. The tunnel bent ahead— long, empty. No signal. No communication. Just him, with no reinforcements.

They were getting away.

Aldric forced a breath through his teeth, clearing his thoughts. He couldn't let them reach the city. Beyond it stood only the perimeter wall.

Relying on the wall made his stomach turn. Not because he doubted the guards, but because he hated the idea of depending on them. The wall was built to keep threats out—not to trap those already inside. He needed to act. Now. Seconds were slipping away.

Jaw set, eyes honed to razor slits, Aldric continued forward, flashlight jittering with each stride.

At last, the tunnel ended at the landfill. Even to Aldric, the sight held the bleak charm of a coal mine—dirt, dust, and workers moving with robotic drudgery. He strode across the open ground toward the first dump truck, every step of not seeing them a heightened notch of frustration and anger.

Without pause, he approached the driver's window, face cut from stone.

"Did you see anyone come from the tunnel?" he asked, voice clipped and icy.

"Good Earth, sir. No," the driver stammered, straightening. "But I just got back from hauling dirt."

Aldric glanced into the truck bed.

Empty.

Without another word, he crossed the field, heading for another vehicle. He repeated the question to the woman in the cab. Her answer was casual, unconcerned.

"Nope. Not a soul."

"How long has this bed been filled?" Aldric asked, scanning the heap like a predator sizing up his prey.

The woman blinked, her demeanor shifting as she realized who stood at her window. "Good Err—"

"HOW LONG, I ASKED?"

"Ten minutes ago. It's just excess, Sir. I'm waiting on the green light to haul it out of the city."

Aldric's brow furrowed, patience wearing thin. "You sure it's just dirt? No one hiding in there?"

"In the dirt?" She frowned. "I don't think so. I'd have noticed."

He didn't like her words. "Think? I want certainty. Grab a shovel. Check for stowaways."

She jumped out, fumbling for a spade near the truck.

"Report back if you find anything unusual," Aldric said, already turning away.

The landfill stretched before him—a grid of holes punched into the ground forming a matrix, some capped, others black and open. He couldn't afford to miss a single one.

Aldric began down the first row, mind calculating the pattern that would ensure he checked them all efficiently. He shined his flashlight into the first shaft—only darkness. Empty. A vertical grave. No place to hide. He moved to the next, then the next. Some filled, others waiting for a load. He ignored the packed ones—dead ends. Irrelevant.

Then—something.

He noticed one of the openings ahead. It tugged at his instincts. Breaking his pattern, he veered toward it. A smock.

Neon purple. Hanging over the edge like a careless flag.

Unmistakable. Other coats ringed the rim, forming a crude, thoughtless fringe.

A spike of satisfaction lanced through him.

This was it.

He stepped onto the fabric, leaned forward, flashlight slicing through the shadows below.

There they were. Looking up at him.

Trapped.

His fugitives.

Perched atop the rubble, barely ten feet down.

He nearly drew his weapon. One shot. End it. But no—why waste the protein? They looked unarmed.

Aldric allowed himself a quiet, amused breath. "And here I was worried. I can't imagine a more juvenile hiding place. Pitiful, really."

They didn't answer. No sound. No motion. Just stares.

Then, without warning, they yanked on the purple smock.

Hard.

The coat slid out from under his boots.

Aldric lost his footing—slammed sideways, crashing hip-first onto the pit's edge. Pain exploded through his side as he tumbled in, barely missing a jagged rock.

Zev towered over him now, coat still in hand. The trap had worked.

Aldric's weapon was gone.

Luna followed, crouching beside the rock his head had nearly struck. She grabbed it with both hands, lifting it above him—calm, certain, brutal.

Aldric lay on his back, stunned.

Zev bent down next to her, grinning. "You, young lady, are not only beautiful—you're brilliant." He kissed her forehead.

Luna smiled, the compliment received without flinching, her voice steady despite the rot beneath their boots.

"Thank you, Zev."

Then she turned her full attention to Aldric, crouching over him, eyes burning.

"I'd like to offer you an alternative to death," she said.

Zev was beside her, pistol now in hand.

"But it's the only one you're going to get."

Chapter 70: Kylo

A woman in orange stepped forward to face Kylo. Her jumpsuit was streaked with solvent and grime, a stained bandage wrapped around her left hand. "There's a door up ahead that only Greens use—after Stage Seven. I've never been inside. Once they go in, we never see them again. It might be a way out."

Kylo nodded. "We'll follow you."

She led the surge of mostly orange-clad workers toward the door until they bunched in front of it. Kylo took a deep breath, then pushed it open.

The space beyond felt out of place. Leather chairs. A polished conference table. Warm lighting filled a room faintly scented with vanilla. A side table held coffee and tea dispensers, small plates of fruit and pastries, and a basket of metal utensils. It looked like a boardroom airlifted from another world.

On the far end, two guards stood tense on either side of an elevator, hands twitching near their rifles.

Some rebels in the group had no weapons and quickly seized the butterknives to arm themselves.

They were outnumbered. Over thirty workers now crowded behind Kylo, some climbing onto the table, armed with anything they could carry—wrenches, paint rollers, even a bucket of bleach. Tension crackled in the air like static before a storm.

Kylo stepped forward, voice calm yet commanding. "You've got the guns. But we have the numbers. Set your weapons down on the floor, and I give you my word—you'll be treated fairly. If you don't, you might shoot me and a few others… but it won't end well for you. Surrender now, and no one has to get hurt."

The guards stood frozen—caught between their fear of the mob and their fear of Aldric.

Then Remi stepped forward, her voice steady and firm. "Gentlemen. I'm Senator Remi McCarthy. I strongly recommend you do as he says."

The taller guard eyed her with suspicion. "If you're really McCarthy, why are you in red? For all we know, you're a Morlock pretending to be her. We've only seen her on screens."

A hot flush rose to Remi's cheeks. Not shame—fury.

She opened her mouth to respond—

But a man from the back pushed forward, voice raw with rage. "You think we won't charge? We've been starved down here. We've watched our friends vanish—you think we don't know you're killing them? Disgraceful."

He stepped up and jabbed a finger into the shorter guard's chest. The guard panicked.

His rifle went off, point-blank.

The second guard fired too, aiming at Kylo—but missed. The bullet sang past Kylo's ear, grazing his hair, and struck the woman who'd led them—she was still standing on the table behind him.

She crumpled with a painful cry, clutching her shoulder.

Screams erupted. The room detonated into chaos.

The workers surged forward in a wave of orange, overwhelming the guards and dragging them to the floor. It was over in seconds.

Kylo grabbed the rifles, checked the chambers, and handed them to the front line. "Now we've got something to fight with."

The man who had initially confronted the guard lay dead, a bullet through his chest. No one even knew his name, just his number. He hadn't hesitated—he'd just snapped.

The injured woman was luckier—still breathing. She slumped in one of the leather chairs, face pale and drawn, blood soaking her sleeve.

Kylo crouched beside her. "We'll patch you up. You'll be fine."

She gave the smallest nod.

He stood, surveying the room—and the people. Not a soldier by training, but he thought like one now. There was no choice.

"Yeah," he muttered. "This'll do just fine."

He scanned the room. This was war, and they needed leadership. Everyone looked to him—as did Remi.

Chapter 71: Luna

Luna climbed out of the landfill hole first, using Aldric's back as a stepladder. Aldric was down on all fours, Zev's gun pressed to his temple. Zev followed, and only then was Aldric helped out from above. Luna looked at Zev, a hollow pit still in her stomach.

"I need to find Karli. She's somewhere in the city. I'll need a green smock."

Zev's eyes skimmed across the barren field.

"There's a woman shoveling dirt over there, in green. Let's make ourselves known."

Aldric led the way reluctantly, an unwelcome third wheel. They crossed the field toward the truck driver. She glanced up, pausing her work as dirt slipped from her shovel. Fatigue showed in her face as she addressed Aldric.

"No one found in the pile yet, sir. I'll keep digging."

Aldric's sneer cut the air.

"They're right here, stupid."

The woman froze, eyes wide, catching sight of Zev's gun aimed at Aldric's back.

Luna's voice was calm, controlled.

"I'm gonna need that smock."

The driver glanced at Aldric, who gave a curt nod.

"You heard her."

They exchanged clothing without a word—green for orange. As the woman changed, Aldric couldn't hold back his fury.

"Not once did you look up—no awareness, no instinct. If you'd seen what was happening, maybe you could've raised the alarm. When this is over, red's your new color. A Turnip, in fact."

The woman's eyes glistened with tears.

Luna stepped forward.

"What's a Turnip?"

The woman whispered, "A Red. But one who's worked before disposal. Comes from 'can't get blood from a turnip.'"

Luna's foot slammed into Aldric's groin with brutal force.

"You can assume your new colors are black and blue."

He collapsed, gasping. Zev grabbed her arm before she could strike again.

"Easy."

Luna whirled on him, voice rough.

"He's a killer. God knows how many."

Zev's voice remained steady.

"I get it. That's what the judicial system is for. Otherwise, we're just vigilantes. Focus—Karli's out there."

The name pierced through her rage. Luna turned back to Aldric.

"Where are they keeping her?"

Aldric groaned, doubling over before straightening slowly.

"Probably in the nursery. But they won't just hand her over. Guards are posted at every observation tower along the perimeter. You've got no shot. If you really care about that kid living a full life... you'd stop now. Surrender. It's what's best for her."

Luna kicked him again, harder this time. He crumpled.

"What's best for her is a mother." She glanced at Zev, sheepishly.

"Sorry."

Zev stared at Aldric, writhing in the dirt.

"He's right about one thing—we're outnumbered and outgunned. One weapon isn't much."

Luna hesitated, then nodded.

"I'm going alone. You stay here and watch him. Bringing him will only draw attention and ruin everything."

Zev frowned.

"Then let me go instead."

"Absolutely not. I'm her guar..." An unmistakable change overwhelmed her.

"Mother."

Zev paused, smiling, then held out his gun.

"Then take this."

Luna shook her head.

"No. Two reasons. One—you need it to keep him under control. Two—if I show up in green carrying a gun, I'll get shot before I speak. I need to blend in, look harmless. If they catch me, maybe you can use him as leverage."

Zev looked at her, the awe unmistakable in his expression.

"I misjudged you. You're stronger than I thought. You get fiercer every moment."

Luna glanced away, voice low.

"I'm surprising myself."

He whispered,

"Don't be long."

To her surprise, he stepped closer and pulled her into his arms. She didn't resist. Her hand pressed against his chest, steady and strong beneath her palm. His lips touched hers—brief, almost hesitant—but the jolt of it surged through her, leaving her breathless. The danger around them didn't vanish, but for that instant, it no longer mattered. When he drew back, she was left smiling faintly, eyes on his, unable to find her voice.

Luna walked to the truck, steps uneven, a tentative smile tugging at her lips.

But as she drove away, clarity settled over her like a cold wave. The odds were stacked against her, and she knew it.

The truck rumbled through the tunnel. Exhaustion clouded her senses, warping the world into something unreal. Ahead, a pale light marked the tunnel's incline. Two guards flanked the exit but didn't spare her a glance. She passed through the gate and into the walled city.

She parked in a small lot at the city's northwest edge and stepped out. The rest would be on foot.

Luna walked beside the paved road, eyes fixed on the perimeter wall. Every tower was manned, weapons aimed outward.

That was their vulnerability.

The city stretched before her. She'd imagined quaintness— stone cottages, thatched roofs, trees, and fields. Reality was far colder.

Boxy white houses, more like a trailer park, stretched in every direction, windowless and identical. Solar panels covered every roof.

Efficiency had stripped away any charm.

Steel turbines spun overhead, humming a harsh lullaby. The city felt industrial—sterile, more prison than sanctuary. Luna saw now that Felicity's design mirrored its ethos: minimalism instead of character. Vanilla instead of the other thirty flavors.

Adjusting to the monotony, she passed modular buildings— each interchangeable, able to become a school, a store, a home, or a nursery.

People in green moved around her—carrying groceries, jogging in sweats. Then she spotted it: a woman cradling a baby, crossing from Town Hall into another building. No knock.

That had to be it.

Luna followed, heart hammering. She hesitated at the door, then pushed it open.

The woman inside screamed.

Luna froze, hands raised in apology.

"I'm so sorry! I thought this was the nursery—I didn't mean to scare you."

The woman's tension eased.

"You startled me. But I don't know why—it's a crime-free city." She smiled. "You must be new. Come in on the last train?"

Luna nodded, it was actually true.

"Yes."

"Congratulations. Makes sense you're confused. Everything looks the same. The nursery's just two doors down."

Relieved, Luna hurried out. She found the right building and opened the door. The crying inside confirmed it.

A man behind a desk looked up.

"Hello. May I help you?"

Luna's voice was steady, measured.

"I'm here for Q25."

Chapter 72: Kylo

Kylo welcomed sharing command—Remi had proven more than capable. No one questioned her authority or resolve. For Kylo, this wasn't just about getting free. He carried the weight of his family's fate on his shoulders. He wanted control over his own destiny—and he intended to shape the course of a war he believed was inevitable.

He pointed to the dead man and instructed two young men in orange, his voice low but firm: "Take this poor soul out of the room. Find a respectful place to lay his body. Wrap him carefully."

Then he turned to the small crowd that had gathered. "Does anyone here have medical experience?"

A brunette in blue raised her hand. "I used to be a nurse."

"Good. If you're willing, get her"—he pointed to the woman with the bullet wound in her shoulder—"to the supply room. See if you can cobble together a bandage with what's on the shelves. If she can't walk, get help—grab a couple of people, maybe use one of these rolling chairs."

The nurse nodded and moved toward the wounded woman.

Kylo's eyes dropped to the two guards, still restrained on the floor. He addressed the men holding them. "Let them go."

They hesitated, glancing at each other.

"Not to free them," Kylo clarified. "For their camo and gear."

The men stepped aside, allowing the guards to strip off their uniforms. A minute later, the two stood in their underwear, pale and uncomfortable.

Kylo, once a master at diplomacy, now found that intimidation cut straighter and deeper. He stepped in close to the shorter guard, invading his space until his face hovered inches from him.

"We just sustained our first casualty because of you," he said, his voice low, teeth clenched. "Don't say I didn't warn you."

He turned, repeating the same stance with the taller man. "I said there would be consequences."

Then he stepped back and addressed the men in orange.

"Walk this scum to rendering—Stage Ten. Through the double doors, you'll find an abattoir. Brace yourselves."

His stare grew cold. "When you reach the chamber, lock them in with the corpse. If they resist, shoot them."

He looked the guards dead in the eye. "The body waiting inside is your treasurer. Your leadership is crumbling."

Without another word, the prisoners were marched away.

Kylo turned back to the conference table, his mind already racing. He yanked down a large orientation poster from the wall— a schematic of the building. He knew it was incomplete. The diagram concealed more than it revealed.

He spread it out flat. It showed the layout of Town Hall, its rooms and functions. Several sections—mostly on B2 and L2— were marked "restricted."

Kylo scribbled in a blank space near the chamber where the dead treasurer lay, then handed the marker to Remi. "Senator, you said you were given a tour. I need you to fill in every inch of this building you remember."

Looking up, he addressed the rest of the room. "Once she's done, I want everyone else to add what's missing—anything you've seen, heard, or guessed." He took in the surroundings, feeling a quiet satisfaction. "This room will now serve as our command center."

After a brief pause, his eyes swept over the group once more. Then, simply: "One last thing—I'll need paint."

Chapter 73: Luna

The man behind the desk in the Nursery fixed Luna with a scowl. "Who are you, and why do you want this new resident?"

Luna had rehearsed this since the moment she left the truck. She kept her voice steady. "The baby missed her inoculation during onboarding. It's mandatory before any transfer."

His frown deepened. "Never heard of that. Where did you come from?"

"Immigration. I was sent to retrieve her."

He sneered, suspicion heavy in his tone. "By whom? You have no authority here."

"By our CEO, Aldric Heister." Luna's fingers edged toward the phone on his desk. "He left me his number in case of resistance."

His eyes narrowed. Then his hand shot out, covering hers. "Hold on. What's the child's ID again?"

"Q25."

He snapped, "You mean Q0025."

She blinked, masking her confusion. "Of course."

His fingers hammered the keys. "Alright, yeah. Little girl, about a month old. How long will this take? Her foster family is expecting her soon."

Luna forced calm. "You do realize they're still processing train passengers? The backlog's hours long. I can't say. I'll return after she's had her shot."

He grunted, then disappeared behind swinging doors. Luna braced, half-expecting the sound of security's boots on the wooden floor. But he returned, holding the baby with stiff arms, still trying to assert control. "Be quick. We've got piles of paperwork to get her registered as a Sustalia citizen."

For the second time, it was pointed out that Sustalia wasn't part of the United States—and Luna didn't think that was an accident.

She took the child carefully, fighting the urge to cradle her and smother her in kisses. She walked out as if Karli was just another cog in the machine—a machine that sifted and filtered the unfit through a cold genetic sieve.

Once clear, Luna quickened her steps. She climbed into the truck, then finally let herself collapse, cradling Karli and releasing the breath she hadn't realized she'd been holding. Tears slipped down her cheeks—tears of relief and raw joy.

"Hello, beautiful." She brushed her cheek with her hand. "Did you miss me?"

A tiny curl of a lip and a gentle squirm felt like an answer. Luna's hands moved carefully, inspecting her from scalp to toes. "You're perfect." She pressed Karli close, inhaling the soft, warm scent that anchored her in this hostile city. Or country.

She tucked Karli low beneath the dash, wrapped in a blanket to prevent her from rolling, and kept her hidden from any wandering eyes. Then she started the truck toward the tunnel.

But as they neared the checkpoint, anxiety coiled in her chest. The scene had changed—sleek SUVs blocked the entrance, and armed guards moved forward with clear intent to stop her.

Instead of slowing, Luna slammed the accelerator. The dump truck shuddered as it clipped two vehicles, metal scraping against metal with a harsh screech. One SUV lurched sideways, tipping over with a thunderous crash, its wreckage tumbling onto the road and forming a jagged blockade behind her. Dust and exhaust fumes choked the air as Luna's heart hammered in her chest. The only thing on her mind was reaching the fields.

Steam hissed from under the hood. The radiator was shot.

Figures I'd end up with a combustion engine—everything else is electric.

She slowed as she approached a narrow pass and dumped the truck's dirt load to form another barrier.

Finally, she reached the clearing where Zev waited. Relief flooded her chest.

He was there—alongside Aldric and the woman whose smock she had still worn.

Luna jumped out, cradling Karli like treasure. The three embraced tightly, Luna weeping into Zev's arms, oddly feeling safe.

Zev's voice steadied her. "Let's head back inside. We've got a lot to do." He raised his weapon at Aldric. "Move, you two."

Aldric and the driver walked ahead. Luna and Karli lagged behind, crossing through the field to avoid other workers.

"I don't know how you did it," Zev said, "but I'm glad you're back. I was worried. Still not sure how we're going to get out of this mess."

Aldric sneered. "Well, if you keep stumbling across idiots like this driver, maybe you'll manage."

For the first time, the driver spoke up. "I'm not the idiot. You're the one who lost track of them, not me."

Aldric snapped, "They escaped because of another fool—our treasurer. He's dead now, by the way, and soon you'll join him."

Suddenly, Aldric vanished—his body slipping into a hole.

A soft voice murmured mockingly, "Oops."

The driver stood still, arms folded. She had pushed him.

They rushed to the edge and shone a light into the pit. Aldric was wedged about fifteen feet down, the shaft continuing deeper beneath him. His body was grotesquely contorted—head bent to his knees, one arm twisted behind his back. He grunted, his breath shallow and labored.

The driver shrugged. "He earned that. Right?"

"Help," Aldric wheezed. "I can't move my arms or legs. Get a rope—hoist me out."

Zev looked at Luna. "We don't have much time. What do you want to do?"

From below: "That bitch pushed me."

Luna turned to the driver. "How deep is that hole?"

"More than a hundred feet."

Luna eyed her. "I'm guessing he hired you for a job?"

The driver nodded. "I fill the holes with waste from the abattoir."

Luna turned to Zev. "I think we let the lady do her job."

She took Zev's hand and began walking briskly toward the Town Hall, Karli held tight in her other arm. They were nearly to the tunnel when curiosity made them turn for one last look.

A dump truck hovered above the hole.

Its bed tilted.

Waste poured in, smothering the CEO's final cries.

Chapter 74: Kylo

Kylo ascended the stairs from B2 to B1, fully armed, his movements slow and deliberate. The next objective was clear: take B1, lock it down, and continue the climb.

As they met guards along the way, most dropped their weapons the moment they saw the Senator. The few who resisted didn't last long—they were quickly overpowered. Rebel losses were minimal.

Kylo watched as their improvised force grew, swelling with each surrendered weapon and every narrow victory. Momentum was on their side.

By the time B1 was secure, an orange-clad fighter ran up, breathing hard. "The B2 chamber is packed with prisoners—cramped—they've barely any room to breathe, let alone sit."

Kylo felt a shift inside him—cold and calculating. No sympathy, just clarity. His words tasted bitter as they left his mouth. "Let them rot. Karma has sharp teeth."

Just then, the young man tasked with recruiting fighters approached, flanked by squad leaders, his pride barely contained.

"Sir, we're now over a hundred strong."

Kylo nodded. "You did well, son."

The young man hesitated. "There's… been a request."

Kylo raised a brow. "Go on."

"We'd like to call ourselves 'Citizens.' If that's alright. It'll keep morale up. We refuse to be called 'illegals.' Or worse—Sustalians."

Kylo allowed himself a rare smile. "That's the perfect moniker. We'll adopt it."

The recruit's face lit up. "We've organized into eight squads—two platoons. We're ready to function as a company under your command."

Kylo paused, then said, "We have much more than just weapons and numbers."

The young man blinked. "What do you mean, sir?"

Kylo looked over at Remi. "We have the Senator."

The recruit smiled. "True enough. What's our next move?"

Kylo glanced around. "We're buried underground. Like coal miners after a collapse."

He muttered, half to himself, "Morlocks... I get it now. Living beneath the earth, eating human flesh, like in *The Time Machine*."

Nearby soldiers traded confused looks, but Kylo's focus quickly shifted.

"I don't want them watching us."

He turned to the recruit. "Disable the security cameras. Paint them, smash them—I don't care how. I want every lens blind."

"Understood, sir," the recruit said, rushing off.

The Senator's voice cut through the moment. "It's great that we've reclaimed some ground, but we've got a lot of hungry, thirsty people—especially those pulled from the trains."

Kylo nodded. "Good point. We'll start with water."

He turned to another squad leader. "Get volunteers—collect what you can in buckets in case they shut it off."

Remi added, "And food?"

Kylo rubbed his jaw. "That's trickier. No pellets—now that we know what they're made of."

He looked back at the squad leader. "Check the mixer room. Look for raw supplies—barley, wheat, anything sealed and untouched. All the processed stuff goes to the disposal fields. That place is already a mass grave."

Remi's concern shifted. "We have injured people—some sterilized. They need care."

Kylo's expression softened. "Agreed. Find a room. Start an infirmary. Can you lead that?"

Remi nodded. "Thanks for trusting me."

Kylo gave a brief nod and stepped away.

His thoughts wandered—past the walls, past the rebels, to history. The Alamo came to mind—850 miles south. Was this going to be his last stand too?

As he saw it, Felicity's leaders had two options: starve them out, or send a wave of soldiers in a lopsided slaughter. Either way, it would be ugly.

His mind turned to his family. The note he'd left behind—it ate at him. He hadn't explained anything. What would they think? So many questions—no answers. It had only been a day, and yet everything had shifted. He pictured their sleeping faces, safe and unaware. A sudden wave of loneliness hit him.

He missed them. God, he missed them.

But there were no phones in the basement levels.

With no other option, he sat down, pen in hand.

He paused, breathed, and began to write.

When he finished, he signed it, folded it carefully, and placed it in his pocket, next to Alma's birthday gift.

He hoped the letter would never need to be delivered.

Before he could gather his thoughts again, an orange-clad squad leader appeared, urgency in his step.

"Sir. As you predicted—they've cut the water."

Kylo pulled his hand from his pocket. No time for reflection.

Action was the only way forward.

He rejoined the squad leaders and the Senator, about to issue his next command—when the lights cut out, plunging everything into darkness.

Chapter 75: Luna

Luna and Zev found the forklift exactly where they'd left it—jammed into Town Hall's entrance, its steel nose wedged into the frame of what used to be a door. The vehicle was half in, half out.

With the lift blocking their return path, Zev fished the keys from his pocket. "Still got 'em." He glanced at the single seat. "We'll have to reverse into the abattoir. There's only one seat, so you'll need to sit on my lap."

Luna shot him a look—half amused, half skeptical—as if suspecting he'd engineered the seating arrangement. She climbed aboard, cradling Karli in her arms. Zev winced as her weight settled on his injured leg. Clenching his teeth in pain, he backed the forklift just far enough to let them slip into the slaughterhouse.

As they reentered, the stench hit like a wave—a foul mix of blood and bleach, strong enough to sting her eyes and throat.

Luna gagged, her hand snapping over her mouth. "Let's get out of here."

Zev nodded grimly. "Agreed."

They climbed off the forklift, careful not to brush against anything, and started toward the abattoir exit.

Then—without warning—the lights cut out. Blackness slammed down around them like a lid.

Luna's voice trembled. "Oh God. Not here. Anywhere but here. Please don't tell me we have to feel our way out... through all these... bodies."

Silence.

"Zev?" she called, tension rising.

Nothing.

"Zev, are you okay?"

Finally, she heard him—his breathing ragged.

"Yeah," he said at last.

"What's wrong?"

"A childhood nightmare, replaying itself. It happened on Halloween, a prank that started just like this. Later that night, my brother choked on a balloon. I saw it—I could have helped, but I didn't."

"How old were you?"

"Seven. After that, my mother never looked at me the same. Years later, when she died, her last words were his name—she only longed to rejoin him, her favorite child. Never me."

"That's not your fault."

"I'll be fine—just give me a second. Take my shoulders—I'll guide us. That way, you can carry Karli."

Luna exhaled shakily. "I'm so sorry. And thank you."

Zev took a shallow breath. "Let's focus on finding the Senator. We need to head right—toward rendering."

Luna placed a hand on his shoulder, letting him lead.

"I feel like a sleepwalker in a morgue," he muttered. "Arms out like Frankenstein, but praying I don't brush against anything."

"I know," she whispered. "It's horrible."

She couldn't even see her own hand resting on his back.

Suddenly, Zev recoiled with a yelp. "Ew."

"What is it?"

She felt him shiver. "Something... mushy. Cold. What part—I don't want to know."

"I'm sorry," Luna said, her stomach turning at the thought of someone's liver.

"If that was your stomach," Zev whispered, "I'm barely holding it together myself. I'm switching to feet-only navigation. No more touching anything."

Moments later came a metallic clang, followed by the dull rolls of multiple objects hitting the floor and rocking.

Luna groaned. "Tell me you didn't just kick over the bucket."

"What bucket?"

Her voice dropped to a grim murmur. "Never mind."

Heads.

They crept forward in the dark. Suddenly, Zev sprang back with a shriek, followed by the repeating squeak of something swinging.

Luna swallowed hard. "What now?"

Zev's voice was tight with revulsion. "My face just hit something fleshy. Torso on a hook, I bet. Left slime on my nose. God, how could anyone work here? There aren't enough carbon credits in the world to justify this."

After what felt like a slow-motion nightmare, Zev finally found the double doors to the rendering area and shoved them open. They slipped through—relieved to be free of the abattoir.

"Well," Zev muttered, "I'm strangely happy we're back where I got shot."

In the distance, a flashlight beam cut through the dark. Not knowing who it belonged to, they ducked behind a hopper—the same one that had swallowed Simi.

From the glow, they spotted a man in orange, hauling a heavy sack over one shoulder.

Zev called out, "Hey you! Friendlies—over here!"

The man turned the flashlight on them. "Who are you?"

Luna stepped forward. "We're looking for the Senator."

"Just left her," the man said. "She's trying to figure out how to reach the ground level. She sent me down to get rid of these pellets… er, remains—to the landfill."

Luna dipped her head. "She's with someone named Kylo."

The man nodded. "Kylo's leading the resistance. He and the Senator think they'll eventually try to starve us out. That's why I had to remove the remains—no temptation. They've shut off the water, and now the power too. Kylo's trying to find a way up to the ground floor, but everything's locked down. No way up."

Zev glanced at the sack, lips drawn in.

"I think," he said slowly, "I know a way. Can you take us to them?"

The man set the sack down. "Yeah. No problem."

He led Zev and Luna toward a new command center on B1, his flashlight cutting through the darkness ahead. Occasionally, the light swept across the broken forms of Felicity's victims. Most wore orange, but a few had red, blue, or even green smocks. They passed people sprawled or slumped across the cold cement, suffering alone or in small groups steeped in obvious anguish.

At times, Luna caught brief glimpses of their faces—flashes no longer than a strobe at a dance party—but most looked sullen and anxious. The images of pain were fleeting, but the sounds of anguish clung to the air: moaning, crying, and hysteria echoing off the factory walls, a constant undertow of despair.

Luna flinched when she felt a tug on her pants, the memory of her nighttime encounter inside the Mall IDP flaring back to life. She jerked her leg free.

A man's voice pleaded, "Water, I need water."

The guide's flashlight landed on a middle-aged man lying on the ground, his missing front teeth barely visible in the light.

The man leading them said, "Rations will be here soon, sir."

Luna's face flushed with embarrassment. Her knee-jerk reaction felt cruel now, just a reflex left over from older fears—fears of the unhoused, of their unpredictability, their smell, their germs. She looked at the man and quietly resolved to do better, seeing him not as a threat, but as someone deeply human.

They continued on, crossing B2 toward the stairwell on the eastern side of the immense building. The flashlight caught a slight figure with long blond hair, her head bobbing as she wept. Something about her struck Luna with instant familiarity.

"Can you hold the flashlight on the crying girl?" she asked.

The guide obliged, and Luna stepped closer, eyes narrowing. She grabbed Zev's arm. "I know her—from the train. She was with her father. They were separated in the showers."

Luna moved closer. "Hi, honey, do you remember me from the train? Where's your father?"

The girl's voice trembled. "I don't know."

Luna helped her up. "You're coming with us. It'll be okay." The girl nodded, clearly grateful. Luna hugged her with her free arm.

Now a group of five, counting Karli, they continued to the stairwell and climbed one flight to B1. Luna sniffed the air, her nose wrinkling.

"Do you smell that?"

Zev took a shallow breath. "Yeah. Like burnt garlic."

Luna nodded. "Or onions. My eyes are burning. Yours?"

"Same," Zev replied.

He wiped at his face. "Whatever it is, it's airborne. Let's keep moving."

Chapter 76: Kylo

Kylo could hear the Senator breathing hard and fast, but he couldn't see her. Lifting his palm to his face, he felt the air stir—but even inches from his nose, all he saw was black.

"Senator, you can't see either, right?" The question was meant less for her than for himself—a way to confirm he hadn't suddenly gone blind. It was just too dark.

Remi's voice cut through the silence. "It's pitch black. I can't see a thing, and I hate it."

Kylo wasn't surprised. "They've killed the electricity. Once we disabled the cameras, they had no reason to leave the lights on. On a floor with no windows, no power means total darkness. Even when our eyes adjust, we'll barely see a damn thing."

"What now?"

Kylo paused. "We need a flashlight. I think I know where one might be—but we'll have to walk."

"Then I'm coming with you," Remi said, her tone steady despite the tension hanging in the air.

Kylo extended his hand, waving it slowly until it brushed something soft. The Senator yelped and jerked away. "What the hell are you doing?"

Kylo felt a rush of embarrassment. "Apologies, ma'am. I thought you might want my hand. Maybe… maybe you should find mine instead."

Remi was quiet for a beat. "All right. Let's just agree never to mention you felt up a senator in the dark."

They both chuckled—awkwardly.

The Senator reached out, higher than him, until her fingers jabbed Kylo's nose. "There. Could've been worse." Finally, they found each other's hands.

Kylo mentally reconstructed the layout of the packaging room—the path to the lift. A guard had been subdued there, stripped of his belt. Kylo was certain it had been left just outside the doors.

"We need to head toward the elev—"

A loud boom cut him off, a deep, concussive roar that rattled the walls and stilled the air.

They froze—statues in the dark.

"What was that?" Remi whispered.

Kylo gripped her hand for silence. "Shhh." He strained his ears. "Do you hear that?"

Remi sounded mildly irritated. "May I speak now?"

"Sorry, ma'am. I just… I think I'm hearing something. Something bad. Do you hear it?"

Remi sighed. "The explosion? Of course."

"No, after that," Kylo said. "Since then."

Remi fell quiet, listening. "I hear people in the distance. Clamoring—screaming. They're panicked. Understandable—trapped in a dungeon built in hell."

Kylo's grip on her hand tightened. "This is closer. Something's hissing—thinner. Higher pitched."

There was silence, then her voice came again, elevated now. "Yes. I hear it. What is that?"

Panic clawed at Kylo. "How are your eyes?"

Remi's answer came slowly. "Interesting question… they're starting to burn."

Kylo's voice dropped. "And your lungs?"

"Burning too," she admitted, fear creeping in.

Kylo coughed and began moving. "There's a supply room nearby—they stock a lot of bleach and ammonia. If they're mixed, we're looking at sulfur mustard. Mustard gas. I think it was meant for the chambers, but they probably figured it'd spoil their meals."

Remi's voice rose in pitch. "What are you saying?"

Kylo fought to breathe. "I'm saying they're using it now. They're gassing us out." He patted his pockets—finding nothing. *No inhaler?*

A flashlight beam carved through the dark. Luna emerged, cradling a baby, Zev close behind, while a young girl clung to her side like a lifeline.

Remi offered Luna a warm but strained smile. "Congratulations—you found your child."

But Zev's attention snapped to Kylo. "What's wrong with you?"

Kylo tried to answer, but his breath caught.

Remi stepped in. "He thinks they're using mustard gas. I was about to suggest we take him downstairs—air might be better. I think he's got asthma. He's getting worse by the moment."

Kylo coughed violently, then forced himself upright. "I'm fine. The real issue… is figuring out how…" He doubled over, a dry, scraping sound rattling up from his lungs. "…how to get upstairs. If we reach the PA system, the Senator can speak—to the prisoners, the guards, everyone. I think they'll listen. But there's no way up."

Zev furrowed his brow. "Actually… maybe there is. There's a dumbwaiter leading up to the kitchen. They use it to lift food from B1 to the ground level—avoids pushing carts through restricted zones. Pretty sure it's big enough for two."

Kylo shook his head. "No good. Power's out. It won't work."

Zev shook his head. "It's manual. Operated by a hand pulley."

Kylo looked up, hope stirring. "Yeah? Show us."

Zev led them to the pulley system. He hesitated. "Whoever goes up should be in a guard's uniform. To blend in."

Kylo nodded, coughing again, a deep, wheezing exhale. "Smart. There are uniforms by the exits—we stripped the guards."

They found them quickly. Kylo knelt, still winded, and checked the collars. "One's a medium. The other's large. No good for me— I'm an extra-large."

Zev stepped forward. "If only two can go, the Senator has to be one. We need her voice. She'll fit in the medium. I'll take the large." He glanced at Luna. "Stay with Kylo. He'll need help."

Luna nodded. Zev and the Senator quickly changed.

"I'll need a weapon," Zev said.

Kylo looked up, face flushed. "Ever used one before?"

Zev looked away. "No."

Kylo pointed. "This is the safety. And this…" He gestured at the muzzle, forcing air into his lungs. "…keep it pointed away from anyone you care about. Works better that way."

Zev tested its weight, grinning nervously. "I'll keep it pointed at the bad guys."

He climbed into the dumbwaiter first, curling tight. The Senator followed. They gave a thumbs-up.

Kylo, looking pale, gripped the rope. His breath strained, strength draining fast. "Let's hope this thing holds. Please… be careful," he rasped.

The Senator gave him a faint smile. "You'll know we made it when you hear my voice on the PA."

Kylo thought, *I'm not sure I will.*

He pulled downward hard, watching them rise—hauling the rope hand over hand. In time, each pull slowed. His strength was failing.

He glanced at Luna, cradling Karli in one arm, flashlight in the other—a sight that struck him harder than expected, stirring a memory of Alma as a baby, eyes wide, her mom holding her, hair tousled from sleep.

Stars began to swim in the dimly lit space. He forced himself to hyperventilate, trying to reset his oxygen levels, but energy drained from his limbs. His lungs burned. His vision blurred.

He saw Ingrid—heard her voice, soft in his ear.

"You need to go downstairs."

"I can't let go," he whispered. *"They need me."*

"But your family needs you too. Alma needs you."

"There's no other choice. I'm gone either way."

"I love you, cloud hopper."

"I love you."

Luna's voice broke in. "Are you talking to someone?"

He didn't answer. He couldn't. He had to pull—had to hold on. Every instinct screamed for him to stop, but he hauled until the rope went taut—felt it catch.

They made it.

With what little focus he had left, he hitched the rope around a cleat bolted to the wall.

Then the world pitched. The flashlight spun. His knees gave out.

The floor caught him, hard.

He dimly sensed Luna dropping beside him, passing the flashlight to the young girl.

Oxygen was out of reach. Each gasp dragged fire through his chest, offering no relief. His hand trembled as he reached into his pocket, drew out a folded letter and a small box, and held them out to Luna.

She stared at him, frozen.

He whispered in her ear, instructions meant only for her.

Luna listened carefully, then said, "I promise."

"Thank you."

Everything went black again—but this time, darkness had nothing to do with Felicity's power grid. Barely conscious, he felt the tug of the letter and box being pulled from his hand.

And he knew it was time to let go.

Chapter 77: Zev

Zev and Remi climbed out of the dumbwaiter. No alarms. No shouting. The corridor outside was silent.

They were now on the main floor, closer to their target. Remi had taken the tour before and remembered clearly: the elevator led straight to the control room on Level Two. No ciphers, no locked doors. Just a ride up.

But Zev held back, eyes narrowing.

Something was off.

He scanned the hallway, instincts alarming. "Where is everyone?" he murmured. "No Greens. No guards. No workers." He peered deeper into the stillness. "It's like they've abandoned the building."

That's when he spotted it—a portable ventilation unit on wheels, thick ducting snaking down into a vent in the wall. The machine was outfitted with two cylindrical plastic tanks, one filled with a pale green liquid, the other with yellow. A faint chemical tang hung in the air.

He stepped in, crouched. "This is it," he said, his voice rising. "Kylo was right. They're gassing the whole level."

He yanked the plug. The machine died with a soft whine.

"That was easier than I expected," he muttered, glancing at Remi. But she wasn't listening.

She was already pointing—to another unit across the hall.

Zev's mouth pressed into a thin line. One machine was targeting a specific area. Two meant part of a darker plan.

He crossed to the next one and drove his heel into the outlet. The crack of plaster echoed through the corridor. They continued their search, finding five more ventilators. Each was shut down in turn. No resistance. No interference.

When the last one powered off, Remi gave a tight nod. "Elevators."

They moved fast. The ride to Level Two was brief. A short walk brought them to a wide doorway overlooking the control room.

Inside, two operators sat at their consoles—far fewer than expected. Both wore hazmat suits, with visors dull with fog. Their gloved fingers hovered over screens, tracking information fed by the building and the compound.

Zev noticed that their masks narrowed their peripheral vision. *Perfect.*

Zev slipped in, silent as a wisp of air, and tapped the nearest man on the shoulder. The operator jolted, spun, and froze—face-to-face with a muzzle. His hands shot skyward, dropping his computer mouse. The second man looked up, saw the weapon, and followed without a word.

Zev didn't blink. "This woman behind you?" He nodded toward Remi. "I hope you know who she is. She's about to speak. You're going to help her. That, or I ventilate your suits with bullet holes."

They nodded—panicked, compliant.

"Good. Power up the PA. I want every single person in the city to hear her. No delays. No clever ideas. Do you understand?"

More nods. Eyes wide. Breathing fast behind their filters.

Zev kept the gun raised.

People like this always behave—until they don't.

Chapter 78: Remi

Remi cleared her throat, steadying her voice, fighting a rare level of insecurity in her mind. This would be the most important speech of her life. Failure meant thousands might never see daylight again.

"To the citizens of Felicity," she began, her words echoing through loudspeakers across the city. "This is Senator Remi McCarthy. I speak to you not just as your elected official—but as a fellow American."

She paused, hoping the weight of that claim bought her a moment of open ears—maybe even open hearts.

"Most of you are living under an illusion," she said. "You've been misled by those in power. Aldric Heister, your CEO, has deceived you—and the truth will shake you. He has met his fate. And though it pains me to say it, I share in the blame." Her voice didn't waver. "But it's never too late to choose what's right. I'm choosing that now. I ask you to face two hard truths."

There was no turning back.

"First," she said, "Heister claimed loyalty to the United States. He said he was one of us. But in truth, he led a secret rebellion— an attempt at secession." She leaned into the mic, willing her voice into every home, every mind. "If you doubt it, think back to your arrival. He took your passports. No city leader—no matter how powerful—has the authority to strip you of your citizenship. That was your first warning—one too often ignored."

Her voice grew sharper.

"Second—and this is harder—his so-called utopia was built on the torment of others. On blood. On the suffering of the innocent." She swallowed, forcing back the stomach acid. "I won't describe what we found beneath the soil of Sustalia—beneath the Town Hall. Words fall short. But understand this: it rivals the worst horrors of human history."

She glanced at Zev. He was watching, jaw tight, eyes locked on hers. It gave her steadiness.

"I know many of you are afraid. Fear brings out the best in some, and the worst in others. I appeal to your conscience—to your decency." Her tone changed, not softer, but deeper, grounded. "Let your outrage find its rightful target: those who orchestrated these crimes. And if part of that blame falls on me—and it should—then I will bear it."

She took a breath.

"What now?" she said, her voice quiet but clear. "To the guards especially—lay down your weapons. If you didn't know what was happening, as I believe many of you didn't, you have nothing to fear. If you were forced to take part, you will find peace. But if you chose this—if you embraced it—then justice will find you."

A long pause.

"I ask that you each gather outside the Town Hall. I will meet you there—in person."

She hesitated, then signed off.

"May God bless America."

The words fell into silence. She was deaf to the city's response, unsure whether it had shifted toward belief—or disbelief.

Remi turned to one of the men in a hazmat suit. "Take me to the front entrance," she said quietly.

He nodded and led her out—through a hallway, into the elevator, and down to the ground floor. Zev followed, weapon slung low, eyes alert and scanning the area.

Remi braced herself. For a mob. For a rope. For a hook like Mussolini.

But what she saw brought her to a halt.

No violence. No chaos. Not even anger.

It was something else. Something impossible.

A heap of weapons lay at the threshold of the building.

And beyond them, a crowd stood in silence.

Not with the verdant fist-in-palm.

But with the American military salute.

Part 5: Migration

Chapter 79: Zev

Friday, August 13, One Year Later

A Ruby-throated hummingbird hurtled through the air at thirty miles per hour, already deep into its long journey south from Canada. No heavier than a nickel, it would soon cross the Gulf of Mexico in a single, seemingly impossible stretch—an act of instinct and endurance that defied its size. But for now, the land still stretched beneath its wings. Spotting sanctuary below, the tiny creature dived toward it.

A feeder had become a lifeline. It hovered and darted, sipping sugar water from the vessel that swayed gently beneath the low branch of a tree.

Zev watched the hummingbird, its wings a blur—eighty beats per second—caught in the golden afternoon light. Its grace held him still. To witness it felt like a stroke of luck: a flash of iridescent green and blue, suspended in flight.

A year had passed since the fall of Felicity. He stood behind a newly installed window in a modest house tucked safely inside the city walls. Glass wasn't energy efficient, but it offered a view of the world beyond—and that glimpse made him feel more human. Not every choice had to be practical. Some were permitted, if only because they simply felt right.

Luna had hung the feeder on impulse, never imagining her small gesture would offer exactly what this fragile traveler needed to keep going. But it had. Her kindness had tipped the balance—just enough—for survival.

He thought of Luna. She had found her fierceness—a strength that had always been within her, waiting to be discovered. But in her decisions, there was always empathy. They both shared this trait, a compassion for others, even for his mother, though it wasn't always returned.

His heart often pulled him down difficult, sometimes tragic paths. He would struggle with his mother's rejection for the remainder of his life. But he was learning to live with that. He liked where he was in his journey.

And the path forward would soon reveal itself. He had submitted the request months ago, and the answer was expected today. Despite it being a Friday, he was hopeful. It was Friday the Thirteenth. He sat beside the phone, a little excited, a little fearful.

Waiting.

Chapter 80: Remi

Remi stood in front of the mirror, adjusting her hair and plucking away invisible specks from her dress. After a moment, she walked the short distance from Aldric's old office to where the television crew waited. It had been decided that the interview would take place on the second floor of the Town Hall in Felicity, with the war room's whiteboards as a backdrop.

Once seated between the two interviewers, Remi resisted the urge to squint beneath the harsh lights. The blue-haired woman sat to her right, while the redhead positioned herself on the left, to provide the proper configuration from the viewer's perspective. Behind the cameras, cables snaked across the floor in an intricate mess. Sound blankets hung over chairs, and the crew worked quietly, attending to every detail to ensure a smooth transmission. A makeup woman stepped forward, holding a tray of powder. "One last touch-up, ma'am."

Remi smiled. "Sure."

A man raised his hand and began the countdown. "5, 4, 3." He stopped speaking at three, only using his fingers until he closed his fist, signaling that they were live.

The blue-haired woman spoke first. "Welcome once again to 'In the Mix at Six.' We're honored to have Sustalia Senator Remi McCarthy with us today. A survivor, rescuer, and whistleblower of atrocities conducted within the very building we're broadcasting from. She has become one of America's most admired figures—a beacon of hope for those still suffering. Welcome, Senator."

Remi smiled. "It's great to be here today."

The redhead leaned forward slightly. "Remi, we've heard rumors that you're considering a bid for president. Is that true?"

"Those rumors have been out there for years, but I haven't given them serious thought."

"Interesting. Let's dive into your beliefs for the viewers."

"I'll do my best to answer everything," Remi responded.

"First, we'd like your views on the new mayor position."

"Well, as you know, many of the Felicity residents have remained in Sustalia and demanded the city be led by an elected official—a mayor. There's been strong support for Ms. Luna Brighton to take on the role. If she chooses to run, I would back her without hesitation. She knows their pain and has shown strength and leadership."

The redhead nodded slowly, lips pursed. "We all know what happened in Felicity. As horrific as it was, some people still live here. Why?"

Remi explained, "Many refuse to leave the place where others made their final sacrifices. They want to give meaning to the loss. Most importantly, we must remember the atrocities so they're never repeated. We've converted the mass gravesite into an underground memorial—a sacred space where families and friends can honor the lost."

The blue-haired interviewer softened her voice. "One of the reasons this place existed was fear of overpopulation. With the global population now over fifteen billion, many still defend the suspended Carbon Laws. Do you share that fear? As their original author, where do you stand now?"

Remi was prepared for this question. "It's clear the Earth can only support so many people. When I was a child, my biology professor ran an experiment with fruit flies in a sealed jar. We watched them multiply until there was no space left. Food dwindled, waste built up, and eventually, they all died." She paused, voice quieting. "I still remember the silence in the room when they were all dead. It wasn't just a science lesson. It was a warning."

She took a deep breath.

"Our Earth is no different. But if we maintain balance, it can sustain us. If any one species grows unchecked—ours included—extinction becomes a real threat. So yes, I share a concern about population."

The redhead leaned in. "And the Carbon Laws?"

Remi's tone grew more serious. "The Carbon Laws were too broad, leaving enforcement to local jurisdictions. That was our failure. The devil truly was in the details. While I believe in addressing overpopulation, Aldric Heister became a tyrant. The murder of innocent people is never justified. He weaponized those laws to mask his atrocities."

The redhead raised a brow. "You wrote the Carbon Laws. Now you're condemning them. Isn't that political convenience?"

Remi's jaw tensed, but she held her ground. "Not in their current form. The laws were well-intentioned but allowed for terrible abuses. We do need to limit our growth—through measures like limiting family size or calculating carbon impact—but not through genocide. Natural selection belongs to nature, not human decree. Aldric relied on algorithms that led to mass death. They turned out to be—well—deadly equations."

She stopped, lips pressed together. For a moment, she thought to say more, but didn't.

The blue-haired interviewer leaned forward, her tone more cautious. "Then where does that leave us? How do we control human expansion?"

Remi paused. "That's the hardest question. I've wrestled with the contradiction between our survival instinct—to create life—and the need to protect the planet. It's written into our DNA. It's what helped us survive the Ice Age, build civilizations. But now we must find balance. Somewhere between nurturing the future and preserving the present."

The redhead pressed again. "So what's the sweet spot?"

Remi hesitated. "I don't know. Maybe a two-child policy per couple—similar to China's more restrictive approach, but voluntary and globally supported. That would allow a gradual, more humane population decline."

The blue-haired interviewer didn't let up. "What about sterilization? That was enforced in Felicity, wasn't it?"

Remi nodded. "Yes. And it wasn't the first time. Over sixty-four thousand people in the U.S. were sterilized without consent under eugenic laws—even as late as 1963. In 1927, the Supreme Court upheld forced sterilization in Buck v. Bell. They called people 'feebleminded.' They stripped away humanity. As for my position—I don't know how anything like that could ever be done fairly. It would mean playing God, and that's never ended well for us."

The blue-haired interviewer glanced toward her colleague, then returned to look at Remi. "Many overcrowding challenges stem from immigration. Even if we slow procreation, growth might continue. What about border control?"

Remi expected this. "Aside from Native Americans, all of us came here from somewhere else. Tightening our borders feels harsh, but it may be necessary." She exhaled through her nose. "I hate saying that. It goes against everything I believed growing up. But I've seen what happens when we ignore the limits."

"So, zero?"

"Certainly not, but more restrictive. We can't control the policies of other failing countries or hostile regimes. It's like being on a plane—if the oxygen masks drop, you put yours on first. Our people are suffering. We need to tend to them first. Only then can we help others."

The redhead asked one final question. "What's your outlook?"

Remi exhaled slowly. "You've asked tough questions. Like many extinct species, some couldn't adapt to the very changes they triggered. Will we be different? Can we anticipate what's coming rather than react too late? I believe overpopulation is one of Earth's gravest threats. Every new life demands food, land, energy. Without limits, we invite famine, conflict, pollution. Yet we must also cherish life. But the Earth pushes back—through disease, wildfires, storms, scarcity. These are the great correctives. Our burden is real."

She leaned back slightly, her voice quieter now. "I was taught in Girl Scouts to leave a place better than we found it. We can't blame those before us—they didn't understand the cost. But to answer your question—yes, I still believe in us. I think humanity will adapt. I think we'll find a way."

With that, the session was wrapped up. Remi was escorted by her entourage, and she found herself in the rear seat of an Escapade. Gone was her limo. Gone were her refrigerator and imported snacks. She'd stripped those things from her life deliberately.

It wasn't just conviction. It was optics. And every adjustment, every small discipline, brought her one step closer.

The White House was in her sights.

Chapter 81: Ingrid

Ingrid had just said goodbye to Luna—grateful for her visit, though quietly unraveling inside. Trevor also left, continuing his family's tradition of honoring officers lost.

In one hand, Ingrid carried something that felt impossibly heavy: a box. In the other, a leash—at the end of which trembled a nervous border terrier pup with white patches across its body, blinking uncertainly at his new home.

She walked to the sofa, placed the puppy on Alma's lap, and sat down beside her, the box resting across her knees. Drawing her daughter close, Ingrid curled around her like a shield. A child, a mother, a trembling pup, and a container destined to break their hearts—this was the shape of their small huddle.

Ingrid decided that since Alma was eleven, she was old enough.

"Open the box," she said softly.

Alma, teary-eyed, stroked the puppy's back with one hand and lifted the lid with the other.

Inside were three items: a ring, a smaller box, and an envelope.

Ingrid's breath caught. She recognized the ring immediately. Without saying a word, she slid it onto the fourth finger of her left hand, until it met her own. His ring was nearly large enough to swallow hers whole. She was caught between anger and loss.

You ring swore.

With shaky hands, Ingrid retrieved the envelope. Inside was the letter—a letter she had read hundreds of times, but never aloud to Alma. It had been emailed to her, images and words attached, but never the original that her husband had scrawled. The physical evidence had taken a year to reach her. She drew a slow, steady breath.

To my dearest family,

If you're reading this, it means something good, yet costly, has happened.

First, I'm sorry I left without a proper goodbye. I didn't even wish Alma a happy birthday. I know that must have been confusing. The truth is, I had to solve a mystery—a murder I didn't commit.

I'm sure the police came to the house asking questions. Maybe you wondered why I ran. Maybe—just for a moment—you wondered if I was guilty. I hope you know now that I am not.

I didn't want to put you through a trial, a scandal, or worse. So, I left to find the killer on my own. The atrocities I've uncovered… they're beyond imagining. I can only hope the truth, and this letter, will find daylight.

If fighting this evil costs me my life, please understand: I didn't just fight for justice. I fought for you. For a future you both deserve.

And no—I didn't forget Alma's birthday. The small box is for her. The dog? You were right, our family can always use a little more love.

Though, my love is infinite.

With all my heart, Dad, Kylo, the cloud hopper

Ingrid's voice faltered at the end. She let the letter fall gently to her lap, then looked at Alma with tear-stung eyes.

"I think that small box is for you."

Alma's shoulders were jerking with emotion, but she managed to reach for it and pull open the lid.

Inside was a necklace with a heart-shaped pendant. She flipped it open. On the left, a photo of her with her parents. On the right, the puppy.

Alma began to cry. "Can we call him Cloudy?"

Ingrid wrapped her in a fierce, full-bodied embrace. They wept together—the kind of crying that empties you, that comes from the center and leaves silence in its wake. Ingrid held her daughter, wanting to protect her from everything the world had already taken. And for a moment, in their shared grief, they clung to the love that was still theirs to keep.

Chapter 82: Luna

Luna glanced at the slender plastic stick resting on the end table and smiled. Then she returned to the more somber task of labeling the last box in her D.C. apartment. She left it on the floor, careful not to lift anything too heavy. It wasn't what she had packed that stirred the sadness—it was what she had to leave behind. Sentimental objects had been sacrificed. Movers were expensive, and she needed to focus on the future, not the past.

The hardest decision had been selling her grandmother's settee. As a child, she would curl up on the overly firm two-person sofa, with Bubba softening it using fluffy blankets, a plush pillow, and her teddy bear. They would sit together, snuggled, telling stories that led her into fantastical worlds—*Alice in Wonderland*, *Harry Potter*, and other beloved classics. Luna missed that sense of security—the warmth, the constant love that had once filled her childhood. She lifted her phone and snapped a few photos of the settee. Memories captured in pixels would have to do.

Thoughts of family brought many tears. Earlier that day, she had visited Kylo's wife and daughter to personally deliver his handwritten letter—and the dog she'd been instructed to buy for Alma. Beforehand, she'd taken a photo of the puppy—a terrier, just as he'd requested—and tucked it inside the pendant.

Luna had been the last person to see him alive, and she needed to be there in person—not just a flickering face on a screen. She wanted to offer them more than condolences: her presence, quiet grace, genuine empathy. It had been frustrating to wait nearly a year for the investigation team to release his belongings—only then could she fulfill the promise she'd made.

"Yes, he fought valiantly."

"Yes, he died a hero, saving lives."

"Yes, his last words were that he loved you all."

She added her own touch, but nothing that betrayed the truth.

"Most of all," she'd said, "he believed in you. The best way to honor him is to live well. Be strong." They needed to hear that.

It had been hard enough watching Kylo's wife fight to stay composed. But it was the daughter who truly unraveled Luna. She was old enough to grasp what death meant—but not old enough to understand why life could be so cruel. To her, grief had no fairness. Calling her father a hero didn't soften the blow. It wouldn't bring him back. Still, Luna hoped it gave her something to hold onto—the idea that maybe, somewhere, he was watching over them.

In the end, they cried together, holding each other, searching for meaning in the unthinkable. She left them with the box filled with his memories—and their privacy.

Luna knew she had to hold on to the good, too. She thought of the young girl who'd once been separated from her father—one of the rare, redemptive stories that hadn't ended in sorrow. Luna had been there when they were reunited. Now, a year later, they were gone, choosing not to stay in Felicity.

Thinking of the city, her mind returned to her recent conversation with Senator Remi McCarthy. Remi had urged her to run for mayor of Felicity. Public support was growing—people saw Luna as someone who stood up to injustice. She was still considering it. It would be her first time in elected office, and she had to make sure it wouldn't conflict with another calling—one closer to her heart.

A quote came to her—one of her favorites from Confucius:

"Choose a job you love, and you'll never have to work a day in your life."

Over the past few months, she'd been weighing whether she could shoulder both responsibilities. But first, she needed to know if her dream had taken root.

She didn't yet realize the answer was already trying to reach her.

The phone rang. She looked at the screen.

Zev.

She answered, smiling. "Hi, honey."

Zev's voice came through, warm and grounding. "Hello, beautiful. How's it going?"

Luna sighed. "It was rough, talking to Kylo's family. Just... heavy. And letting go of almost everything I own—it's hard."

Zev responded gently. "Well, you've got a new place here in Felicity. And someone who can't wait to have you home."

"Thank you," she murmured. "I needed that."

His voice brightened. "I also have some news. Ready?"

Luna's heart fluttered. She had a feeling, but she needed the words. She sat on the settee for the last time, feeling its familiar firmness beneath her. "Okay. I'm ready."

Zev didn't hold back. "Approved. The adoption letter is in the mail."

Tears rose again, but this time they were filled with joy.

Zev's voice beamed. "Someone wants to say something." A pause followed—soft, expectant. Nothing but silence.

He laughed. "I held up the phone to Jade's mouth, but she must have fallen asleep. She was full of babble earlier. So... how does it feel to be a mom?"

The title rang through her, profound and new. The first time anyone had said it aloud.

And it fit.

"I'm so glad we chose the name Jade," Luna whispered. "Out of respect for her…"

"We'll make sure Jade knows what her birth mother gave up," Zev said quietly.

Then there was another pause—gentle, intentional.

She drew a slow breath, her fingers drifting unconsciously to her stomach. "By the way… I have something to tell you, too."

A pause. "What?"

"You're smart. Easy as two plus two."

Another beat of silence. Then: "How do you know?"

"I took a test. I'm looking at the stick now. Pretty conclusive."

Zev didn't speak right away. Just breathing over the line. Then: "I went from no kids to two in a day. Come home. I love you."

"Soon," she whispered, ending the call with a soft smile.

She set the phone down and stared at the end table, her thoughts already drifting far ahead.

The test was still sitting where she'd left it—small, silent, and full of promise.

Zev's child was growing inside her, and the glow she felt now was impossible to contain.

She thought back to the bridge, and her journey. How one moment—a simple glint—had changed everything. A butterfly effect.

She was a different person then. She had transformed, like a butterfly herself.

She was thankful for the forces that guided her.

But she no longer waited for signs.

She would choose.

And this time, the path ahead would be hers to define.

Did you love Deadly Equations?

About the Author

Jeffrey Rosoff grew up in central California, moving through cities that serendipitously start with 'S'—Sacramento, Salinas, San Jose, San Carlos, and Stockton—all close to Silicon Valley and the settings of Steinbeck's stories. Influenced by classic sci-fi series like *The Twilight Zone* and *The Outer Limits*, Jeffrey continues to be drawn to reruns and finds inspiration in their timeless intrigue.

He holds degrees in computer science and business administration from the University of the Pacific and San Jose State University. His career at Lockheed Martin spanned over thirty years, culminating in a director role where he managed major defense-related projects in Washington, D.C.

Though writing is a lifelong passion, Jeffrey's greatest joy is his family—his wife, children, and four grandchildren. When he isn't writing, he enjoys traveling the world, gardening, engaging in spirited conversations, and seeking out unique restaurants.

The Glass Fountain was Jeffrey's first novel, while *Chipped* became his first published work. *Deadly Equations* is his third book, with all three falling into the realm of speculative thrillers.

If you enjoyed his work, please consider leaving an honest review on Amazon, Goodreads, or your favorite retailer's website—it makes a tremendous difference.

You can reach Jeffrey at JeffreyRosoffBooks@gmail.com and follow him on:

- instagram.com/jeffreyrosoffbooks/
- facebook.com/JeffreyRosoffAuthor
- goodreads.com/Jeffrey_Rosoff
- amazon.com/Jeffrey_Rosoff

Acknowledgements

Before I began writing books, I immersed myself in my family's ancestral history, uncovering stories of resilience, survival, and unimaginable hardship. I was profoundly moved by the struggles on my mother's side of the family—tales that were both heartbreaking and inspiring.

Among the many stories I heard, one stayed with me the most—the story of a Russian Jewish woman. Separated from her husband, who had gone to England to build a better future for them, she was left behind—pregnant—to care for four young children. Unfortunately, World War I broke out just after he departed, preventing her from joining him. The money he sent never reached her. Instead, she was left reliant on her father-in-law, who passed away from cancer within the year, leaving her destitute.

Now penniless and facing pogroms and the upheaval of the Bolshevik Revolution, she fought tirelessly for her family's survival. Though frail in body, she spent seven long years battling to protect her children. She did whatever was necessary, scrubbing front porches for money, even begging. She endured the heartbreaking loss of a child to diphtheria. In the end, she crossed hostile borders and reunited with her husband. Against all odds, she triumphed.

Had she not possessed unimaginable inner strength, her story—and by extension, my own—could have taken an entirely different turn. The decisions made by her and my other ancestors shaped the course of my life, and yet, for so long, I had no idea who they even were. This is my chance to thank them, especially this one remarkable woman—my great-grandmother, Sarah

Trashinsky. I regret that I've lived this long life without ever having honored her—until now.

As my journey of discovery continued, my interest expanded to the atrocities of World War II and the depths of human cruelty. Of course, I had learned about the Holocaust since childhood, but the horrors were always distant—until seeing the names of the relatives lost, with entire branches of our family erased. It left me profoundly shaken. On a more personal level, I began to truly understand the difficult decisions my ancestors faced.

It was through this lens that I met Harold Gordon, the author of *The Last Sunrise*—a memoir of his survival during the Holocaust, including Auschwitz. Harold had been a close friend of my father's, and he bore the tattooed number on his forearm, a permanent reminder of the hellish childhood he endured. One day, when my young children were present, they asked Harold questions that many adults might have avoided. His answers, raw and unflinching, gave me a rare, intimate glimpse into the horrors of Nazi Germany.

Much of what I learned from Harold's experiences echoes throughout this narrative. It serves as a somber tribute to the human spirit and a warning that the atrocities of the past should never be forgotten—or repeated.

I must acknowledge that the horrors of the past are not limited to the Holocaust. Cruelty has surfaced in many places, including slavery, genocide, and so much more. It's also important not to hold people accountable for actions they had no part in. Descendants are not responsible for their ancestors' deeds, nor should they be expected to apologize. Wounds must heal to move forward, with the scars only serving as reminders so we can recognize the signs—and not foster more hate. Harold himself was the owner of a Volkswagen as his personal car, a nod to moving toward a brighter future.

As for this manuscript, I'm deeply grateful to those who were willing to review this dark meditation on human nature. I hope it serves as a warning against any future atrocities.

In particular, I must thank:

- **Frani Rosoff** – for reading all my drafts, keeping me on the path to success, supporting me always—the highs and the lows—and never complaining. You are my rock.

- **Niki Snyder** – for your meticulous attention to detail and tireless proofreading—a truly thankless job, but a job you did so well.

- **Marilyn Rayman, Julia Rosoff, and Steven Rosoff** – for your unwavering support and encouragement.

- **Madelyn & Max Snyder, Lucas & Calvin Rosoff** – for giving me the spark and inspiration to write.

- **Sarah Trashinsky and Harold Gordon** – in memory of their resilience, serving as perfect models of the human spirit."

- **Thomas Fonner, Melissa Meyers, Rebecca Payne, Joyana Peters, Robert Romano, Bryce Snyder, and Kelly Sunday** – for unselfishly reading my early drafts and providing invaluable feedback along the way.